frame by frame

frame by frame

CJ Murphy

Desert Palm Press

frame by frame

by CJ Murphy

© 2017 CJ Murphy

ISBN (book): 9781942976622
ISBN (epub): 9781942976639
ISBN (pdf): 9781942976646

Desert Palm Press
1961 Main Street, Suite 220
Watsonville, California 95076
www.desertpalmpress.com

Editor: Kellie Doherty
Cover Design: TreeHouse Studio, Winston-Salem, NC

Printed in the United States of America
First Edition November 2017

Acknowledgements

Where to even begin? There's only one place and that's with the woman who married me twice. The second time after knowing exactly what she was in for, having married me the first time thirteen years earlier. Thank you beyond measure to my wife Darla who has anchored my soul through the turbulent storms of life, showing me a love and family that I never knew could exist. I also have to thank her because she uttered four little words that I am fairly sure at times, she regrets now..."write me a story."

With our incredibly busy lives, it's difficult to take the time to sit in one place for hours, crafting characters and scenes, when the lettuce needs harvested, the carrots need dug, or the grass needs to be mowed. Thank you, my love, for allowing me to carve out time to feed my creative spirit.

To my numerous friends who beta read for me and said, "you have to publish". To Marion, Myra, Dava, and Jeannie I am deeply in your debt for your belief in me and your unending support. To M. E. Logan for the encouragement to write for my mental health and your friendship in general, I am forever grateful. A huge thank you to my beta reader and friend AE, who had the foresight to introduce me to AJ Adaire, who in turn performed a 'splenectomy' with a wicked sense of humor, a velvet glove, and a twenty-pound sledgehammer. This book would not be worth a dime without your initial guidance, encouragement, and mentorship.

Thank you, Kellie Doherty for your editing skills to make this a better story.

Finally, to Lee and Desert Palm Press for taking a chance on an unknown, raw novice by saying, "I would like to publish your manuscript." I will never forget reading those words after I submitted my 'first born child' to you. Thank you for making the leap of faith with me and guiding me through this process.

To the reader, I hope you enjoy the tale I've woven. The little tourist trap in this book truly does exist and inspired the story 'frame by frame'. The characters are based on people I know and the area I call home. It deals with two things I care deeply about breast cancer awareness and PTSD. I've lost important people in my life from breast cancer and it will always be one of my deep passions. I'm not a veteran like Val, but I respect our military a great deal. I've spent close to thirty years on the line as a firefighter. I know unseen trauma in those that witness such incredible sorrow and tragedy, is real. Lastly, I can't end this acknowledgement without reminding you to check those smoke detectors and have an escape plan in case of an emergency. Yes, it's that important and it's part of my mission in life.

Dedication

To Darla

.

Chapter One

VAL MAGNUSSON ROLLED HER wrist back and opened the throttle on the big Indian Chief. Mile after mile of asphalt ribbon glided beneath the gleaming wheels of the black iron horse. The pavement shimmered with the heat of summer. Rivulets of sweat trickled down her back under her leather jacket. The farther the bikes climbed into the mountains, the less oppressive the temperatures were. This was her fourth year making the 'Ride to the Wall,' each year riding with a different group from a different starting place. This group of veterans started in Columbus, riding to pay tribute to the fallen at the Vietnam Wall in Washington D.C.

As a former marine photographer for *The Marine News*, her camera now captured scenic vistas, instead of soldiers armed with the weapons. As a freelance photographer, her main body of work was for The Great Roads section of *Rider Magazine*. One focus was on organized rides like this one. Other pursuits took her to various riding opportunities in the United States. Her stories were told through the lens of her camera followed by a few descriptive lines preceding her photo credits. There was no office space where her awards hung, having long since abandoned the conventional work environment for a custom leather seat with the roadway inches below her dusty black boots. Honorably discharged from the service, her current work was far away from the battlefield horrors. Far too many of those images still crowded her mind.

The powerful vibration of the bikes in unison served as a common voice for those who never made it home. Lulled by the rumble so reminiscent of a Humvee traveling the unpaved roads of Iraq, her subconscious drifted back to those battlefields and the one image she couldn't forget. A soldier holding a small, dark-haired child, orange and yellow flames surrounding them. Thick black smoke arose out of the carnage. The soot stained face of the child, tear tracks revealing tanned skin, permeated her nightmares. An arm hung from the body, a pack of crayons clasped tightly in its hand. The small figure showed no signs of life. Her vision tunneled down to the taillight in front of her, and she shook her head. *Focus dammit.* She dragged herself from the vivid memory and forced herself to focus on the road that continued to climb into the mountains of West Virginia.

The communication device inside her helmet crackled to life. A voice filled her ears. She wasn't sure if it was Dave, who had led the last leg of the trip, or Mike. The two Vietnam veterans often changed lead bike positions. "We're coming up on those hairpin curves where your taillight and headlight might meet up. Stay awake, everyone."

Val raised her hand, as did the others. These miles were her favorite part of the famed transcontinental highway. In another twenty minutes, they would stop at the quirky roadside diner and gas station at the top of Cheat Mountain. Cool Springs was one of the most unique places she'd ever been. The sign boasted 'good food, groceries, ice cream, hardware, feed store, taxidermy, gifts, and gas. If we don't have it, you probably don't need it.'

Val followed the rumbling bikes around the last few hairpin turns. Loud pipes echoed off the rocks and reverberated around her. Riding mid-way back allowed her to watch the centipede-like continuum straighten out as they came to a whitewashed building. The wide front porch was full of well-used wooden rockers. *This must be where Cracker Barrel got the idea,* she mused. She flipped down her kickstand and turned off the ignition. Almost in unison, dozens of riders took off their helmets. After pulling off her gloves, she scratched her scalp and ran her fingers through her short, thick, blonde hair. Pushing her bangs back, she pulled the US Marine patrol hat out of her leather jacket and fixed it low on her brow. This was the only ride she wore this hat on.

Val looked around her surroundings. Ancient equipment, from steam engines to old iron tractors, peppered the land. Tall oak and maple trees shaded the area as sunlight dappled through the leaves. A small stream that gave the establishment its name, ran through the tourist trap. On hot days, you could find any number of children walking barefoot through the water while others climbed over the equipment. Parents lounged on swings, eating ice cream, taking a break in their travels. It had a wide parking lot filled with motorcycles and rusty pickup trucks with Farm Use spray painted on their side. The other vehicles in the lot were a license plate game bonanza. Plates from all the surrounding states, as well as more distant ones from Canada, often took up space on the cracked pavement. She took a deep breath, inhaling the scent of fried food, allowing the familiar surroundings to calm her jangled nerves.

"Hey, Viking, you going to sit on that bike all day?"

Val looked up from the bike to see the face she'd been longing for. Leaning against the support column stood a woman with long chestnut hair loosely braided and hanging across one shoulder. The smile crossing Laurel Stemple's face was warm and inviting. The mere sight of her fired Val's blood.

"The older I get the slower I move." Val straightened, placing her hands on the small of her back. The bikes hadn't made a stop in three hours. The last twenty minutes were spent navigating a mountain famous for 'cheating' men out of their lives. She twisted side to side loosening the stiff muscles.

"If you plan to get any of Gram's rhubarb crisp, you better find your way to the kitchen. She's been waiting on you."

Swinging her leg over the bike, she pulled off the black leather motorcycle jacket and hung it on the handle bar over her helmet. Taking long strides to the porch, she smiled at Laurel, drawn to her like a moth to a flame. Laurel wore a checkered blue and yellow sleeveless blouse over a pale blue t-shirt. Her shapely legs were clad in a pair of faded cut-off shorts and a well-worn pair of hiking boots. A rip in the front of her shorts showed the white pocket beneath. She looked so comfortable and damn sexy.

"It's good to see you, Laurel." Val wrapped the smaller woman in a hug, lifting her feet off the ground. "How is Ree?"

"Full of spitfire and sass, like always. It's good to see you too. It's been at least eight months since we've seen you ride through here," Laurel chided. "Don't you have snow tires for that bike yet?"

"Snow I'm not afraid of. It's that ice you guys get up here. Never was good on skates."

"I guess the thought of four wheels never crossed your mind." Laurel tilted her head sideways. "Come on. I know you won't be here long. Oh, by the way, thanks for the subscription. She loves seeing where you've been, since it's the only way she's going to know."

"You could take her on a vacation." Val winked, a small smile escaping her lips.

"Gram leave? You're dreaming, Viking." Laurel shook her head.

Val grinned. She'd always liked the nickname ever since Laurel had tagged her with it on one of her first trips through, right after she had found out Val's full name, Valkyrie Magnusson. Her father was a university professor specializing in Scandinavian studies at the University of Washington. Much like him, she had pale skin and Nordic blue eyes. On one of her trips, she'd stopped in only to be presented with a plastic Viking helmet fully equipped with horns and long braids of yellow yarn. They'd all had a good laugh over it, and Gram proudly wore it the rest of the visit. Before she left, it was enshrined on top of the mounted deer head above the women's restroom.

As they walked side by side through Cool Springs, she raised a hand to Tilly, Beth, and Wunder, all the people she'd come to know who kept this place running. Mule, a string bean of a man, wearing faded overalls and a stained John Deere ball cap, lounged in the corner. Bobeye joined him. Bobeye, aptly named for his one wandering eye, read something out of the local paper to a scowling Mule. They sat in the wooden rockers around a currently unused potbelly stove and a checkerboard.

"Hey, boys." She tipped her hat, slowed, and waited for the two men to finish some argument.

"Well looky here, Bobeye. See what the cat drug in that the dog won't drag back out?" Mule rose and shook her hand with a great laugh. The sound resonated throughout the store, causing curious looks from newcomers. Mule's laugh sounded much like a donkey braying. Val was used to it, the uniqueness of it never failing to bring a grin.

Val held his hand a second longer. "How are you, Mule?"

"Fair ta middlin'. You?"

"Shiny side up."

"You're doing better than some," Bobeye interjected. "I've already hauled two crotch rockets and one Harley off the mountain in the last two days."

Bobeye owned the local towing service and kept busy between the tractor trailer wrecks and the flatlanders that had a hard time handling the curves of the mountain roads.

"Damn, hate to hear that. Anyone serious?" Val asked.

"Nope, nothing too busted up exceptin' their pride and their fancy motorcycles. They's lucky." Bobeye sighed.

"Same old story then?" Val arched an eyebrow.

"Same shit, different day. Be careful out there. I'd hate to put that old Indian on the hook, you know?"

Val nodded. "Not if I can help it."

Mule looked over the diner. "How many in your group this year?"

"Close to fifty. Half went on over to Dot's Diner so as not to over-run the help. We're meeting back up at 1:30 to finish out. Should be at the wall around four or so. Covering some events this evening." Val looked at her watch.

Mule's brow furrowed. "You'll say hi to Dale for me?"

"As always, Mule." Mule's brother Dale had died when he was shot in Quang Nam.

"Safe travels, Viking." Bobeye raised a finger in a wave.

"Always."

Val and Laurel continued through the swinging doors into the kitchen where two identical women with salt and pepper hair worked at the grills. Faye and Kaye were as fast and efficient as any line cooks Val had ever seen, and their food second to none. The twins had worked at the diner for thirty plus years, preparing the simple menu made with top ingredients. The women bickered like old hens but could talk in tandem and finish each other's thoughts. *Freaky,* Val thought. They waved their spatulas at her.

At the back corner, a slight statured, white-haired Ree Stemple snapped green beans from her apron into a big metal pan. "Land sakes, I thought you wasn't coming. Figured ya might have found somewhere the food was better and the girls prettier. Let me look atcha."

"Not a chance." Val hugged Ree and placed a gentle kiss on her lined temple. "Somebody said I could score some rhubarb crisp if I made my way back here."

Ree pushed a strand of hair behind Val's ear. "Think you're something special?"

"I don't know about that. I just know what I can smell." Val's cheeks heated.

"With or without ice cream?"

"Is that a rhetorical question?" Val's laughter brought a smile to the elderly woman's face.

"If you mean was that a joke, of course it was. Sit down and I'll fetch it."

"Thank you, Ree."

"Pretty sure you've earned the right to call me Gram." The frail woman stood to make her way over to the stove where a fresh pan of rhubarb crisp sat cooling. She scooped some into a bowl and walked out to the diner area to add vanilla ice cream on top.

Val faced Laurel. "She looks good."

"Better than she was four months ago. That pneumonia about

wiped her out. And me." Laurel shivered.

Ree Stemple was a spry eighty-five-year-old who took no guff from anyone. She'd run this local tourist trap since the mid-fifties, expanding the business to what sat here today. With everyone else gone, it was Ree and Laurel that kept it a thriving business along with a host of characters that beat any variety show ever contrived.

"Can't imagine her not being here," Val whispered reverently.

Laurel wrapped an arm around Val's waist and pulled her close. "She's pretty fond of you, too, Viking."

"I consider myself lucky to have met her."

Ree came back through the swinging door and sat the dessert and a ceramic white mug of black coffee down on the wooden table sitting in one corner of the kitchen.

"It's not gonna eat itself. Get at it." Ree pinched Val's arm with her wizened fingers. "You're too damn skinny as it is. What the thunder do ya eat when you're out on that bike traipsing across the country?" Ree sat back down in her rocker and motioned for Val to dig in.

"Nothing as good as this place serves." Val grinned, holding up a huge spoonful of the crisp.

"Guess them boots haven't found a place to light yet?"

Val shook her head. "Too much left to see."

"I keep up with where ya been. Laurel here has me all fixed up on that faceybook thing. I liked ya, now I can keep track of where ya are, and I don't have to wait for my magazine to come."

Val nearly snorted coffee out her nose and broke into a coughing spell. "You're on Facebook?"

Ree rolled her eyes. "I am. I don't do that bird watchy thing. Laurel shows me where ya been on her smartypants phone."

"Gram, that's smart phone," Laurel groaned. "And it's Twitter, not bird watchy. Don't let her fool you, Val, I got her a tablet and I've seen her scrolling."

Ree rolled her head from side to side. "You say potato, I say potato."

"You two crack me up." Val tried to take another sip of coffee without it going down her windpipe.

Tilly, their waitress, stuck her head in the kitchen. "Hey, Laurel, can you come run the register? Viking's crew has the tables full and both Beth and I are hustling to get their orders in."

Laurel sighed. "I guess that's my cue to get to work. Val, you want anything else?"

Ree waved Laurel on. "Don't worry about her. I've served a few dishes around this joint in my time. Get out there before Tilly breaks her pencil lead."

Laurel walked past Ree and ran her hand over the hunched shoulders of her grandmother.

Val recalled that Ree's daughter Sara had died a month after Laurel turned nine. With no father in the picture, Ree raised Laurel. Val marveled at their close relationship. The fact that Val was a lesbian had driven a deep, unbridgeable divide between her and her father. The relationship with her mother wasn't much better. *At least Mother and I are on speaking terms.* Val watched as Laurel leaned over and kissed the top of her grandmother's head and felt a pang of longing.

"How could I forget, Gram? Here I was thinking you were a new hire."

That made Val smirk around her cup, not wanting to draw the ire of the matriarch.

"Who in their right mind would want to work in a nut house like this?" Ree squinted her right eye at Val and then turned to Laurel. "Thunder. Be lucky if I remember my own name tomorrow. What was it I told ya to remind me of?"

"Which time?"

"Don't you get sassy with me, young whip. I'll warm your britches like I did when ya were ten."

Val laughed at the back and forth between the two. She'd shared a similar closeness with her own grandmother.

Laurel put her hands on her hips. "Gram, I know I cut a dozen forsythia twigs for you to tan my hide, but I don't remember you ever using one." She held her pinky finger up at her grandmother and narrowed her eyes as the woman held hers back.

Their voices spoke in unison. "Better not be smaller than my pinky."

She kissed her grandmother's cheek. "You wanted to ask about the Punkin Chunkin contest."

Val remembered her article she'd written last fall about the event in Delaware.

Ree wrung her hands. "How could I forget something like that?"

Laurel's jaw tightened, and Val winced. *Is she that concerned?*

But then Laurel's face softened as she hugged the elderly woman. "Gram, you've forgotten more things than I'll ever know."

Ree grinned. "Get out there. I can see the line from here. Now, Val, about this bunch of folks that destroy perfectly good pumpkins."

Val never took her eyes off Laurel as she went through the swinging doors back into the restaurant. She turned her gaze to Ree. "A bunch is right, last year thirty thousand people went to watch it."

"Land sakes, don't people got anything better to do than watch pumpkins fly?" Ree shook her head, wide eyed as she crawled out of her rocker. "Whatcha want besides that crisp? And don't tell me ya ain't hungry 'cause I'm not buying it."

Val chuckled at the tough older woman, whose speech was razor sharp and filled with Appalachian slang. Val loved paying attention to the dialect and inflection in the places she traveled. This and the low country were some of her favorites. Ree's still held a bit of the German prevalent in the historically German community of Aurora, West Virginia. She also loved the Creole of the low country while in Louisiana. The way it rolled off people's tongues in the bayous made her smile with envy.

She'd picked up enough Arabic to keep herself out of trouble while in Iraq, but it hadn't been enough to understand the venom-filled protests. For a moment, she felt the searing heat of the desert again and reached into her pocket for her lip balm. It was habit, formed from long days of stifling temperatures, not enough water, and the futile attempt at keeping her lips from splitting.

"You're getting a foot-long dog and a large chocolate milk," Ree said.

Val rubbed her face. Looking around, Ree wasn't where she'd been before, having moved over to the stove to pour chili over the hot dog. Val screwed up her face when Ree picked up the lid on the coleslaw and sighed in relief as she put it back down. Apparently, her sigh didn't miss the elderly ears.

"I might have forgotten about that Punkin Chunkin, but I haven't forgotten your ill will toward coleslaw." Chuckling, Ree turned and sat the foot-long hot dog slathered in chili and mustard in front of her then crossed the kitchen to the large refrigerator. Pulling the glass jug of chocolate milk from the shelf, she poured the rich mixture into a tall mug resembling a mason jar. After replacing the jug, Ree carried it over and sat it in front of Val.

Val chewed the hotdog, a third of it already devoured. The seasoned tomato sauce merged with the ground beef perfectly. With her mouth semi full, Val held the icy mug close to her lips. "If I stayed around here long, I'd have to buy bigger pants you know." Drinking some of the thick chocolate milk, she rolled her eyes in pleasure.

Ree laughed at the milk mustache Val always left there for her amusement. "Might be good for you. Wipe your mouth. You're worse than Wunder. And don't wipe it on your sleeve like he does."

Val used the napkin on her leg to wipe off the milk. Wunder was Tilly's twenty-year-old son. "I'll say this, I've had a lot of chocolate milk across the country. There's none as cold or as thick as what you serve."

Ree pointed her crooked index finger at Val. "That's because I won't serve low fat junk. Ya want to drink that, go somewhere else. Here, we serve the high-test made less than two miles away at the dairy." Ree had lost her husband, Johann, at the age of twenty-four. The dairy she spoke of had been her father in law's business.

"Why didn't you two take over that instead of starting this place back then?" Val asked taking another bite of her chilidog.

"Johann's father, Fritz, held to a lot of his German ways after he came over. Fritz believed his oldest son should inherit the business. He did help us get this place going, and it was an outlet to sell things from the dairy. That's why to this day, we still do, including that ice cream ya love so much."

Val was envious, thinking of how long Laurel's family went back in this area. She chewed her last bite of chilidog and washed it down with the rest of the milk. Hot dogs and chocolate milk, by most people's standards, wouldn't be considered comfort food. To her, it was better than a steak served in the finest restaurant.

Ree brushed her hands together. "So, about that Punkin Chunkin thing?"

Val spent the next fifteen minutes explaining the intricacies of hurling a pumpkin through the air for distance and the throngs of people that paid money to see it.

"People must be starved for somethin' to do. Land sakes." Ree shook her head in disbelief.

"It's big business and its good for the local economy. Personally, I'll take sitting out there on your front porch over it any day." Val watched as the older woman smiled at her and felt blessed to have ever had the chance to really get to know her.

***

Laurel had looked through the windows into the kitchen a few times to see Val and her grandmother in conversation. Watching her grandmother laugh and carry on with the traveler, reminded her how much they both loved the biker dropping in. Val stopped in a few times a year on her travels and always took time to talk with her grandmother. Watching the easy friendship between the two women always made her heart warm. The line at the register finally slowed, allowing her to go back into the kitchen to catch a few minutes with them.

"Val says people pay money to see how far they can chuck a pumpkin. Maybe next year we should have our own contest here with the pumpkins left over after Halloween." Ree turned away, indicating she didn't need a response. Her grandmother's reaction to the event didn't surprise her. Running the store left little time for pointless activities. As Laurel made her way over to her grandmother, she ran her hand across Val's shoulder. The touch she used held great fondness. The two women timidly flirted whenever they were around each other. She had a hard time trying to categorize how she felt about Val. It was more than friendship, and yet it lacked an actual label. "You coming back this way after the ride on Sunday?"

"That's the plan. I left out of Columbus with this group. I've got an assignment down in Tennessee. I figure this will be their stopping point on the way back too." Val scraped her second bowl of crisp noisily, savoring every bite.

"Guess I'll need to make another crisp Sunday morning so ya can get your fill on the way back." Ree watched Val clean her spoon. "Want to lick the bowl too?"

Val shook her head. "You don't have to go to any trouble for me. I don't expect anything."

"I know. That's why it'll be ready when ya come through. I figured you'd be dropping off another rubbing for Mule," Ree replied, a knowing smile on her lips.

Laurel was aware of this act of kindness Val performed and the impact it had. She'd witnessed the first one Val presented Mule. She'd never forget the tears he'd tried to hide.

Val nodded. "It's become kind of a tradition for me to do it for certain people. Mule appreciates them the most though."

"Gram, how old was he when Dale died?"

"Twelve. Followed Dale everywhere. Never seen a child grieve so." Ree's voice became soft and low. "Always said he wanted to make a trip over to the memorial to see his name on the wall. Other than the day they buried Dale, he's never gone farther than Oakland. Worked his daddy's farm his whole life. Wasn't a good piece of land, but somehow them potatoes kept the family fed and the bill collectors away."

Val tilted her head. "Mule never married?"

Ree looked at Val with questioning eyes. "Not unless she was deaf as a post. You've heard that man laugh. He's pretty solitary except for his daily sit here with Bobeye. Been rocking by that stove for a few hours every day for the last forty years. His daddy brought him in to try and bring him out of his grief the year his brother died. My daughter Anna told him a joke and made him laugh. His daddy said it was the first time any sound had come out of his mouth since he heard the news. I've never heard tell of him ever even going out with anyone, never mind marrying them."

Laurel realized she couldn't remember a time in her life that Mule hadn't been around. To her, he was part of the framework of the building. He was as much a part of the store as the faded red booths.

The kitchen door swung open and Tilly leaned in. "Val, your buddies are loading up. See you back in here on Sunday?"

"Count on it." Val flashed her a killer smile. "I'm going to hit the head before it's time to go. I'll be back in a minute."

Those dimples are going to be my undoing. Laurel watched her walk across the store. *I count on it more than you know Viking.*

***

As Val made her way to the restroom, she looked around the tourist trap. Souvenirs lined the shelves and bins providing shoppers the chance to take home a small reminder of their time. She ran her finger over a coffee mug with a man wearing buckskins, a coonskin hat, and holding a musket. Dried corncobs on dowel rods, lumps of polished coal, and t-shirts declaring "Miners do it in the dark" lay before her. Various mounts and game heads lined the walls. Above the women's restroom, the plastic Viking helmet with yellow braids still sat regally on a twelve-point whitetail deer head. She pulled out her smartphone, snapped a few photos, and posted them to her social media account named IronhorseOORAH with the hashtag, #CoolSpringstheresnoplacelikehome. She grinned as she entered the restroom beneath the yellow braids.

Val came back to the kitchen and carried her dishes over to the sink. She began helping Laurel load up what was in the last plastic tub on the counter. They finished, and she walked back to her hat rolling the bill in her hands. It grew increasingly difficult to leave and always proved to be the hardest part of stopping in.

Ree got up from her rocker and walked around the table. "Now, you be careful." She poked Val's shoulder. "I been to Washington D.C. one time, and that was one time too many for me. Come back soon." She patted Val's arm and headed into the back office.

"Time for you to saddle up, Viking," Laurel said as Val turned to her. "Thanks for taking the time to talk to her. She loves being able to fuss over you."

"I enjoy her company and the fussing just as much. Although I missed you ganging up on me."

"You rode in with a bunch of hungry hooligans. I assume you'll plan on staying a little longer on the ride back?" Laurel finished drying her hands with the dishtowel and meticulously folded it into a small square.

Val watched the absent-minded action. Wondering if her departure pulled at Laurel as much as it did her. She walked a few steps closer, reaching for Laurel's hand. Her attraction to the beautiful woman became stronger each time she visited. "Yeah, I'll split off from the group here and head south to my next assignment. Gives me a little more time to visit before I have to be down there since I won't have to backtrack."

"We'll keep the crisp warm and the ice cream cold." Laurel tapped Val's hat bill with one hand while using the other to squeeze the hand holding hers. "Strap that helmet on tight. Cheat Mountain's had a lot of big rig wrecks on it of late. New trucking company has been doing transport down it, and their drivers apparently don't realize you still need brakes when you get to the bottom of a mountain. Someone forgot to tell them there are seventeen curves to negotiate."

"I'll do that." Val stepped forward and hugged Laurel. Feeling her body this close always made Val long for more. They walked out with their arms around each other, Val's slung loosely around Laurel's shoulders and Laurel's hand under the wide black belt circling Val's waist.

The two women made it to the porch and Val looked at her Indian Chief. "You'll have to take that ride with me someday."

"Someday maybe I will, but not today." Laurel had told her the same thing numerous times over the years.

Val was reluctant to let Laurel go, holding her and resting her chin lightly on Laurel's head breathing in the faint vanilla and coconut scent that reminded her of the beach. "Always someday. I've been trying to figure out what day of the week that is. Does it come between Wednesday and Thursday or Saturday and Sunday?"

"Get out of here, you nut."

"See you Sunday." Squeezing Laurel's hand, Val released her and stepped down onto the cracked blacktop.

***

Laurel stood on the storefront porch, watching the tall, lanky woman deftly swing her leather jacket on. The movement briefly tightened the white t-shirt across the muscled shoulders and caused Laurel's breath to hitch. "God, she's sexy," she whispered.

Beth, her best friend, walked up beside her, wiping her hands on a blue striped kitchen towel. "She is. When the hell are you going to get around to telling her that?"

"Beth, she's got wandering feet like the father I never knew did. Besides, you of all people know why I don't." Laurel had a touch of impatience in her voice.

"You spend too much time worrying about something that might never happen instead of living. Never took you for a fatalist, but it's not like you listen to me anyhow." Beth turned and walked back into the restaurant.

"No sense stirring something that's never going to happen." Laurel raised her hand in goodbye as Val and the rest of the bikes roared back out onto US Route 50, heading east. Spinning on her heel, Laurel strode into the store to help bus the tables and booths that sat in the center of the building. Walking over to the empties, her shoulder brushed the woman who was like a sister. "I'm sorry, Beth. I know you care."

"You and I have been close since we were five years old. We've been through our share of spats. That one didn't even register. Laurel, someday you're going to wake up and find your whole life has passed by and you've barely noticed." Beth shook her head. "Some things are worth taking a chance on. That Viking might be one of them."

Laurel watched her grab the plastic tub of dirty dishes and glasses and disappear into the kitchen. She wrung out a dishrag to wipe down the table, still thinking about Val. She finished resetting the placemats and silverware and made her way back to the kitchen. Her grandmother sat with her tablet in hand using the stylus to scroll. The arthritis left most of her fingers gnarled and misshapen, but Laurel had learned there was little this woman couldn't do regardless of her age, aches, or pains.

However, she had noticed that the double pneumonia Gram had suffered, appeared to have sapped much of her reserves. Laurel could still taste the palpable fear she'd felt when Gram had been sick. Gram was her only blood relative and the thought of her not being around still chilled Laurel to the bone. Looking at her now, Laurel could tell she was well down the path of recovery. She'd purchased the tablet so Gram could have something more immediate to interest her while she recovered. She tried not to think about her grandmother not being in her life.

Ree gave her a smile. "Liebchen, come here. Our Viking's already let the world know she stopped in." Ree held up the tablet for Laurel to see.

Laurel looked the post. It wasn't the picture that caught her eye, but the hashtag line. *There's no place like home. Val thought of this place as home?* Val had never even spent a night here that Laurel knew of. *But she thinks of this as home?* Laurel rolled the thought around in her mind and caught her grandmother looking at her with suspicious eyes.

"A fox that watches its prey too long might miss a meal."

Laurel squinted at her. "What's that supposed to mean?"

"Just saying, you look a little hungry to me."

"Gram!"

"Don't Gram me. Never known ya to be a coward. I sure as thunder didn't raise ya to be one." Getting up and pushing through the diner door, she left Laurel alone in the kitchen, dumbfounded.

Am I a coward? She'd never thought so. She'd never done anything brave like go off to war like others she knew, but she'd always considered herself a little on the daring side. Like the time she was seventeen and jumped off the railroad bridge into Blue Hole. She'd skinny dipped in the Cheat River with Beth and a few other friends. Looking back, spending a night in the haunted cemetery on Halloween seemed stupid and foolish now, not brave. Muttering as she emptied half full glasses into the sink, Laurel looked up to the ceiling. "Not by Val's standards."

"Not by Val's standards what?" Beth asked as she brought in another tub of dirty dishes.

"Oh, I was thinking about us jumping off Seven Islands Bridge."

"God, we were stupid. That thing is twenty-five feet in the air. Good thing Blue Hole is damn near bottomless. How we didn't die as teenagers, I'll never know." Beth laughed and bumped Laurel's hip with hers. "What got you thinking about that?"

Laurel waved her hand back and forth. "Oh, something Gram said about not raising a coward."

"Boy, that woman has you pegged dead to rights. If we'd have listened to half of the stuff she told us, we might've done something with our lives."

Laurel raised an eyebrow at her friend.

"Not that working in this classy joint sixty hours a week wasn't what I spent those years in college to do," Beth said with a wide grin on her face.

They both broke out into laughter. Hearing their chortling, Wunder walked into the kitchen and over to the big counter. "Whatcha laughing at?"

"Just girl talk, Wunder." Laurel looked up at him.

He stood for a second then cocked his head sideways. "I wonder, why doesn't glue stick to the inside of the bottle?" Looking over, he saw the plate with his name on it holding the sandwich his mother had made for him. Grabbing for the thick slices of homemade bread heavily laden with peanut butter and jelly, he took a huge bite on his way out of the kitchen.

"And people ask us why we call him Wunder," Beth whispered.

"I still thank God we hired him four years ago. Gram always said she knew he'd have trouble getting a job after he dropped out of school. Think of all the groceries he's carried out and the gas he's pumped for those who can't. He's a godsend for Tilly. Those questions of his make my head hurt, but somehow I couldn't imagine this place without him." Laurel smiled thinking about how lucky they were to have him.

Wunder helped bus tables and kept all the machinery running in the place with his mechanical genius. They paid him a decent salary and while he was at work, he could drink all the chocolate milk he wanted. His sister had gotten hooked on heroin and was now a resident of the Hazelton Federal Prison for the next ten years, after being sentenced for possession with intent to deliver. Her three children lived with him and his mom.

Laurel frowned. "Tilly says he watches those kids like they were his. Not sure how she'd work that second job at the Dollar General without him. He feeds, bathes, and reads them all bedtime stories before he tucks them in. She doesn't get home until 11:00 pm and told me it's not unusual to find him passed out, a story book open on his chest and one of those kids curled up at his side. Wunder wouldn't hurt a soul. One of the kindest people I know." Laurel found the young man's innocence endearing. "What a place it would be if there were more Wunders in the world."

Chapter Two

VAL AND HER FELLOW riders arrived in Washington D.C. about 4:00 pm. The local VFW treated them to a memorial presentation and after, they made their way over to the Vietnam Wall. She had her camera out, respectfully capturing moments as men and women of all ages reached out to the granite monolith to touch the lettering on a name that had once been a friend, a comrade, or a loved one. It was difficult to watch, the grief still palpable some forty years later. Her camera lens focused on the veterans clothed in remnants of bygone uniforms bearing their unit insignia. In their faces, she saw a study in grief and regret and—she saw herself.

I imagine I wear that look a good bit. Your body is standing on home soil while parts of your soul lie bleeding in a foreign land. After a while, the sight of the unspoken pain became too much. She walked away to find a warm ray of sunlight to break through the darkness. Pulling the small artist pad from her bag, she let her hand move across the paper. Sketching was one of the exercises Liz had her use to capture the confusion struggling to the surface. More than one person had commented that the sketches showed a great deal of artistic talent, but that wasn't something Val could see. Her pad held page after page of sketches chronicling her visits to this hallowed place. As she sat there, a haunting image began to find its way onto the blank paper. Small fingers, a crayon, and a blood-soaked uniform. Her fingers traced the fine pencil lines, blurring them as her mind did the memory. Dubbing it *Collateral Damage*, it was an image Val had drawn from a dozen different angles. A mystery she couldn't solve. She put her hand across her face. *Why can't I let this go?*

Val finished and brushed her hands on her pants. She checked her camera settings and made her way to the large polished granite panels. That was where her own respects would be paid using a small piece of artist charcoal she rubbed across the engraved surface. Her hope was that in doing so, the token created would bring comfort to her friends who couldn't be there to do it for themselves.

Val stopped at Panel 05E-Line 47. 2LT Elizabeth Ann Jones, died in a helicopter crash in Saigon. This was the aunt and namesake of her psychiatrist and friend, Dr. Elizabeth Ruston-Romano. Mailing the pencil rubbing to her had become a ritual. Without Liz's help, Val wasn't sure she would've escaped the memories that plagued but no longer bound her. Although less frequent now, they still persisted. If they got bad enough, a trip to Maryland for an 'in person' visit was necessary instead of their monthly phone conversation.

After placing the rubbing in her sketchpad, she found Panel 29E-Line 98. Reverently, she touched the name of 1LT Randall D. Shaffer, Mule's brother. He was a newlywed at the time. A few years after his death, Mule's sister-in-law remarried and moved away from Aurora. His remains were among the thousands of white crosses in Arlington National Cemetery. She ran her finger across the name, feeling the smooth stone and the indentation of each letter. It didn't matter that she hadn't known Dale. She knew his death had deeply affected Mule. That was enough. After making the rubbing, she filed it in her sketchpad and decided to take a few pictures of the name. Taking a second rubbing, she placed it alongside the first while her mind rolled over something special for Mule. How to accomplish it would come later. For now, Val stared at the name and wondered if she'd ever meant that much to anyone.

That evening, there was another ceremony and a concert by the Lieutenant Dan Band, led by Gary Sinise. In *Forest Gump*, he'd played Lieutenant Dan Taylor. Val had a press pass providing her backstage access to capture some of the events as part of her story. She was to meet up with Tess Arnold, who had worked with her over in Iraq.

Val remembered meeting Gary for the first time finding out that he did a great deal for the troops and veterans. He'd also co-founded Operation Iraqi Children, a program designed to 'Help Soldiers Help Children' with author Laura Hillenbrand. The program purchased and shipped school supply kits to soldiers in Iraq and eventually to other areas in which troops were deployed. It had been Val's job to photograph the events while she was embedded with different units in Iraq. During one of the donation events, Val's life changed forever. Walking around the back of the stage, Val heard a voice from her past.

"Hey, stranger, how are you?" Feminine arms enveloped her into a hug and soft lips met her own in a greeting kiss. "I wondered when you would show your mug around this place."

"I'm like a bad penny that keeps showing up. I'm good, Tess. You?"

"Busy as always. More to do than I have time for." Tess held Val at arm's length, a questioning eye appraising her.

"I'm fine, Tess. Leg doesn't give me any trouble or the elbow. Call me the bionic woman," Val assured her.

"How about the head?"

"Still have some migraines. They're manageable."

"I'm not talking about the headaches, and you know it." Tess stepped back and crossed her arms.

Val chuckled and shifted her weight from foot to foot, staring at a particularly fascinating tile on the floor.

Tess persisted. "Not kidding. This is me, not some doctor or someone who doesn't know you."

Val thought about the petite woman standing before her. For a few months, they'd been more than friends. To save their friendship, they chalked it up as two people needing to connect. "I still have some nightmares, some flashes during the day. I go see Liz if they get bad. Mostly I get on the bike and ride away from them."

"Still sketching?"

Val managed to muster a hint of conviction in her voice. "Of course, it helps get the pictures out of my head. I don't know that I'll ever forget what I saw, though it's been a long time since I crawled across the floor on my hands and knees in the middle of the night."

Tess had held her many nights as the terrors chased her from the bed and under a table. She'd seen the worst of it and suffered a few bruises bringing Val back to reality. They would still be together if Tess had her way, but Val couldn't bring herself to lie to this beautiful woman. No matter how hard she tried, she wouldn't ever be in love with her. Saddling Tess down with the demons while not giving her what she deserved was unfair.

Tess ran her hand gently down the side of Val's face, stopping to cup her jaw. Val leaned into the touch, drawing strength and warmth from the caress. "Honestly, Tess, I'm happy. How about you?"

Tess looked away. "Kelly and I've moved in together. I don't know if it's forever. What we have is comfortable, and she's good for me."

"That's great. You deserve someone to be good to you." She was relieved Tess was finding happiness with someone. Her head pounded, familiar regret racking her from the emotional and physical pain she'd inflicted on Tess.

Tess pulled Val against her again. "I deserve someone to make me feel like you did. I know you aren't going to let that happen, so I'll keep trying to find something close."

"You deserve so much more than me. Now, where's Kelly?"

"She's working a twenty-four-hour shift at Arlington. She's been promoted to captain."

"Tell her congratulations for me next time you see her." Val put every bit of sincerity in her voice she could.

"One of these days, Val, you're going to realize you're enough. If not for me, for someone. You have to let someone in, babe."

"Maybe someday, for now, I have—"

"Miles and miles to go before I sleep," Tess finished.

"Exactly." She squeezed Tess one more time, kissed her forehead, and broke the embrace as she walked away knowing she'd never be her lover again and hoping that a friendship would do.

That night, Val took a ride to quiet the voices that threatened to pull her back to that dark place. She let the miles slide by, driving the dark voices back into a box. She pulled into her hotel a little after midnight. Taking a long hot shower, she let the pulsations ease her tired muscles. Her body ached, reminding her to take her over-the-counter pain meds before lying down. The decision to go without prescription painkillers had become a mandate as the desire for the pills overcame the necessity. Having her mind clouded while she rode was a bad idea.

Hopping out of the shower, she dried her body. Riddled with scars, it told the story of how her life had taken a dramatic left turn. Though not painful, her right calf muscle was missing a large chunk where shrapnel had torn it away. A long scar ran from her triceps down the underside of her left forearm where they'd replaced the elbow joint. The most devastating injury she suffered that fateful day was having her left leg nearly blown off, amputating it just below the knee. The vest and helmet saved her life.

Standing naked at the sink, both hands grasping the edge of the counter, she balanced on her right leg as the laughter of children, angry foreign words, and the deafening sound of an explosion bombarded her senses. Her prosthesis rested by the shower. It bore her Marine Corp insignia and various images from her career. One was taken while she was embedded with her unit. Displayed on the socket was a picture of her surrounded by Iraqi children. Shutting her eyes tight against the images, Val shook herself to rid her mind of the vestiges of that former life.

She pulled on a soft blue t-shirt and a pair of loose boxers, pushing her stump into the prosthetic leg. Walking out of the bathroom, she sat down on the edge of the bed and pulled a bottle of Makers Mark out of her bag, pouring three fingers into a clear glass she found by the bathroom sink. Throwing four ibuprofens into her mouth, she took a healthy swallow of the amber liquid. Despite being smooth, it burned going down. Restless, she rose and walked out onto the balcony of her hotel room, staring at the tiny dots of light. Feeling the pulse of the city, the vivid memories of searing heat and the bitter taste of blood pushed back into her memories. She stood there for several breaths and closed her eyes. *Let it go. It's only a memory from your past, not your present.* Stepping back into the room, Val picked up her laptop. The email she typed to Liz had one line: 'Got time for a face to face? Val.'

There was little doubt that her psychiatrist and friend would look at her schedule and then set up an appointment. Seeing Tess had stirred the memories she tried to keep at bay. There was a weary understanding that sleep would have a steep price tonight. Payment would be in the form of a full-color movie of the worst day of her life or a hangover. Looking at her glass, she poured another three fingers and started counting out the cost.

Chapter Three

LAUREL STOOD AT THE prep table and folded the ends under the loaves of dough in the stainless-steel pans. She covered them with a clean cheese cloth to allow them to rise before baking. Her grandmother sat at her side on a stool.

"I'm glad ya got the inner webs turned on here at the store, honey. I can see what our travelers a doin' even if we aren't home. Got something I want to show Mule when he comes in today." Ree turned her tablet around for Laurel to see.

"It's the internet, Gram, not the inner web. I'm glad, too." Laurel looked at the tablet. On the screen was a black-and-white photo Val had taken of Mule's brother's name. The stone around it was so polished, you could see the reflection of a veteran standing at attention and saluting the wall. Val had titled it *Remember the Fallen*. Wiping her hands on the blue and white cotton dishtowel slung across her shoulder, she walked over to a long preparation table. "Mule will be touched."

"Mule will be. What time ya figure she'll be coming back through?"

"She really didn't say." Laurel rubbed her grandmother's back.

Ree looked up at Laurel, her eyes narrowed. "Ya really like her, don't you?"

Laurel felt her cheeks heat and turned to avoid Ree's questioning gaze. "Of course, I like her. She's given the store a lot of great advertising over the years."

"Now ya know that's not what I'm talking about. I might be eighty-five, but I'm not senile. I've seen the way the two of ya look at each other."

"Gram!"

"I remember what it was like to feel my heart speed up at the sound of a voice and for my palms to sweat anytime Johann was near me." Ree's sharp tone made Laurel wince. "I want to see ya happy and as far as I can tell, no one else's even ruffled your feathers for years."

"I'm not talking to you about this, especially not here. Last thing I need is more talk about me in this place." Laurel headed toward the walk-in cooler.

Ree chuckled. "Ya can cool off in there all you want. I noticed ya didn't deny it neither. If I'm not blunt with ya, who will be?"

***

Ree clucked her tongue in disapproval and watched her granddaughter shake her head as she disappeared into the cooler. Making her way out of the kitchen, she hobbled toward the potbelly stove and heard Mule's distinctive laugh. Bobeye already had the paper and held it in one hand with a coffee cup inches from his lips. Something had caught his eye. Mule ordered a sandwich from Tilly as Ree reached him.

"Afternoon, boys. Anything good in that rag, Bobeye?" Ree lowered herself down in the third rocker, falling the last few inches onto the well-worn cushion. She rubbed her knee. "Somethin' amiss, fellas. My knees a thumping."

Bobeye finally took a sip of his coffee. "Paper says the weather's supposed to be good. Can't be that. What's ailing you, Ree?"

"I'm not rightly sure, but somethin's a coming." Ree often had this phantom pain predicting some major event that was about to take place. It had started the night Johann had been killed and had continued over the years. She'd known when Mule's brother had been shot in Vietnam. She'd felt it the day Sara was going to give birth to Laurel, even though she wasn't having any contractions. Her knee just told her. Now it was thumping again.

"Maybe it's arthritis. Doesn't always mean something important." Bobeye dismissed the notion.

"Ree ain't never been wrong if'n her knee takes to aching," Mule countered.

"Thank ya for the vote of confidence, Mule. Come here, I wanna show ya something."

Mule rose out of his chair and knelt beside her. She showed him Val's photo, and a smile came across his face. "Our Viking's something, isn't she?"

"That she is."

Mule brayed his boisterous laugh. "I can remember the first time she came riding in here. Not sure she'd ever been in a place like this."

Ree laughed too and thought back to the first time the tall blonde had stepped foot in the store. It had been nearly five years ago.

Looking through the window on the swinging door, Ree watched a tall woman dressed in black leather pants and a white t-shirt approach the register. She cracked the door to listen. "Would it be all right if I took some pictures in here for a story I'm doing about this trip?"

Laurel looked up and back down quickly, her face flushing. "Sure, that's part of the charm we have around here. Anything else I can help you with?"

"Can you give me a little history on this place?"

Laurel smirked. "If you want that story, you'll want talk to the owner."

"Is he here?"

"She is. Her name is Marie Stemple. She and her husband Johann started running this place back in 1956. Let me see if she's got time talk to you. She's frying apple pies."

Ree backed away from the doors as she watched Laurel approach.

A few moments later, Ree came out of the back, straightening her apron and adjusting the tight bun pinned to the back of her head. Smoothing the rest of the strays back, she brushed flour off her arm. "How can I help ya?"

"Yes, ma'am, sorry for interrupting you." The woman looked around. "I believe this diner might be the most interesting place I've ever been."

Ree laughed and waved the woman over as she made her way to the rockers by the warm potbelly stove. There was still a little chill left from a late snowfall, and the fire chased the dampness from the air inside. "Forgive me, I hafta sit. I can't stand for long periods no more. Mind's a willin'...the body, that's another thing. And don't call me ma'am, makes me feel like I've got one foot in the grave. Name's Marie, but ya can call me Ree like the rest of these fools."

The woman replied, "Ree. I like it."

"It's the only one I got besides Gram, and I only got one who calls me that."

"My name is Val. Val Magnusson. I do some photography for Rider Magazine and I'm not sure I've ever been in a place that advertised ice cream and taxidermy in the same sentence. I know I've never been in a

place this awesome." Her smile widened as she looked around, landing on the mounted game animals. "Who did all those?"

One corner of Ree's mouth curled up. "Who do ya think, kid?"

Eyes wide, Val shook her head. "You're pulling my leg."

Ree held up three fingers. "Scout's honor."

Val belly laughed. "Ree, you're a fascinating woman. How did you come to own the store?"

Ree turned the thin gold band on her left hand. "When I married Johann, he was working on his father's dairy farm. He wasn't in line to run it so, sometime after we got married, his father helped us start this place. It was a little place then, a single Texaco pump and a little store. For the first five years, we lived in two rooms in the back. Then the babies started comin', so we bought the house Laurel and I live in. Since we didn't need the living space any more, we added the diner. My daughters were still little the night Johann went out to help Mule's dad. He slid into the ditch on a bad stretch of road up here on the mountain. Another car came by and clipped him. He died right there on the highway." She paused for a minute and dabbed her eyes with a thin floral handkerchief she pulled from her white apron pocket. "Had to take care of my girls, so I started making this place into something everyone needed."

Diners filled the booths of the restaurant with heaping plates of food in front of them. People stood in line at the register with ice cream cones and treasures in hand.

Val cleared her throat. "It looks like you managed to accomplish exactly what you set out to do."

"Half the kids in the community have worked the diner at one time or another, and thanks to the likes of people like you traveling through, we do all right."

"I'd say better than that. We had a heck of a time finding room for the motorcycles."

"We're pretty popular with your two-wheeled friends in the better weather. Pretty good stopping place for those needing to stretch their legs." Ree chuckled and stretched her own legs out.

"I can agree with that. Will it be okay if I do a little story on this place? I have a pretty good following among motorcycle riders. We're always looking for interesting places to stop."

"Honey, it's a free country last time I checked. Make sure ya get something to eat before ya go." Ree pushed a menu toward her visitor.

"What would you recommend?"

Ree had explained the specials and remembered the way Val's face twisted at the mention of coleslaw. She chuckled at how she'd introduced Val to Laurel.

"I'll send my granddaughter out with something for ya."
"Which one is your granddaughter?" Val asked, looking around.
"The prettiest one, of course. She looks just like me." Ree smoothed her hair back. "Laurel, behind the counter. Sweeter child never been born. Not sure what I'da done without her all these years. She keeps this place running, and I keep the wolves at bay."
"Sorry?"
"Not like it's a secret. She's never been ashamed of who she is and neither have I. She bats for the other team, as the boys say. We get a lot of men through here that think only with the head they got between their legs, if ya get my meanin'. Some don't take no for an answer too easy. Some of 'em get downright mean. That's where I come in. I remind 'em of their manners and show 'em the exit if they can't find 'em somewhere."
"Ree, you truly are one of a kind. Wish there were more of you out there. Think we can clone you?"
"Land sakes, child, one of me in this world is too much for some people. You go find your way to the counter, and Laurel will bring ya your food. Now, ya make sure ya come back through here as you're traveling."
"That, you can count on." Val held three fingers up. "Scouts honor."

The memory made Ree smile. Val had cleaned her plate and groaned in pleasure at the first bite of a fried apple pie. Ree used dried apples from her own trees and a special syrup recipe stuffed into a hand-made dough, folded over and pinched closed with a fork. They were fried golden brown and dusted with sugar. Val had devoured it.

Pulling herself from her first memories of Val, Ree rocked, scrolling through the Facebook travels of the woman she'd become fond of. It was apparent Val had been through a great deal, and Ree always felt life was too short not to eat dessert first. She was dead sure that her granddaughter was even fonder of the tall woman. Unless she missed her mark, Val had feelings for Laurel also. "Both too stubborn to go after what they both want and need."

***

Laurel finished rearranging the cooler for the third time while she considered her grandmother's words. It was hard to admit her feelings. Her heart did beat harder at the sound of Val's voice and her palms weren't the only things that got wet. The memory of the first time she'd laid eyes on Val still sent shivers up her spine. They'd shared a great deal about themselves in that first meeting, things she couldn't imagine sharing with any other stranger in the store. The attraction had been immediate and grew stronger every time Val was anywhere near her. She anticipated her visits as much as her grandmother did. If she knew Val was coming through soon, she watched the calendar like an expectant mother and searched her closet for what might catch Val's eye. She'd never done that for anyone.

She looked forward to their walks and placing her hand under Val's belt. To be honest, she kept an eye on Val's social media account just to be able to see her, to feel connected in some way while Val rode through warmer climates. Spring brought anticipation of many things, but none more than knowing Val would be stopping in. She ached for even the briefest of embraces where she could feel Val's strength and smell her sharp cologne. Just the thought of it raised goosebumps on her arms and she rubbed them with her hands. What she felt for Val was no passing phase. She'd fallen for Val that day over a meal and good conversation. Every time she thought of Val, she understood what her grandmother meant about the heart knowing what it wants, even if the mind doesn't.

***

Val went back to her room after the morning's activities. She found it disgraceful that fifteen years past 9/11 and the thousands of casualties later, there was no memorial for the Iraqi or Afghanistan veterans. Those who made the ultimate sacrifice in bringing to justice the terrorists behind 9/11 deserved recognition. Those who died knew they were fighting a war, no matter what Washington called it. Those people were brave. Val never considered herself brave and wanted her fellow soldiers recognized for their sacrifices. Bringing attention to the lack of a tangible memorial was her way to honor them as she rode to the Vietnam Wall for Memorial Day. It was well past time for the politicians to recognize the true cost of war. The VA hospitals were overrun with mental health issues and serious lingering injuries. Everyone screamed from the mountaintops at the treatment of veterans, and yet no one wanted higher taxes or to pay that unseen cost of war in the treatment of long-term brain injuries. Val's temple pounded and her jaw hurt from being clinched. Her hands ached from being balled into fists. She opened them and rubbed her face.

She shook herself, dispelling the anger. She knew dwelling too long on these subjects would drive her into a bottle, or the arms of someone she really didn't want. After Tess, she'd kept her sexual liaisons brief and without any real meaning. She didn't get serious or leave things with a question regarding the next time the woman would see her. Val had been honest with them about her needs and tried to make those she was with satisfied.

Since meeting Laurel almost five years ago, she hadn't even taken a woman to dinner. The attraction to Laurel was so strong, but she couldn't bring herself to move past the casual flirtation. Something about Laurel kept her from doing it. Hurting Laurel, or Ree for that matter, was a greater concern than her need for sexual release and the oblivion losing herself in a woman's body would bring. No, she knew what it would be with Laurel, and she was both exhilarated and terrified at the prospect. Doubts caused her to believe she'd fall far short of what Laurel deserved. Instead of taking that chance, she always swung one leg over Maggie's black tank and rode off into the sunset. Time and time again, Laurel Anastasia Stemple drew her back.

Her cellphone rattled across the table, alerting her to a notification. It was Liz with a date and an appointment time. Val added it to her Google calendar and sent a simple 'thanks' in response. Closing her eyes, she put her phone in the chest pocket of her leather coat. She'd plug it into her audio system on Maggie. She finished rolling her clothes into the leather duffle bag she'd attach to the seat. She picked up the cup of coffee and stood at the window overlooking over the city. Her mind drifted to the memory of Laurel leaning against the porch post. Thinking of how it felt to hold her caused her to smile. She looked at her watch, finished the coffee, and picked up her gear. Within thirty minutes, she'd start back along the same route they'd taken the few days before. The way she had it planned out, she could spend about four hours at the diner visiting with Ree, Laurel, and the gang, while passing on the rubbing of Dale's name to Mule. She looked forward to these visits with all the anticipation of a child at Christmas. She could see them every day and her reaction would be the same. These people were like family, and she craved the warmth of their embraces after her absence like an addict. She bounded down the stairs, imagining walking into the diner's kitchen. The yeasty smell of homemade rolls, of fresh coffee and tangy chili sauce. Her mouth watered. She wanted to do more than just think about being there. She wanted to get on the road, now.

Val's group met in the parking lot and the lead riders gave instructions while everyone secured their gear. "Hey, John. Marion, you get a good night's sleep?"

Marion, a short woman with a warm smile, tucked a stray strand of brown hair back into her helmet. "We did. You ready to get back on the road?"

"You know it. I'm not much for hanging in the concrete jungle. I've never much liked city life."

Val watched Marion's husband John, a gentle giant of a man, gather his gray hair back into a ponytail and slip on his helmet while she strapped her bag to the bike. She pulled on her own helmet and threw her leg across the wide leather seat. She reached for her camera as he settled in on his seat and brought his Harley to life.

John put on his sunglasses. "I'm ready to get out of here. Too many damn politicians for my taste."

As the bikes roared to life, the ground trembled like a massive beast. The percussion of the exhaust beat against Val's chest. She loved this moment, seconds before the incredible horsepower would be unleashed. She snapped several shots of the group as they pulled out onto the roadway. Tucking the camera into the special pouch near her windshield, her retreating hand touched the small photo of Maggie and Lorraine for luck. As she made it to the roadway, her body settled into the familiar rhythm. The farther they rode, the more her nerves settled. Cool Springs drew her back, like a magnet, to Laurel.

Concrete, high rises, and traffic congestion gave way to green rolling hills and tree lined blacktop. Dodge pickup trucks replaced the BMWs of the city. As soon as they crossed the West Virginia border, a smile crossed Val's face. Her mind conjured up John Denver's tribute to the mountain state that was its unofficial battle cry. She sang the familiar tune that called her to travel this twisting winding road. *It's like this road leads me back to the place my heart belongs. It leads me back to her.* Just the thought of spending even a few hours with Laurel brought her true happiness.

It was a thing of beauty to watch the bikes be so in sync. Some of this group had been riding together almost twenty years. She particularly enjoyed watching John and Marion who rode in front of her. Milliseconds separated their movements. She watched as John's bike would roll left or right, with Marion mimicking the fluid movements.

Turning her radio to John and Marion's talk channel, she spoke aloud. "You know, watching you two ride is a lot like watching synchronized swimming."

After a second of silence, Marion's voice filled her head. "That's what riding together for over two decades will do for you."

They'd previously owned a motorcycle shop together and started a large motorcycle rally in South Eastern Ohio that carried on to this day. Their son John Jr. ran the shop so they could enjoy retirement riding around the country at their leisure. John and Marion had become her good friends. They frequently took trips together including being with her the first time she'd stopped at Cool Springs. It was a comfortable friendship. Still, they didn't know as much about her as Laurel and Ree did. *Strange.* Val probably spent more time with the couple, but it was always about the bikes, or John's plane, or Marion's musical abilities. She knew quite a bit about them, but they only knew the surface of her.

She was almost positive the couple didn't know her leg was amputated below the knee. Neither did Laurel or Ree. Having her natural knee and wearing a top of the line prosthesis allowed for no noticeable limp. Pants and boots allowed her to easily conceal the metal and fiberglass. Learning to live with the loss hadn't been near as hard as finding her grace in surviving the blast that killed her friends. The bile rose in her throat, choking her. She focused hard on the back of Marion's bike, forcing her feeling of guilt into the background. Her mind shifted to her next destination. Knowing she'd see Laurel and Ree soon allowed her to shake off the melancholy.

The miles to Aurora rolled by easily, the traffic passing in the opposite direction was sporadic. Large green fields dotted the landscape. A green tractor pulling a wagon passed by. Looking up, she saw a sizable break in the line from the lead bikes. As they passed the fire department, a flash of yellow caught her eye. She jerked her head sideways in time to see a sports car run through the stop sign at the intersection of US Route 50 and County Route 26. She braked hard and steered to avoid the impending collision, her heart leaping into her throat. The car's momentum was too great, and it caught the side of her bike. Her vision tunneled into a stop motion effect. Each frame a second of her life. The sound of squealing brakes and smell of burnt rubber, the groan and pop of metal bending and giving way, all assaulting her senses. *Oh shit!* The collision sent her into a slide, sparks flying into the air as metal ground against pavement. The force of the blow ripped the handlebars from her grip and she was thrown off.

Her head hit the pavement with a bone-jarring thud as she went spinning into a field along the roadside. Her body rolled over and over, finally sliding to a stop. Too shocked to feel the pain, her ears rang. She tasted the tang of copper. She spit out a mouthful of blood, spraying the inside of her visor. Everything spun.

She felt the weight of the helmet as she tried to lift her head. Her vision blurry, she tried to focus, tried to find her company commander. The sounds all around her were foreign and unrecognizable with her blunted hearing. Heat, searing heat, and the unmistakable smell of blood. She hurt all over. *Where had the blast come from? Where was the danger? She reached for her service weapon, missing.* Her training coming back to her. *I need to move, find cover. How many hostiles? Identify. Eliminate.* Muffled voices she couldn't understand, closer. *Danger. Need to find cover!*

Val tried to get to her feet, but her leg refused to obey. Her body reeling, she rolled onto her stomach and searched for a purchase point so she could crawl to safety. Her lungs screamed. She tried to take a deep breath, finding she couldn't. The pain started to hit and for some reason, she couldn't push with her left leg. Exhausted, she strangled out one word before the blackness overtook her.

"Medic!"

Chapter Four

ALL DAY THE BIKES rolled in and out of the store. They barely got the tables bussed before the next crowd came in. Each time the bell over the door rang, Laurel looked up, anticipating Val to come strolling in. It was nearing 5:00 pm, and Val's crew was overdue. Laurel looked at Ree who sat rubbing her knee as she ran the cash register. *Her knee has never been wrong. Maybe it's not about Val.*

Finally, around 6:00 pm, Laurel recognized John and Marion come through the door. They looked grim. Laurel dried her hands and walked toward the couple. She kept watching, praying for Val to come in behind them. Val never did.

Laurel's pulse raced. "What's wrong? Where's Val?"

John ran his hand through his hair, and Marion put her hand on his shoulder. The couple had stopped here many times with Val. Marion's voice shook. "Honey, there's been an accident."

Laurel's hand covered her mouth and her legs nearly buckled. Her mind raced. *Accident? She'd be here if she was able. Please let her be ok. She has to be ok.* Her stomach sank, and she felt sick. Thank goodness for Beth. Her friend was at her side in an instant, putting her arm around Laurel's now shaking form.

John rubbed his forehead. "We just left the scene. Some car ran the intersection from Route 26, hit Val and the two bikes behind her."

Even with Beth holding her, Laurel reached out for a chair to steady herself. "Is she all right? Where is she?"

"They flew her someplace. I'm not sure where." Tears rolled down Marion's cheeks. "I won't lie to you, Laurel, it's bad."

"I've got to find out where they took her. Beth, call your brother. Maybe he was there at the scene and can tell us where she is," Laurel implored. Beth's brother Mike volunteered for the local fire department.

By this time, Ree had made her way over to Laurel. "Liebchen, come sit down. We'll find her. Beth, go make that call. Tilly, call Bobeye to see if he knows anything, and call in a few of the part timers. This day isn't over yet, but it is for me and Laurel."

They led Laurel over to the rockers, and she looked up at the couple. "What did you see?"

Marion took a deep breath. "She had blood on her face and was thrown pretty far from her bike. They were putting some kind of splint on her right arm. They put her on a backboard and strapped her down. Her helmet was still on, but they cut the visor away. She was wearing her leathers, so I didn't see a lot of road rash."

Laurel sat shaking and stunned, taking in the information. She felt like her world hung on the edge of a cliff. She tried to categorize the injuries. *How bad is it? They said she was bleeding. Head injury. Anything could be wrong.* The panic rose to a fevered pitch, her mind running wild. *She said they were splinting her arm. What about her back?* She felt hot, unable to breath, and light headed. She had to get to Val. She needed to see her for herself. Sweat ran down her neck. Her chest heaving, she struggled for breath. Tears burned her eyes. She needed air.

Ree rubbed small circles on Laurel's back. "Honey, calm down. Slow your breathing or you'll pass out." Ree looked to the couple. "Was she talking?"

A look of sadness dropped across John's face. His shoulders slumped. "No."

"Thunder," Ree said. "Beth, what did Mike say?"

"They took her to Morgantown. Mike says she's pretty busted up, but alive." Beth stopped at Laurel's side and put a cool towel on the back of her neck. "Mom's coming down to help at the store. I'll drive you both over there."

Laurel looked at Beth, unable to say anything. The tears welled and fell in earnest now. She reached for Beth's hand and squeezed. She found her voice. "Thank you."

"Let's get going," Ree said.

It took over ninety minutes to arrive at Ruby Memorial Hospital. As they walked through the automatic doors, a blast of cool air hit them. The lobby smelled like industrial cleaner. People milled around, phones to their ears, oblivious to everything around them. Rows of chairs sat filled with people talking. A small food counter buzzed with activity as the attendant filled large Styrofoam cups with steaming liquid.

Laurel stepped toward the busy information desk, nearly running into a woman in blue scrubs pushing a janitorial cart. Apologizing, she stepped back, allowing the woman to pass. She shook her head, trying to clear the fear filling her body. She turned to her grandmother, her hand in front of her mouth. "God, Gram, how in the hell are we going to find out how she is?" They were unlikely to get much information on Val given they weren't blood family. All the new privacy laws prevented the hospital from giving out patient conditions.

Beth squeezed her shoulder. "Honey, try to remember anything you can that Val might've said about her family. Maybe we can track them down, and see if they'll give us permission."

Laurel wiped the tears from her cheeks and tried to think. "Her dad's a professor at the University of Washington. Norse history, I think. There can't be that many Magnusson's there that teach that subject."

Beth pulled her phone out. "That's a place to start. Let me see what I can find on their website. Do you remember anything about her mother?"

"Only that she's a journalist out there. I have no idea where."

"Let's see." Beth's finger scrolled down the screen in her hand. "There is a Professor Hallsteinn F. Magnusson. It's got to be him. I'll call the school." Beth stepped to the side and started to make the calls.

Laurel and Ree made their way through the line at the information center in the emergency waiting room. A silver-haired woman sat behind the desk, looking something up for a gentleman standing at the counter. After a few seconds, she wrote on a piece of paper, handed it to the inquirer, and pointed down the hall. As they stepped up to the woman, Laurel started to speak but she choked up.

Ree put her hand on her granddaughter's forearm. "Ma'am, a friend of ours was brought in by helicopter from a motorcycle accident in Aurora. We aren't blood family, but that doesn't mean we don't think of her like one. I know ya got rules, but she's got no one around here. She's from out west, and we're trying to reach her parents. So, with all that being said, we're looking for Val Magnusson."

The silver-haired woman in a bright-pink smock smiled and looked around. She typed at her computer and wrote on a piece of paper, directing them to the fourth floor. "Wish I could help more. I could get in trouble for even giving you this much."

Laurel's tears began to fall again, still unable to speak. She whispered a strangled 'thanks' to the woman, grateful for the act of kindness.

"Thank ya, and if ya do get in trouble, ya come find me." Ree, still holding Laurel's arm, led her back over to where Beth stood.

Ree looked at the paper and put her hand to her chest. "Looks like she's in surgery. Not sure what we can do until we get in touch with her parents, but at least we'll be near."

"I'm on hold right now with the university operator." Beth held her phone to her ear as they headed for the elevators.

After they reached the surgical waiting room, Beth spoke to the receptionist telling her they were attempting to contact Val's parents in Washington, Laurel standing close at her side. As she was giving her their names, Beth stopped to speak into her phone.

Laurel leaned in, trying to decipher the one-sided conversation. She held her arms tight around her middle. The fear turned her stomach over. Her head pounded, and tears continued to trickle down her cheek and drop off her jawline. *Please God, let her be okay.*

The receptionist looked up at them. "Did she say Laurel and Marie Stemple?"

"Yes." Laurel raised a questioning eyebrow. "I'm Laurel Stemple."

"Sorry to have eavesdropped. You said you weren't family. The information I have, has you both listed as contact people in her information. Let me see if I can find out more." The receptionist picked up her phone and began dialing.

Beth stepped closer to Laurel and Ree. "Okay, I got through to the operator at the university. She's going to try and contact the Magnusson's. I gave her my number."

After about fifteen minutes, the receptionist walked over to them. Laurel's eyes rose to the woman. She felt tears trickling down her cheek and she wiped them away.

The receptionist tilted her head as she read from a notepad. "Apparently, Ms. Magnusson was conscious in the E.R. and gave her consent for you to be updated on her condition. According to the staff, she was pretty adamant about it."

Laurel stared at her in disbelief, trying to understand the meaning behind the woman's words. The one thing she held on to was that Val was conscious. Conscious enough to remember her and her grandmother's names.

The receptionist continued. "Someone's going to come and update you in a bit."

"Thank you." Laurel bit her lip to keep more tears from falling. Obviously, Val thought of them as important to her. She sat down on the couch beside her grandmother and folded into the comfort of her arms.

"Our Viking's tough, honey. Ya gotta believe she's gonna be okay."

"I'm trying, Gram, I really am."

She felt her grandmother pull her closer and place a gentle kiss on her temple. *Val has to be ok. She still has to take me for a ride someday.*

Waiting without any answers to Val's condition was the hardest part. Too much time passed with nothing to do but worry. She paced back and forth near the windows while her grandmother looked through an old *Taste of Home* magazine. Beth had gone to get coffee for them. Her mind was on Val. Her visits were never long enough. In all the years she'd been stopping in, they'd always taken time to talk, getting to know each other in short conversations that veered off into unknown tidbits of information that filled in the blanks. *Valkyrie Vör Magnusson.* She whispered the name, remembering the conversation that revealed Val's full name and led her to nickname her Viking. She let her thoughts roam into one of her fondest memories.

Laurel stood behind the counter as Val sat her coffee cup down.

Val pointed to it. "Can I get another?"

Laurel squinted at her. "It'll cost ya."

"Name your price, milady," Val countered.

"Val is short for what?"

Val blushed. "Oh, I can pay that price, but you might not believe it."

"Try me."

"Valkyrie. Valkyrie Vör Magnusson."

"Ah, we have been graced in our little hole in the wall by a Viking god." Laurel bowed her head in mock worship. "Let's see if I can decipher that. You're one that brings the slain to Valhalla for Odin and … Vör … what was it?" Closing her eyes for a moment, she tried to recall a distant memory. "The careful one? Goddess of oath and promises?"

Val's mouth fell open. "How in heavens name do you know any of that? I'll bet I couldn't find twenty people who know who Vör was."

"Majored in business administration. Minored in Greek mythology. I dabbled in Norse mythology. And I read. A lot. I've always been fascinated with lore." Laurel grabbed the coffee pot and poured her another steaming cup.

Val shook her head, spinning the coffee cup on the Formica top.

Laurel slid a warm fried apple pie in front of Val. "Here's to having the most unique name I've heard in a long time. Eat up."

Looking around the diner to see if anything needed her attention, she sat down beside Val on an adjacent stool. Between bites and satisfied moans, Val explained her father was a professor of Norse history at Washington University. Her mother had been a journalism professor at the same university but now freelanced for the Washington Times.

"Ok, your turn. Your first name is Laurel. What's the rest? By the way that," Val pointed her spoon at her now empty plate, "was delicious."

"Wait until you taste her rhubarb crisp."

"Rhubarb?"

Pointing at her stomach, Laurel winked. "Do you have any more room in there?" Val tipped her head in affirmation, and Laurel made her way to the kitchen where her grandmother sat peeling potatoes with a Cheshire grin. Walking over to the stove where a large pan of crisp sat, she pulled down a bowl. Eyes burned a hole in the back of her head. She turned to her grandmother and narrowed her eyes.

"What?" Ree turned toward the twins working the grills. "Girls, did ya hear me say a peep?"

"Not a," Faye started.

"Word, Ree," Kaye finished.

Laurel rolled her eyes at her grandmother and placed a hand on her hip. "It's what you're not saying that's screaming, Gram." Picking up the bowl, she walked over to the small woman and kissed her on the cheek. "You're such a troublemaker."

"Say what ya will, but I saw this coming long ago in a dream. I'll just see if it plays out the same." Ree went back to her peelings. "You go on now, Liebchen, if that don't knock the socks off of her, we'll have to pull out the big guns."

"Oh, I think she's already impressed with you, Gram. No need to have her going around barefoot." Laurel pushed the swinging doors open with her back.

"Not yet anyway." Ree wiped her hands and set the bowl on the table.

"I heard that."

Laurel placed the dessert down in front of Val and ran her hand through her hair. She pulled her hair to one side so that it lay over one shoulder. The woman beside her unsettled her, so she calmed herself by running her fingers through the strands.

Val looked up, spoon held in mid-air, mouth open. The second the sweet concoction hit her tongue, she groaned.

"That good huh?"

"Stunning." Val shook her head and pointed to the crisp, blushing. "I mean, it's delicious."

"I'm glad you like it."

"I might be in love with your grandmother. Or at least her cooking." Val grinned and scooped up another big spoonful into her mouth.

"Gram is single but unavailable. She gave her heart long ago and even though he's been dead over sixty years, she still misses him like it was yesterday." Laurel's eyes grew soft. "Gram's been waiting a long time to hold his hand again."

"How about you? Anyone have your heart?" Val asked around a mouthful.

"Gram would tell you not to talk with your mouth full."

"You won't tell on me, will you?"

"Not a word, Viking." Laurel smiled, not meaning to give her a nickname, somehow finding it naturally rolling off her tongue.

"Viking, I like it. When I was in the service they called me Click, because of the camera. Most of the time you couldn't see my name on the uniform." Val stared off for a moment.

"What branch?"

"Marines. I worked for Marine News, embedded with a combat unit until..." Val stopped abruptly and spooned another bite of the crisp in her mouth.

Laurel saw the far-away stare. A few seconds passed as she watched the shadows travel through Val's eyes. Not knowing what put them there, she wanted to pull her out of it. "Tell me about that bike you rode in here on. Not sure I've seen too many like that."

Val shuddered for a second. "I can't imagine you have. It's fairly rare. It's a 1946 Indian Chief. Completely restored. Found it on one of my travels. I stopped to take some pictures of this farm's gorgeous red barn. I knocked on the house door to ask permission. The owner, probably about Ree's age, and I struck up a conversation. Believe it or not, it was her motorcycle. What a pistol. She and her companion had ridden all over the place on it before she died. After that, she parked it in the barn and covered it up. Didn't have the heart to ever ride again without her partner. Offered it to me for a fraction of what it was worth. I gave her more than she asked for and stayed around for a few months helping her with things that needed doing. I was fresh out of the service and had no place to be. I finally got it running, sold mine, and took off on

'Maggie May.' The real Maggie died about six months after I left. She and Loraine are probably riding around on the highways up in heaven."

"That is an incredible story. Did you do an article on them?" Laurel liked the wistfulness in Val's voice as she spoke.

"I did. A whole series called Miles with Maggie. It was pretty popular. I could never get her to take a ride with me, but I did get her to pose, holding an old black photo of her and Loraine with the bike."

"I'll bet she was glad to see someone else keep their memory alive." Laurel tentatively reached out and touched Val's forearm.

Val looked down at Laurel's hand. "You've avoided two questions of mine. Time for you to pay up. Full name, please."

Laurel grinned. "You've got a mind like a steel trap. Full name, Laurel Anastasia Stemple."

"Anastasia. I'm guessing there's a bit of German in your family?"

"A lot more than a bit."

"And anyone special in your life?" Val asked, a curious smile on her face.

"No one has claim on my heart."

"And how on earth can that be with a smile like that?" Val placed her hand on her heart and turned her head in mock disbelief.

Laurel looked off into the distance. "I guess I'm holding out for someone who makes me feel like my gram said my grandfather did. I just haven't met her yet."

"Your gram said you play for my team."

Laurel crinkled her nose and quirked an eyebrow. "I think that's a story for another day. Eat your crisp. Looks like your crew over there is itching to get back on the road, Viking."

Laurel was abruptly drawn back into the present by the entrance of a young woman wearing scrubs and a surgical cap into the waiting room. They were the only people occupying the space. "Are you the Stemple's here for Val Magnusson?"

"Yes," Beth said.

"May I sit down?" the woman asked.

Laurel felt her anxiety ratchet up as her heart began to race. Sweat formed above her lip and the hair on the back of her neck stood up. "Yes, of course. My name is Laurel, and this is my grandmother, Marie. This is my friend Beth."

The doctor pulled off her surgical cap and ran her fingers through her sweaty hair. "Thank you, it's been a long day. My name is Dr. Ellis.

I'm the trauma surgeon on her case. I'm sorry I haven't made it out to see you yet. I've been in the operating room. She's in the recovery room right now."

Laurel watched as her grandmother wrung her hands. Still missing vital information, Laurel probed. "How is she?"

"Stable," Dr. Ellis replied.

Beth put a hand up. "Wait, let me take notes. I'm waiting for a call from her parents." After digging around in the massive purse that Laurel had always made fun of, she produced a small pad of paper and a pen. "Okay, go ahead."

Dr. Ellis held her stethoscope in her hands, fiddling with it while she spoke. "It seems she had some injuries from her military service. We didn't see any further injury to her amputation. She was bleeding internally. Her spleen had to be removed, but she can live without that. She also has a fracture of her right scapula and several severe tears in her rotator cuff. Those issues will have to be addressed in a future surgery after she's more stable. It's a good thing she was wearing a helmet, because she still has a pretty serious concussion. Other than that, there's no major brain trauma. Overall, she's pretty damn lucky. She's beat up, but alive, and I intend to keep her that way. Right now, I need to get back and review a few more of her tests. She'll be in the SICU, so I can't tell you how soon you can see her. Do you have any questions that I can try to answer?"

Laurel looked up at the doctor, confused and searching for questions that should be asked. "God, a million things. I'm assuming the blood loss and spleen injury are her most critical issues?"

The surgeon nodded. "For now. I'll consult with the other surgeons as to what to address next and when. Right now, her body needs to heal a bit," Dr. Ellis said as she rose. "If her parents call, I'll be happy to talk to them if I'm available. Just have the hospital operator page me. If I can come, I will."

Through her quiet tears, Laurel said, "Thank you, Doctor Ellis." She tried to process the new information that seemed improbable. *Prior military injuries? Amputation? What the hell? That doesn't make any sense. Val never mentioned any of those things.* Her mind felt like it was in the industrial blender they had back at the diner. She rubbed her temples.

"You're welcome. In the meantime, there are some private waiting areas that are much more comfortable. I'll have the receptionist direct you to one."

41

"That's mighty kind of ya.". You take care of our girl. Sounds like she's got a rough road to travel. Apparently, she's no stranger to that." Ree's voice dropped off, revealing her own sadness.

"From the looks of her previous injuries, I'd say you're right, ma'am."

Dr. Ellis left them while the receptionist directed them into a private waiting room with a coffee pot and comfortable couches. As she walked to the door, she turned to them. "If there are any major changes, you'll be updated as soon as possible. Let me know if there's anything I can do."

Laurel couldn't sit. She felt queasy and unbalanced. Questions ticked off in her mind as she walked to the windows looking out onto a practice field. Flashes of blue and gold faded in and out of her field of vision. She pressed her warm forehead to the cool glass, trying to process the information and falling far short of any answers.

Beth came up beside her and wrapped her arms around her from the back, resting her chin on Laurel's shoulder. "It's going to be ok. Don't make yourself crazy. Want a cup of coffee?"

Laurel shook her head no and started to pace, trying to push back the panic that bubbled below the surface.

Twenty minutes later, Beth's cellphone rang. Laurel came over to sit on the couch beside her. "Hello, this is Beth Abernathy."

The voice on the other end was so loud Laurel could hear it just by sitting next to Beth. Their conversation seemed to ring throughout the quiet room. "Ms. Abernathy, this is Amanda Magnusson, Val's mother. How is she?"

"Please call me Beth, Mrs. Magnusson." Beth told her all they knew so far.

"That damn motorcycle. If she hadn't been on it in the first place, she wouldn't be hurt." Val's mother sounded distraught, her voice pitching louder.

Laurel winced at Val's mother's shouting and watched her friend try to be sensitive to Mrs. Magnusson's distress. She defended Val, though, too. "The accident wasn't her fault. Someone ran an intersection and hit three of the riders."

"I'm sorry. I know Val is careful. She's my only child. I almost lost her to the war and now this." There was a long pause, and Laurel had to strain to hear Val's mother's next words. "Do you have children, Beth?"

"No, I don't. That doesn't mean I can't understand your fear. Val's important to us."

"She almost died in Iraq. I'll be on the next flight east." Amanda's voice trembled slightly.

Laurel tried to put in yet another piece of new information about Val's past. *Her mother said she almost died. How could I not know any of this? Have I just not been listening or does Val not talk about it?* She leaned forward, her elbows on her knees, pressing her thumbs to her temples. She had more questions now than she'd ever had.

Beth hung up her phone. "Seems her mother will be on the next flight east."

"Sounds like she's mad at our Viking." Ree pointed to her ears. "Even with these old ears I could hear her shoutin'."

"She's upset. I don't think she cares much for Val's love of motorcycles." Pantomiming, Beth rolled her wrists back like she was riding one.

"Unless I miss my guess, our Viking doesn't give a damn what others think, including her momma." Ree chuckled, coming to sit by Laurel, rubbing her back. "She's gonna be okay."

Laurel, who'd barely gotten herself under control after listening in to the phone conversation, stood and walked to the windows looking out at the football stadium. "In all the conversations we've had over the years, she's never mentioned anything about her parents other than what they did for a living. I have no idea if they're even close. Somehow, I'd think if they were, we'd know more about them. She made sure the hospital would tell us about her injuries. Don't you think it's strange she never mentioned to the staff about calling blood relatives? I hope this wasn't the wrong thing to reach out to her parents."

Ree walked up to her and put her arm around her waist. "No matter what, honey, they're her family. They should be told. What happens after that is up to all of them."

Laurel whispered now. "I'm scared, Gram. She could have died, and I've never told her how I really feel."

"Sometimes it takes us almost losing something to realize how important they are to us. Ya still have that chance. What happens now is up to you two." Ree walked away from her, leaving her standing looking out at the white lines marking each yard on the practice field. Laurel vowed that if she got the chance, she'd tell Val how she felt.

Chapter Five

VAL WOKE UP FROM the anesthesia haze in a great deal of pain. Her mouth was as dry as it had been while she was in the desert. Mindlessly searching for her lip balm, a surge of white-hot pain shot down her arm. The pain cleared the haze, and she tried to raise her head to look around. Monitors hung above her, droning out steady beeps of her heart on the screen.

"Oh, what fresh hell can this be?" she murmured, quoting Dorothy Parker. The fog began to clear a little more, and she looked at her right arm. It was in a large bulky immobilizer. *Well that sucks. I'm fucking right handed.* Her throat felt like she'd swallowed ground glass. She'd been intubated. Her head felt like it had been used as a soccer ball. Each time she tried to look around, the light caused knifelike pain. On the top of the scale was an intense pain in her abdomen. Val used her left hand to gently seek out the source of the pain.

A soft voice broke through the equipment noise. "Hey, look who's joined us. Welcome back from your nap, Rip Van Winkle." A warm hand captured her exploring one.

She squinted, unable to focus or recognize the voice. Somehow it was familiar. She knew it, and yet, it just wouldn't come to her. "Can I have some water?"

"I can get you some ice chips, no water yet. I'll be right back."

While the voice was gone, Val again tried to take inventory of her pain. Her left foot hurt. That had to be phantom pain because that foot had been gone for a long time. There were times she'd wake up in a nightmare and forget. Jumping from the bed to run, she'd crash to the floor trying to take a step on the limb that no longer could perform that duty without the prosthesis. From her inventory, she cataloged three major areas of pain: head, shoulder, and belly. She struggled to remember what had happened. A spoonful of ice chips appeared in front of her lips.

The voice she was still trying to identify came again. "Not too many now. Just let them melt in your mouth."

Laurel. Turning her head to look at the figure by her side, she croaked, "What happened?"

"There was an accident. A kid ran an intersection and hit you and two other bikes."

It all flashed back in a second with terrifying clarity. The impact, the sound of crunching metal and squealing tires came rushing back. "Laurel, are John and Marion okay? They were right in front of me."

"Shhh, you'll get me thrown out of here. They only let me in because you wouldn't settle down." Laurel put a gentle hand on her uninjured shoulder. "John and Marion are fine. The bikes behind you got a little beat up. Unfortunately, you took the brunt of it."

"How bad?"

"You're pretty beat up."

Val furrowed her brow, irritated. "Not me, Maggie May."

"I don't know who you're talking about."

"My bike." Val tried not to be petulant.

"Oh. I don't know. I'll call Bobeye later. He picked it up. We were only worried about you, you blockheaded Viking." Laurel stroked her fingers through Val's locks that fell haphazardly across her forehead.

Val chuckled at the nickname, gasping as the movement sent pain shooting through her body.

"Be still now or I'll have to leave. That pain in your belly is from the operation to save your life. You nearly bled to death." Laurel held another spoon of ice chips to Val's lips, which Val sucked on gratefully.

"Do you have anything to put on my lips?" Val raised her left arm and ran her finger across her dry lips. "They feel like I'm back in the desert."

Laurel reached into her pocket, pulled out the small tube, and rubbed the soft stick across Val's dry lips. "Better?"

"Much, you're an angel of mercy. Now how about you tell me how bad this all is in a little more detail, now that I know Maggie May's in good hands," Val said, her eyes roaming her own form that lay under the bleached white sheet covered by a thermal blanket.

Laurel explained what her condition was in more detail. She looked down at Val's left leg. "You've got a lot of bumps and bruises that will have you sporting several lovely shades of blue, purple, and yellow soon."

With the humor fading, Val replied, "Funny, a real comedian you are. How messed up is my prosthesis?"

"Pretty messed up. Took a direct hit and came off in the melee."

"Fuck. It'll take me forever to break in a new one. Took me almost six months to get that one the way I wanted it where it wasn't causing sores." Val scowled, raising her left hand to her forehead, shielding her eyes to look at Laurel.

Laurel's eyes grew soft. "Of all the things we've talked about in the last few years, you never mentioned you'd lost your leg."

Val sighed and closed her eyes. Few people knew outside of her doctors, her family, and a few women she'd let close enough to see her au naturel. "It's not that I didn't want you to know, I just never talk about it. I've spent a long time perfecting my gait. I don't need anyone to pity me. I don't talk about it, because I don't like to remember how it happened. For the record, my elbow is a replacement, too, titanium. I guess if they have to replace my shoulder joint, you can call me Borg instead of Viking." Val tried to summon a smile that fell short.

Pointing to herself, Laurel quirked a smile. "Trying to take my new job?"

"What?" Val said.

"Comedian. I think we'll stick with Viking. You're a warrior. Get some rest. Your mom should be here in a few hours."

Val tried to rise from the bed, her pain the only thing forcing her to lie back down. Her head swam. "Oh, for fucks sake! How does she know about this? How long have I been out?" Her relationship with her mother was strained under the best of circumstances. This would likely be the straw that broke the camel's back. She didn't need her condescending tone or her self-centered attitude, especially not now.

The monitors began beeping all around the hospital bed. Laurel rushed to calm her. "Hey now, don't make me bring Gram back in here to put you in line."

"Ree is here? You've got to be kidding me." Val forced herself to be calm, though anxiety still flowed through her. Val knew Ree rarely left the mountain and worried about her.

"No, Beth drove us over here. I've sent her to the hotel to rest. Beth's going to pick your mom up at the airport and bring her over." Laurel placed a cool palm against Val's heated cheek.

Val leaned into the touch, drawing strength from the woman beside her. She tried to release her clinched jaw. "Just tell me my father isn't coming?"

"I don't have any idea. Beth talked to your mom, but there was no mention of your dad."

Val tried to put it all together and rubbed at her face. Her head throbbed. The thought of her mother's arrival left her nerves raw. "How did you guys even know to call her? I don't even have her listed as an emergency contact in my phone."

Laurel filled in the pieces. "You told me that your dad was a professor of Norse history at the University of Washington when we first time we met. Beth looked up the contact number for the school and called. They took Beth's information and eventually, your mother called her back."

"I'll bet that was pleasant conversation." Val rolled her head back and forth. She stopped as a wave of nausea hit.

"You could say that. Beth did say she was concerned, though she did curse your preference of transportation."

"She hates it and never fails to tell me about it as I pass through."

Laurel winced. "I'm sorry, Val, we didn't know."

Val closed her eyes and reached for Laurel's hand. Their fingers entwined, and a small wave of peace washed over her. She thought about the family drama she didn't wish on her worst enemy. She knew how her mother would be. Amanda Magnusson craved attention and adoration. Neither of which she got from her only child. She garnered it from her many fans as a popular award-winning journalist. The infamous Mrs. Magnusson would come in like a hurricane, full of crocodile tears and looking for someone to fawn over her.

"It's not your fault...we haven't been close in a long time. I guess I followed somewhat in her footsteps by becoming a journalist. That's about all we have in common, aside from our looks."

"You look like your mom?"

"Almost identical, other than hairstyle. Mother is much more to the feminine side. My build and height come from my father." She pointed to her cheek. "This face is all hers."

"So, I'll get to see what you'll look like as you age?"

Val rolled her head to the side slowly, her long bangs falling over her brow. She and her mother did share the pale blond hair color, although she was sure by now her mother's was the result of a pricey Seattle salon. "Hardly, let's just say she looks more like my sister than my mother. She keeps the plastic surgeons busy."

Laurel stroked the stray wave of hair out of Val's eyes. "Oh, Val, that's cruel."

"Truth hurts. She's never gotten over me enlisting and coming home less than whole." Val closed her eyes against the light.

"I'm glad you came home. I'm sorry, Val, I really am."

"It's not your fault. My family has always been dysfunctional. I'll be surprised if my father even knows. Mother will want all the sympathy for herself." Val fought a yawn.

"Why don't you rest? I'll go." The monitors once again raised an alarm. "Hey, calm down."

Val held Laurel's hand tighter. "Don't go, please."

"Ok, settle down. Sleep now. I'll be right here." Laurel interlaced her fingers with Val's.

Val lay back and closed her eyes, trying to process everything. Sleep and exhaustion eventually claimed her, the hand she still held tightly in her own anchored and grounded her in her sea of pain and anxiety.

.

Chapter Six

EVEN THROUGH A LIGHT doze, Val could tell her mother had entered her room. The smell of her signature perfume enveloped her, overwhelmingly familiar and sickeningly sweet. "Hello, Mother." She felt Laurel's hand shift in hers. She used the touch to calm her anxiety.

"Oh, Valkyrie, what have you done now?" Amanda Magnusson held her hand to her mouth.

"I went a few rounds with a stretch of pavement," Val droned, "and it's Val."

"I carried you inside me for nine months, I'll call you anything I damn well please." Amanda's voice rose as her face grew hard, her lips pursed in a frown. She narrowed her eyes. "Valkyrie, I didn't come here to fight. When I heard you were hurt, I jumped on the next flight and flew across the country. The last time I did that..." She stopped, digging through her purse. She withdrew a bottle of pills, shook a few out, and pulled a small bottle of water from her bag.

Val watched as Amanda's hand trembled as she took the pills. Her mother was visibly struggling to get her emotions under control, which was out of character for the normally composed journalist. Val let her head drop back to the pillow. "I was coming home from Germany, I know. It's okay, Mother, I'm not dying. I'm simply missing another body part," She hadn't considered the full ramifications of her new injuries. She'd survived worse in Iraq.

"You and that damn motorcycle."

Val had a death grip on Laurel's hand and the monitors around her began to scream. Val looked closely at her mother. Their features almost mirrored down the straight lines of their nose and jaw line. *Hell, she looks like she just walked off of Rodeo Drive not eight hours on a plane.* She stood at the side of Val's bed, her hair and makeup flawless, impeccably dressed in tailored charcoal pants, a pale blue blouse, and a dark blue velvet blazer over top.

"Mother, if this is your way of making me feel better, then you can get back on the damn plane right now."

Standing, Laurel cleared her throat. "Mrs. Magnusson, my name is Laurel Stemple. I'm a friend. I'm sorry to meet you under these circumstances."

Amanda turned to Laurel, reaching for Laurel's hand. Laurel was forced to release Val's to shake the one in front of her. The loss of the physical connection disoriented Val. A second later, the perfunctory greeting was complete and her hand found its way back into Val's. Her anxiety settled. The two women looked like they were sizing each other up in a battle of wills.

There was a long pause before Amanda broke her gaze and spoke. "May I have a few minutes with Valkyrie please?"

"Sure." Laurel looked down at Val, pulling her hand to her lips and kissing the scraped knuckles. She released her hand. "I'll be outside."

Val missed the contact and braced herself for the brewing storm. "It's okay. If she was going to eat me, she'd have done it when I was a child," Val joked, though it fell flat in the room.

***

After Laurel skirted around Amanda, she walked past the nurse's desk. The nurses were busy looking at monitors spitting out vitals of their charges. Shaking her head, she offered an apologetic look to one of them, knowing they were going to have to deal with the effects Val's mother was going to have on both her attitude and her well-being. Val's visceral reaction to being told her mother was coming, coupled with the brief exchange, didn't bode well for future interactions.

The nurse offered a knowing look of sympathy, briefly resting a hand on her forearm. "Mother-in-law?"

Laurel chuckled and shook her head at silver-haired nurse. Watching her pick up a box of files, she saw the woman's bicep muscle bulge. *Maybe she can put Amanda in a headlock.* "Val's mother. I'm not sure they're that close. I'll be outside if she needs me."

"Go get some coffee, honey, you look like you could use it. She's out of danger. If we can keep our patient from having a stroke, she's going to be fine."

"Thank you," Laurel looked at her gold name badge with hospital logo, "Myra. I'll be back in a bit."

Laurel pushed through the doors to see Beth sitting in the small waiting room. "Come on, I could use some air. God, if Gram treated me like that I'd be devastated. She could have died."

Beth looked at her. "You need more than air. You look exhausted. We're getting something to eat, too. Ree is tucked in over at the hotel. You haven't eaten since lunch today. If I remember right, that was a sandwich."

"I know. I haven't felt like eating. I'm not sure if I can eat with Cruella in there with Val."

"I take it the reunion didn't go well?"

"That's an understatement. Val's lying in a hospital bed with serious injuries. She never even asked Val how she was. She went straight into the 'I'm disappointed in you' routine." Laurel emphasized the point making air quotes. "Val almost broke my fingers she was squeezing them so tight. I didn't want to leave her, but Amanda wanted to talk to her in private."

Playing devil's advocate, Beth offered another possible explanation. "Well, maybe that's what her mother's afraid of."

"What?" Laurel crossed her arms and furrowed her brow.

"Val could've died from this and from what her mom said to me on the phone, this isn't the first time. She nearly got killed in the service. Maybe she's scared shitless and has a rather peculiar way of showing it."

Laurel made her way to the elevator passing by a small waiting room. The air smelled stale and artificial. She needed to get outside.

"Believe me, if it hasn't gotten better by the time I go back, I'm going to ask her to leave. Val needs support and time to heal. If her own damn birth family won't give her that, then her family of choice will." Laurel stepped over to the silver doors of the elevator and jabbed the button to take them down to the cafeteria.

Chapter Seven

VAL STARED AT HER mother, trying to calm her nerves by taking a few deep breaths as Liz had taught her during their sessions. It wasn't working.

"Can we start this again without swords at the ready, dear?" Amanda asked.

"Mine wasn't drawn before you came in. I didn't get my shield up fast enough to deflect your first blow." Val clenched her jaw and then relaxed it. She took another deep breath. "I'll call a truce for now. Hello, Mother." Val willed her pounding heart to quiet. It was always like this with her mother. The fact she'd refused to wear dresses, makeup, date boys, or do anything her mother had wanted kept them at odds since she was six. She had no false illusions that it would be different now.

Amanda gestured to the chair at her side. Val nodded. Amanda moved it so she could face her and sat. "Really, how are you?"

"I'm sore as hell and feel like I've been hit by a truck. However, by all accounts, it was a yellow convertible. I don't think that mattered much. From what I've been told, I've once again escaped the clutches of my namesake. Odin will have to wait for my soul." Sighing, she brought her hand to her throbbing head. "I'm weak, pissed off, and had no idea they'd called you. I'm sorry you found out like that. Thanks for coming, Mother. I really do appreciate it. I haven't felt this busted up since Iraq." Val paused, seeing the look of discreet distress in her mother as her eyes shut and her brow furrowed. "I'm sorry. I know you don't like to talk about that."

"It's more than that. I don't like to think about how close we came to losing you, then or now."

"Where's Father? Off on some European quest to raise some Viking ship from its watery grave?"

"I don't keep up much on your father anymore. He lives his life, and

I live mine. I simply chose not to live it with him and the young college girls sharing his bed." Amanda's tone grew bitter. "I'd divorce him, but I prefer to write the news, not star in it myself. I won't have my life destroyed as he tries to preserve his precious name. For now, he continues to live in an apartment near campus, and I have the house."

"I'm not surprised. At least you're free to do as you please. We both know he's a bastard, better we live on in spite of him." Val chuckled but stopped because it caused pain in her stomach and shoulder. The pain nauseated her and she pursed her lips, breathing in through her nose to stave off the sick feeling.

"Do you need me to get the nurse? Is it time for your pain meds?" Amanda searched for the call button tied to the bed rail.

Trying to breathe through the pain, Val relaxed. "No, I've got a pump and I can dose myself when it's time. I have a while yet." Val tried to center herself. "Mother, what are you doing here? I do appreciate you coming, but there isn't anything you can do."

"Valkyrie." Amanda paused.

Val rolled her eyes but listened.

"Whether you like it or not, I'm still your mother. You may not be able to see it, but I do care. I watched you suffer after the attack and how hard you fought to regain your independence. I flew across the country, because I was told my only child had been in a serious motorcycle accident. As a mother, that tends to pull out all the maternal stops in the hopes you might have the chance to tell your only child how grateful you are to find them still among the living. I didn't come to clash with you, Val. I came because I love you."

Val heard her chosen name and lowered her defenses. She looked at the woman beside her. Upon closer inspection, she could see the shadows beneath the makeup and regretted her insensitivity. "Mother, I'm sorry." Trying to analyze her mother's about face at this point required more energy than she had to put into it. For now, she'd accept it at face value.

Amanda rummaged through her purse. "I brought you a peace offering. Candy cane if I remember correctly. Difficult to find given it's not Christmas."

Val's mother held up a string of small red and white lip balms. Val reached out to touch them. She looked at her mother, eyes soft now. "You remembered."

"You're my daughter. There's little I don't remember about you, at least the parts you've let me see."

Val watched as her mother broke their eye contact, dropping her head. *Maybe it's me that needs to work on my bedside manner.*

Their attention was drawn to the door as Dr. Ellis walked into the room. She picked up the chart and read through the reports. Val watched as she underlined something on one of the papers. She turned to the nurse's station, signaling for Myra's attention. The nurse joined her and Dr. Ellis pointed out something on the chart. "Let's repeat that in two hours and see if those values change. If not, I want to hang blood."

Val craned her neck, wondering if she needed to be concerned.

Amanda looked up at the doctor. "What is it?"

Dr. Ellis walked over to them, pulling up the sheet to examine the incision and looking at Val. "How's your pain?"

A knowing grin lifted the corner of Val's mouth. "Tolerable with the pain pump. This is my mother, Amanda Magnusson. Ignoring her question is likely to bring out a rather unpleasant and unrelenting banshee."

"That may be true. You're conscious and as a doctor, I find that after the age of thirteen, my patients prefer I talk to them and not their mother," Dr. Ellis said, smiling back. "If you're under the age of thirteen, then you've had a pretty tough few years."

This brought a laugh from both Val and her mother, causing Val to gasp in pain again. Amanda stroked back an unruly lock of hair from Val's forehead. She found it strange that her mother's touch didn't elicit the same warm reaction that Laurel's had doing the same thing earlier.

Dr. Ellis nodded to Amanda but kept her gaze on Val. "Since she asked so nicely, here are the basics. Your blood counts are still lower than I'd like even after a transfusion while you were in the ER. Because you have a particularly hard to get blood type, I want to get more on hand before you might actually be in trouble.

Val watched as Amanda raised a single eyebrow and looked at her. *And in rides the heroine to save the day. I'll be hearing about this for the rest of my life.*

Amanda turned to Dr. Ellis. "Despite her feelings to the contrary, it appears it's fortunate that I came. We have the same blood type, and although she tends to think I'm heartless, I think I have enough to spare her a few pints."

"Mother." Val shook her head. Her mother was right; they did share the same blood type. She reached out and squeezed her mother's fingers. "Thank you."

Rising, Amanda smoothed the side of her hair and adjusted an earring. "As I've told you, Valkyrie, there isn't anything I wouldn't do or give for you. Care to direct me to the blood bank, Dr. Ellis?"

Dr. Ellis looked at Amanda, a quirky grin on her face. "Yes, ma'am, step out here at the nurse's desk with me, and we'll make arrangements."

As they stepped out, Val shut her eyes and tried to take stock. *I wonder where Laurel is. Has anyone let my boss know about this? I'll have to take a leave of absence until I recover. What the hell am I going to do about Maggie May? I hope she isn't too bad, but taking a direct hit had to do some major damage. Shit.* She threw her head back into the pillow, bringing back the roaring headache that had started to abate.

"Thinking pretty hard there, Viking, I can see the smoke rolling," Laurel said.

Val opened her eyes and sneered at Laurel who held a cup of steaming coffee in her hands. "You're a cruel woman bringing that around me."

"Oh, you mean this delicious cup of hospital poison? Trust me, you aren't missing anything." Laurel took a small sip and scrunched her face up. "It's hot, wet, and has some form of caffeine in it."

"Hot and wet, huh?" Val's smile broadened as she wagged her eyebrows.

"You must be feeling a little better, either that or those pain meds are better than the last time I was here." She took another sip. "Where was your mother off to on such a mission?"

"To be the hero, of course. Apparently, my blood count's low. If it doesn't get better in a few hours, they want to transfuse me. We're a perfect match for an unusual blood type, so it makes sense for her to make a direct donation."

"Will you be okay?" Laurel's voice quivered.

Val heard the tremble. *Was that fear? She has enough to worry about.* "Sit down." Val pointed at the chair beside her bed. Reaching out her hand, Laurel took it. "I'm going to be fine. I've survived worse."

"I knew you'd been in Iraq. Somehow, I never knew you'd been injured that badly. Care to tell me what happened?"

Val stared up at the ceiling, the familiar tightness settling in her chest. She was back in the desert, searing heat all around her. She shook off the dark shadows of memory trying to envelop her. "Maybe someday. Can you put more lip balm on for me? There are some new ones that Mom brought."

Laurel found the string of candy cane lip balms on the small bedside table. She pulled off the cap and ran the tube along Val's lips, as if she'd done it a million times before.

Val closed her eyes, inhaling deeply. "A bit more, please?"

Laurel again ran the smooth waxy stick across Val's lips. "Is it like an aroma therapy for you?"

"Sort of. My lips have never recovered from the desert, that's why I'm constantly applying it. My grandmother used to carry this tin of salve in her purse. The nights I'd stay over, she'd always put it on my lips before I went to sleep. If I had a bad cold, she'd rub it on my chest, too. I've never been able to find the tin, but I remember that it had red and white stripes on it, like a candy cane. Sweetest woman I've ever met. Reminds me of Ree." Val drifted back to the present.

"Gram used to rub Vicks salve on my chest, so I know what you mean. I want you to get some rest now. I'm going to the hotel for a few hours, but I'll be back. I'll leave the number where I'll be if Cruella gets to be too much for you." Laurel raised an eyebrow and pulled her lips back in an exaggerated smile.

Val laughed. "Don't let her hear you say that. She'll put a restraining order on you."

"Let her try, Viking. I'm pretty sure you were fighting with the ER staff to call me and Gram. And more than a little pissed we'd contacted your mother. I think I've been raised with the stuff to take on the likes of her. Can you tell the nurses that you give us permission to call and check on you? Beth is going to run Gram home in the morning, and I know she'll want to call. I swear some days, she loves you more than me." Laurel grinned, standing to lean over the bed rail. "Get some rest, Viking, I'll see you in the morning." She kissed Val's forehead, holding her cool lips to the heated skin.

Val soaked in the contact. Her attraction to Laurel had always been strong. Now it was reaching a new level. One of a deeper connection on an elemental level. *I need her.* She reached up with her good arm and directed Laurel's head down so she could look into brilliant green eyes. She cupped Laurel's jaw and traced her cheekbone with her thumb. "Thank you for being here for me, all of you. Tell Ree and Beth I said so, too."

"I will."

"And thanks for not pushing me about Iraq right now." Tentatively, Val gave her a gentle kiss, tender, full of emotion, and all too brief.

Laurel kissed Val again and pulled away. "Sleep, Val, I'll be back in the morning."

"Promise?"

"Count on it."

"I'll hold you to that."

"Please do. Now get some rest." Laurel picked up her coffee cup. She lifted their clasped hands to her lips, kissed Val's knuckles, and walked out of the room.

Val felt delicate for the first time in her life. It was as if she was made of thin strands of glass. She'd survived Iraq, but she wasn't sure she would survive the night without Laurel by her side.

***

Laurel tried to be quiet as she climbed into bed beside her grandmother. She didn't want to disturb her if she could avoid it. Beth slept on the pullout couch in the other room. After their bite to eat, Laurel had driven her over here and taken the car back to the hospital.

Ree rolled over to face Laurel. "Our girl okay?"

"I'm sorry for waking you, Gram. She's stable. Her blood count is low, so her mother is donating blood in case they need it. That woman is a trip. Did Beth tell you?"

"Yup, Beth said she came in with both guns blazing. She's scared, honey. No parent is meant to bury their child. I should know. When your kids are sick and there isn't anything ya can do, it tears your soul apart. Sounds like it's only by the grace of God that we ever got to meet Val. Whatever happened to her over there must have been pretty bad. Ya can't mend a fence if the fence is gone. Now, how are ya?"

Laurel was grateful it was dark. She knew her grandmother always saw the truth in her, even if she didn't tell her everything. "You also can't build a bridge if the other side doesn't exist. I don't know what I'd have done if I'd lost her. I'm all jumbled up inside. You, of all people, know why I don't get involved. I can't put someone through what we went through with Momma." Laurel was near tears thinking about her mother's death. She'd watched her struggle and suffer. The memory of her illness was a constant reminder to be vigilant with her own health.

"Liebchen, ya love that woman, and she loves ya too. Everyone around ya can see it. For some reason, you two are bound and determined to not take a chance. I only had your grandpa for a few short years. Ya have a chance to spend your life with the one ya love, no matter how long that is. Listen to what your heart is telling ya to do.

Now, get some sleep. Tomorrow is another day, and Val's gonna need us. Love ya." Ree leaned in, kissed her Laurel's head, and rolled over, pulling the covers over her shoulder. "Never did like sleepin' in a strange bed. Damn thing is harder than a river bed full of rocks."

"Night, Gram." Laurel adjusted the covers around her. Gram was such a homebody. The finest hotel wouldn't have satisfied her. She was a child of the mountain and had no desire to roam.

Trying to fall asleep, Laurel's mind drifted to Val and her wandering soul. *Could she ever be happy in one place? Could she be happy with me?* Val traveled everywhere for her job and had told Laurel there was really no place she'd ever settled other than the seat of her motorcycle. Laurel sighed, remembering Val's tagline she had posted during her visit. *There's no place like home. Cool Springs seems to hold some place in her heart. Could Val be content with Gram and me?* Laurel thought about all the gentle touches she and Val had exchanged over the years. None had been overtly sexual, and yet still intimate in their own way. Her hand fit so naturally in Val's. Val would always pull her close, an arm wrapped around her waist or shoulders anytime they were near. Tonight was truly the first time they had ever kissed beyond a greeting. Laurel was no virgin, but that kiss had ignited her more than any other sexual experience. *That kiss set me on fire.*

With a start, she remembered the reason she hadn't been with anyone in years. The fear of dying from the same cancer that took her mother, paralyzed her ability to love. She scowled at her earlier musings. *How could I do that to Val? She's already lost too much.* Tugging her hair into a loose twist, she held it in her hands and settled her cheek against the cool pillows. Closing her eyes, she sent a silent prayer into the heavens that Val would be all right. She'd figure this out after the current crisis had passed. Right now, Val needed to heal, and she was bound and determined to make sure that happened.

Chapter Eight

OVER THE NEXT SEVERAL days, Val continued to get better. They were fortunate that one infusion of her mother's donated blood had helped bring her counts back up. Dr. Ellis had upgraded her condition to stable, and she was moved out of the SICU and into a private room. This allowed her mother and Laurel to visit more frequently. Laurel was there every afternoon once she'd finished the morning shift. Val had asked her mother to pick up a new smartphone, as hers had been smashed in the accident. Luckily, they could extract the SIM card and all her data and contact information had been salvaged. They were also able to bring her laptop to her. Upon inspection, it appeared to suffer no damage because of the hard-sided saddlebags, but after using it a few times, Val could tell it was on its last leg. She had her mother purchase an external hard drive for her.

One day, while her mother was out, she called Liz to reschedule the appointment with her the following week. Val was fairly sure she'd flashed during the accident. Still pictures spidered out from her memory. *I can remember the taste of blood in my mouth, pain all over my body, even the impact itself in a way.* The last thing she remembered was yelling for the medic. She shook her head, clearing the thoughts. Trying desperately to keep the strength in her voice, she spoke to her friend. "Sorry, Liz, I'm going to have to reschedule on you."

Liz's voice lowered. "That's not like you. You haven't dodged an appointment with me since our first few sessions. What's going on?"

Val stared mindlessly at the TV. She wasn't much of a fan. She flexed her right foot and then bent her knee, bringing her foot to rest flat on the starch white sheets. "I'm not dodging anything. I was in a pretty serious motorcycle accident after I left D.C. I'm pretty busted up in a hospital in West Virginia."

"Oh, Val, I'm so sorry. Is there anything I can do?" Liz asked.

Val heard the shift in her tone. "You can get my mother to go home."

"Your mother is there? How in the hell did that happen?"

"Some friends remembered where Father worked and the university got in touch with her." Val sighed. "Luckily, he didn't come back from overseas, so I've only had to deal with one of them."

"How's it going with her?"

"It was rough going the first day or so, but it's settled down. Laurel's been running interference, and it torques my mother off to no end." Val laughed. "She calls her Cruella behind her back. I need more pain meds just to not die from laughing."

Liz laughed, too, and then paused. "How are the nightmares?"

Val sighed again, knowing that she couldn't bullshit Liz. "I think I flashed during the accident, but it's pretty fuzzy. My helmet prevented a serious head injury, but I still ended up with a concussion. It feels more like snapshots of memories. I'm not sure if they're from Iraq or the wreck." Liz had seen her at her lowest points. Times that she didn't care about living or dying. The nightmares had been so bad she had to be sedated heavily to sleep even a few hours. She only had to live through the physical pain once. The pain from the memories, she lived over and over and over. She still occasionally woke up screaming from a vivid nightmare of the day that stole her military career and parts of her body. Liz had been there all along the way. Val diverted. "How's Jo?"

"My wife is fine, busy creating some kind of metal art from scrap pieces of steel. She has a show coming up soon and has several pieces to complete."

With true admiration in her voice, Val replied, "She amazes me all the things she can do from that robotic chair of hers. I remember she had that conventional one she tricked out after we went through rehab. Designed it herself and built the damn thing with spare parts. She always told me she wouldn't let her paralysis keep her from doing..."

They both finished in unison, "anything I fucking want to."

Jo Romano was Val's best friend and one of the most important people in her life. Having been her chief antagonist, Jo was just as responsible for Val walking as her physical therapists. They met in Bethesda while they were both recovering from active duty injuries. Jo's Humvee had taken an RPG in Iraq. After the vehicle went airborne and overturned, she'd been paralyzed. She'd already been at Bethesda for seven months when Val came in. Jo pushed Val to quit feeling sorry for herself and *get the fuck up,* as she had so elegantly put it. Jo had damn near dumped her out of bed and then kept pushing her wheelchair away from her. Each time Val got close, Jo would push it farther away and wheel herself over to it.

And so, it began, day after day, week after week until Val no longer needed Jo to piss her off to get up. After the amputation healed enough, Val was fitted for her prosthetic, and the cajoling started again as Val learned to walk using it. Over the months, Val and Jo became good friends, moved into the same room, and Jo saw the full extent of Val's nightmares. Val resisted any type of counseling until a particularly bad night that ended with Jo crawling out of her own bed across the floor to hold Val. Several ego slams later, Val finally agreed to see someone. Lieutenant Colonel Elizabeth Ruston worked with Val for over a year to root out the triggers to cope with the nightmares. At the end of that year, Liz retired from the service and set up a private practice in Annapolis.

Slowly, Val became aware of Liz's voice bringing her back from her musings.

"You're diverting, Val," Liz said.

Val, confused by her lapse, quickly recovered. "I'm not. I really did want to know about Jo. The nightmares are tolerable right now. Traveling to the wall and attending the ceremonies always stirs things up. I had a pretty bad flashback one day. I grabbed my sketchpad and worked it out."

"Still seeing the boy?"

"Always. I can't see the soldier's face, no matter how much I try."

"Need a visit? Jo's always up for a ride in that tricked out Hummer of hers," Liz offered.

Val chuckled. "You know it's a little ironic she lost the use of her legs in a Humvee and now as a civilian, she's still driving one."

"She says that if she hadn't been in a reinforced Humvee, she might not have lived long enough to meet the woman of her dreams and marry me. I can't argue with that logic, so if you can't beat them, join them." Liz laughed. "I'll let you slide for two weeks. After that, I'll have no choice but to turn my bulldog loose on you."

Val groaned. "I'll be coming back to Bethesda soon. My peg leg was mangled. I'll have to go see the good folks at The Bodyshop about repairing it."

"That trip better include time to stop in and see me, capisce? Doctor's orders." Liz's tone left no room for argument.

"I promise. If I need to, I'll call. Tell that pain in the ass you married hi from me."

"Will do, and don't be surprised if she comes to see you whether you want her to or not. She'd be up for a good game of catch me if you can. Although with that new chair, I'm not sure you could, even on your motorcycle. Rest, Val, we'll work on the mind after the body heals. Sketch when you need to. If it gets bad, call."

"Thanks, Liz."

Val's shoulder ached, and she adjusted the immobilizer. She wasn't looking forward to having another major surgery or another metal body part. She knew her shoulder wasn't going to heal on its own and not having it fixed, wasn't an option. Another thing she needed was for her mother to go home. They hadn't spent this much time together in ten years. They were barely tolerating one another, and her mother was trying to make more and more decisions without Val. *That has to stop. I'm not a child anymore.* If it got to be too much, Laurel ran interference for her. Seeing her so frequently had become the one positive thing in all of this. Ree had even been to visit a few times, bringing chilidogs, chocolate milk, and a large helping of rhubarb crisp. Val had groaned in appreciation.

She looked up to see Laurel leaning in the doorway watching her. She looked delicious in a pair of worn jeans and a form fitting polo shirt. Carrying a thermal tote in her hands, her smile went straight to Val's heart.

"How are you, Viking?"

Seeing Laurel warmed her from the inside out. "In Mule's words, 'fair to middlin.' Please tell me you have something from the diner in that tote for me? I think they're trying to starve me." Val's mouth watered in anticipation.

"Oh, Gram has made sure you won't starve. I'm pretty sure she's planning to come over here to the hospital cafeteria and give them a piece of her mind after she saw your tray the other day. Tonight, you dine on roast beef, potatoes and gravy, peas and crisp." Laurel looked around. "Where's your mother?"

"I sent her back to the hotel. She's on my reserve nerve and it's close to snapping. I want her to go home." Val pushed her head back into the pillows.

Laurel entered the room and arranged supper for Val on the bedside table. Val reached over and clumsily grabbed the fork with her left hand, spearing a piece of the roast beef. Stuffing it in her mouth, she chewed. "Heaven."

Laurel laughed. "There's a reason the diner has done so well over the years. Gram can out cook anyone in the county." Laurel slid the table in front of Val and pulled out the thermos.

Val was right handed, so doing things now required concentration. Left handed, she couldn't quite spear the peas on her plate. *I had better motor skills when I was three.* Frustrated and hungry, she huffed.

Laurel took the fork from her and moved the table to the side. She sat on the bed and fed Val one bite after another, stopping to let her take a drink. It was so easy between the two of them. "I think you like me taking care of you. What are you going to do after you get out of the hospital?"

Val put her head back and chewed. "Honestly, I really don't know. I could get an apartment over in Annapolis near Liz and Jo, which would mean I'm close to someone for help if needed. I'm going to have to go back to The Bodyshop for repairs. I'm sure there will be therapy after surgery on my shoulder. I'm definitely not going back to Washington State. My mother is driving me bat shit crazy as it is."

"What about your dad?" Laurel asked.

Val answered with thick sarcasm in her voice, rolling her eyes. "Oh, I'm sure you've been able to witness how close we are. You can tell by how many times he's been here and his daily calls."

"I guess that's all the answer I need."

Val held up two fingers. "Judging by the amount of times we've spoken in the last ten years, I'm not even sure I'd say we're on speaking terms. He's an overgrown teenager who never had time for a family if it didn't suit him. In college, I never knew whether someone wanted to be my friend or get close enough to score points with him. Going my own direction infuriated him." She rolled her head left and right against the pillow. "You don't deserve to have this dumped on you. I'm sorry."

Reaching out for the hand clutching the bedding, Laurel used her other hand to cup Val's chin, forcing Val's eyes to hers. "Val, I think we're close enough that you can say whatever you need to. That's what family does and as far as Gram and I are concerned, you're family."

"I—" Val started, but her words stuck in her throat.

Laurel dropped her hand and began clearing the remains of the dinner. "It's okay if you don't feel the same, doesn't stop us from caring about you."

Val caught her arm. "I do feel the same. You two and that crazy bunch from Cool Springs are more important to me that anyone in this world. I only have a few close friends." Shaking her head for emphasis.

"Few people know anything about me. Liz, Jo, and Tess are about all I have. The rest are acquaintances. Don't ever think you aren't important to me."

Laurel cleared her throat. "If that's so, Gram and I have a proposition for you. We want you to come and recuperate with us after your release. Over in Thomas, there's a fantastic little nursing home with a top-of-the-line outpatient physical therapy unit run by a friend of mine. I know you have to go back to Bethesda. I'd like to take you. Beth's offered to take over for me at the diner, and Gram's threatened to make you go cut your own switch if you don't agree."

Val shifted in the bed looking away. Returning her eyes to Laurel, she swallowed hard. "Laurel, that's a lot to take on." *You've already got so much to do. The last thing you need is to babysit me.*

Laurel cupped Val's cheek in her hand. "Think we can't handle it? Come on, Val. Even if it's temporary, you need a place to stay and people who care about you. It's going to be a while before you can ride again, and we want to help. I want to help."

Leaning into the touch, the years of isolation melted away. "Let's see what tomorrow brings. If I need surgery on my shoulder, I don't know how soon my doctor at Bethesda will be able to do it." *You don't know how badly I want to say yes. There's so much of me you haven't seen.*

"So, you'll at least think about it?"

"Your offer is one of the kindest things anyone has ever done for me. I'll think about it. Mother isn't going to like it at all." Val used her good hand to squeeze her temples. She didn't look forward to starting World War Three with the formidable woman.

"I've had her eating out of my hand since the second day. You're not the only one who has been entranced by Gram's crisp."

Val laughed so hard she was forced to grab her side. "Of that I have no doubt."

***

Amanda and Laurel sat down in a quiet area. Val's mother still looked like she'd stepped out of the pages of *Vogue*. Her eyes, however, held a shadow under them that she tried to conceal with makeup. Even with all their discussions, Amanda revealed little about herself or her relationship with her daughter. Laurel had promised she'd get Amanda to go home, and she needed to get started on that. "Amanda, what are your plans from here?"

With a great sigh, Amanda brought her eyes to Laurel's. "She's had enough of me, hasn't she?"

Laurel dropped her gaze and studied her hands. "That's not what I asked."

"I know you didn't. I also know my daughter. We've never had the mother-daughter relationship that some are lucky to have, though she's actually let me in farther this time. As much as I'd like Val to come home with me, I have no illusions that lead me to believe she ever would. She's never stayed in one place long enough to put down roots. I think that's why the military appealed to her. She could see the world and piss both of her parents off at the same time." Amanda shook her head. "I think she already has everything she needs. I know she's out of danger now. I'll start working on booking my return flight this afternoon. Has she told you what she'll do?"

"I've made some suggestions, like for her to stay with Gram and me so we can help her. There's a top-notch therapist in our area. She hasn't given me an answer, so I don't know what she's going to do yet."

"I'm grateful to you and your grandmother. I don't want to see her slip down the rabbit hole again. After she healed, she jumped on a motorcycle and hasn't stopped since. I'm going to let her know I'm planning my trip home. That will let her relax about me asking her to come home." Amanda rubbed her temples, laughing bitterly. "Home. It hasn't been home for her since she started college. I don't know where home for her is, and I'm not sure she does either." Amanda wiped at her eyes. "Thank you, Laurel, for tolerating me. I know we got off on the wrong foot. I'm sorry. Almost losing your only child twice tends to make you lose your grace."

Laurel was grateful for the small crack in the ice that had developed between them. She still didn't like the way Val's mother treated her, but she was learning that much of her bluster was a defense mechanism. "Amanda, I don't know what Val will do. All I know is I want to help her. She seems comfortable enough with my family. If I can convince her to come and stay with us, you can be sure she'll be well taken care of."

Rising from her chair, Amanda reached out her hand and clasped Laurel's forearm. "I've never been the best parent, but she's about the only thing her father and I did right. She didn't grow up watching a happy marriage. If her father had looked at me the way you look at her, maybe our lives would have been different. Maybe she would've felt about our family like she does yours. I don't know."

Amanda turned and walked down the hall toward Val's room, leaving Laurel stunned, reflecting on Amanda's observations.

*　*　*

Val was gazing down at her phone, slowly trying to answer correspondence. She looked up hearing her mother enter the room.

"I'm going to book my flight home. You don't need me here, and I have an interview with the president of the Puget Sound Partnership. They're trying to get more stringent permits to prevent environmental issues in the Sound." Amanda's eyes narrowed. "I'm not even going to ask you to come back to Seattle, because I know you won't. All I ask is that you let me know how you're doing on a regular basis."

Val pursed her lips and let out a long breath. "I will, Mother. I don't know what I'm doing yet."

"I think you should take Laurel up on their offer."

"That's a lot for someone to take on that isn't family."

Crossing her arms, Amanda continued to probe. "Aren't they? I've read the blogs you write after you stop at their diner, Valkyrie. I'm not sure I've ever heard you describe anyplace or anyone with such affection."

Val did consider them family. *More importantly, they consider me family.* "I'll think about it."

"While you're thinking about that, try being a little more honest with yourself on a few other things." Amanda kissed her daughter on the forehead and walked out of the room.

As Val watched her walk away, she marveled at the way her mother could drive home a railroad stake with very little effort.

Chapter Nine

LAUREL APPEARED IN THE doorway, and Val shook her head. "Do you have magical powers?"

Laurel grinned mischievously as she patted her hands together and then separated them in a gesture of full disclosure. "A good magician never reveals her illusions."

"If getting my mother to go home is an illusion, then David Blaine needs to hire you. I'm not sure which is the bigger miracle, that she's going or that she seems to be going without a fuss." Val squinted one eye. "What did Ree put in her crisp?"

"In the words of Sipsey from *Fried Green Tomatoes*, 'secret's in the sauce.'" Laurel grinned.

"I love that movie." A smile graced Val's lips.

Deciding to take another stab, Laurel broached the subject on her mind. She wanted to convince Val to come home with her. "Well, maybe once I get you home we can have a movie marathon of all our favorites?" *Please let me help you.*

Val fidgeted in the hospital bed, running her hand through her hair. "Laurel, I don't know. That's so much on you guys."

It was time to change tactics. *Let's see how you react to a little assertion.* "Suck it up, buttercup. You're coming home with me when they spring you from this joint. I'll help get you wherever you have to be, including Bethesda. We'll take it one day at a time." She held her breath and searched Val's face for any signs of irritation.

Val chuckled and rubbed the back of her neck nervously. "It doesn't sound like I've got much say in this. I can see I'm not going to win this battle."

Laurel raised an eyebrow, smirking. "Oh, you have a say. You can say yes now, or in a few days when they let you out."

Val raised her arm in surrender. Laurel reveled in her triumph. *In the words of my favorite Pittsburgh Pirates announcer, "Raise the Jolly Roger, game over."*

Another week passed as Val recovered in the hospital. She signed her release papers and Laurel helped her into her Jeep to drive them to her home in Aurora. Val had completely given in after another visit from Ree, who threatened to use her considerable powers of persuasion and make her cut her own sprig of forsythia if she wouldn't listen to reason. Val agreed after saying she'd help out at the store once she was recovered.

Laurel drove slow, taking care to avoid as many potholes in the road as possible. They pulled up to the modest home, the exterior covered with native field stone. She ran around and helped Val into the companion wheelchair. Grateful for the ramp built onto the house leading to a side entrance, Laurel wheeled Val into the house. *She looks pale. I bet she's in pain.* Laurel, relieved to finally have Val home, helped her into the guest room. The room was warm and inviting, decorated with antiques and pieces of local pottery. The physical therapist had shown her how to help Val stand so that she could transfer in and out of the wheelchair without inflicting injury on either of them.

"How are you? Comfortable?" Laurel examined Val. Beads of sweat dotted her forehead and upper lip. Her eyes were full of pain and she grimaced as she settled Val onto the bed.

"I'm ok. Just tired."

Laurel retrieved a cool cloth that she placed on Val's forehead. "Rest, ok?"

After seeing Val nod, Laurel retreated, but left the door ajar so she could hear if Val needed her. She made her way to the kitchen where her grandmother sat with a sharp paring knife, cutting peaches into small chunks.

Laurel ran her hands through her hair, pulling it up off her neck. She rolled her shoulders in an attempt to release the tension that had formed during their ride home. Dropping into a chair at the table, she rested her head on her palm. "She's settled in for now. I'll take her something to eat later." She looked at her watch. *She'll need a pain pill, too.*

Ree looked at her. "Going to take her a while to get her gumption back. What's your plan?"

"Tomorrow, if she's up to it, we'll drive over to Annapolis and stay with her friends Jo and Liz. The following morning, I'm taking her to someplace called The Bodyshop, to see if we can get her prosthesis fixed. I think she's more worried about that than anything. From what she told me, the last time it took her over a year to get the fit right. Later that afternoon, she has an appointment at Bethesda for her shoulder." Laurel yawned.

Ree waved her knife through the air. "They must know what they're doing. Tarnation, I never even knew she had one. My Uncle Henry was missin' a leg. Some logging accident he had as a kid. Had this great big wooden thing with metal brackets and a wide leather strap that went up and over his shoulder. He hitched it to walk, but walk on it he did for sixty years. They just kept whittling him a longer one as he grew."

Laurel stifled a laugh, worried she would wake Val. She shook her head in disbelief. "Gram, just when I think I've heard every one of your stories, you pull one out of your hat."

"Honey, once you've lived as long as I have, you'll have stories too." Ree laughed and went over to the stove. "I'm going to do something that will be easy for her to eat one handed. No peas."

Laurel rose and ran a hand down her grandmother's arm, kissing her temple. She paused. *I hope you're around for a long time. I need you so much.* "Thanks, Gram, I'm going to go check on her." Laurel made her way down the hall and pushed the door open a crack.

Val was asleep but not resting well if her furrowed brow and jumping jawline were any indication. Laurel stepped in, pushed a few locks of hair off Val's forehead, and adjusted the throw she placed over her. As she rose to close the blind a bit more, a hand caught her wrist.

Looking up from the bed, Val said, "Stay, please?"

Laurel peered into the blue eyes clouded with pain and walked over to the other side. Val rarely asked her for anything. She wanted to be close to Val, to comfort her and reassure her she'd be all right. Though they'd never done more than embrace and share a few tender kisses, Val had asked her to stay and there was little Laurel wouldn't do for her. Pulling off her shoes, she carefully crawled onto the bed. Val lifted her left arm up in invitation. Laurel moved in until her own head rested on Val's shoulder, tucked under her chin. She caught her breath as Val's right hand, still confined by the immobilizer, clasped hers. *This feels so right.* She relaxed into the touch and within minutes, both were asleep.

***

Ree stole down the hallway as quietly as she could, trying to avoid the creaky boards. Peering in, she saw exactly what she'd expected. Laurel curled up in Val's arm with her own thrown across Val's body. They looked like they'd been together forever. Ree backed up and walked away with a smile on her face. Now if she could just get them to see what she did—love.

***

Val woke with Laurel in her arms. She didn't move, afraid to wake her and lose this moment. Before Laurel joined her, her pain and her mind refused to let her rest. A peace had come over her once Laurel had lain down beside her. She couldn't remember the last time she felt this way. *Maybe because I never have before.* Stroking the soft skin of Laurel's arm, she marveled how her fingers tingled. She didn't care if they ever moved.

Laurel stirred and rolled her head to look at Val. The smile she offered warmed Val to her core. Laurel sat up looking down into Val's eyes. "I think I smell dinner. How do you feel?"

"Actually, pretty good. Some pain, but it's tolerable." She watched Laurel rise from the bed. "I need to go to the bathroom."

Laurel stepped around the bed and helped Val sit up, helping her to the bathroom and waiting outside for her. Unconsciously Val tried to use her right arm to slow her descent into the chair and winced at the pain. *Damn.* She closed her eyes and breathed through the burning in her shoulder.

"Thank you." Val took an appreciative sniff to the air. She could make out the fragrance of chicken and bread. It smelled heavenly and Val's stomach grumbled. She needed to put back on the weight her accident and hospital stay had cost her. She knew getting too skinny cost her strength she needed it to hold up the big bike. *If I ever get the bike back in shape to ride.*

They made their way to the dinner table in the comfortable kitchen and Laurel helped her into a seat at the table. Worn wooden chairs creaked with every weight shift. A cheerful red and white checkered tablecloth covered the surface and real cloth napkins sat with the silverware. She held one up to Ree with a questioning look.

"I just like em' better than those paper ones. These I can scrub my hands good after a good round of barbeque," Ree said, handing a glass bowl to Laurel. She carried the main course to the table herself and uncovered a roasting pan full of chicken and dumplings.

Val's mouth watered in anticipation.

Ree took her seat and said a word of grace, then they dug in. She placed her napkin on her lap. "How are ya, hon? Ya in much pain?"

Val shook her head. "Not as much as I would expect. My head is still a little fuzzy, and my arm bothers me if I do something I shouldn't. Good thing I bounce. Don't worry, I'm alright." She reached out and patted Ree's hunched back, trying to ease the concerned look on her face.

Ree's eyes searched hers. "You've got a big trip tomorrow, so eat up and get rested for that. Mule and Bobeye have been asking about ya. I'll give'm a report tomorrow."

Val speared a piece of homemade bread. "Damn, I just thought about my cameras and the rubbings from the wall. They were in my saddlebags. Anyone know if that stuff is okay?" *I hope some of my things survived.*

Laurel shook her head. "I know Bobeye towed it. I'll check with him tomorrow."

Val tried to relax, knowing there was nothing she could do about her things if they were destroyed. "My sketchpads are in there, too. Any chance we could drop by there on our way out in the morning?"

Laurel finished chewing her bite of food. "Sure. It's on the way. That companion wheelchair's easy to get in and out of the Jeep."

They ate and enjoyed small talk about the diner and who had said what. Ree got tickled. She composed herself as she relayed the latest Wunder story. "So Wunder came in the other day with that look. We all waited 'cause we knew this was gonna be good. He turned his head sideways the way he does." Ree mimicked him perfectly. "He asked, if they find plane crashes in the ocean, how come they don't find submarines crashes in trees?"

Val held her side as she laughed. Laurel shook her head while she cleared the plates. She came back with three bowls of peach cobbler topped with milk.

Val's eyes lit up as she raised her spoon. "I'm not going to have to worry about putting weight back on around here. I'm going to gain three hundred pounds eating like this," Val said, as she shoveled the cobbler in her mouth.

Laurel giggled. "I guess we'll have to find a way to work it off you."

Val couldn't resist pushing the envelope a bit. "And how, pray tell, do you plan to do that?"

A blush rose up Laurel's neck. She grabbed at her shirt collar and pulled it. Turning back to the refrigerator, she picked up the tea pitcher. "Pretty soon you'll hook up with Fallon and she's likely to work your ass off in therapy. My bet is you can eat all the crisp you can handle without fear of needing to go buy new jeans."

Val had noticed the blush, thinking Laurel beyond adorable when she was embarrassed. By the time Laurel made it back to the table and filled their glasses, Val could barely see the blush. She tried to change the subject, letting her off the hook. "What day do I get to meet Fallon?"

"I guess that will be up to your surgeon once we get your wing fixed, and I assume after you get your leg back in working order. We'll also need to check with Dr. Ellis to make sure you don't have any restrictions."

Val sat with a spoonful of cobbler millimeters from her lips, staring at Laurel. Her mouth curled into a smile. *I guess I'll just follow her lead.*

Ree laughed at them.

After finishing dinner, they all sat around the table and played a few hands of cards. Val had never spent a more enjoyable evening. *Funny, no one's staring at their smart phone, no reality TV droning on, just honest interaction around a kitchen table. I could get used to this.*

"Gin." Ree fanned her cards out. "I'm pretty sure if we were playing for coin, the two of you would be washing dishes at the diner until ya got to be my age." Rising from the table, she looked at both of them. "Goodnight, girls, these old bones would like a lay down and to spend a few hours seeing what Agatha Christie has Miss Marple up to. See ya when ya smell the bacon." Ree kissed Laurel on the temple and did the same to Val. Ree let her weathered hand rest on Val's shoulder. "Nice to have ya with us, Val. I like having ya in person compared to seeing ya on a little screen."

Val closed her own fingers around those of the older woman. Ree's fingers were soft, and yet Val knew they were working hands. This simple gesture made her insides go to mush. Her words stuck in her throat, and she coughed. "Thank you, Ree. I don't know if you will ever know what having you and Laurel there for me during this has meant to me."

"Night." Ree kissed Val on top of the head again and moved out of the kitchen and down the hall.

Val closed her eyes tight to keep the tears threatening to escape from rolling down her cheeks. She felt Laurel's hand close on hers.

"She's something isn't she, Viking?"

"She's amazing and so are you." She opened her eyes and looked into Laurel's green ones. "So, how about that movie marathon you promised, or at least one of them?"

"Only if you'll watch it lying down. You need to rest and that strap has to kill your neck," Laurel replied. "What do you want to watch, chick flick, classic, comedy, or thriller?"

"I think you promised me an evening with Idgie Threadgoode, if I remember correctly," Val said using an exaggerated southern drawl.

"So I did." Laurel retrieved the wheelchair. "Your chariot awaits. Towanda!"

Val laughed. "I'm with you." *And I've never been happier.*

***

They made their way to Val's new room. Laurel settled her on the bed, then left to make a huge bowl of popcorn and some tea. The movie played and they both laughed as Idgie let the prosecutor have it. Once they'd finished the popcorn, Laurel moved into Val's arm, with her head resting on Val's chest. The steady relaxed rhythm of her breathing told Laurel that Val was asleep. Not wanting to disturb her, Laurel stayed where she was, warm and comfortable.

As the movie continued, she watched Idgie's soul shatter at the loss of Ruth. Laurel gained perfect clarity about why she hadn't crossed the imaginary line she'd drawn on her heart. She was dancing dangerously close to allowing an impossible dream to take hold. *The cancer might already be inside me, waiting.* She wanted to stay in the small cocoon she currently found herself in. The warmth of Val's body drew her in and for the first time, she questioned herself. *Why not? What if?*

Chapter Ten

THE NEXT MORNING VAL woke up alone to the tantalizing smell of bacon. Looking over at the bright red numerals on the clock, she could see it was 5:30 am. *Early risers in this house.* That suited her fine. She'd always enjoyed the morning hours. Trying to make her own way to the bathroom was going to be a chore. She threw back the covers in a huff. Unfortunately, the wheelchair was across the room, and she wasn't sure how she was going to hop over there. She pushed herself into a seated position, groaning at the stiff muscles and the nagging pain. She swung her legs over the side of the bed. Not having her prosthesis grated on her. *I could crawl*, although she wasn't sure about getting back up. She scooted to the foot end of the bed and noticed the large bedpost. *That'll work.* She pulled herself up with her good arm into a standing position. It made her incision hurt like hell, but she was upright. *Now how can I get over to the bathroom? Ah ha!* Spotting a small rolling office chair under the desk, she pulled it to herself and rested the bent knee of her amputated leg on it, then propelled herself across the hardwood floor to the bathroom.

Val heard clapping as she reached the doorway. She turned to the sound and saw Laurel standing in the bedroom doorway in a pair of loose boxers and a t-shirt. *God, she's beautiful.* Her mouth curled up in a sheepish smile.

Laurel shook her head. "I wondered what you were going to do after I saw you sit up. Bravo, Viking, bravo."

Val blushed feverishly, dipping her head in thanks. "I'm not good at being dependent on anyone. Not that I don't appreciate it, honestly. There are just some things you want to be able to do on your own. Hopefully after we get to The Bodyshop, they can either fix my current leg or put a new one together quickly. I could've at least used crutches until they fixed my leg, but this bummed up shoulder makes that a no go."

"The good thing is this house is already universally accessible. As my mom got sicker, we remodeled to make it easier for us to care for her. The grab bars are already there, and it's a walk in, roll in shower with a chair. If there's anything you can't reach, let me know." Laurel walked over and made up the bed.

A wicked grin came across Val's face as she looked back at Laurel. "Like my back?"

Laurel bent over laughing, her blush already apparent. "God, you're bad. I suppose that could be arranged."

Heat seared up her cheeks. "I think I've got it. I'll need some help getting this contraption off to get in the shower. After that, I'm good."

"Ok. Breakfast is ready if you want to hold off on that shower. I was coming in to see if you were awake or if we needed to keep it hot until you got up. Bacon wake you?"

"It's a great alarm clock. Nothing like the smell of bacon frying, although I'm usually up this early anyway." Val yawned and stretched her good arm out. "I need to hit the head. I'll yell for you if I need help. If it's okay, this office chair works pretty good. I should be able to navigate to the kitchen."

Laurel nodded. "It's fine by me, but please be careful. I don't mind helping you, honestly. I know it's important to be able to do it for yourself, but for now, let us help you when you need it."

"Thanks for understanding. I promise, I'll ask. See you in a minute."

***

Laurel smiled and headed back to the kitchen. *Do it myself or die trying. Stubborn cuss. It's not a sin to ask for help.*

Ree eyed her as she stole a piece of bacon. "What's that grin all about?"

"Oh, Gram, that's one persistent woman. She figured out how to use an office chair as a scooter. Wait until she makes it in here. So damned independent." Laurel shook her head but the smile remained.

"Think about it. Having something ripped away from ya causes ya to fight tooth and nail to get back what ya can and hold even tighter to what ya have. Remember, she's not used to being part of a family like we are. To us, it's a helping hand. To her, it's doing it for her. She'll see the difference once she's been here for a while. Trust me, I plan to give her a few jobs as she's able."

"I have no doubt about that." Laurel turned slightly to the hall. "Here comes Miss Independent now."

Val managed to wheel herself fairly easily into the kitchen and with help, moved to a seat at the table. Her hair had been wet down and combed, but she had an adorable rooster tail sticking up in the back. She looked up at the two women with a smile on her face. "Morning." She caught Laurel's attention and furrowed her brow. "Miss Independent, that's cute. Not."

Laurel shrugged. "If you say so."

Ree chuckled. "All right, you two, breakfast is on the table. Val, ya take your coffee black, right?"

"Yes, ma'am. I used to take cream, but that was a luxury in the desert. I learned pretty quick to drink it without."

Ree sat a large mug down in front of her with a glass of orange juice. Laurel rose and walked over to the counter looking at the medicine bottles the hospital sent home with Val. She got out the dosages of antibiotics, anti-inflammatory, and pain meds. Bringing them over, she placed them by Val's left hand and sat down at the table to eat. She could feel Val's eyes on her as she took her seat.

"You're an awesome nurse," Val said, in a playful voice.

"Funny." Laurel pointed her butter-laden knife at Val. "Eat."

Twenty minutes later, her belly full of biscuits, bacon, and eggs, Laurel leaned back with a satisfied moan. Val did, too, which Laurel was happy to see. With the same precision and speed they used at the diner, the table was cleared and the dishes done.

Beth stopped in to pick Ree up. Grabbing two biscuits on the run, she bent down, kissing Laurel on the cheek on her way by. Backing up, she planted a sloppy kiss on Val's cheek, too. "You're part of this madhouse now, might as well get used to it. You two be careful on your travels. Text me later." She was out the door, Ree on her arm.

Laurel kissed her grandmother on her way out and turned to Val. "I'm packed, but I need to shower. We can stop by Bobeye's and get what you need off the bike. I'm sure we'll probably need to do a little shopping for you. You really need some button up shirts so you don't have to pull them on and off over your head until you get that shoulder fixed. How long you will have to wear that contraption?"

Val sighed. "When we see my surgeon tomorrow, then I'll know more. Cat will want to get this done sooner than later. And probably bitch that I've waited this long."

Raising her eyebrows, she looked at Val, stunned. "We just got you out of the hospital yesterday. I don't think we could have gotten you there any sooner."

"Yeah, but you don't know Cat. If she could get you into surgery before you had the accident, it wouldn't be soon enough. She's a battlefield surgeon. Out there, the quicker she gets the bleeding stopped and the bones reset, the faster your recovery. Pretty amazing by anyone's standards."

Laurel crossed her arms. "If you say so. Anything I can do for you before I jump in the shower?"

"Nope, I'm good." A crooked grin came across her face. "Will you need any help?"

Laurel pulled her shirt away from her neck to release the rising heat. "I think I've got it covered, Viking." She was enjoying this playful flirty side of Val and wanted it to continue. She was still feeling a little conflicted, though. Her heart was telling her to see where this road led. How far she would travel it was still yet to be determined.

***

An hour later they pulled into Bobeye's garage. Laurel helped Val into the chair and wheeled her into the area where Maggie May sat. Val felt like someone had ripped muscle and skin away from her body. The big Indian Chief sat upright on deflated tires. Dirt and clumps of grass littered the chrome and black paint. The bold oversized fenders once gracefully curved down over the tires, were bent at odd angles. The paint was scarred where the rocks and blacktop scraped across their surface. Gel leaked out of the comfort pad of her custom leather seat. One mirror hung from the handlebars while the other was missing completely. The large glass headlight was busted. The insurance company would probably total it. Tears came to her eyes at the destruction. She felt sick. She couldn't imagine not riding it ever again. *No matter how long it takes, this isn't the end of the road.*

She rolled over to the machine that had been more like a friend than a mode of transportation. Her hand grazed the tank, fingers coming to rest on the picture of Maggie and Loraine, still intact in its place of honor. It was one of her more treasured possessions. It'd taken a good bit of convincing for Maggie to give Val a picture of her and Loraine after she'd bought the bike. The older woman couldn't believe Val wanted to carry it with her. The photo was an old black and white with scalloped edges. Maggie sat straddling the bike, her outstretched arm resting on the handlebar with a cigarette between her fingers. Her other arm was around a beautiful woman with dark hair and dancing eyes. Loraine stood at her side, one hand resting in the center of Maggie's chest, the other around her waist. *I'm so sorry, Maggie, I'll fix it, I promise. We'll all ride again.* Val felt a hand on her back.

She looked up at Laurel. "This is the original Maggie May and Lorraine. The two of them have ridden hundreds of miles with me. I'm glad this survived. Seeing the bike like this hurts me more than any of my injuries."

Laurel knelt and took Val's face in her hands, pulling her gaze away from the wrecked machine. "The good thing is, we're going to get you both fixed up. I'm positive Maggie May has many more miles left in her. I'm even more positive that you do. What do you need off of her?"

Val proceeded to show her what to grab, including the large rucksack and everything out of the hard saddlebags. Checking the case that carried her camera, she could see the damage. *My longest lens is beyond repair, but at least the body survived.* Her small external hard drive was busted. *Maybe the data can still be recovered?* Most of what was on it had been saved in the cloud, but unfortunately some files weren't.

Val's voice grew soft as she cleared off a clump of mud from the gas cap. "Bobeye, keep her safe for me, will you?"

Bobeye covered her hand with his. "I always told you I never wanted to see this Indian on the hook. I'm glad if it had to be done, it was me doing it. I did my best not to do any more damage than the idiot who hit you. She'll be here, no charge on storage. You get back on your feet, and we'll make everything as good as it ever was."

"Thanks. We better get a move on, Laurel. Maggie May isn't the only thing that needs new parts. See you later, Bobeye." Val watched as Laurel loaded the gear from the bike into the Jeep. "When we get to Liz and Jo's I'll need to do some laundry. I'd been on the road for a week before the accident happened. I hate that I lost my favorite leather pants. Any clue about my jacket?"

Laurel laid a hand on Val's shoulder. "They had to cut them both off you. We have them back at the house, but I didn't think you'd want to see them."

"I guess I don't need them. Not like I'm getting on the bike anytime soon anyway." *Shopping never has ranked high on my to do list.*

Laurel stepped around the front of Val's chair and placed both hands on the armrests. She met her gaze and put a hand on her cheek.

"You will ride again. You've been through worse. This'll be a walk in the park for you."

Val found that Laurel's touch grounded her and pulled her back from the ledge. "Don't mind me, I get to feeling a little sorry for myself on occasion. Seeing my bike torn up is sort of like the proverbial straw breaking the camel's back. I promised Maggie I'd take care of her."

"You will. Accidents happen, and a sixteen-year-old kid in a convertible happened to you. Let's get this show on the road so we can start fixing what we can."

Val lost herself in Laurel's green eyes, drawing confidence that everything would work out, one way or another. *Including my feelings for you.*

***

After two hours of travel, Laurel started looking for a place to stop. Val's color had paled and a light sheen of sweat shone on her brow. She held her injured arm. *That brace probably needs adjustment.* Wheeling the Jeep into a small roadside diner, Laurel wanted to give Val a break and she needed a cup of coffee for herself. Heading inside, Laurel helped Val move close to the table in her wheelchair and she sat in a chair across from her. The waitress stopped by their table offering menus and white ceramic mugs of steaming coffee.

Laurel pulled one of the medicine bottles from her purse, retrieved a pill, and handed it to Val. "I know you don't like taking these, but you'll only delay your healing. Your body needs to recover, and it can't do that if it's fighting pain. Trust me, I know."

Val was looking at the menu but stopped to accept the pill. "Ah, my faithful nurse is back."

Laurel rolled her eyes and lifted the coffee cup to her lips. Val threw the pill in her mouth and gagged. A sour look came across her face as she took a drink of coffee to wash it down. Dark shadows still showed under her eyes. She wasn't well. Thoughts of how close they'd come to losing her drifted in and a shiver ran down Laurel's spine. *So close.* She didn't want to think about life without Val, no matter what their relationship would become. Resting her chin in her hand, she looked at the blonde woman sitting across from her. Val had always looked so alive, so strong. Now it looked like the wind had left her sails—drawn and gray. *I'll bring that light back into your eyes. I'll help you heal and get back to what makes you happy.*

The waitress took their order for two pieces of apple pie. Val pulled her phone from her pocket and Laurel watched her struggle to type left-handed and resisted the urge to offer her help. Their pie came and Val put her phone back in her pocket. Laurel watched her struggle without her dominant hand. "Need some help?"

"Thank you, but no. I might be a little slow, but I've been feeding myself for a long time, although I think I made less of a mess back when I was first learning to hold a fork." She took the bite into her mouth and put down the utensil. She rubbed her hand across her neck while she chewed.

Laurel reached over and pulled Val's hand down and held it in her own. She stroked the soft skin with her thumb. "I know you can do it. I'm not pushing you. I just want to help."

Val took a deep breath and looked at her. "Thank you, Laurel. I appreciate everything you do for me."

They sat together in the small diner and finished their coffee. Val scraped up the last crumbs of the slice of apple pie. She shook her head. "Doesn't hold a candle to Ree's."

"Not much does. At the Buckwheat Festival, she's taken the blue ribbon every year she's entered as long as I've been alive." Laurel left money on the table for the bill. "I'm not sure there's a dessert she makes that I don't like."

They made their way back out to the Jeep, and Laurel adjusted Val's brace to make her more comfortable. Val fell asleep almost immediately. Laurel drove and placed her hand over Val's, smiling as she drew Laurel's hand to her lap. Laurel was sure it was an unconscious gesture. She liked the way it felt, so she made no attempt to pull it away.

Chapter Eleven

AN HOUR LATER, THEY were in Annapolis, Maryland. It was just after 1:00 as Laurel pulled the Jeep into the driveway of the beautiful Georgian style home. It was red brick with large shuttered windows and a gorgeous staircase leading up to the front door. Laurel looked at it and wondered how in the world she'd get Val in there. There was no way she could get her up those steps in the wheelchair. The answer became apparent as a dark-haired woman came out in a wheelchair from behind the attached portico. Her black sleeveless t-shirt showed off her defined arms. Her legs were strapped to the chair. The broad smile told her that she was more than a little happy to see them. Laurel waved.

She gently shook Val, who jerked awake, blinking rapidly. Grasping Laurel's hand tighter, she arched an eyebrow and yawned.

Laurel pointed out the window. "I think someone is glad to see you, Viking."

The woman staring through the window was giving them the finger. Val released Laurel's hand and waved her pinky up and down at the grinning woman. "You're looking at Jo Romano, my best friend and that," she said pointing at her, "is her standard greeting." A few seconds later, a short red head, dressed in a tan business suit, stepped beside Jo and shook her head. "And that's her wife and my psychiatrist, Liz Ruston-Romano."

Laurel raised an eyebrow and stepped out of the car.

Jo opened Val's door and grinned. "Hell, I thought you were too chicken to get out. Afraid I'll whip your ass in a race, or are you trying to keep that fine-looking filly all to yourself, Jarhead?"

Laurel bit her upper lip to stifle a laugh. Jo was proving to be quite the comedian. She tilted her head and looked to Val.

"I'd leave you crying in your beer, Dogface, and you steer clear of that filly or I'm pretty sure Doc will cut off the balls you've never had. Plus, I know that ring on your hand also has a matching one in your nose."

Both Laurel and Liz shook their heads at the two friends. Liz stepped around the Jeep and stretched out her hand. "Hi. Since those knuckle draggers are too busy trying to one up each other, we'll introduce ourselves. I'm Liz."

Laurel took the hand and shook it. "Laurel Stemple, nice to meet you."

Laurel pulled the wheelchair out of the back of the Jeep and brought it around for Val.

Jo reached out her hand, cocking an eyebrow at Val. "Holy shit, Val. You have someone waiting on you hand and foot and you haven't proposed? Your head took a harder hit than you let on."

Still trying to stifle her laughter, Laurel shook the outstretched hand. "I'm Laurel."

"Hi, nice to finally meet you." Jo pointed to Liz. "And my wife is wrong about one thing. I don't need to one up this jackass. I'll always be a step in front and above. Taught her everything she knows."

Laurel did laugh this time and let Liz hold the chair while she helped Val from the Jeep. Val hopped on one foot until she could turn enough to sit down, sweat pouring down her pale face. Laurel was sure she was trying to hide how much pain she was in. Laurel turned a quick glance to Liz, her eyes wide, hoping Liz would see her concern.

Liz spoke up. "How about we get everyone inside? I imagine the car ride hasn't been easy on someone involved in an accident as bad as yours."

Val looked at Liz then closed her eyes. "That'd be great. Thanks."

Jo led the way into the house. "The house should make it easy on her. Everything is universally accessible. There's a small elevator back here that allows access to any of the three floors. The bottom floor is our living area and the bedrooms are on the second. The top floor is my studio and workshop."

Laurel was relieved that the house was set up to handle someone with mobility issues. "Let's get you settled down for a while." Laurel leaned down to look at Val. "You're white as a sheet. Are you going to be sick, or is it the pain?"

"Just the pain." Val peered up at her friends. "Hey, Liz, got a place I can rest? The trip took more out of me than I thought it would."

"Excellent idea." Liz led them through the gorgeous house. Wide plank floors gave the house a warm solid feeling. Rich burgundy and gold accents played in the wainscot and crown moldings. Pictures of Liz and Jo at the beach lined the walls. The house had been lovingly restored. Stepping into the elevator, Laurel pulled Val's chair toward her. She placed her hand on Val's shoulder, giving it a gentle squeeze. Val leaned her head back and rested it on her arm, eyes closed.

Laurel settled back against the elevator wall, holding back tears that threatened to spill out. She felt a hand squeeze hers and looked down to see Liz's slender fingers curled around her own. She watched as Liz mouthed, "it will be okay." Laurel nodded to acknowledge she understood. Liz led them to a large room with muted earth tones and a four-poster bed. She turned on a small lamp on the bedside table and pulled down the bedcovers.

Val cleared her throat and quietly said, "I need to go to the bathroom first."

Laurel pushed her into the spacious bathroom equipped with handicap grab bars, locked the wheelchair, and went around to the front. "How do you want to get up?"

Val considered her options. "I think if we butterfly our hands together and you lean back, I can use this arm to pull up without straining the bum one."

"Ok." Laurel reached out her left hand and Val slipped her clammy one in hers. With a little effort, they had Val standing.

"I can take it from here. Thanks."

Laurel exited to give Val privacy and walked back into the hall where Liz was standing.

Liz reached out and lightly grasped her forearm. "Are you ok?"

Laurel pulled her hair up off her neck, trying to cool down. "I will be, when she is."

Liz shook her head.

Laurel rubbed her neck, trying to relieve some of the tension that settled there. After a few minutes, Val called out and Laurel returned to the bathroom and shook her head seeing Val already seated in her wheelchair. They made it to the side of the bed and they repeated the earlier procedure. Laurel put her other arm around Val's waist to steady her and Val nearly sank into her arms. They pivoted, and Laurel helped Val sit and then lie down. Val's face was completely white. Rivulets of sweat rolled down the side of her skin and she collapsed with a sigh. Laurel went one step further and pulled off Val's boot for her.

Liz turned the wide slatted blind so only a small amount of light filtered into the room. "Laurel, your room is right next to this one, unless you two want to share." Grinning, Liz headed for the door. "I'll see you later. I've got a patient that'll be here in twenty minutes. If you two need anything, yell at Jo. If she can't help, she'll get me. Val, doctor's orders, get some rest."

Val softened as she looked at her friend, her eyes slowly closing. "No choice, Doc. Thanks for putting us up."

"Val, you're family. Laurel, that means you, too. Anyone who can put up with her has to be good people. See you later."

Laurel followed her to the door. "Thank you. She's not so bad. I've wrangled kittens that have given me more of a fight." She turned back toward Val in time to see her grimace. She whispered this time, hoping Val didn't hear. "This trip was hard, and she's hurting more than she's saying."

Liz nodded and replied just as quietly, "Don't let her push you away. She will at some point. It's her nature."

"Don't worry, I've been expecting it, but I'm made of tougher stuff than that. Thanks for the warning, though." Laurel squeezed Liz's hand as she made her exit.

She returned to the bed, putting a few pillows under Val's injured arm to support it and loosening the strap around her neck. Sitting down on the bed, her fingers brushed damp strands of thick blonde hair off Val's pale forehead. "Need a sip of water or anything?"

Val grabbed her hand. "No, I'm fine but..."

"What? Don't be afraid to ask. It's what I'm here for."

"Will you stay?"

Laurel struggled with the overwhelming desire to do just that. Her barriers she'd erected long ago were fast disappearing, as were her reasons to believe she needed them. "Val, all you have to do is ask. I'm here for you, but I don't want to keep you awake. I want you to get some rest."

Val nodded. "I'll sleep, I promise. I just need something to hold on to right now."

Laurel reached out and cupped the side of Val's face. "Then let it be me."

Slipping off her hiking sandals, she climbed into bed. She snuggled under the raised arm and into Val's side, careful not to put pressure on the incision area. She put her hand on Val's chest so she could feel the subtle changes in Val's body. Moments later, Laurel felt the tension start to drift from it. Val's breathing evened out, and the hand that had been caressing her, stilled.

Laurel took in the sharp citrusy cologne that hung on Val's skin. She felt her own thoughts drifting at the rise and fall of Val's chest. A need welled within her to hold Val closer, to protect and heal her. Her heart wanted Val in a more intimate way. In contrast, her head told her she had no business having those feelings, knowing she might not be able to offer Val a lifetime. There wasn't even a guarantee she could offer her a few years. The demons that lived within her cells could make themselves known at any time. Could she dare to dream that she wouldn't develop cancer? Could she allow herself to dream of a future with this tall Viking? *Does Val even want someone in her life this way?* The questions swirled in her mind as she drifted off, a comforting warmth and steady heartbeat beneath her cheek.

***

Val felt Laurel leave the bed as the mattress dipped and then settled. She kept her eyes closed, listening to the quiet sound of Laurel moving around the room. Hearing the door creak shut, she opened her eyes. The second Laurel's body pulled away from her arms, she felt the loss. It was like someone snuffed out a fire on a cold winter's day. *She hasn't been gone five minutes and I already miss her.*

She remembered leaning her head against Laurel's arm in the elevator. She'd felt both protected and grounded. She was growing to rely on Laurel more and more. The unspoken understanding was something she had with few people and none like this. It both frightened and soothed her. She tried to remember if she'd ever felt like this and for the life of her, couldn't. She'd lived with Tess for a short time and could never remember missing her warmth like she did Laurel's. Ever since her accident, her need for this one woman, had intensified tenfold. She put her hand on the bed in the spot Laurel had just vacated. The heat from her body was cooling fast. A faint aroma of coconut and vanilla lingered. She closed her eyes and tried to reign in the desire that was fast overcoming her better judgment.

Val shifted on the bed, trying to get comfortable, and got her shoulder in an awkward position. The pain was instantaneous, a white-hot bolt shooting through her back. *Shit!* Val lay quiet for a few minutes, breathing deeply in through her nose and exhaling through her mouth to hold back the acid that rose in her throat. *I will not throw up. I will not throw up.* She smacked the bed with her good hand in frustration.

She pulled a deep breath in and tried the relaxation techniques Liz used during their sessions. Clearing her mind, she felt the anger dissipate. Pictures of things that comforted her flashed like she was watching an old-time slide show, Cool Springs front porch, Ree in the kitchen making pies, and Laurel standing on the porch, drop dead gorgeous in a tank top and a pair of cutoff jeans. Her mind settled, and the nausea passed. She was floating on a memory or maybe a dream. One way or another, she felt peace as she drifted back to sleep, content to see Laurel in any form she could.

***

Laurel left Val sleeping and walked down the stairs, following the smell of something delicious. Making her way to the kitchen, she saw Liz standing at the stove stirring a large pot while Jo sat at the small dinette drinking a beer.

Laurel pointed to the beer. "God, that looks good. Wouldn't know where another might be found, would you?"

"Praise Jesus, another beer drinker. I was afraid you were going to ask for a glass of red wine like my refined better half." Jo wheeled over to the refrigerator, grabbed a beer, and popped it open with the underside of her wedding ring. "Here you go."

Laurel took the cold bottle from Jo and pulled in a long drink. She looked at the bottle, an amber microbrew. She took another drink deciphering the unique flavor, nutty with caramel overtones and a hint of chocolate. It was really good.

Liz placed a hand on her hip. "Jo, please tell me you didn't open that with your wedding ring?"

A sheepish grin escaped Jo's lips. "I can't help it. It's handy."

"Unlike that really nice opener I had installed right beside the refrigerator." She looked at Laurel, who was smiling at them. "We've been married six years and twice a year it has to go in for repairs. I'm not sure there's much left of the original band."

Jo rolled over to where Liz was and pulled her into the chair with her. "The real ring, as Val pointed out, is in my nose and you know it." Jo kissed her wife.

Liz pulled back from the kiss and lifted Jo's left hand. "Yes, but this, my dear Josephina Danielle Ruston-Romano, is the one your adoring fangirls see while pretending to be in love with your art and not you. This ring tells them that you're spoken for."

Jo put both hands on the wheels of her chair and spun them around. "You're the only fangirl I care about."

They kissed again, and Laurel cleared her throat, uncomfortable.

"Need me to leave so you two can burn the house down without an audience?"

"Shit!" Liz jumped out of Jo's lap and back to the stove where she began madly stirring the pot.

Laughter filled the kitchen and Jo motioned for Laurel to sit down.

Laurel sat, her heart warming. "Val said you two were the real deal."

"It took me long enough to convince her of that." Jo pointed at Liz. "I chased that woman for over a year before she finally agreed to go out with me."

Liz stared at her. "And you know why. I told you several times during that year of chasing me around the hospital, I didn't date patients or anyone else in the military."

"And I told you I wasn't your patient and without the ability to stand on two legs, Uncle Sam was done with me."

Liz shook her head and rolled her eyes. "But you were still enlisted and technically a patient at the hospital."

Laurel loved the back and forth and listened to the married couple go through what was obviously a tired argument that in the end, both had won. They were together, and by all appearances, still madly in love. She gradually realized that Liz had asked her a question.

"Sorry, daydreaming. What did you ask?" Laurel shook her head in embarrassment.

Liz rested her hand on Laurels forearm. "You've had a lot on your plate helping her. I can't imagine why you'd be distracted. I asked how's Val doing?"

"She's really beat up. I was scared to death we were going to lose her in those first few hours. She almost died in the emergency..." Laurel's voice disappeared, and she trembled as the terror came rushing back. She started to cry and covered her face with her hands, embarrassed. "I'm sorry."

Jo wheeled around, pulling one of Laurel's hands into hers. "It's okay. Jarhead up there is damn tough. Has she told you what she lived through in Iraq?"

Laurel wiped at the tears that fell off her chin and shook her head. "She said she would sometime, she just hasn't been able to do it. She's exhausted and weaker than she wants to let on. I get the feeling allowing others to help her isn't in her nature." Laurel took another drink of her beer and began to absent-mindedly pick at a loose corner of the label.

"No, she's a stubborn ass." Jo smiled fondly at some distant memory. "The day I met her, one of the docs asked me to look in on her. I'd tried to engage her a few times. She shut down. Finally, I figured the only way to get her up and moving was to piss her off."

Laurel filed that piece of information away for future use. She'd been able to gently persuade Val into doing what was needed without a great deal of fuss.

Jo gave a low whistle. "If she could have gotten ahold of me that first day, I think she'd have strangled me. Once I got her out of that bed, I knew I had her."

"Honestly, it hasn't taken much to get her out of bed or moving. But she's drawn in right now. She lets me in as far as she can, I'm sure."

"That's a plus, and you didn't even have to piss her off. My wife might not agree, but I'm going to tell you some of her story, at least the important parts. I want you to you know what you're up against."

Shaking her head, Liz said, "Don't put words in my mouth, love. I'm a believer that everyone tells their own story in the way and time they need to. If they don't, I help them find their way to do it. That's my job, you know. I've been told I'm pretty damn good at it."

"She's a spitfire, isn't she, Laurel? Trust me, I married up." Jo pulled Liz to her and kissed her. "Let's go outside. Val's going to sleep for a while longer." Jo grabbed two fresh beers and led Laurel out to a paved stone deck looking out into the back yard.

They settled in around a small table and Jo began to fill in Val's past. "I assume you know she wrote for the *Marine News*, or should I say she was a photographer." She looked to Laurel for confirmation. Laurel nodded and she continued. "Val was embedded with a group of marines who were trying to make inroads with the Iraqi's by delivering school supplies donated by Gary Sinise's charity, Operation Iraqi Children. The unit was delivering these school supplies as a good will gesture. They were gathered in an interior courtyard with teachers and probably fifteen kids. Some guy walked in with a suicide vest on. He detonated it in the middle of them all. Val was front and center taking pictures and lucky to survive. They had to replace her elbow and remove the lower part of her leg. She had a pretty severe concussion and still suffers migraines from the blast. I worry this latest concussion might make them worse."

Liz joined them and sat beside Laurel with a glass of red wine.

Laurel leaned back and took it all in. She'd seen some of the scars but had no idea it had been that bad. "I guess that's why Cruella was in such a snit after she got there."

Jo and Liz both burst out laughing. "Oh my god, that's hysterical. Does Val know you call her that?" Jo covered her mouth in disbelief.

Laurel grinned sheepishly. "Yeah. Told me that if her mom knew she'd probably slap me with a restraining order."

"When I called to talk to her in the hospital, she told me she needed more pain meds to keep from laughing too hard about it." Liz took a sip of her wine.

Laurel glowed at the fact that Val had mentioned her to Liz when they had talked. "Oh, can I use your laundry? We picked up her duffle on the way here. She's pretty thin on clean clothes."

A smirk crept across Jo's face. "She never has been much for material things other than her cameras and bike."

"I'm learning that every day."

Liz stood and walked back toward the patio door. "I'll show you where it is."

Following, Laurel said, "Then I'm going to go check on her. It's about time for her pain meds."

Jo's eyes widened. "She's actually taking them?"

"Yup, like a trooper, and the antibiotics."

Jo grinned. "Wow, that's progress. She tried to suffer through the last time. I was ready to put them in her mouth and pinch her nose to get her to take them. Good for you. I think she's met her match in you, Laurel Stemple."

Liz murmured under her breath, "And I bet it scares her to death."

Laurel raised an eyebrow at the mumbled phrase. It might not have been something she was meant to hear, but it rang in loud and clear. *Then that makes two of us.*

***

Val felt a soft touch and heard a gentle voice. Slowly, she opened her eyes.

Laurel rested next to her, running a finger down her cheek. "Hey, sleepy head. It's time for some meds. I brought your stuff in and tried to sort through what looked clean and what looked like it needed to go in the laundry. In the end, I decided they all needed a trip through."

Val put her hand on her face and groaned. "You sorted through my dirty clothes? I'm so sorry. I'd have done that. Thank you. That's above and beyond."

Laurel laughed. "What? You afraid of me seeing those sexy boxers you wear?" She threw her hand over her mouth, stifling the comment. Val grinned wide. "No, but geez, you aren't my maid. You're already doing way too much as it is. Doing my laundry is too much."

"No, I'm not." Laurel sat down on the bed beside her. "I'm simply someone who cares about you, and you need clean clothes. Eventually we're going to have to go shopping, because you're going to be in one place a little longer than you normally are. Two pair of jeans and four t-shirts aren't going to do it, even if you do look sexy in them." Laurel teased. "You'd do the same for me."

Raising an eyebrow, Val smirked. "Yes, I would. Sexy is the last word I'd use for me right now. Sorting through your underwear would be a lot more exciting."

Throwing her head back, Laurel laughed. "You think so, huh?"

"Oh yeah. I see you as a lacy lingerie kind of girl. Tough and tomboy on the outside, but on the inside? All woman." Val reached out and traced Laurel's upper lip.

The touch elicited a smile from Laurel, but she turned away, a blush rising on her neck. "That remains to be seen." Holding a few pills and a bottle of water, Laurel helped Val sit up.

"We're a pretty good team, you know?" Val noticed that Laurel blushed again. Trying to cool the moment, she offered a different topic. "Where are Liz and Jo?"

"Working on dinner. They said it'd be ready in about twenty minutes. I figured that was enough time for you to move around and get your meds in you. Need help to the bathroom?"

"Please?"

A few minutes later, they made their way downstairs and into the kitchen. Val pulled in a deep breath, enjoying the smell of garlic and tomato sauce. "Please tell me you made Noni's lasagna?"

Jo flourished the large wooden spoon she was mixing the salad with. Liz was bent in front of the oven looking at its contents. "For our most honored guest, of course. Noni sends her love and says you're in big trouble if you ride through without stopping. The only one she adores more than you, is my wife. Liz could get away with murder. I've never seen anything like it. Swears she's an angel in human form sent down to make me fly right."

Val laughed, thinking about Jo's grandmother. "And unless I missed my guess, she's been able to do that, so I wouldn't give Grandma Josephina a hard time about being damn accurate. You were a hellion before this woman caught your eye." She turned to Laurel. "I swear, she'd give Brad Pitt a run for his money on how many women she had hanging on. Then in walks this spit and polished Lieutenant Colonel, and Jo lost her shit. Can't say anything and damn near trips over her own tongue."

Liz blushed, and Jo's rich laughter filled the room. "She knocked me out of my chair. I'd never seen anyone with those steely gray eyes like hers. Lips to die for and legs that went all the way up and made a beautiful ass."

Liz smacked Jo on the head. "Stop that! You're incorrigible."

Jo pulled the petite woman into her lap and wrapped her arms around her. "Yes, and you married me anyway."

Liz melted into her wife's embrace and her hand entwined in Jo's dark hair. "Yes, I did, after you actually got brave enough to ask me out and not have your sidekick do it for you." She leaned over and eyed Val.

"Hey, now, don't drag me into this. I kept telling her what you said about not dating patients!" Val looked at Liz who was about to object, holding her hand out to stop her. "My turn to add to this story as a witness to the courtship."

Liz quirked a smile and shut her lips, wrapping her arms around Jo's neck and nestling into her arms a little more. "Go on."

"Thank you." Val nodded and turned to Laurel. "After Jo and I were discharged, Jo was still asking me to get Liz to go out with her. During one of my sessions, I told her that Jo was dying to ask her out. Liz just shook her head. After my session ended, Liz tells me that if Jo wanted to go out with her, she'd have to find the courage to ask her."

Jo interrupted, finishing the story for her. "And the rest is history. I literally swept her off her feet and rolled her down the boardwalk on our first date. After that, she couldn't resist me."

Val's eyes warmed with true affection. "These two are too much. They're the happiest couple I know." Val looked at the two women she'd come to consider her true family. She had very few people in her life that had any real meaning to her. These two women meant more to her than most of her birth family. Liz and Jo were the center of her support unit. *If it hadn't been for these two, I'd probably be homeless, sitting on the curb in Seattle rocking back and forth reciting the bus schedule out loud.* She shivered and ran a hand across her face. Laurel and Ree had joined that same circle and were increasingly becoming more and more important to her well-being.

"I waited a long time for the best. I know a good thing when I see it. Liz was and still is."

Liz leaned down and kissed her. "Thank you love, now go."

"I'll set the table." Jo spun a few circle wheelies and headed for the cabinet to grab the dishes.

Val sat back and enjoyed the entire banter back and forth between her two friends. Sarcastic humor was one of her strongest coping mechanisms. Without the ability to deflect the anxiety constantly hammering at her psyche like a battering ram, she knew she might well lose her mind. *Or worse, put a gun in my mouth.* She sat watching the smile grow on Laurel's face. She looked at ease. Val glanced down. At some point, Laurel had taken her hand in hers. Their fingers entwined without thought as if it were the most natural thing in the world.

"Anything I can do to help?" Laurel asked.

"Not a thing. You sit there and enjoy the show." Liz pulled the lasagna and the bread out of the oven.

Val felt Laurel's thumb brushing the top of her hand. It was strange that she hadn't even realized she'd clasped Laurel's until the soothing motion penetrated her awareness. *It fits. She fits like nothing ever has.* It felt so right and yet scared her to death. The demons of her past still haunted her, and she was nervous about exposing those she cared about to it. The post-traumatic stress disorder didn't rule her life as it once had, but that didn't mean it wasn't there. She had no idea what might happen during a major flashback with Laurel near. The minor ones she'd suffered in her presence were nowhere near what she was capable of. It had happened before, and she still winced at the memory of the bruises Tess had worn after trying to pull her back from the darkness. *I couldn't live with myself if I did that to Laurel.* Distracting herself from the warmth emanating from her chest, she looked over at Liz. "It all smells so good."

Liz grinned, and Jo carried the salad from the kitchen, disappearing into the dining room with it. After a few minutes, Liz called them to dinner, and Laurel wheeled Val to the table.

Val looked at her immobilized right arm and clenched her trembling left hand. She glanced at her fork. "Forgive me if I make a mess of myself. I've never been good at feeding myself left handed. I'm getting better. If I flip a tomato at you, I beg your pardon in advance."

They ate and talked throughout the meal. Liz sipped a glass of red wine while Jo and Laurel chose beer. Val considered the pain meds she was on and settled for iced tea. Several times throughout the meal, Val lost what was on her fork and reddened as some fell onto the tablecloth. She abandoned her fork and placed the hand that trembled beneath her thigh to still it.

Val's eyes met Liz's. Liz knew her, knew how close she was to the edge. She knew the trembling was becoming more noticeable, and an uneven rhythm had taken hold of her breathing even though she tried to stop it. Beads of perspiration dotted above her upper lip. She'd applied several layers of lip balm in the last few moments trying to calm her jangling nerves. Though she struggled with the cap, Laurel had reached out to help. Val had politely declined. She apologized, but Laurel didn't seem bothered by it. *You're such a jackass. She's just trying to help.*

Liz touched Val on the arm. "How about you and I let these two tell stories on us while they clean up? I'd like to see your latest sketches, if you don't mind."

Val took a long, shuddering breath trying to calm the approaching storm. She looked at Laurel. "Hon, could you go get my sketchbook out of my messenger bag?"

Laurel looked wary, her brows drawn together. "Sure. I'll be right back."

Jo waited until Laurel was out of the room. She dropped her chin to her shoulder and threw Val a questioning look. "Hon?"

Val flipped her the feathers and got rewarded with the middle finger salute.

Laurel returned in time to catch the exchange and shook her head. "Please don't make us put you two in time out."

Liz covered her mouth, nearly choking on her own laughter, and Val rolled her eyes. Taking the sketchbook from Laurel, Val and Liz made their way into the study. Liz said, "I like her. She's good for you."

Val wiped a shaky hand across her face. "Yeah, I'm probably no good for her. I don't like Laurel taking care of me like an invalid." Val grimaced as the pain flared up in her shoulder when Liz helped her out of the wheelchair and into a plush leather chair across from hers.

"You're far from an invalid, and from what I've seen, Laurel enjoys taking care of you. Need anything?"

"Yeah, a new body if you have one. I've pretty much worn this one out."

"It's just well broken in."

"Broken being the optimum word." Val laughed without humor and looked around the study. She'd always loved this room. The shelves were lined with leather bound books and photos of Liz and Jo. Pieces of

Jo's art sat around the room. Val ran her hand across the buttery leather chair that molded around her as she settled herself more comfortably. Picking up a framed photograph on the end table beside her, she felt warmth wash through her. "God, this seems like a lifetime ago," she whispered. It was at the wedding, and the three of them were holding their champagne glasses high. Val remembered the toast she'd made to the happy couple. The photo captured a moment of joy she rarely felt.

Liz leaned forward, her arms braced on her knees. "Not a lifetime, but certainly a few years ago. How are you feeling really, Val? I've seen this brave face of yours too many times today. I need to know."

The photo now replaced on the table, Val looked at her shaking hand. Anger and despair warred within her. "Maggie May is in shambles. I can't work. I feel like shit. I hurt all over, and I'm pissed as hell that I can't do anything for myself right now. How's that?" Frustrated, Val ran her hand through her hair. "Hell, I can barely feed myself and wipe my own ass. I'm a freaking mess, Liz."

"And you almost died two weeks ago. Again."

Val grew silent and closed her eyes. She was losing the battle, trying in vain to get her breathing under control. The more she tried, the faster the panic rushed at her, closing in around her like a dark veil. Faking her way through it worked with everyone but Liz. Fingers tightly gripping the armchair, she tried to center herself. She felt the heat of the desert against her skin as a familiar voice reached out to her.

"Val, you're in no danger right now. There are no IED's, no suicide bombers, no children in danger, and you're not dying. You're right here. I want you to lift your index finger on your left hand if you can hear me." Liz used a soft but commanding tone as Val lifted her finger. "Val, I want you to count, out loud, back from five and exhale after each number, slowly.

"Five, four, three, two, one." She breathed out each time.

"Now I want you to tell me your full name, how old you are, where you're from, and where you are now."

Like a bright light showing her the way, Liz's voice broke through the dark veil in Val's subconscious. She followed the soft reassuring voice through the panic of darkness enveloping her and back into the safety of the present. "My name is Valkyrie Vör Magnusson. I'm forty-four years old. I'm from Seattle Washington, and I'm in your home in Annapolis Maryland." Val recognized this technique.

"Val, I'm going to count down from five and after I reach one, you'll open your eyes and feel at peace. Five, four, three, two, one."

Val opened her eyes and noticed that her hand was sitting relaxed in her lap. She took a deep breath, her eyes clearing as she met Liz's gaze. She shook her head. "How did you know?"

"Throughout dinner, I watched as you struggled to hold the panic at bay. The professional in me wasn't fooled, although you were trying hard. I've been treating you almost seven years now, Val. I've seen every coping tactic you have. I knew you were close to losing it, so I figured you needed a safe place to do that." Leaning forward, she placed a hand on Val's shoulder. "You've been through hell, and this had to feel frighteningly similar to coming home from Iraq."

Val laid her head back on the chair. "God, Liz, this is such a nightmare. If it wasn't for Laurel—" She stopped herself, biting off her next words.

Thankfully, Liz let the comment slide, browsing through the sketchpad.

"Let me see what you've been doing."

Flipping through the pages dated over the last few months, she analyzed the images drawn on the textured paper, various angles of things Val knew Liz had seen before. A child's hand holding a box of crayons. A dark-haired child held by a soldier with indistinct features. The Vietnam Wall with a man leaning against it, tears on a note card. Val knew that more recent dates would show a completely different perspective, including a Viking helmet adorning a deer head hung above a restroom sign, a potbelly stove with a checker board set up beside it with a game in progress, and a pair of aged hands pinching a pie crust. The last one was the backside of a body with a feminine hand tucked into the waistband of a pair of jeans.

After she browsed through them, she lifted the potbelly stove sketch. "Tell me about this."

Val looked at the picture and could vividly recall the setting it portrayed. Cool Springs Store. Mule and Bobeye arguing over the upcoming baseball season. The first time she and Ree had enjoyed a conversation. She'd sat in those chairs with Laurel playing checkers many times. "It's part of the store that Laurel and Ree own. They have this corner that's out of the way of the main floor traffic. Locals and some visitors come in, sit down in the rocking chairs to share news or a game of checkers."

"What does it make you think about?"

Frustrated by her inability to control her flashback, Val was irritated, almost petulant. "Dammit, Liz, I don't know." Pausing, she closed her eyes and collected herself. "I'm sorry, Liz, that was uncalled for." She took a deep breath. "What's the date on that?"

"March 2016."

Val thought about what she'd been doing that March. If she remembered correctly, she'd been riding through parts of Colorado. It'd been bitterly cold and many miles lay ahead before her planned stop. She couldn't actually remember what assignment she'd been headed to. "I honestly can't remember exactly where I did that sketch or why. I think I was in Colorado. It'd been a pretty long trip, and I hadn't stayed in one place for too long. I do remember wishing I could get warm. The Rocky Mountains up there are pretty damn isolated and cold."

Liz continued to look over the sketch. "I'll bet that stove throws off the heat."

Val grinned. "It does. Personally, I think the people there give off the most warmth. This one guy, he's been coming in to sit every day near that stove for over forty years. Then there's Bobeye. You never know where he's looking because one of his eyes doesn't sit quite right. They have a young man in there they call Wunder. He's like a savant with machinery. I've told you about those questions he comes up with. And then there's Ree. She's not like anyone I've ever met. The place is like a bag of Skittles, variety at its best. Trust me, you've never been anywhere like it." Val grinned and spoke at ease about these people like they were more than friends. She noticed the trembling in her hand had stopped and her cheeks grew warm.

Liz watched her. "I assume Ree did the deer head with the Viking helmet on it?"

"Yeah, they did that as a joke for me one year, and it became part of the backdrop. Laurel started calling me Viking after she found out my name."

"Laurel's pretty special," Liz replied.

The second Laurel's face entered her mind, Val's nerves calmed several degrees. "Yeah, she is. I think the world of her."

Liz nodded. "I can tell. She's good for you, Val."

"She is. I'm not sure I'm good for her." Val looked away and rubbed her hand over the arm of the chair.

"Why do you say that? I see how she looks at you. She's worried about you. All I ask is that you not shut her out. Talk to her. I think you owe her that much. Personally, I think she's in love with you. If you'll be honest with yourself, I think you feel the same." She held up the sketch of the hand tucked in the waistband as evidence. "Pretty good bet that this hand is hers and that backside's yours."

"It is. Each time I ride through, we always try to take a walk. If we do, that's where her hand rides." Val felt the warmth spreading through her body.

"It's pretty intimate."

"I know." Val ran her hand through her hair again. "Hell, Liz, I don't know what I'm doing. I'm forty-four years old and I wouldn't know love if it slapped me in the face. All I know is being around her stops the nightmares and the flashbacks are rare. She makes me smile. With her, I feel settled. They said I gave the ER staff one hell of a fight until they agreed to tell Ree and Laurel how I was, but I don't remember doing it. In all of the thousands of miles I've ridden, I've never stopped as many times as I have at Cool Springs. There's no place I call home. I've got a few things in storage at work in California and a few things here that you guys keep for me. Other than that, I keep moving."

Liz put the sketchbook down. "What do you think you're looking for? And are you so sure you haven't already found it?"

Val thought about Maggie and Loraine. They fought for a love that wasn't acceptable and wasn't convenient. They stayed together until Loraine died, her death nearly killing Maggie. Val restored and rode Maggie May in honor of their love. *Why can't I stop long enough to find love myself?* "I tried with Tess."

"Did you now?" Liz arched an eyebrow.

Val let her head rest against the cool leather and put her hand over her eyes, squeezing. Liz was right. She hadn't. As much as she loved Tess, she hadn't been in love with her. Now, her days were spent feeling like an empty shell of her former self, broken and desolate. She had nothing left to give. And yet, there was Laurel, giving freely of her time and affection and asking nothing of her. She'd left Ree, the most important person in her life, in the care of someone else to drive her sorry ass to Maryland to help her get her life back on track. *Do I love Laurel? No question in my mind, I do. Am I in love with her?* That was a much harder question because admitting it could change everything. The longer she deliberated with herself, the clearer the answer became.

"Liz, I'm afraid I'll hurt her. I can't always control what I do in a flashback. I hurt Tess and I could hurt Laurel. I'll never forgive myself for hurting Tess. If I did that to Laurel, I couldn't live with it."

"And there's nothing that says you will hurt her. You're not in the same place you were then, Val. From what I can see, she's just as nervous about her feelings for you. You weren't in love with Tess. You need to admit it to yourself, even if you can't admit it to me." Liz uncrossed her legs and held out the leather-bound sketchbook to Val. "Being in love with someone doesn't require you to be perfect. It requires you be all in with whatever you have. Don't hold back because your parents were assholes, or that you're afraid she doesn't know what she's getting into. Let her make her own decisions. Let her see all of you."

Val was tired. Raising her head from where it rested, she looked at Liz. "And if once she sees all of it, she runs for the hills?"

"Then you chase her down the way Jo did me."

"Thanks, Liz. I don't know where I'd be without you. Probably wearing a really nice white jacket with extra long sleeves that buckle in the back."

Liz put her hand on Val's. "Yeah, but the only white you've ever looked good in is a button-down oxford. Now, let's get back to our girls before Jo has Laurel over the edge and I have to do a session with her. All kidding aside, I want to see you again before you guys go back to West Virginia."

"Sure thing, Doc." Val had a lot to think about. *Maybe I can find that backbone I left with my leg somewhere in Iraq.*

***

Laurel busied herself helping Jo put away the leftovers. Hearing quiet voices entering the kitchen, she eyed Val, relieved to see she was no longer pale or trembling.

"Why don't we make our way to the patio? It's going to be a beautiful night." Liz headed toward the back door and Jo followed.

Laurel lingered, needing a moment to collect herself. "I need to flip that last load of laundry. I'll be right there. Val, you want some tea after I finish?"

Val signaled for Laurel to stop. "Don't worry about the laundry. Come join us."

"I'll be right there, I promise. It won't take a minute."

"Okay."

As the trio made their way out the door, Laurel rested her back against the counter. She ran her hands through her hair and shook her head. *I hate seeing her look so depleted.*

Liz came back inside. She reached for Laurel's hand and without giving her a chance to object, led her to her study. "Come on." They settled in the chairs close to the empty fireplace. "Please don't think I'm dragging you in here for a forced session. I'm looking at a face full of stress, and I'm a damn good listener."

Laurel stalled the forthcoming conversation by getting up from the chair and walking around the room, looking at Jo's sculptures and the pictures. "This isn't your work office, is it?" She needed time to collect and organize her thoughts, her feelings.

"No, Jo and I spend a good deal of our time here in the winter in front of the fire. Believe it or not, we're both readers. Most nights, you'll find us curled up together here on the couch with books in our hands." She grinned. "That is, if we're not at one of her shows where I have to use a piece of her art to beat fangirls off her."

"She only has eyes for you. Back home we call that gut hooked. Can't imagine she'd want it any other way." *Can't imagine I'd want it any other way either.*

"I wasn't so sure at first. I'm fifteen years older than she is and I was willing to let her go at one point. I thought I wasn't the woman she needed." Liz ran her finger along the edge of a picture frame.

Laurel picked up a framed photo of Liz sitting in Jo's lap, laughing while Jo looked like she was singing.

"You know the chair fades away when you look at how happy you two are." She thought about Val's missing leg and how she'd never known about it before the accident. Nothing about Val seemed out of place. *We all have pieces of ourselves we hide away.* She put the photo back.

"I know. Jo's probably the most well-adjusted person I've ever met when it comes to the loss of her legs. In all the time I've known her, I've never seen her let it hold her back. She's found amazing ways to overcome it and live for who she is, not what she was." Liz's voice grew soft. "I worry about the future. Right now, she doesn't need me to care for her. As I age, it'll get more difficult and she may not be able to do things for me the way someone with two legs could. But I know my Jo. She'll build something. She doesn't live for what will or won't be. She lives for what is."

"She's pretty amazing."

"She is. Each day, we find a way to deal with whatever comes next." Liz leaned forward resting her elbows on her knees and clasped her hands together.

Laurel gathered her hair in her hands. "I'm not sure I'm that strong."

Liz shook her head. "I think you're wrong. I'm not sure what's holding you back from telling Val how you really feel about her. Looking at you, it's easy to see you're in love with her. It's also easy to see you're holding back even as your heart pleads with you to let go."

"I won't deny I adore Val. Every time I know she's coming by, all I want to do is put my arms around her the minute she pulls in." Tears welled up in Laurel's eyes, drowning her in the memory of Val's accident. Raising a shaking hand to her mouth, she gave voice to her internal battle. "I'm afraid. Val lost so much because of the war. I don't think she trusts love. Given what she told me of her childhood, I'm not surprised. I don't want to hurt her, and I'm afraid that's exactly what I'll do someday." Laurel came back to sit on the couch. Turning her head to the end table, she spotted another photo. She picked up the framed picture of the three of them. "Your wedding day?"

Liz rolled her eyes. "Yes. Val was telling Jo that even a blind dog finds a bone once in a while."

Laurel laughed. "You should see the two of them when once my gram gets going."

"Val's mentioned Ree many times. She adores her. She finds great comfort that being there makes her feel like family. After one of her visits, we get color commentary about some conversation with..." Liz hesitated, tapping a finger to her chin. "Mule, Bobeye, Beth, the twins, Tilly, and oh what does she call him? The kid with the questions?"

"Wunder?"

Liz nodded. "Yes, that's him. I know more about the people at your store than I do about her mother and father. You're all like family to her."

"She is family to us. Gram adores her. She actually learned to use the internet on a tablet so she could keep up with Val on the road." Shaking her head, she pointed to a remote on the end table. "I can't teach her how to use the remote control for the TV, and yet somehow she can pull up Val's magazine and Facebook page with no help at all." She couldn't hold back the giggle.

"You're kidding?"

Laurel put her hand in the air, palm out. "Swear. Gram's the one who pushed so hard to have Val stay with us. Wouldn't take no for an answer."

"She sounds pretty formidable."

"Gram's another one that's been through a great deal, raised me and managed to keep me from losing my mind when..." Laurel trailed off, closing her eyes again.

Liz prodded. "When what?"

Laurel sat up and opened her eyes. This was painful to talk about, and it held all the reasons why she couldn't love Val the way she wanted to. Because of this, she couldn't think about building a future with her, even if she could let herself believe Val wanted it. "I'm going to tell you something about me that I've told few people. My mother died of breast cancer just after I turned nine years old. Gram raised me. While I was in college, I found a lump in my breast. They did a biopsy and found precancerous cells. We did some genetic testing, and the results showed I'm BRCA 1 positive, meaning..."

Liz finished the statement. "There was a strong chance you might develop breast cancer."

Laurel took a deep breath, wiping at the tears rolling down her face. She nodded. "I decided to have radical mastectomies and had both of my breasts removed at twenty. There's still a possibility that I'll develop some kind of cancer, but removing my breasts cut those chances substantially." Laurel's voice dropped to a whisper. "I remember watching my mother die. It was agonizing to let her go, and I can't imagine how hard that would be on a lover. Val deserves to have someone who'll be around for the long haul. I can't take the chance that in five or ten years I might die and leave her alone. What right do I have to put her through that? On top of everything else she's lived through, it just seems cruel." Gasping for air through her sobs, bands of agony tightened around her chest. Loving Val was easy. Loving her enough to let her go might be the hardest thing she'd ever try to do.

Liz was silent for a few seconds. "You know, I could drop dead tomorrow of a heart attack or an unknown aneurysm. Jo could develop a kidney infection and not realize she was sick until it was too late. The difference between could and will is vast." She held her hands up far apart. "I hate to say this, Laurel, but what you're doing is preventing both of you from having happiness because of what might happen. You had statistics that showed what your probabilities were. You took action to alter those statistics, but you're living as if you're already dying. Even if Val were to stop riding through, could you forget her? Would you want her to forget you? If you're worried that Val will see you less than whole, is that how you see her? Less than whole because she doesn't have a left foot or because she has scars?"

Shock and anger ripped through Laurel at Liz's insinuation. Her voice rose. "No! I didn't even know she had a missing leg until this accident."

"And she doesn't know your breasts aren't the ones you were born with."

Hot tears tracked down Laurel's face, dropping from her eyes faster than she could wipe them way. Liz got up, retrieved a box of tissues, and handed them to Laurel. Sitting down beside her, Liz pulled her into her arms allowing Laurel cry for her own loss and shed tears of doubt at how she'd been handling her feelings for Val.

Laurel melted into the comfort of Liz's embrace, releasing the pain of the past and trying to sort through the uncertainty of the future. Trying to plot a course in the present was proving to be the greatest challenge. The words of her grandmother floated to her in a whisper, "What happens now, is up to you two."

Chapter Twelve

VAL AND JO SAT enjoying the evening breeze blowing through the back yard. Jo tapped the table between them. "Val, this is me here. Tell me what's rattling around in that Jarhead mind of yours."

Val let out a long breath, sighing into the darkness. "Got any Makers Mark hanging around? And don't lecture me about my pain pills and alcohol please."

Jo turned her chair back into the house, returning in a few minutes with a bottle. She poured three fingers of amber liquor into a short tumbler and pushed it toward Val. "If I get in Dutch for this with my woman or yours, you threatened me with your bionic elbow, capisce?"

"She's not my woman."

"Cut the bullshit. I remember you with Tess. She adored you, and I never saw you look at her the way you do Laurel. You're in deep, my friend, whether you want to admit it or not. I spent many years dissecting everything around me trying to recognize friend from foe to keep from dying. What I see watching you and Laurel, that's real. Like it or not."

Val rubbed her temple. "I don't know. I have no experience in healthy relationships. I never know if I'm going to wake up back in Iraq, fighting to stay alive. I've worked hard to be able to take care of myself. I feel like my whole life's been put in a shredder again, and I'm trying to sort the bits and pieces."

Jo sipped her drink. "What's the one thing you're holding on to right now?"

Val became silent, recognizing Jo's tactics. It wouldn't be the first time, nor would it be the last.

"I'm not one to let you off the hook about anything. We call bullshit when we see it with each other. We all want things to be different. You think I don't wish that rocket never hit my Humvee? That somehow, I didn't come out of it paralyzed? I don't like Liz having to do things for me because I can't. I've learned that in loving her, I have to let her love me, her way. I wish I could stand, take my wife into my arms, and carry her to our bed. I wish I could walk with her hand in hand. I wish I could look her in the eyes without having to look up." Jo took a swallow of her drink, slamming the glass back down. "But if I had to choose between having my legs back and my life now with Liz, I wouldn't change a single fucking thing. I don't know why things happen the way they do, but what I have now is incredible and more than I ever deserved. If I'd held back because I thought about what it meant for Liz to be with someone like me, I'd have never even taken the chance. So, I ask you again, what is the one thing you're holding on to right now?"

Val took a sip of the whiskey and turned the glass in a small circle on the table. The drink burned on the way down, flooding her system with warmth. The answer was easy. "Laurel and Ree."

"Exactly. I think you know what you need to do. I just wonder if you're going to find the courage to do it, or be a coward and ride away."

Val looked at the colors of the sunset streaking across the sky. Reds and pinks blazed a trail into the dusk. She threw back the whiskey and sat the glass off to the side. She didn't answer Jo. She couldn't. Was she being brave by denying herself? *Or am I being a coward?*

***

Laurel and Liz came back outside. Liz grazed her fingers across Jo's shoulders as she bent down for a kiss, settling down in the seat next to her. Laurel watched the exchange and found a seat near Val, but not close enough for them to touch. She didn't trust herself right now.

She felt Val's eyes on her in the darkness, and she looked at the sunset and the broad strokes of color in brilliant hues of pink and orange. "Beautiful. Where we live, we have this view where you can see all the way across the mountain ridge and the colors paint the sky. Gram and I love to sit out there in the evenings. Of course, there's usually a pan of beans to snap in my lap or apples to peel. We have some of our best conversations sitting there in those rockers."

"I'll bet it's beautiful. We'll have to visit sometime, Laurel. I've driven through West Virginia, but we've never had the time to really explore it," Liz said.

"It's beautiful in any season, but I think fall is my favorite. The mountains absolutely come alive. When the wind blows, the red and yellow leaves look like tongues of flame. Everywhere you look there's a brilliant palette of amber and scarlet. You can stay with us. We have plenty of room, and the house is already wheelchair accessible. We did that for my mom while she was sick. It makes it easier for Gram to get around now. Anytime you want to come, let me know." Laurel spoke from the heart. It gave her great pleasure to share things about her home. So many people hear West Virginia and immediately picture the stereotype hillbillies with no shoes. She knew West Virginia for all its treasures and wasn't shy about singing its praises.

"We'll have to set a date to come in the fall then. I've seen some of Val's pictures of it and it's spectacular. I'd love to experience it for myself," Liz said.

Laurel beamed with pride. "That would be great. I can promise you a feast prepared by an eighty-five-year-old woman who would put Emeril to shame."

Val patted her stomach. "That I can attest to. I've told Laurel if Ree keeps feeding me like she does, I'm going to have to buy bigger pants."

Laurel thought about Val's words. After the appointments here, they'd travel back to her home. Back to a place she hoped was becoming more like home to Val, too. Only time would tell and that's one thing she'd always been concerned about. How much time would there be to tell. She didn't have the answers, but she hoped to find them soon.

***

Val yawned and fidgeted, shifting her shoulder strap a little and rubbing her drooping eyes.

Laurel looked over at her. "I think someone needs to go to bed, and I'm not far behind. Val, you ready to go up?"

"Yeah, I'm beat, and between The Bodyshop and the appointment with Cat, it's going to be a long day tomorrow. Guys, I can't thank you enough for putting us up and feeding us. I really appreciate it."

"No problem. Hopefully we can have dinner tomorrow night together. I have appointments all day and Jo has a show she needs to finish pieces for. If either of you need anything, just call our cells." Liz watched as Laurel got up and unlocked Val's chair. "Goodnight."

"Laurel, it's been great to chat with you." Jo looked at Val, "Night, Jarhead."

"Night, Dogface."

Riding up in the elevator, Laurel massaged Val's neck. Val put her head back and relaxed into the touch, allowing the skilled fingers to work up and down her neck. The strong thumbs ran from the base of her skull to her shoulders.

"God, you have magic hands."

"I hope your surgeon will give us some good news tomorrow."

"Cat's going to chew me a new one." Lieutenant Colonel Catherine O'Neil was a battle tried and true surgeon who had earned the birds on her collar. She'd operated on Val all those years ago and was one of the few doctors that Val trusted to play it straight with her. Val shook her head. After Val had been completely patched up, Cat made no bones about her interest. Val's mind drifted on a memory.

"Go to dinner with me, Val."

Cat was petite and one of the most feminine women she'd ever met as long as she wasn't in a battlefield hospital tent. She was short, but once she put those 'come fuck me heels' on, look out. She could maneuver in those as well as she did in her combat boots.

"Cat, I think you're an incredible doctor, but I think we need to keep things simple."

Cat stalked around Val, running a polished nail across the back of her neck making her shiver. "What I'm proposing is simple, Val. Dinner and then we go back to my place for some wine and other pleasures."

Val had declined and that hadn't been the last offer. There'd been a weekend of insanity in P-town she still regretted. She'd told her persistent suitor it would never happen again, but that didn't keep Cat from hitting on her and trying every time they met up. She wasn't sure how that would play out with Laurel. Unless she missed her guess, Fourth of July fireworks wouldn't hold a candle.

Laurel helped her into her room. The nighttime basics completed, they got her undressed and settled in bed. Val was surprised with how comfortable she was with Laurel. Leaning over, Laurel kissed her lightly on the lips. Drawing back, she whispered, "Sleep well, Viking. We've got a big day tomorrow."

Val pushed her head up to meet those lips again. She whispered, "stay," and kissed her a bit more firmly.

"Val," Laurel protested.

Val closed her eyes against the rejection and fell back onto the pillow. "See you in the morning?"

Laurel kissed her again and pulled away. "You can count on it."

"Ok, good night."

Val lay there as Laurel walked across to the door and flipped off the light. As she lay there in the darkness, a feeling of recognition washed over her, and she finally admitted to herself that she was in love with Laurel and had no idea what to do about it. She wasn't even sure she knew what it took to have a good relationship, she'd only witnessed it with Liz and Jo. *Would I hurt Laurel?* Closing her eyes, the questions bounced off her mind like a pinball stuck between two bumpers. She willed sleep to come. Val settled back to try and relax, giving her body all the incentive it needed to reach that goal.

Chapter Thirteen

LAUREL REACHED HER OWN room, pulled off her clothes, and slid into the boxers and t-shirt she'd brought to sleep in. Like Ree, she never slept well in a bed that wasn't her own. Since coming home from college, she'd rarely done so. This was for Val though, and she'd do whatever needed to be done. It had taken all she had to not crawl into bed beside Val tonight. Her body and soul longed to lie beside her and that scared her to death. After her talk with Liz, her heart told her she needed to make a decision while her mind cautioned her to hold onto her fear. She needed to focus on getting Val well and then they could talk about what came next. She crawled under the cool sheets and twisted her hair in her hands. She turned on her side and closed her eyes.

Laurel didn't feel like she'd been asleep long when a crash and shouting from the other room made her sit up. Rubbing her eyes, she tried to clear the cobwebs of interrupted slumber from her head and swung her legs out of bed. Disoriented, she held her head and tried to get her bearings. Again, she heard a shout and then a cry of pain along with more crashing. *Val's room.* She raced to the room next door and saw Liz running toward her. Jo wasn't far behind in her wheelchair.

Laurel started to hit the light when Liz yelled, "No!" A light turned on in the hall and Liz held her arm out to stop Laurel from going in. "Let me go in first."

Jo stopped beside her wife, holding on to her arm. "Be careful, baby, broken wing or not, she's strong."

Liz stood at the doorway, the light from the hallway shining into the room. It was still too dark for Laurel to make anything out clearly, especially from where she was tucked behind Liz and Jo. The bed was empty, covers strewn on the floor.

Liz called out in a strong voice. "Val, it's Liz. You're in my home, and you're in no danger. There are no suicide bombers, there are no children in danger, and you aren't dying. You're all right. I'm coming in." She paused. "Val, I want you to call out to me. I'm going to turn on the bathroom light. The light won't hurt you. You're in no danger."

Laurel watched as Liz crossed the floor to the bathroom. A soft white light illuminated Val huddled in a corner, a wingback chair on top of her. She let out a cry. Laurel's stomach twisted with guilt at the scene before her.

Liz motioned for Laurel to approach. "Laurel, talk to her. Remind her where she is and that she isn't in danger."

Laurel took a few steps closer. "Val, honey, it's Laurel. We're all okay. There isn't any danger. You're okay." She stepped closer and watched as Val's left leg tried to find purchase. With one missing foot, she was unable to do so. "Val, baby. I'm going to come down beside you. You're at Jo and Liz's. We're all okay." Val cried out in pain, and it nearly broke her. "You're going to hurt your shoulder. Please let me help you. Can you hear me?" Tears began to trickle down her face as she pushed the back of the chair up. She saw Val wide eyed, lying on her injured arm, her right hand clutching the chair as her left searched on the side of her leg for something.

Jo whispered, "She's looking for her side arm."

"Val, honey, it's Laurel. You're okay. Let me help you. You're okay, I promise, we aren't in any danger." Finally, Val's death-grip on the chair loosened, and Laurel lifted it off Val. Laurel made her movements slow and purposeful. "Val, honey, it's going to be ok." Laurel looked at Val's unfocused eyes that flitted left and right. She was soaked with sweat, her fear palpable.

Liz cautioned and placed a hand on Laurels arm. "Be careful. She hasn't come back to herself yet. She may hurt you."

"No, she won't." Laurel reached out for her. "Val, it's Laurel. We need to get you off your shoulder. You're going to hurt yourself and then Gram is going to kick my ass. Val, can you hear me?" Recognition flashed in Val's eyes and some of the fear receded from her face. Laurel moved closer and touched one hand to Val's cheek, forcing Val's eyes to hers. She wanted Val to see that she wasn't afraid of her, that she trusted her. She watched as Val began to tremble and then a cry of anguish came over her as she pressed into her hand. Laurel pulled the trembling woman into her arms, rocking her. "Honey, did you hurt yourself? It's all right. I'm here. Nothing is ever going to hurt you again. I'm right here, Val. You're safe."

Val sobbed, and Laurel whispered, "That's it. Come back to me. Your arm has to be killing you." Laurel's heart raced, but she fought to keep her voice low and even.

Val trembled as she struggled to regain control. "I'm so sorry," she whispered, tears choking her words.

"Val, there isn't anything to be sorry for. I'm sorry I didn't stay with you like you asked. If I'd been here, this wouldn't have happened." Laurel felt sick to her stomach, anguished at Val's state. "We need to get you up off the floor so we can look at that shoulder, okay?"

Val nodded. Together, Liz and Laurel got Val up and helped her back into the bed. Laurel watched as Val took deep breaths in through her nose, exhaling slowly through her mouth. They examined her arm. The incision on Val's side looked fine. Unfortunately, the shoulder was warm and red. Liz cursed. "I can't tell if she's done any more damage, only a scan will tell us that. Val, can we take you over to the ER?"

Val shook her head. "It's fine. It hurts like hell. Trust me, it doesn't feel as bad as it did after the accident."

"Honey, are you sure?" Laurel frowned, worry coursing through her.

Jo made her way to the bathroom and retrieved a wet towel that she handed to Laurel. Wiping Val's sweaty face, she examined Val's eyes. They were clearer, but still dilated. She caressed Val's back and shoulders.

Val looked at Liz with a face full of apology. Her body trembled, still not under control. "Honestly, guys, I'm okay. I should've known what we talked about would bring this on. It's been a while since this happened. I thought maybe I was getting over them. Obviously not."

Liz stood beside Val and touched her forearm. "I was afraid it might. I should have kept a closer eye on you."

Laurel shook her head, remorse still twisting inside her. "No, Liz, I should've."

Val grabbed Laurel's hand, kissing the fingers that had been caressing her. "Laurel, you've never seen one of my flashbacks. This isn't your fault. I've been having them for years. This whole trauma has it all stirred up, and it's nobody's fault."

Laurel closed her eyes for a second, trying to find her voice through a throat thick with anxiety. She was scared and knew that if she showed even a hint of it, Val would take it on herself.

Jo had rolled up to the bed. She wagged her finger and smirked at Val. "Hey now, I didn't try to take the blame for any of this, Jarhead. I was just snuggling with my wife, and you had to try to remodel my guest room."

Liz smacked her. Jo rubbed her arm in mock distress. "What was that for?"

"Go get her an ice-bag, you jackass." Liz leaned down and kissed her. "I love you."

"Love you, too. Be right back."

Laurel climbed on to the bed and held Val in her arms. She was grateful for the banter between the couple. It lightened the mood, and she saw Val break a smile. They seemed adept at putting Val at ease and she relaxed a little.

Liz went about quietly examining Val, checking her pulse and respirations. "My blood pressure cuff is out in my office. I think we can skip it. Val, can you tell me about it?"

Val bit her lip, but took a deep breath and the words came tumbling out. "It's always the same. The kids are so excited, and the teachers are there. I'm trying to find the best camera angle so I'm not interfering. Lieutenant Gamble and Sergeant Layfield are passing out the supplies to the kids. I see that bastard walking up in his robes, and something doesn't feel right. Angry words, upset kids, and then all hell breaks loose. I'm knocked back. I try to get up, but I can't. My leg is blown to bits and I can hardly move my left arm. Shouts everywhere. Then it's a kaleidoscope of images until I see the kid with the crayons."

Laurel was horrified, never having heard what happened in Val's own words. She held her tighter and kissed Val's damp hair. How close had she come to never having known this woman? How close had she come to not ever having felt this way about someone? She made up her mind right then that Val would never suffer another flashback like this one alone.

***

Val rubbed her free hand across her face and through her sweaty hair. She was still jittery and skittish after the flashback. After everyone settled down, Liz and Jo went back to bed. They told Laurel to call for them if she needed anything. It was clear she wouldn't be leaving Val alone again tonight.

"Can I have a pain pill?" Her shoulder was screaming, but she didn't want to frighten Laurel. She was sure she would never get to sleep without it. Whatever damage had been done this evening could be fixed after Cat tore into her tomorrow. The pain was making her sick, and all she wanted to do was curl up in Laurel's arms. Laurel handed her a bottle of water and the pill. "Thank you."

"You're welcome. Now get some rest." Laurel kissed her head and settled Val down at her side.

Val sighed. If she couldn't sleep, then she'd draw strength and peace from the woman holding her and the easy rise and fall of the soft chest her head rested against. Knowing that Laurel had now seen her at her worst and hadn't run, eased her fear. "I don't like feeling helpless."

"You're not helpless. You're hurt, and it's been a hell of an evening. Going through what you did, most people would be curled up in a corner. You've pushed through it and come out the other side. This is nothing more than a speed bump."

Val raised her head to look at Laurel and smiled at the twinkle she saw in the eyes that met hers. Laurel's hand cupped her cheek, her thumb softly stroking it, and Val pushed herself up enough so their lips were millimeters apart. She licked her lips and wished she had her lip balm, afraid her lips would be rough. Laurel brought their lips together. She wanted heat, but what Laurel brought to her was tenderness. The kiss was gentle and yet held more passion than any kiss Val had ever experienced.

Val wanted more, so much more, but she needed to feel in control of her life first. *I need to be able to hold her with both arms and be able to touch her everywhere.* Even though her arm was restrained, she could brush her hand across Laurel's breast. Surprisingly, she didn't react the way Val would've expected. She crushed her lips harder to Laurel's and leaned up to move her head closer. She felt Laurel melt into the touch and for the first time in a long time, Val knew what she wanted. She could enjoy this kiss and every one she could manage after this. After her arm was healed, she'd do so much more.

Laurel pulled back from the kiss, gasping for air, a smile escaping her lips.

Val could feel her insides clench. *God, I want her. Want to feel every part of her.* She was in no condition to make love though, and she hoped Laurel was stronger than she was right now.

Laurel pushed softly against her chest. "Val, honey, we have to stop. You need to rest. You're safe with me."

Val yearned to make love to Laurel. She couldn't imagine a day without Laurel in her life and yet, she still needed to get past her own insecurities. "I know, this can't happen right now. I need you to know, I want another chance. I want you, Laurel. You're so beautiful." She pulled Laurel in for another kiss.

Laurel pulled back, running her hand through Val's hair. "Behave yourself and try to sleep. It's after midnight and we have to be over at The Bodyshop by 8:00 am because you, my sweet, have an appointment with your surgeon at 10:30 am. Now sleep, love."

Val sighed. "Are you brushing me off?"

"No, I'm trying to get you to rest. I think you can figure out from that kiss how I feel, but this isn't the time or place."

"Then just tell me that there will be a time and a place, and I'll go to sleep."

"We'll see, Viking, we'll see." Laurel settled Val back against her chest and wrapped up against each her.

For the first time in a long time, Val felt safe and complete. She fell asleep content to be exactly where she was in Laurel's embrace.

Chapter Fourteen

THE NEXT MORNING LIZ eyed Val clinically. *Clear eyed but still tired and pale. About what I expected.* Val had made it to the table. She'd been in great deal of pain and cried out as they sat her up. Her shoulder looked inflamed and hot. She struggled to get showered and dressed, requiring Laurel to help her more than ever. Liz gave her permission to take the maximum dosage on her pain meds. Doing so would make her groggy, but without it, Liz knew she'd have difficulty doing much of anything.

At breakfast, Jo created a feast of pancakes, eggs, and sausage. "Breakfast is the only meal I'm any good at. The rest of the time, I leave the culinary skills to my wife, who's as good as any trained chef in my humble opinion."

Liz kept the breakfast conversation light and comforting. No one brought up the episode, and she wheeled Val back to the study while cleanup took place. They settled again in the comfortable chairs and Liz took another hard look at Val. There were dark circles under her eyes. Her face was tight with pain despite the narcotics she had taken earlier.

"How are you?"

"I feel like shit," Val grumbled. "I hate that Laurel witnessed that. It had to scare her to death."

"I'm sure it did, not for the reasons you think though. I get the feeling she's not afraid for herself, rather she's worried about you. Seeing someone you love in that much pain, tears you up inside. During Jo's last spinal surgery, I felt like I was dying."

Val leaned forward in her chair, her left hand grasping the armrest. "I never wanted that for her. Why do you think I avoided any relationships? I hurt Tess more than once, and not just emotionally. I still haven't forgiven myself for that. I couldn't live with myself if I ever did that to Laurel. She's too important to me to fuck this up. It's why I've never told her how I feel or stayed around long enough to let this develop. She deserves someone to care for her without all this baggage. What kind of life will that be, watching me cower against something that isn't there? I carry what happened every day. How could I make her bear that burden?"

Liz knew that part of being a marine was the deep sense of valor and responsibility. Val had seen and photographed things no one should witness. She sat back and spent a few minutes considering her next words. She diagnosed Val with survivor's guilt many years ago. It was her professional opinion that the images from Val's past were embedded in her psyche. The scars were deeply rooted and had nothing to do with her missing leg or other injuries.

They'd made tremendous progress toward exorcising those demons, but some still persisted. Her challenge now was to get Val to the next stage of healing. "Val, you have to believe that who you are right now is more than enough for anyone. You're not less because you left part of yourself in that schoolyard. You couldn't have changed what was going to happen that day. What you can change is every single day from here forward." There was a big part of the equation she knew Val had yet to reconcile, one that she tried numerous ways to bring clarity to. "Have you made any headway identifying the soldier in those pictures, the one that was holding the child?"

Val rubbed her face. "Every time I get close, something happens and I can't pin it down. I know who was there that day and those who survived swear there wasn't anyone else there except our crew. The pictures clearly show someone holding that child, but the angles are so bad I can't tell who it is. It only shows a small part of the uniform, and I'm almost positive it's a marine by the pattern. The only thing in focus is the child's face and those damn crayons."

Liz nodded. She had her own thoughts about who was in the picture. It was nothing she could prove though, and she wanted Val to come to a conclusion on her own. If she didn't, she doubted Val would accept it. "Until you exorcise this demon, you're never going to be free. We need to concentrate on filling in all the blanks. Just as importantly, Val, you need to tell Laurel exactly how you feel. She deserves to know the truth. Don't waste a chance to be happy."

Liz watched Val drop her head back and close her eyes. She wondered which pain was worse, the one in Val's shoulder or the one in her heart.

Chapter Fifteen

VAL SMILED AS LAUREL pulled into the parking lot of The Bodyshop. They made their way inside, she signed in and made small talk with the one of the receptionists. They settled in the waiting area. A spry sixtyish looking older woman walked around the corner, and Val hugged her.

"Hi, Anya, how are you?"

"The better question is, how are you? You aren't supposed to be showing up here in a set of wheels instead of on that bionic leg we made you," Anya chided her.

Val chuckled. "I know. Somehow, I didn't manage to keep the shiny side up this time. Thank a kid in a convertible. Give me a little longer and I'll be good as new. One thing though, I'd really appreciate being able to stand up on my own."

Anya patted Val's shoulder. "I'll bet. Let's see what we can do about that, and who's this?"

Val shook her head. "I'm sorry, Anya. This is Laurel Stemple. She's been carting me all over trying to get me back on my feet, literally. She and her grandmother are like family to me and have sort of adopted me. Laurel, this is Anya Cavender. She and her sons are the magicians who helped me walk again."

Laurel shook Anya's outstretched hand. "It's a pleasure to meet you."

The pleasure is all mine." Anya waved her hand. "Come on back."

They traveled down the hall to a small room with a long table with cabinets beside it. Framed photographs hung on the wall showing patients being fitted for their new arms or legs and children being given a chance to walk or hold a ball. Poignant, but still filled with joy.

Anya and Laurel helped Val get situated on a table and then raised it so she and Val were on even ground. Val suddenly realized that constantly looking up at everyone bothered her. "Nice to be able to have an eye to eye conversation." It felt empowering.

Anya pulled up a small rolling cart and placed her hand on Val's forearm. "I know how important that is. Now, depending on how badly you destroyed our masterpiece, we should be able to get you back up on two feet fairly quickly. Do you have what's left of it?"

Laurel handed her a duffle bag. Anya removed the prosthesis and examined it, moving behind the long table with a bright light. Pulling specialized tools from the cabinets, she began to disassemble the leg. After that was complete, she began to look at the control systems. Several structural pieces were visibly damaged. Val watched as Anya carefully took apart each component, scrutinizing the leg.

Anya looked up at Val. "You trashed this pretty good."

Val gritted her teeth in disappointment. "It came off in the accident. Most of it was protected in my boot, but the socket took a pretty good tumble. Think you can fix it?" Val asked hopefully. Laurel stood close beside her and she felt a hand massage the back of her neck. This woman's touch quieted the churning in her stomach and the turmoil in her head.

Anya raised an eyebrow. "Is that a rhetorical question? Val, we haven't stayed in business for over twenty years because we weren't any good at this. I may be seventy years old, but I still know a thing or two."

Val grinned. "I wasn't doubting you. I'd hate to start all over. It took us a year to get it right last time."

"And you complained the entire time that it was good enough, but I could see it needed adjusting. With the notes from last time, it shouldn't be that hard. Were you having any issues with your sleeve? I'd really prefer we do a new one so it's made at the same time the socket is. We can go with the same materials as last time. You know how critical that is to your comfort."

Val looked at the woman with true affection, admiring her dedication and professionalism. "The sleeve was starting to get a little worn, but it was still holding up."

Holding up the pieces of Val's leg, Anya continued. "Let's get Charley in here so he can get a new mold, and Daren and I'll get started on fixing this." She eyed the lightweight titanium frame. "Depending on how bad this is, we can get it done in a day or two. If we have to create it all from scratch, it might be at least a week before we can get you in to try it out for the first fitting."

"I'm staying at Liz and Jo's, so I'm in town. I'll make it work. Laurel and put her mouth close to Val's ear. "I told you I wouldn't leave you alone, and I meant it."

Anya chuckled and grabbed the tube of lubrication from Laurel. "Oh my God, I think you might've met your match, Val. Charley will be back to do a few measurements and then we'll set you up for your return appointment. Laurel, I'm happy to know she has someone who sees through that bullshit bravado. It's nice to meet you."

Laurel nodded. "Thank you, Anya, it's been nice meeting you, too. We'll see you on Thursday."

Val hugged her. "Thanks for seeing me on such short notice, Anya. I can't thank you enough."

"Val, you'll always be welcome here." Putting her hand on Val's shoulder, she turned to Laurel. "All the photos and news articles you see in here are compliments of this talented photographer. She brought attention to what we could do, not only for veterans but children as well. We couldn't have bought that kind of publicity. There's no way for us to repay her."

Val covered Anya's hand with her own. "It's been my pleasure. You've helped me more than I could have imagined. The joy I've seen you put on a child's face when they take their first steps, or as they're able to pick something up for themselves, that's priceless. I know what that feels like, and I wanted more people to know about those who make that happen every day."

Laurel looked around the room at the incredible photos that hung on every wall. Each one displayed a moment of triumph for the person in the image. Val had captured those moments of beauty and dignity.

"I agree, she's pretty special." She brushed her hand across Val's shoulders and ran her fingers into the hair at the back of Val's head. She looked around the room at the pictures and realized that with every new person she met in Val's life, another piece fell into place. Val was like a puzzle. One that she very much wanted to see in its entirety. She leaned in and kissed Val's temple. *More special than I could have even imagined.*

may have to go back, though. We'll see. I need my leg back, Anya, I really do. I forgot what it's like to be without it. With this banged up shoulder, I can't even crutch my way around."

Laurel shook her head. "Val, you know I don't mind helping you. I'll be around as long as you need me."

Val felt a squeeze. She looked down at a pair of joined hands and had no recollection of reaching for Laurel. She only knew that holding her hand felt so right. "I know you don't. Laurel, you can't be away from the store that long." She raised Laurel's hand to her lips and kissed it.

"You let me worry about that. If I come back to Cool Springs without you, I'm likely to have to go cut a switch."

Anya looked concerned, but Val laughed and held up her hand to allay her unease. "Don't worry, Anya, it's an empty threat by a feisty matriarch of the most interesting place I've ever been. Laurel and her grandmother run a small store and diner in West Virginia."

Anya turned to Laurel. "Is that the place with the deer head with the Viking helmet I've seen in your pictures?"

Laurel chuckled. "One and the same."

"Ah. Let's see what we can do to get both of you back there." Anya left the room.

Val closed her eyes, taking deep breaths, trying to stay positive.

Laurel's soft voice penetrated her consciousness. "You okay?"

"Yeah, I'm worried about this. These guys are the best in the business. They're also perfectionists. I sure hope I didn't destroy it, forcing us to start all over."

Laurel came over to stand in front of Val and kissed her forehead. She moved between Val's spread legs and wrapped her arms around her waist, pulling her close.

Val rested her chin on Laurel's shoulder and breathed in the sweet trace of the tropics she always associated with her. The scent settled Val's nerves and made her think about sitting on a beach with Laurel. Her mind filled with the picture of the waves crashing onto the shore and the water gently flowing over the sand. She could imagine Laurel in a bikini and felt a pulse start deep in her center. God, how she wanted Laurel...wanted to feel her beneath her. Before she could completely lose herself in her thoughts, a knock at the door brought them back to reality. Charley walked in with a bucket dangling from his hand. He sat it down and strode over to Val. "Long time no see. What have you done now to give me the pleasure of dipping your leg in goo? I could think of a dozen other ways I'd like to visit with you."

There was a subtle lilt to his voice and a feminine manner. He was a beautiful sort of handsome. He looked a little like the love child of Bon Jovi and George Michael with a mane full of blond hair feathered back and at his collar. His vibrant green eyes shimmered with mischief.

Val's smile widened. "How are you, Charley?"

"Fabulous, darling. I can tell by that new bondage getup you're wearing that you aren't as fabulous as normal."

Val felt the blush crawl up her neck and her ears felt hot. She looked over at Laurel who had her free hand up over her mouth trying to hide a smirk and stifle a laugh. It wasn't working.

Charley spoke up. "Where are your manners, girlfriend? Who is this beauty you have with you and why haven't I ever seen her before?" He held out his hand and shook Laurel's.

Val sighed. "Charley, this is Laurel Stemple. Laurel, meet Charley Cavender, artist extraordinaire and hair aficionado. Laurel has graciously been taking incredible care of me while I recover."

Charley took an exaggerated bow. "Honey, I have no doubt you have your hands full there. As brilliant and talented as this hunk is, she can be a royal pain in the ass at times."

"Just because I won't let you dress me up and accompany you to the leather bar." Val smirked and Laurel's eyes got big.

Laurel wasn't as successful at hiding her laugh this time. "Why, Val, I'm seeing a totally different side of you."

Charley smiled at Laurel and hugged Val. "A boy can dream, you know. Down to business. Mom said you'll need a new socket and sleeve. Let's start with the sleeve, shall we?"

Val rolled her eyes at him. "Now there's a great idea. Let's get started."

***

Laurel watched as Charley went about mixing up something in the bucket that reminded her of the material the dentist used to create her retainer after the braces. He handed Val a tube of something to rub on her amputated leg. Val shook her head and frowned at him.

"I've only got one wing here dipshit," Val said, whacking him in the head with the tube.

"Watch the hair! Laurel has two good hands, as far as I can tell." He looked at Laurel. "You'll be more than capable to act as my assistant,

won't you, darling?" Charley smiled like a Cheshire cat.

Laurel caught Val flipping him the middle finger of her immobilized hand. She felt her face grow warm as she took the tube from Val. Never having touched Val this way, she tried to calm her pounding heart and rolled Val's jeans up to her knee, exposing the flesh beneath. Without looking at Val, she squeezed some of the gel into her hands and warmed it between them. It had a faint blue tint to it with no odor that she could detect. She placed both hands around the stump, riddled with scar tissue and felt Val stiffen as she rubbed the gel on her skin. The blush crept higher into her cheeks. Closing her eyes for a moment, she enjoyed the feel of the warm skin beneath her hands. She could swear she heard Val whimper, but convinced herself it was a figment of her imagination. Soon, Val relaxed into her touch.

Charley broke the almost tangible intimacy. "Put a couple of coats on that so it doesn't stick when we go to remove her leg after this sets up. Besides, Val is close to orgasming, I'd hate to rob her of a climax."

Something smacked the man and Laurel looked up to see Anya frowning. "Charley, don't be so crass. Laurel isn't used to your teasing with Val."

Charley laughed. "Oh, Momma, I couldn't help it. Val's like a love-sick puppy and after all the shit she's given me over the years, it serves her right."

Anya rolled her eyes. "Be that as it may, Laurel doesn't deserve your teenage antics." Anya handed Laurel a towel. "Forgive my son, Laurel. I raised him better. There's only so much a mother can do."

Laurel's blush grew hotter as she wiped the gel off her hands. "Kids, what are you going to do with them?"

"Ok, Val, dive in." Charley held the bucket close enough that Val could stick her leg in the mixture. He brought a stool over and rested the bucket on it to allow the mixture to solidify. "I'll be back in a bit. I need to go gather the other compounds for the sleeve."

Shaking her head, Anya held up Val's busted prosthesis. "Okay, Val. The microprocessor is shot on your old leg. We've got some boards in stock, so it's just a matter of programming one with your settings. However, replacing the other components will take a few days. Charley will use the measurements and the molds we take today to get to work on your sleeve and socket. We should be able to bring you in for a fitting Thursday afternoon, maybe early evening. Does that work for you two?"

"I don't have much choice. I don't know about Laurel, she—"

Laurel interrupted. "Will be right here with you, Val." She leaned

Chapter Sixteen

VAL TENSED AS A they sat outside of The Walter Reed Military Medical Center. She'd always referred to it as Bethesda. Her stomach knotted. It was time to go see about her shoulder. Val was dreading having Cat and Laurel meet. It'd been several years since she'd replaced Val's elbow. She was the best at what she did or Val would have sought treatment elsewhere. She wanted her shoulder fixed and fixed right. That fact alone had brought her back to the best the VA had to offer.

After they were signed in, they sat in an enormous area with dozens of others waiting to be seen. The noise of a busy hospital beeped, vibrated, and rattled around her. Rows of industrial chairs sat all around the room filled with men and women of all ages. Dull yellow walls fell short of providing a cheery atmosphere. The individuals who sat around her waited their turn to see whatever specialty dealt with their injury. Prosthetic limbs, scarred and misshapen bodies were all around her, the cost of war evident. The vacant, hollowed eyes, clouded with sand and memories, were easily recognizable to those who shared those nightmares. Those scars were harder to treat, if they were treatable at all.

She watched a woman younger than her. Her knee bounced up and down, and she rolled a coin back and forth through her fingers and across her knuckles. A chocolate lab sat between her legs, his head resting on her thigh. She was absently stroking his head with her free hand. Her eyes were blank. Val looked away and blinked back emotions that threatened to overwhelm her. These were the true cost of freedom and democracy. The price that those in this room paid so that others could go about their day not thinking for even a second about that cost. She was brought out of her reverie by a soft voice.

"Is it always like this?" Laurel asked.

"Always. Some are here for routine examinations or prescription refills, some for more serious issues." It still angered Val at the wait many of her fellow veterans had to go through to get the treatment they desperately needed. People who'd lost friends and pieces of themselves in the lands they fought in, now had to fight to see a doctor or to have a procedure in the richest and most advanced country in the world. *Shameful and it never changes.* "If I hadn't already had this appointment scheduled six months ago for some pain in my elbow, I'd still be on the waiting list." Val turned her attention to thumbing through the most recent edition of *Stars and Stripes,* her eyes drawn to a picture taken near Mosul.

Laurel's phone buzzed. Her fingers worked the keyboard texting, a faraway look on her face.

"Everything okay?"

"Yeah, I got a text from Beth. She's giving me shit, because I didn't call last night. Gram's giving her the devil for information about you." Laurel laughed. "Not that's she's concerned about me. You on the other hand..."

Val chuckled. "I have an idea. How about this evening we call, or if Beth can help her, we'll do a video chat on Facebook?"

"Oh, she'd love that. I'll text Beth a time." Laurel's thumbs flew over the screen.

Val checked her own phone and saw a missed call from her mother, a text message from her boss, and another one from Tess. She deciphered her mother's message by using a voicemail to text app. Her mother was concerned that she hadn't called in a few days to give her an update. She'd wait until after her appointment so she'd have more information to pass on. The text from her boss offered a few words of support. She wondered who'd picked up her assignment in Kentucky, guilty that someone else would have to take up her slack. Everything had been such a blur since the accident.

The one from Tess surprised her though. Somehow, she'd gotten word of Val's injuries and wanted to confirm if it was her involved in the accident. One of Kelly's crew moonlighted as a flight paramedic and apparently, was someone who brought Val in. The medic happened to tell Kelly and mentioned Val's vintage motorcycle. Details filtered in about a photographer doing a story on the "Ride to the Wall" event. Tess thought it was a long shot, but she wanted to check. Val knew a text wouldn't suffice for this, but she really wasn't ready to talk to Tess. She'd handle that later.

She sent quick texts to her mother and boss, which really wasn't that quick with one hand. By the time she managed to peck out the messages, the receptionist called her name. She began to sweat. The back of her neck tensed, and she had a feeling like before an approaching storm.

Laurel rose and wheeled Val into an examination room. Val had been in many like this over the years. It looked like it had been recently updated. The tile on the floor wasn't cracked and the walls were a pale blue. She remembered reading an article that blue was supposed to promote calm. In her case, it wasn't working. Her nerves vibrated like a tight guitar string.

She looked at Laurel, who'd taken a position off to her left, sitting in a hardback chair. She appeared relaxed and beautiful. Laurel caught her staring at her and gazed back, reaching out to stroke Val's arm. A nurse entered, took vital signs, recorded the basic issues, and left.

Laurel put a hand on Val's shoulder. "Do you need a drink of water? You look pale."

"I'm a little warm." Val blew out a breath and wiped at the sweat running down the side of her face. "I'm sorry. It's this place. I met some of the most important people in my life in here, namely Liz and Jo. I also suffered a great deal of pain here on my road to recovery. I had to learn to walk again. My left arm was almost useless until Cat replaced my elbow. The concussion caused serious migraines." She paused, lost in her own thoughts, her vision growing cloudy. "None of that was as bad as the nightmares and the terrors that kept me locked inside myself."

Laurel got up and knelt in front of her, placing both hands on Val's face. "Honey, you're not there. Regardless of how beat up you are now, it's temporary. You'll walk on your own again. We'll get your arm fixed and maybe I'll even let you take me for a ride on Maggie May after you get her up and running."

Val looked at the woman before her. Never in her life had she wanted anyone the way she wanted Laurel. She owned no camera capable of capturing how beautiful Laurel looked at this moment. Leaning forward, she ran her fingers through Laurel's hair, cupping her cheek. She brought their lips together in a gentle kiss. "Thank you, Laurel, for being with me."

"No place I'd rather be. Do you want me to leave so you can talk to your doctor in private?"

Val shook her head no. A brisk knock at the door startled them. Laurel was still kneeling with her hand on her cheek as Cat strode through the door, looking at the chart in her hands.

"Val, if I'd known you wanted to see me again, you could've called. I'd have been more than happy to examine you head to toe in, shall we say, more friendly surroundings." She went silent, seeing that Val wasn't alone. Moving over to the counter, she put down the file and turned to the pair, crossing her arms.

Laurel stood and Val cleared her throat. "Laurel Stemple, meet Lieutenant Colonel Catherine O'Reilly. Best damn battlefield surgeon I've ever met."

"Only because I put you back together at a time that you resembled a jigsaw puzzle. Now, what have you done to my masterpiece?" She extended her hand to Laurel. "Nice to meet you. Call me Cat."

Laurel took Cat's hand. "It's a pleasure. She didn't do this on her own. Someone helped her put a ding or two in the paint. The motor and the chassis are still sound."

Cat laughed and looked at Val. "I like her, Val. She's got spunk."

Laurel didn't laugh, but Val's smile widened. "So do I, Cat. Rest assured, I haven't screwed up what you so skillfully put back together. The leg's fine. My elbow was acting up, that's why I scheduled the appointment. Unfortunately," she said, looking at her right arm, "it appears I've managed to do some damage to a part of me that didn't get torn up over there."

Laurel handed Cat a large manila envelope. "Inside you'll find a report from the doctors at WVU. The CD contains the scans of that shoulder. She has a fractured shoulder blade."

Pulling the hospital notes from the envelope, Cat slid her eyes to Laurel and then back to Val. "How long has that arm been in the immobilizer?"

Laurel looked at Val and ran a hand across the restrained shoulder. "They had something else on her while she was in the SICU. After they moved her out to the regular floor, they put this one on. She's been in this one for about a week and a half."

Val shuddered at the intimate touch and felt her insides go warm. She was enjoying the way Laurel was taking charge.

"Damn, you should have called me, Val. You know I don't like to wait on these types of injuries." She turned to the computer and slid in the disc, pulling up the images. "The shoulder blade will heal on its own. Unfortunately, you've torn the shit out of your rotator cuff. It's going to require surgery. I don't know exactly what day I can clear a spot on my schedule and no one else is taking a scalpel to you unless I'm dead. I'll may have to go back, though. We'll see. I need my leg back, Anya, I really do. I forgot what it's like to be without it. With this banged up shoulder, I can't even crutch my way around."

Laurel shook her head. "Val, you know I don't mind helping you. I'll be around as long as you need me."

Val felt a squeeze. She looked down at a pair of joined hands and had no recollection of reaching for Laurel. She only knew that holding her hand felt so right. "I know you don't. Laurel, you can't be away from the store that long." She raised Laurel's hand to her lips and kissed it.

"You let me worry about that. If I come back to Cool Springs without you, I'm likely to have to go cut a switch."

Anya looked concerned, but Val laughed and held up her hand to allay her unease. "Don't worry, Anya, it's an empty threat by a feisty matriarch of the most interesting place I've ever been. Laurel and her grandmother run a small store and diner in West Virginia."

Anya turned to Laurel. "Is that the place with the deer head with the Viking helmet I've seen in your pictures?"

Laurel chuckled. "One and the same."

"Ah. Let's see what we can do to get both of you back there." Anya left the room.

Val closed her eyes, taking deep breaths, trying to stay positive.

Laurel's soft voice penetrated her consciousness. "You okay?"

"Yeah, I'm worried about this. These guys are the best in the business. They're also perfectionists. I sure hope I didn't destroy it, forcing us to start all over."

Laurel came over to stand in front of Val and kissed her forehead. She moved between Val's spread legs and wrapped her arms around her waist, pulling her close.

Val rested her chin on Laurel's shoulder and breathed in the sweet trace of the tropics she always associated with her. The scent settled Val's nerves and made her think about sitting on a beach with Laurel. Her mind filled with the picture of the waves crashing onto the shore and the water gently flowing over the sand. She could imagine Laurel in a bikini and felt a pulse start deep in her center. God, how she wanted Laurel...wanted to feel her beneath her. Before she could completely lose herself in her thoughts, a knock at the door brought them back to reality. Charley walked in with a bucket dangling from his hand. He sat it down and strode over to Val. "Long time no see. What have you done now to give me the pleasure of dipping your leg in goo? I could think of a dozen other ways I'd like to visit with you."

There was a subtle lilt to his voice and a feminine manner. He was a beautiful sort of handsome. He looked a little like the love child of Bon Jovi and George Michael with a mane full of blond hair feathered back and at his collar. His vibrant green eyes shimmered with mischief.

Val's smile widened. "How are you, Charley?"

"Fabulous, darling. I can tell by that new bondage getup you're wearing that you aren't as fabulous as normal."

Val felt the blush crawl up her neck and her ears felt hot. She looked over at Laurel who had her free hand up over her mouth trying to hide a smirk and stifle a laugh. It wasn't working.

Charley spoke up. "Where are your manners, girlfriend? Who is this beauty you have with you and why haven't I ever seen her before?" He held out his hand and shook Laurel's.

Val sighed. "Charley, this is Laurel Stemple. Laurel, meet Charley Cavender, artist extraordinaire and hair aficionado. Laurel has graciously been taking incredible care of me while I recover."

Charley took an exaggerated bow. "Honey, I have no doubt you have your hands full there. As brilliant and talented as this hunk is, she can be a royal pain in the ass at times."

"Just because I won't let you dress me up and accompany you to the leather bar." Val smirked and Laurel's eyes got big.

Laurel wasn't as successful at hiding her laugh this time. "Why, Val, I'm seeing a totally different side of you."

Charley smiled at Laurel and hugged Val. "A boy can dream, you know. Down to business. Mom said you'll need a new socket and sleeve. Let's start with the sleeve, shall we?"

Val rolled her eyes at him. "Now there's a great idea. Let's get started."

***

Laurel watched as Charley went about mixing up something in the bucket that reminded her of the material the dentist used to create her retainer after the braces. He handed Val a tube of something to rub on her amputated leg. Val shook her head and frowned at him.

"I've only got one wing here dipshit," Val said, whacking him in the head with the tube.

"Watch the hair! Laurel has two good hands, as far as I can tell." He looked at Laurel. "You'll be more than capable to act as my assistant, won't you, darling?" Charley smiled like a Cheshire cat.

Laurel caught Val flipping him the middle finger of her immobilized hand. She felt her face grow warm as she took the tube from Val. Never having touched Val this way, she tried to calm her pounding heart and rolled Val's jeans up to her knee, exposing the flesh beneath. Without looking at Val, she squeezed some of the gel into her hands and warmed it between them. It had a faint blue tint to it with no odor that she could detect. She placed both hands around the stump, riddled with scar tissue and felt Val stiffen as she rubbed the gel on her skin. The blush crept higher into her cheeks. Closing her eyes for a moment, she enjoyed the feel of the warm skin beneath her hands. She could swear she heard Val whimper, but convinced herself it was a figment of her imagination. Soon, Val relaxed into her touch.

Charley broke the almost tangible intimacy. "Put a couple of coats on that so it doesn't stick when we go to remove her leg after this sets up. Besides, Val is close to orgasming, I'd hate to rob her of a climax."

Something smacked the man and Laurel looked up to see Anya frowning. "Charley, don't be so crass. Laurel isn't used to your teasing with Val."

Charley laughed. "Oh, Momma, I couldn't help it. Val's like a love-sick puppy and after all the shit she's given me over the years, it serves her right."

Anya rolled her eyes. "Be that as it may, Laurel doesn't deserve your teenage antics." Anya handed Laurel a towel. "Forgive my son, Laurel. I raised him better. There's only so much a mother can do."

Laurel's blush grew hotter as she wiped the gel off her hands. "Kids, what are you going to do with them?"

"Ok, Val, dive in." Charley held the bucket close enough that Val could stick her leg in the mixture. He brought a stool over and rested the bucket on it to allow the mixture to solidify. "I'll be back in a bit. I need to go gather the other compounds for the sleeve."

Shaking her head, Anya held up Val's busted prosthesis. "Okay, Val. The microprocessor is shot on your old leg. We've got some boards in stock, so it's just a matter of programming one with your settings. However, replacing the other components will take a few days. Charley will use the measurements and the molds we take today to get to work on your sleeve and socket. We should be able to bring you in for a fitting Thursday afternoon, maybe early evening. Does that work for you two?"

"I don't have much choice. I don't know about Laurel, she—"

Laurel interrupted. "Will be right here with you, Val." She leaned in and put her mouth close to Val's ear. "I told you I wouldn't leave you alone, and I meant it."

Anya chuckled and grabbed the tube of lubrication from Laurel. "Oh my God, I think you might've met your match, Val. Charley will be back to do a few measurements and then we'll set you up for your return appointment. Laurel, I'm happy to know she has someone who sees through that bullshit bravado. It's nice to meet you."

Laurel nodded. "Thank you, Anya, it's been nice meeting you, too. We'll see you on Thursday."

Val hugged her. "Thanks for seeing me on such short notice, Anya. I can't thank you enough."

"Val, you'll always be welcome here." Putting her hand on Val's shoulder, she turned to Laurel. "All the photos and news articles you see in here are compliments of this talented photographer. She brought attention to what we could do, not only for veterans but children as well. We couldn't have bought that kind of publicity. There's no way for us to repay her."

Val covered Anya's hand with her own. "It's been my pleasure. You've helped me more than I could have imagined. The joy I've seen you put on a child's face when they take their first steps, or as they're able to pick something up for themselves, that's priceless. I know what that feels like, and I wanted more people to know about those who make that happen every day."

Laurel looked around the room at the incredible photos that hung on every wall. Each one displayed a moment of triumph for the person in the image. Val had captured those moments of beauty and dignity.

"I agree, she's pretty special." She brushed her hand across Val's shoulders and ran her fingers into the hair at the back of Val's head. She looked around the room at the pictures and realized that with every new person she met in Val's life, another piece fell into place. Val was like a puzzle. One that she very much wanted to see in its entirety. She leaned in and kissed Val's temple. *More special than I could have even imagined.*

Chapter Sixteen

VAL TENSED AS A they sat outside of The Walter Reed Military Medical Center. She'd always referred to it as Bethesda. Her stomach knotted. It was time to go see about her shoulder. Val was dreading having Cat and Laurel meet. It'd been several years since she'd replaced Val's elbow. She was the best at what she did or Val would have sought treatment elsewhere. She wanted her shoulder fixed and fixed right. That fact alone had brought her back to the best the VA had to offer.

After they were signed in, they sat in an enormous area with dozens of others waiting to be seen. The noise of a busy hospital beeped, vibrated, and rattled around her. Rows of industrial chairs sat all around the room filled with men and women of all ages. Dull yellow walls fell short of providing a cheery atmosphere. The individuals who sat around her waited their turn to see whatever specialty dealt with their injury. Prosthetic limbs, scarred and misshapen bodies were all around her, the cost of war evident. The vacant, hollowed eyes, clouded with sand and memories, were easily recognizable to those who shared those nightmares. Those scars were harder to treat, if they were treatable at all.

She watched a woman younger than her. Her knee bounced up and down, and she rolled a coin back and forth through her fingers and across her knuckles. A chocolate lab sat between her legs, his head resting on her thigh. She was absently stroking his head with her free hand. Her eyes were blank. Val looked away and blinked back emotions that threatened to overwhelm her. These were the true cost of freedom and democracy. The price that those in this room paid so that others could go about their day not thinking for even a second about that cost. She was brought out of her reverie by a soft voice.

"Is it always like this?" Laurel asked.

"Always. Some are here for routine examinations or prescription refills, some for more serious issues." It still angered Val at the wait many of her fellow veterans had to go through to get the treatment they desperately needed. People who'd lost friends and pieces of themselves in the lands they fought in, now had to fight to see a doctor or to have a procedure in the richest and most advanced country in the world. *Shameful and it never changes.* "If I hadn't already had this appointment scheduled six months ago for some pain in my elbow, I'd still be on the waiting list." Val turned her attention to thumbing through the most recent edition of *Stars and Stripes,* her eyes drawn to a picture taken near Mosul.

Laurel's phone buzzed. Her fingers worked the keyboard texting, a faraway look on her face.

"Everything okay?"

"Yeah, I got a text from Beth. She's giving me shit, because I didn't call last night. Gram's giving her the devil for information about you." Laurel laughed. "Not that's she's concerned about me. You on the other hand..."

Val chuckled. "I have an idea. How about this evening we call, or if Beth can help her, we'll do a video chat on Facebook?"

"Oh, she'd love that. I'll text Beth a time." Laurel's thumbs flew over the screen.

Val checked her own phone and saw a missed call from her mother, a text message from her boss, and another one from Tess. She deciphered her mother's message by using a voicemail to text app. Her mother was concerned that she hadn't called in a few days to give her an update. She'd wait until after her appointment so she'd have more information to pass on. The text from her boss offered a few words of support. She wondered who'd picked up her assignment in Kentucky, guilty that someone else would have to take up her slack. Everything had been such a blur since the accident.

The one from Tess surprised her though. Somehow, she'd gotten word of Val's injuries and wanted to confirm if it was her involved in the accident. One of Kelly's crew moonlighted as a flight paramedic and apparently, was someone who brought Val in. The medic happened to tell Kelly and mentioned Val's vintage motorcycle. Details filtered in about a photographer doing a story on the "Ride to the Wall" event. Tess thought it was a long shot, but she wanted to check. Val knew a text wouldn't suffice for this, but she really wasn't ready to talk to Tess. She'd handle that later.

She sent quick texts to her mother and boss, which really wasn't that quick with one hand. By the time she managed to peck out the messages, the receptionist called her name. She began to sweat. The back of her neck tensed, and she had a feeling like before an approaching storm.

Laurel rose and wheeled Val into an examination room. Val had been in many like this over the years. It looked like it had been recently updated. The tile on the floor wasn't cracked and the walls were a pale blue. She remembered reading an article that blue was supposed to promote calm. In her case, it wasn't working. Her nerves vibrated like a tight guitar string.

She looked at Laurel, who'd taken a position off to her left, sitting in a hardback chair. She appeared relaxed and beautiful. Laurel caught her staring at her and gazed back, reaching out to stroke Val's arm. A nurse entered, took vital signs, recorded the basic issues, and left.

Laurel put a hand on Val's shoulder. "Do you need a drink of water? You look pale."

"I'm a little warm." Val blew out a breath and wiped at the sweat running down the side of her face. "I'm sorry. It's this place. I met some of the most important people in my life in here, namely Liz and Jo. I also suffered a great deal of pain here on my road to recovery. I had to learn to walk again. My left arm was almost useless until Cat replaced my elbow. The concussion caused serious migraines." She paused, lost in her own thoughts, her vision growing cloudy. "None of that was as bad as the nightmares and the terrors that kept me locked inside myself."

Laurel got up and knelt in front of her, placing both hands on Val's face. "Honey, you're not there. Regardless of how beat up you are now, it's temporary. You'll walk on your own again. We'll get your arm fixed and maybe I'll even let you take me for a ride on Maggie May after you get her up and running."

Val looked at the woman before her. Never in her life had she wanted anyone the way she wanted Laurel. She owned no camera capable of capturing how beautiful Laurel looked at this moment. Leaning forward, she ran her fingers through Laurel's hair, cupping her cheek. She brought their lips together in a gentle kiss. "Thank you, Laurel, for being with me."

"No place I'd rather be. Do you want me to leave so you can talk to your doctor in private?"

Val shook her head no. A brisk knock at the door startled them. Laurel was still kneeling with her hand on her cheek as Cat strode through the door, looking at the chart in her hands.

"Val, if I'd known you wanted to see me again, you could've called. I'd have been more than happy to examine you head to toe in, shall we say, more friendly surroundings." She went silent, seeing that Val wasn't alone. Moving over to the counter, she put down the file and turned to the pair, crossing her arms.

Laurel stood and Val cleared her throat. "Laurel Stemple, meet Lieutenant Colonel Catherine O'Reilly. Best damn battlefield surgeon I've ever met."

"Only because I put you back together at a time that you resembled a jigsaw puzzle. Now, what have you done to my masterpiece?" She extended her hand to Laurel. "Nice to meet you. Call me Cat."

Laurel took Cat's hand. "It's a pleasure. She didn't do this on her own. Someone helped her put a ding or two in the paint. The motor and the chassis are still sound."

Cat laughed and looked at Val. "I like her, Val. She's got spunk."

Laurel didn't laugh, but Val's smile widened. "So do I, Cat. Rest assured, I haven't screwed up what you so skillfully put back together. The leg's fine. My elbow was acting up, that's why I scheduled the appointment. Unfortunately," she said, looking at her right arm, "it appears I've managed to do some damage to a part of me that didn't get torn up over there."

Laurel handed Cat a large manila envelope. "Inside you'll find a report from the doctors at WVU. The CD contains the scans of that shoulder. She has a fractured shoulder blade."

Pulling the hospital notes from the envelope, Cat slid her eyes to Laurel and then back to Val. "How long has that arm been in the immobilizer?"

Laurel looked at Val and ran a hand across the restrained shoulder. "They had something else on her while she was in the SICU. After they moved her out to the regular floor, they put this one on. She's been in this one for about a week and a half."

Val shuddered at the intimate touch and felt her insides go warm. She was enjoying the way Laurel was taking charge.

"Damn, you should have called me, Val. You know I don't like to wait on these types of injuries." She turned to the computer and slid in the disc, pulling up the images. "The shoulder blade will heal on its own. Unfortunately, you've torn the shit out of your rotator cuff. It's going to require surgery. I don't know exactly what day I can clear a spot on my schedule and no one else is taking a scalpel to you unless I'm dead. I'll call with a time. Are you staying around here?"

"We're staying with some friends. Do you think it will be in the next week? If not, we'll go home. We can be back in about three hours."

Cat turned back around on the heels of her stilettos, the only non-regulation part of her uniform, a pinched lip smile drawn across her face. "Home? Val, I wasn't aware you'd settled anywhere except the seat of that bike."

Val smirked at the feel of Laurel's hand sliding into hers. The perplexed, yet irked look on Cat's face was priceless. "Laurel and her grandmother Ree have taken me in."

She didn't need to justify anything to Cat. The few mornings she'd awakened in Laurel's arms meant more to her than the few nights of passion with Cat or even the few months she and Tess tried to live together. Cat began to remove the immobilizer, startling her from her musings.

"This thing has been on too long in my experience. If you don't at least do some small movements, it'll freeze." She began to manipulate the shoulder gently. Val winced. It was painful from the actions of the night before. She reached deep inside herself to allow the movement. The feeling of Cat's icy fingers on her flesh was uncomfortable and foreign. She squeezed Laurel's hand harder.

Laurel covered the hand in hers with her free hand. "She fell out of bed onto it last night. I was afraid she'd done more damage. It was still hot and swollen this morning."

Cat raised an eyebrow. "I'm not sure she could tear it up much more than the accident did. It more than likely aggravated it. It won't heal right until I've repaired the tears." Cat ran a hand up to Val's shoulder to where it met her neck. Her thumb brushed Val's cheek. "I'll text my secretary to put you on the schedule for Thursday morning. I was supposed to teach at a symposium, however, this takes precedence. I'm a surgeon before I'm a teacher. They can find someone else to do it. You and I have a date, Magnusson. You know the drill, nothing after midnight. No cologne or deodorant. I'll have the nurse bring you the antiseptic wash to shower with that morning. We'll set you up with a rehab schedule after that and—"

Laurel interrupted. "She'll be doing rehab at Backbone Mountain Rehab and Physical Therapy in West Virginia. I can get you all the particulars so you can send whatever you need to Fallon Armstrong."

The tension in the room was thick enough to be cut with a knife. Val raised her chin to look at Cat. *Oh, here's where the claws come out.*

"Well, Val. It appears you've lost the ability to talk for yourself," Cat said, squinting.

Val squeezed Laurel's hand in reassurance. "I haven't. Laurel's been taking care of me since the accident. She was kind enough to make arrangements with a local therapist, who from all accounts, is a miracle worker. It won't be convenient for me to do therapy here. I'm not staying in DC, and there's no way I'm driving back over here three days a week."

"You could always stay at my house. I have plenty of room and with my schedule, I'm almost never home unless I choose to be," Cat replied.

Val could feel the waves of tension rolling off Laurel. She was sure that any second one of them would pee on her to declare ownership like dogs do as they marked their territory. She needed to put a stop to this now. Cat had no claim on her.

"Cat, let's stop dancing. Remember, I only have one good leg. I'm staying with Laurel and Ree in West Virginia. Soon, I'll have my prosthesis back and I'll be able to drive myself if needed. I appreciate the offer, but if we need a place to stay, Jo and Liz have already told me we're welcome there." Val lost the cordiality in her tone and wanted no misunderstanding. She needed Cat to fully comprehend there would be nothing more between them beyond a professional relationship. She felt Laurel's hand relax around hers.

Cat crossed her arms and tilted her head. "It seems you can speak for yourself. I'll have my secretary phone you with the details. Is your number still the same as it was while we were in Provincetown?"

Val gritted her teeth at Cat's inference to familiarity. "Yes."

"Good. I'll see you Thursday." Cat stormed out of the room, her heels punishing the floor with the spikes of her shoes.

Laurel leaned down and planted a searing kiss on Val's lips, her hand tightly grasping the hair at the back of Val's neck. Closing her fingers into a fist, she tilted Val's head up. "I'm not going to ask why she's acting as if you have something current going on. But, just so you know, if she'd have touched you again, it's likely the MP's would have had to be summoned and I'd have been arrested."

Val liked Laurel's possessiveness. Her center clinched. It made her feel wanted and protected. She'd rarely let anyone take control in her life, but there were times she just didn't want to be in charge. "What happened between us was a long time ago. It was brief and only one weekend. I haven't seen her in two years and that was for an appointment. There's nothing between us on my part. I need you to believe me."

"I believe you. I'm not sure she sees it that way." Taking a deep breath, Laurel put one knee on the ground so she was at eye-level with Val.

Val pulled Laurel to her with her good arm and kissed the top of her head. "Doesn't matter what she believes. My dance card is presently full. Let's get out of here. I could use some lunch, and I know a great place."

Laurel kissed her more softly this time. "Anything to get us out of here."

After lunch Laurel stopped in at a Target for a few things. Val stayed in the car to make some phone calls. One of them was to Tess telling her it had been her in the accident. Tess offered to come and help her, even offering to let Val stay with her and Kelly.

"Thank you, Tess, but I'm being taken care of, sometimes too well. I'm not sure how I got this lucky."

There was a long pause before Tess spoke. "You've found her, haven't you?"

"Tess, I..."

"Oh, baby, it's okay. I hoped it would happen to you someday. Be sure to let her in." Tess paused. "Have I ever met her?"

Val let her head fall back against the headrest, closing her eyes. "No, you've read about her grandmother's store."

"Cool Springs. I should've known. Never seen you mention any place so many times. She must be pretty special."

"She is." Val paused, rolling her shoulders, trying to decide if she should say what she was thinking. "And so are you."

The exchange had been brief but exhausting. Tess deserved so much more from her and time after time, she'd failed. It had to be different with Laurel. It just had to.

***

Laurel drove back to Liz and Jo's, worried that the day had exhausted Val, who'd been quiet the entire ride. Thoughts of Cat still boiled her blood. Her jealousy felt irrational. Val told her there was nothing between them, but she didn't trust Cat to honor that. At the house Liz helped Laurel get Val settled, and then took Laurel by the hand and led her to the study.

Walking over to the well-stocked bar, Liz poured them both a highball of Maker's Mark and tonic water. Handing Laurel the glass, she smirked. "Pretty sure you can use this. How did it go?"

Laurel shook her head and accepted the glass. She allowed the smooth liquid to burn away the tension of the day. "It was both inspiring and infuriating. The people at The Bodyshop were incredible. Charley and Anya hope to have her new leg ready in the next few days."

"And her appointment with Cat?"

Laurel narrowed her eyes and took another drink. "She…" She closed her eyes and bit her upper lip. She took a long sip of the liquor she held, opening her eyes.

Liz shook her head. "I take it she was her typical self? She's the best damn surgeon I know. Unfortunately, if she wants something, she lets little stop her. She's made her interest in Val known for a long time. I can tell you from conversations with Jo and me, Val isn't interested. She has strong feelings for you. One drunken weekend doesn't count as anything resembling a relationship."

Laurel took a deep breath. She stirred the cocktail and gathered her thoughts. "That woman is a walking hormone. If I had any say in it, she wouldn't touch Val. You both tell me she's the best surgeon. I must believe that or I would've dragged that woman out in the hallway and showed her that West Virginia women don't take kindly to those who try to take liberties they haven't been given permission to take. Good surgeon or not, I wanted to kick her ass. She had the audacity to try and get Val to stay with her to recuperate."

"That doesn't surprise me. She took a shine to Jo several years ago before we were married. It was my good fortune Jo was already smitten or I might have had to open a can of South Carolina whoopass. Don't dwell on what could have happened, only what will happen. You have a great deal of influence on that."

Laurel ran a shaky hand across her face. "I just want to help her get better. Whatever she decides after that will be up to her. All I can do is be there for her."

"You're capable of much more than that, my dear, whether you know it or not. Val may not have said it in clear terms yet, but I have no doubt she has strong intentions about your relationship."

Laurel sipped her drink, trying to calm her mind. She thought about the exchange. Val hadn't responded to Cat's advances. Actually, she'd rebuffed her repeatedly and reassured Laurel there was nothing between them. *Is she trying to tell me she wants more, or is it me just not ready to accept how I feel?*

She and Liz finished their drinks and Laurel took a walk around the back yard. She tried to sort through her jumbled emotions. What did she want? Was she ready to tell Val everything, all her fears? She wasn't sure, but it felt like the answer was becoming clearer every day. *It's been Val for a long time. Always Val.*

A few hours later, they woke Val up and Liz ordered Chinese for dinner. Laurel insisted on paying. After some good-natured arguing, she prevailed. Laurel laughed as Val attempted to use her chopsticks left handed. After several comical attempts at bringing food to her mouth, Laurel found Val a fork.

She cleaned off a bit of orange sauce from Val's cheek. "Here, try this instead."

Val kissed her. "I was about to use these chopsticks to spear my chicken. Not sure it would have worked too well on the rice. Thanks."

They devoured the food and talked about the store and all the characters there. Laurel's phone chimed with a reminder to go online for the planned chat with Beth and Gram. "That's our cue, Viking. Let's go get set up."

Several minutes later, they both settled around the laptop, signed in, and placed the video call.

Beth and Gram appeared on their screen. "Beth, can you hear me?" Laurel asked.

"Hiya, honey, she might not be able to, but I sure can. How are ya? Val, what're they going to do about that shoulder? What's up with your leg?" Ree wasted no time.

Val and Laurel laughed. Laurel shook her head and ran her hand into the back of Val's hair. "Hi Gram, miss you too."

"Hey, Ree. Thanks for letting me borrow this one. Having Laurel with me is a godsend. I have no doubt you miss having her around."

Ree grinned. "Oh, I miss her all right. But I tell ya, having Beth here to fuss over me is about like having Laurel here. If I shut my eyes, I could swear it's her. Just as big a burr under my saddle."

Beth opened her mouth as if she were going to protest. Shaking her head, she took a good look at them. "You guys look tired."

Laurel glanced at their own reflection in the tiny screen by the corner and noticed deep shadows under both her and Val's eyes. *No kidding.*

Val answered this time. "Neither of us got much sleep last night, and today took a good bit out of me. One good thing is I got that damn immobilizer off. The plan is to put Humpty Dumpty back together again

Thursday morning. Hopefully I'll get my leg after that and be good as new."

"How's the store, Gram?" Laurel looked for any signs of illness or stress in her grandmother's face. Seeing none, she relaxed a bit more.

Ree rolled her eyes. "Falling apart without ya. Not sure how I ran that place before ya was born."

Laurel's eyes widened. "Gram, you know that's not what I mean. I miss everyone."

Ree laughed. "Everyone misses ya, too. Tilly's grandkids were all there today. They missed story time with Ms. Laurel."

Val looked at her, brows drawn together. "Story time?"

Ree spoke up, smiling. "A couple of times a month, Tilly brings the kids in for a treat on her day off. You know, hot dogs and chocolate milk. We give them some small job to do so they can earn some spending money. After that, Laurel reads to them from some book."

Val looked over at Laurel who grinned sheepishly.

"Wunder reads to them at home and I read to them while they have ice cream. They're good kids." Laurel thought about the small faces hanging on her every word. It was just as important to her.

"Val, your room's waiting on ya when they get done poking and prodding ya. I'll have a crisp warming in the oven for ya. Laurel, ya quit your worrying about anything back here. Enjoy yourself for once. I'm fixing to teach this kid to play gin. I think she might be better if we were playing Go Fish." Ree shook her head. "You two get some sleep. Ya look like ya could use it. Love ya both."

Laurel yawned and touched the screen. "Love you too, Gram."

Val added, "That goes for me too, Ree. See you soon. Beth, don't put any money on your game with Ree, she's a shark."

"Don't I know it. You two be careful. Talk to you soon." Beth ended the call.

Val yawned, and Laurel ran a finger down her cheek. "I think it's time we go to bed. It's been a long day."

Upstairs, Laurel helped Val change into a pair of plaid boxer shorts and a maroon t-shirt bearing the immortal words of John Muir, "The mountains are calling and I must go."

"Are the mountains the only thing that calls you?" Leaning forward, she pressed a kiss to Val's forehead. She pulled back, intending to go change. She felt Val grab her arm.

"No. You do too. Please don't go."

Laurel looked deep into Val's eyes, threading her hand into the thick blonde hair. She kissed her softly. "Honey, I'm just going to change and get your meds. I promise, you won't sleep alone again, unless you want to."

"Not a chance."

Laurel left to get changed and returned a few minutes later. Val took her pills and Laurel crawled in beside her. She was exhausted, both physically and emotionally. She curled into Val's side and felt Val's arm come around her shoulders. Both settled in and she felt Val slowly bring her other arm around Laurel. This worried her. "Don't hurt yourself."

"It's fine. This movement doesn't hurt." She squeezed a little tighter. "This is the best medicine. Go to sleep, my green-eyed monster."

Laurel chuckled. "I wanted to knock her down a notch today."

"Oh, I was well aware of that. I think she was a bit taken aback with you, too. Shocked the hell out of her that someone was with me. She never even saw me with Tess." Val stopped and kissed Laurel's forehead.

"Tess?" This wasn't a name she could recall Val mentioning before. Her curiosity piqued. She craned her neck to look at Val.

Val stammered, "Someone...someone I dated seriously after my weekend with Cat. Do we have to talk about this right now?"

"I don't want to know just the part of you that rides into Cool Springs a couple times a year. I'd like to know all of you." Laurel settled her head on Val's shoulder. She didn't want Val to feel pressured, but she wanted to know more.

Val sighed. "I met Tess about six years ago. I was working on a photo shoot for one of Gary Sinise's charity concerts. She's one of the organizers. We hit it off and dated for a while. Even tried to move in together. The nightmares kept me from being who I am now. I wasn't in a good place and eventually we separated. We still run into each other occasionally. I actually saw her during the bike run."

Laurel stiffened a little in Val's arms. Hearing about someone else who'd meant something special to Val was painful.

"She and her girlfriend Kelly moved in together. Kelly's a captain with the Arlington Fire Department. I've met her, and she's terrific, thinks there's no one like Tess. She deserves someone like that."

Laurel hadn't meant to bristle at the mention of another of Val's ex's, but meeting Cat had her on edge. Her head pounded. To think of Val holding any other woman would make her crazy. She knew she had no claim on Val. She also knew she shouldn't be doing anything with Val because they likely had no long-term future. But Laurel couldn't help herself. She wanted something. Something she couldn't explain. Maybe she just needed to make love with Val, but somehow, she didn't think that was it. It went deeper. The things she hadn't told Val were the things that kept her from having any serious relationships at all for years. If the cancer developed, she might not have to worry about a future with Val at all. It was also possible Val would be completely turned off by her secret. Deep down, the thought of Val rejecting her nearly broke her. She stifled a cry into Val's chest, praying she'd think it was over Cat or Tess.

Val squeezed her. "Hey, hey, honey. Honestly, I was never in love with Tess. I cared for her, I did. I could never be what she needed or deserved. Kelly will give her everything I couldn't."

Laurel lay quiet for a long time thinking. Her mind refused to settle. It felt so right to be in Val's arms, like it was the one place she was meant to be. She was conflicted by her physical and emotional attraction to Val in combination with her hesitation to reveal her whole self and what she'd been through. The fear of rejection sat on her chest like a lead weight threatening to hold her down. *I want her so much.* Her jealousy today was proof of her desire to be with Val.

Laurel dried her tears on Val's shirt, her lips inadvertently brushing Val's nipple. She heard Val groan in pleasure. Her desire pushed through the veil of doubt. She needed to feel Val. This time she moved her lips across it deliberately. She felt Val arch into her touch. She raised her eyes to Val's hooded ones and brought her lips to the cotton-covered nipple again. She gently bit the hardening point, enjoying the possessive way Val's hand curled at the nape of her neck, pushing her closer. Her left hand slipped beneath the hem of the t-shirt. Her fingers met soft, warm skin and traced the hardened abdominal muscles, scoring gently with her short nails. She felt the raised scar from Val's surgery running in an arc and skimmed it with her fingertips. She closed her eyes and pushed the doubt into the background. Raising her head, she watched Val's cool blue eyes turn dark and ravenous with desire. Laurel inched up the bed. She captured Val's lips with hers, and then traced them with her tongue.

Peppermint! She captured those lips again and pushed her tongue in between Val's. Val met Laurel's teasing tongue with her own, capturing it in her teeth and pulling the smaller woman on top of her.

"Watch your arm," Laurel whispered.

"My arm is fine. Other parts of me need immediate attention."

Laurel pushed up the t-shirt and kissed the inside curve of her right breast, then her left. She let her lips linger over the taut nipple. She sucked it and felt a hand pushing her head down. "You like it harder, love?"

Val nodded. "Yes."

Laurel kneaded the other breast with her hand and rolled the nipple between her fingers, pinching hard enough to draw a hiss of pleasure and an arch of Val's back. God, she wanted Val. She rose on her knees, kneeling beside Val's hips. Val tried to remove the shirt Laurel wore, but she wasn't ready to bare all and stopped her.

She leaned down to kiss Val and whispered against her lips. "This is for your pleasure. Let me do this for you."

She removed Val's boxers and marveled at the soft wisps of blonde hair forming a triangle between her legs. The intoxicating smell of Val's arousal flooded Laurel's senses as she ran her hand through the curls. Kissing Val's lips, she whispered, "How quiet can you be?"

Val moaned and used her good arm to push Laurel down her body. "Please."

Laurel let a purely predatory grin cross her lips and slid down until she could reposition herself between Val's legs. She skimmed her stomach with her lips reverently kissing the scar. She lingered in Val's soft curls, using her tongue to taste a hint of Val's pleasure before lifting her eyes to the blue ones staring back at her. She wanted to see what her touch did. She wanted to know that in taking her, Val knew how much she was wanted. She lowered her lips to Val, using her tongue to part the warm folds. Covering Val with long strokes, she teased. She drank in the evidence of arousal and felt Val's body tense beneath her. She kissed her inner thighs and held her lips inches from Val's center.

Val's right hand made her way into Laurel's dark hair, once again making a strangled plea for release. "Please, baby," she whispered.

Laurel needed no more encouragement. She sucked Val's clit and drove her tongue into Val's depths, moaning at how wet Val was and how urgent her hip movement had become. She could tell Val was trying to be quiet, as muffled sounds of pleasure escaped her lips. The more Laurel sucked and bit her clit, the more vocal she became. At this point, she didn't care if Jo and Liz heard. She wanted to draw the guttural sounds of pleasure from this woman like she'd never wanted before. She drew her right hand between Val's legs and ran a finger through the wetness.

"Laurel, oh God! Don't stop!"

Laurel reveled as she watched Val's back arch, sweat glistening on the body bending to her will. She withdrew her fingers and slipped her tongue inside. She could feel the tension, but it felt like Val was holding back. Laurel raised her head. "I'm not done yet, and I can tell you aren't either."

"No, I still need more," Val gasped.

"Tell me what you need, love."

"I need...I need..."

Laurel climbed up beside her body and kissed her. "Ask. There's nothing I won't give you."

"I know. I just don't know if you can."

Laurel put her hand in the middle of Val's chest and held her down. "You need me to do this?" Somewhere deep inside her, she felt Val's need to be taken. She wanted to be the one to bridge this gap and allow her to surrender to the pleasure.

"Yes."

"And this?" She didn't wait for Val to answer as she drove three fingers deep inside her. Val arched her back on the bed. Laurel stroked in and out, increasing the speed, all while driving deeper and deeper. She curled her fingers at the end of each thrust before withdrawing for the next stroke. She kissed Val and bit her lower lip as the woman below her struggled to hold back the final release. Laurel found Val's eyes and demanded they stay on hers.

Laurel moved her lips close to Val's ear. "Come for me."

Her lover slipped over the edge and cried out in her release. "Laurel!"

Laurel collapsed beside a heavily breathing Val. Her own breath was rapid as she lay reveling in the feeling of what had happened between them. "God, baby, I've never made love to anyone like that." Val still hadn't spoken, and she rose up on one arm to be able to look in Val's eyes. She found them swimming with tears. Alarmed she sat up. "Honey, what's wrong? Are you all right?" *Shit. Did she hurt her shoulder?*

Val bit her lip. "I've never let myself go where we did or ever voiced those desires. Being with you is so different. I can't...I need..."

Laurel watched her visibly struggle to rein in something unspoken. "Honey, you're safe. It's okay. Let your guard down. I won't hurt you. I'll be right here." She watched as a cloud veiled Val's eyes. Val's breathing became rapid, and her body tensed as she blindly reached out. Laurel grabbed her hand and held it to her chest. Her mind tried to process what she was seeing. Val's eyes were now wild, unfocused. *She's flashing.* "Val baby, look at me. Look at me. Slow your breathing. I'm right here with you. You're in no danger. You're in my arms and we just made love. Val, look at me." Within seconds, Laurel saw the blue eyes before her clear and focus. Smiling, she leaned down and kissed Val.

Val shook and her voice came out on a whisper. "I'm sorry. I don't know what happened there."

"It's ok, whatever it was has passed. You're ok, and you're here with me."

"I can't explain it. Laurel, there's never been anyone in my life I've ever trusted the way I do you. I'm constantly trying to stay in control. For once, I needed to allow someone else have it."

Laurel calmed her own breathing and settled down. "I'm honored. I'm not sure what's in store for us or where this is headed. I do know I've never felt anything like this. I know that's so cliché, but it's true. Being with you, I feel complete, and that's a rare thing for me. There are things I want to tell you, things I need to tell you, but not tonight. Tonight, I need to hold you and be held by you."

Val reached up and traced her jawline. "Don't you want me to touch you?"

"Yes, I do, but not tonight. Tonight, I just want this." She kissed Val, and snuggled into her neck, feeling warm skin beneath her cheek.

Val pulled her closer. "Then this is what you'll get."

Laurel wrapped her arms around the taller woman. Tonight, none of her own fears mattered. Even with all her doubts, she realized she was exactly where she wanted to be.

***

Muted sunlight slipped through the partially open blinds, rays falling across Laurel's face. Val pushed a lock of chestnut hair away from her mouth, and then lightly traced her lower lip with her thumb where a small smile formed. "Morning."

Laurel opened her eyes and wiped a hand across them. "Hi."

Val kissed Laurel, her heart melting with each tender caress. She was sure she'd never get tired of looking into those eyes, the color of spring grass. "How'd you sleep?"

Smirking, Laurel ran a finger along Val's jawline. "Like a rock. I think you wore me out."

Val laughed. "I wore you out? I think it's the other way around."

"My part required a little effort, if I do say so myself."

"Your part was outstanding." Val smiled and then caught Laurel's bright green eyes. "No one has ever been able to read my desire the way you do." She sighed. Her eyes followed the dip in her shirt that exposed Laurel's collarbone. She reached out and let her finger glide across it and enjoying the shiver it elicited. "Laurel, I've never let anyone as close to me as I've let you."

Laurel reached out and ran a hand down her arm.

"I don't just mean physically. I mean in here." She pointed to her head. "And here." She pointed to her heart.

Laurel leaned up on an elbow. "Why?"

Val let her fingers trail small circles on Laurel's side. She tried to put her thoughts into some sensible order. *How can I explain my inadequacies and fear?* "I've spent my life trying to gain some form of control. Control I didn't have as a child, control I didn't have in Iraq, and control I still don't have over the memories. I've never let anyone close because I'm afraid."

"Afraid of what?"

Val rolled over onto her back and put a hand over her eyes. "Afraid of what I could do. You saw how close I came to flashing. If I'm," she stopped and paused for a long moment collecting her thoughts. "If I'm not in control, I could hurt you." She choked back a sob. "I hurt Tess, physically. If I ever did anything like that to you, it would kill me."

Laurel reached up and placed her palm against Val's cheek and lifted Val's hand. She held it in hers. "I've seen your episodes. I'm more afraid of not being there than I am of you hurting me. I'm tougher than I look. Let me be there for you."

"I have no doubt about how tough you are." Val kissed her hand. "I'm trying, Laurel, I really am."

"That's all I can ask. Now, as much as I'd love to stay in bed with you all day, how about we find our way to the coffee I smell?"

Val rolled over and kissed her again. "If we must." She took a deep breath, pulling in the buttery aroma of Liz's favorite Kona bean Val knew she ground herself. "It does smell good. She orders it from a single source bean roaster in Hawaii. Liz isn't extravagant about much, but coffee? She's a snob. Lucky us."

Chapter Seventeen

AFTER WASHING UP AND dressing, they made their way downstairs for breakfast. Jo had a piece of toast shoved in her mouth as she wheeled up to the table to a waiting cup of coffee. She eyed them and smirked. "Morning. Want coffee?"

Laurel kissed the top of Val's head. "I'll be right back. I forgot your meds."

Val closed her eyes at the touch and turned back to Jo. "Always, thanks."

Jo headed back to the coffee pot and poured Val a cup. Jo whispered, "With a side of exorcism."

Liz scowled and smacked her on the arm. "Stop."

Val smirked over her coffee cup. "Funny, Jo. Not like I haven't heard a few things coming from your room on nights I've stayed over. Now don't you dare say a thing to Laurel or I'll chock your wheels."

Jo put her hand to her lips and pretended to lock them, throwing away the key as Laurel re-entered the room. She put Val's pills down in front of her and ran her hand down Val's arm.

Liz moved the conversation to a safer subject. "So, surgery Thursday?"

"Yeah, Cat wanted it out of the brace, thank God. She said it won't heal on its own. It's pretty trashed. At least I have use of both my hands now."

"Just in time," Jo said.

Liz glared at her.

"What did I say?" Jo protested. "She'll need both her hands to put her leg on once it's fixed."

Liz rolled her eyes and pulled a cup of yogurt from the refrigerator. Laurel had a look of confusion on her face until she had her first sip of coffee. Val watched as clarity came over Laurel's face, and a blush slowly began to creep up her neck. Val reached out and put her hand on Laurel's leg. Laurel smiled and that was enough for Val to know she was ok.

"It'll feel good to be out of this chair. I don't know how you do it, Jo," Val said, admiration filling her voice.

"I've gotten used to it. It's like a part of me. With the new robotics, I can stand as I need to. It helps me work with the sculptures. I created a frame to hold the piece and allow me to turn it in any direction. It makes it possible for me to work on larger pieces. Are you guys going to be able to stop by my show this evening?"

"That would be wonderful," Laurel said, clapping her hands together. "I'd love to see some of your art."

"Great! I'll put your names on the list at the door." Jo grinned as she finished her toast and filled a travel mug to take upstairs. "I've got some detail work to do on a commissioned piece. Laurel, why don't you come up with me and take a look at it."

Laurel looked at Val. "Will you be okay?"

"Yeah, I'm going to sit here and drink my coffee. I need to check my email, too. Liz, can I borrow your computer again?"

Liz finished the yogurt she'd been eating. "Sure, the one in the study would be easiest for you to get to. I'll take you to it after you finish your coffee."

Laurel started to rise but sat back down. "Val, you need to eat something with your meds."

Val started to speak, but Liz cut her off and looked at Laurel. "I'll get her something, how about you?"

"I'm good with this for right now. I'll have something in a bit." Laurel followed Jo upstairs and left Liz and Val at the table.

"Go ahead, Liz, ask." Val sipped her coffee.

Liz raised an eyebrow went to the refrigerator for another cup of yogurt. "How are you this morning?" Liz handed it to her.

"Good. Great in fact. This feels different. It feels..." She spooned a few bites of yogurt into her mouth.

"Feels like what?"

"Like coming home." Val thought about the meaning of her words while she ate. *Home meant laying your burdens down.* She'd never given herself over to anyone or relinquished complete control. She put the spoon in the cup and looked at Liz. "I did something last night that I've never done." She paused while she gathered her thoughts. "I gave complete control to her."

Liz's eyes brightened. "That's a big step for you. I will assume then, what I was hearing last night were cries of pleasure?"

Heat crawled up Val's neck reaching her ears. "Uh...yeah." She sighed, lost in memory of making love with Laurel. "I don't ever remember feeling so safe and yet so totally helpless." Val looked past Liz to the hall where Jo and Laurel had disappeared and played with the spoon in the empty yogurt cup.

"Control is an interesting principle," Liz mused. "Traffic lights control movement to reduce the risk of accidents. Valves control the flow air or fluid or completely stop them. In a more personal relationship, control can be both a good and bad thing. Controlling yourself while you're angry, can keep you from saying something that will hurt. Letting go of control can allow you to see the other person's point of view. It's a bad thing if it's used as a weapon. In a much more intimate setting, it can heighten pleasure. It's not the control itself but how it's used."

Val knew about control as a weapon. She'd been controlled to the extreme as a child. What she'd wear, whom she'd associate with, even down to what activities she'd be involved in. The one thing they hadn't been able to control was her sexuality and that drove her father into raging fits. She'd refused to wear dresses after the age of twelve. She rubbed her eyes with her left hand.

"Control in the hands of a self-absorbed bastard can lead a sixteen-year-old girl to run five miles to her grandmother's after he backhanded her for not going out with his associate professor's son. Grandmother threatened to disinherit father after she saw my bloodied lip and swollen eye." Val's tone grew hard, and she shuddered at the memory. She'd collapsed in her grandmother's arms, crying uncontrollably. The woman was furious. To ensure her safety, Harriett Magnusson threatened to call social services if he ever touched her again. At the age of seventeen, Val had gone to live with her grandmother, who'd encouraged her to pursue her love of photography. After high school, she obtained her journalism degree and shortly thereafter, enlisted in the United States Marine Corp. "The good Professor Magnusson valued his chance at being a multi-millionaire from his inheritance and moved out to an off-campus studio apartment. Of course, Mother accused me of driving him away, turning the entire episode into the latest in her 'poor me' act. From that day on, I never let anyone control me again until I went into the service." Val closed her eyes against the memory.

Liz knew Val's childhood had been unhappy from the many hours of therapy. "Our past influences us, Val, but it doesn't have to define us."

Val's mind drifted back to the control she'd given Laurel last night. "Liz, I've had sex. Enough of it to know that until last night, no one has ever touched me like that. I've always been a top. Last night, she took the dominant role." Val paused and sighed. "And I let her, willingly." Val was quiet for a moment, allowing her admission to sink in.

"Was Laurel ok with it?"

"She initiated it. To be honest, she figured out what I needed even though I couldn't say it out loud. She didn't even ask for reciprocation. All she wanted was for me to hold her. It terrified me. I want to hold her and so much more, but I'm afraid of what I feel. What if I hurt her?"

"I don't think that's going to happen. You're so much more in control of your flashbacks now. You'll always have triggers, but you have to forgive yourself for what you think you should've done over there. Until you come to terms with it and what happened with Tess, that day will forever be in control of your future. The fact that you allowed Laurel to take control at your most vulnerable moment, is telling. You obviously have deep trust in not only her, but in what you feel for her. Embrace it and realize that you still have the ultimate control that allows you to love and to be loved."

Val dropped her head into her hands. Liz was right. Her fear still held power over her and as long as she gave in to it, it always would.

Her cellphone rang. She checked the display, rolled her eyes, and hit the answer key. "Hello, Mother."

Amanda's polished voice filled her ear. "How are you, Valkyrie? I know you were supposed to see your surgeon yesterday, and I called to see what she said."

Val rubbed her hand across her forehead. "It could be worse, so I'm trying to be thankful. The rotator cup is shredded. She'll be operating tomorrow. It'll be outpatient unless there's a complication. My new leg should be ready to go soon. Other than some general soreness, I'm fine. How are you?"

"Fine, darling. I wanted to check in with you. Try to get some rest. You'll let me know how the surgery goes, won't you? I'm supposed to be interviewing a visiting dignitary this afternoon or I'd fly in. The paper insists I handle this personally."

Val listened with one ear as Amanda droned on. Placating her mother was easy. "Perfectly understandable, they want the best. I'll have Laurel call you after the surgery and give you the update. I'll be way too loopy."

"How is Laurel?"

"She's fine, Mother. Looking at Jo's latest creation."

"You're staying with Liz and Jo?"

Val rubbed her eyes with her thumb and forefinger. "Yes, they offered us a place to stay while I get this done. Sometime Friday we'll head back to West Virginia, if I can. Then I'll start rehab at the place Laurel lined up."

"Do you need anything?"

Val thought for a moment. "A tin of that peppermint shoe polish Grandmother used to use."

"Peppermint shoe polish?" Amanda grew silent. "Oh, the lip salve she carried. I haven't seen it for years. I'll look for it. Get some rest. You sound tired."

"I am and I will. It was a busy day yesterday, and I haven't quite recovered from the drive over here."

The silence between them grew. Val had long since given up the typical pleasantries most close family members used as they said goodbye. Though they had made strides during the time her mother visited her in the hospital, she still couldn't bring herself to say the things most daughters said to their mothers.

"Take care, Mother."

"You, too, Valkyrie."

They ended the call, and Val closed her eyes, the phone pressed to her forehead.

"That bad?"

Val opened her eyes and took a deep breath. "The call was tolerable."

Laurel appeared and sat by Val. "What call?"

Val melted into the warm voice. "Mother. She was checking in on me. I told her you would call her after the surgery."

Smiling, Laurel ran her hand through Val's hair. "Of course, if that's what you want."

"Better than having her calling every five minutes, trust me." Val tilted her head. "What did you think of Jo's piece?"

Laurel's eyes sparkled. "It's incredible. She does something with heat that makes the steel change colors as the light hits it from different angles. I've never seen anything like it."

Liz beamed. "Jo's always been talented."

"And that's before I even leave the bedroom." Jo wheeled by Liz who was still seated at the table, stealing a kiss.

Liz blushed and ran her hand down Jo's arm. "There, too. So, what are you two doing today?"

Val looked at her phone as it buzzed in her hand. "I just got a text from Charley. They need us to come over to The Bodyshop so they can do a fit check on my sleeve and socket."

"Looks like I have my marching orders. I need to catch a quick shower." Laurel ran her hand across Val's shoulders, leaning down to kiss her temple. "Let me take care of that and I can help you get ready if you need me."

"I'll need a shower, too."

Val watched Laurel head upstairs, and Liz wheeled Val into her office so she could use the computer. Val spent the next half hour catching up on some email. After that, Laurel assisted Val into the shower and then helped her dress. They headed to The Bodyshop.

Laurel reached across the console and took Val's hand. "You okay?"

"I'm better than I've been in a long time." She lifted Laurel's hand and kissed it.

Laurel curled her fingers tighter around Val's. "You know, last night was special for me, too. I've never felt like that."

"Last night was something I've never experienced." Val bit her bottom lip. "But I want to feel that way again. And I need to touch you." She sucked two of Laurel's fingers in her mouth.

Laurel shivered. "Love, you're recovering from one accident. Let's not have another."

Val lowered her voice and slid her fingers around Laurel's ear. "Only if you promise me a rain check?"

Laurel shivered. "I'll promise you anything you want. You've got to stop that or I'm going to lose it."

Val's laughter filled the Jeep. "Oh, that could be dangerous. For now, let's get to The Bodyshop so I can get at least one part of me fixed."

***

Twenty minutes later, Laurel helped Val onto the lift table in Charley's work area. She walked around the room and looked at the sculptures nestled on shelves and display cases. "These are amazing."

Val added some insight. "Charley's multi-talented. Beyond his abilities to create one of a kind sockets, he's quite the artist."

Charley displayed a few sockets in glass cases with pictures attached. One was of an athlete in ski gear at the Paralympics appearing on the gold medal stand. A note indicated the socket had been given to Charley in thanks.

Val waved her hand at Charley. "Go on, tell her."

Walking across the room, Charley pointed to a small socket standing in a place of pride in the room. "This one's my most prized possessions. It's the one my sister took her first steps in after they took her leg. I made it at nineteen." His eyes grew misty. "That one made my little sister Hanna happier than I'd ever seen. Eventually, she outgrew it and I put it in a case to remind myself of why we do this." He nodded in Val's direction. "The last one I made her had special meaning to me. It'll go in its own case, too."

Laurel looked across the room at Val. "She's pretty special."

Charley's lip curled in a smile. "She's amazing, and we consider her family.

Laurel hugged her arms. "I think she feels the same about all of you."

His voice dropped almost to a whisper. "We've known her a long time. I remember the first time she came to see us. She was locked inside herself, but Mom had no intention of letting her stay there." He ran a hand down Laurel's arm. "Now she has you. Let's see if we can get her back up on her feet."

"Excuse me, patient here in the room. Remember me. Don't fill her head with lies, please." Val sat with a hand on her hip, one eye closed, looking at them.

Charley turned and looked at Laurel. "It's always about her. You'd think she needed her own staff to wait on her. Although I don't think she's minding it near as much with you playing nursemaid." He quirked an eyebrow and rocked on the balls of his feet as he looked at Laurel. "If I had some young stud fussing over me the way you are her, I might have to break my leg." He turned at the sound of the door opening. Anya walked in, carrying the soft rubberized sleeve that would fit over Val's amputated leg. If the sleeve was right, they could check the fit on the socket.

"Let's see how this goes, Val." Anya walked over to her and together they slid the flesh colored sleeve onto her leg and checked it to see if it was snug enough.

Laurel thought the sleeve looked soft and pliable. She was fascinated with all the pieces. Never having been around anyone who had lost a limb, she watched Val's face for any signs of distress. She didn't see anything but anticipation.

"Fits like a glove. How about the socket?" Val looked at Charley expectantly.

Charley opened the small case he retrieved from his workbench. The socket gleamed glossy black. The painting on it showed the view over the front of a motorcycle. Off in the distance was a mountain ridge, a sunrise coming up over the peaks. The tank displayed the Indian Motorcycle logo. A small photograph stood out on the top of the tank, and Val's Nikon camera rested on a jean clad leg.

Val held it in her hand and looked at her friends. "Charley, I don't know what to say."

"That spread the magazine did of you a few years ago was the inspiration," Charley said proudly. "I wanted to give you something special."

Laurel watched Val turn it in her hands.

"Laurel, can you help me? I don't know that I can get it on by myself."

Laurel knelt before her and took the socket in her hands. She guided Val's leg into it and gently shoved. There was slight vacuum noise as Val hit a button on the side. Only then did Laurel notice the delicate pattern of mountain laurel etched under the painting. She smiled.

"Pull on it," Val told her.

Laurel did, but the socket didn't come off. She rose, stood in front of Val. She rubbed Val's neck before leaning down. "Won't be long now and I'll have to look up at you again."

Charley rubbed his hands together. "Now to bring in the boy genius. Daren will be right in."

***

Val looked at Laurel, wanting to kiss her. She always seemed to know what to say to make her feel like they were moving forward. A noise pulled her attention to the door as a sandy haired Daren Cavender came in with something under his arm. She lit up. "Hey, Daren, how are you?"

Daren walked over to her and stuck out his hand. "The better question is, how are you?"

Val clasped the outstretched palm. "I've been better. I've also been a hell of a lot worse. Daren, this is Laurel Stemple."

"Nice to meet you, Laurel. Val, you know you're supposed to keep the shiny side up. That one has pissed and moaned for the last twenty-four hours how you destroyed his artwork." He pointed to his brother who looked as if he was about to protest. "It appears it's given the artistic one a chance to create another masterpiece."

Laughing, Val ran her hand along the socket. "It does resemble a piece of art. Now that we know this part works, how long before I get the working end?"

"Funny you should ask." Daren stepped forward and presented her with his latest creation, a high tech prosthesis. "It's the most advanced leg we've ever done. I stayed up all night getting this thing tuned up. Let's try it out, shall we?"

Val's eyes widened. "Please."

Daren attached the working end and lowered the table. Val carefully stood, Laurel at her side. The first steps were awkward and timid. Within seconds, she found her balance. They stepped into an adjoining room with parallel bars used for patients to try their new prostheses. Daren sat on a rolling stool beside the bars to make changes as needed. In one hand, he was holding a small Allen wrench for precision adjustments, while using a laptop on a rolling table beside him with his other.

Val took a few more tentative steps. "Laurel, can you stand in front of me so I don't pitch forward? It feels like it's jumping ahead."

Laurel moved in front of her and walked backward between the bars.

Daren touched a few keys on his laptop connecting the Bluetooth feature of the microcomputer within the prosthesis. A few keystrokes later, and he told her to try again. After another ten feet and one more adjustment, Val walked the length of the bars without noticeable issues. They moved into another section of the room designed to practice stairs and different style ground cover. Val didn't stumble and grew more confident with every step. *God, it feels good to walk again.* She looked at Laurel's face. *Just the ability to look Laurel in the eye means everything.* Her heart lurched as she saw tears slide down that same face.

Val drew her in and kissed her. "What's wrong?"

"Nothing. I'm happy for you."

"I wouldn't be here without you. Thank you." Val kissed her temple and held her tighter.

Laurel shook her head. "I didn't do anything. These people are the miracle workers."

Val looked at those gathered in the room with her. "I don't know what I'd do without any of you. Thank you."

Anya stepped forward and drew Val into her arms. "It's the least we can do for all you've done for us, honey. You're family."

Val fell into Anya's embrace, while Daren and Charley pulled Laurel in with them. It was a moment full of emotion that threatened to bring Val to tears again.

Daren stepped back from the group. "Val, I want you to keep track of how this is responding. I've programmed it to send data back to us at regular intervals. If I see that we need to adjust the code, I can do that remotely, while you're asleep and make minute adjustments by what the data is telling me."

"That's amazing," Laurel said. "The device will tell you if her gait or motion is off?"

"It should. If she's putting too much pressure on one sensor or another I can adjust for it until we get it exactly right. That way she doesn't develop any sores. You'd be surprised at how having your gait off a fraction affects the rest of the body." He patted his laptop. "With this baby, she won't have to keep coming back for minor tweaks. Pretty cool, huh?"

"It's unbelievable. How does it feel, Val?" Laurel asked.

Val tested it with some small movements. "Really comfortable."

"Computer science has come so far, as has this technology," Daren said.

Val smiled, watching the woman she loved and her friends conversing so easily. After a few more minutes to evaluate Val's gait, the team determined she should be fine. Anya said her goodbyes as Charley and Daren walked them to the exit.

Charley interlocked his arm with Val's and whispered into her ear. "What did you think of the background pattern?"

A knowing smirk crossed Val's face. "Mountain laurel, I presume."

"Correct as always." Charley grinned. "I figured you might appreciate having a little reminder of her no matter where you are."

"It's brilliant. Trust me, she's always with me no matter where she is." Val placed her hand over her heart.

"I have no doubt." He leaned in closer. "She's hot. If I was straight, I might try to charm her with my rugged manly ways."

Val snorted. "The only manly thing about you is the Y chromosome you were born with."

Charley belly laughed. "You're so charming."

Laurel and Val said their goodbyes and walked hand in hand back out to the Jeep. It was nice to be able to stand beside Laurel again, to look into her eyes and not up at her from a chair. She'd fought so hard the first time to trust the carbon fiber and metal. This time came so much easier. She couldn't thank the crew at The Bodyshop enough. They'd made this possible. On her own, she climbed into her seat and grinned at Laurel.

"Happy?" Laurel asked her.

Picking up Laurel's hand that rested on her thigh, she kissed it. "More than you could ever know."

Laurel slid her sunglasses on. "How about we take some time to go pick out a few clothes for you? Feel up to it?"

Val rolled her eyes at Laurel. "Shopping, really?"

"Yes, shopping. You need a few things. I promise, we won't buy a lot.

"You're in charge."

"Oh, that's dangerous."

Val leaned her head back and shook her head. "No, I'd say it's a safe bet." *For once, I don't need to be in control of anything but the way I feel about you.*

The two of them spent the rest of the morning shopping. Neither had brought outfits nice enough for Jo's show. Val traveled only with jeans and t-shirts. Laurel helped Val pick out a new pair of black jeans, a robin's egg blue button down shirt, and a black leather suit jacket. Val sat in a waiting area at the front of the store while Laurel shopped. Finally, Laurel walked toward her, bags in hand.

Val arched an eyebrow. "Not going to show me what you bought?"

"Nope, you'll have to be surprised." Val yawned, knowing Laurel saw it. She covered her mouth as another escaped. "I'm sorry."

Laurel ran a hand down Val's arm. "How about we go back and lay down?"

"I'll second that motion."

Back at Liz and Jo's, they climbed into bed for a nap. Val settled Laurel against her, stroking her hair as she let the day's stress melt away.

Laurel ran her hand under Val's t-shirt, touching her skin. "You nervous about tomorrow?"

Val tried not to groan with pleasure. "Nah, this is a piece of cake.

I'll be sore. Therapy will get the arm moving, and I'll be back to normal."

Laurel kissed her neck. "What will you do after you heal up?"

"I have no idea. Maggie May's busted up worse than I am." She remembered what the bike looked like in Bobeye's shop. She closed her eyes and shook her head.

"Will you go back on the road?" Laurel's voice sounded small and tentative.

She took a deep centering breath and let it out slowly. *Hell, I barely know what I'll be doing five minutes from now.* "Right now, all I can think about is the surgery. After that, we'll take it one day at a time. You know what I'm looking forward to, though?"

"What?"

"Lots of time with you and Ree."

"Now that I can get into." Laurel kissed Val and settled her head under Val's chin. "Sleep, love."

Val breathed in deeply, taking in soft vanilla and coconut she always associated with Laurel. She closed her eyes and wrapped her arm around her a little tighter. "With you at my side, piece of cake."

Chapter Eighteen

A FEW HOURS LATER they woke, and Laurel was happy to see Val walk to the shower on her own for the first time. From her hesitant steps, it was evident she was still learning to trust the new prosthesis. From everything Val told her, the adjustment period seemed to be going much better this time. After they'd both cleaned up, Laurel watched from the hall as Val tried to dress without assistance. Her arm still hindered her in doing certain things. Fumbling with the row of small blue buttons below her breasts, Laurel could see her frustration growing and her brow furrowing. Laurel placed her hands in her back pockets and crossed one leg over the other as she leaned against the doorframe.

"You look like you might need some assistance there, Viking." She watched as Val's eyes traveled the length of her body. The simple peasant shirt, coffee colored pants, and above the calf riding boots were having their intended affect.

"Damn." Val bit her lip. "You look beautiful."

Laurel slowly pushed off the doorframe and sauntered over with the moves of a graceful cat stalking her prey. She pushed away the hands that lingered on the buttons. Running a finger up the center of Val's chest, she slowly let her finger land on the cleft in Val's chin. Closing the gaping mouth, she pressed her own lips to Val's. The kiss went from gentle to smoldering within seconds.

Laurel ran her hands into the still open shirt and splayed her fingers across Val's broad chest. Her tongue entered Val's mouth, tasting mint and heat. Val's hand settled on the back of her head and pulled her even deeper into the kiss.

Val's motions were becoming frantic, and she could feel her own temperature rising. Laurel's hand glided down Val's chest to find a hard nipple beneath her hand. She rolled it in her fingers, eliciting a primal growl. Her brain told her she needed to stop or be prepared to miss Jo's opening. She broke the kiss and leaned into her. They breathed hard.

"Holy shit, Laurel. I want you so bad right now."

"I take it you like the outfit?"

Val stroked the back of Laurel's neck. "I do. I like what's inside the outfit even better. For a nickel, I'd stay right here and take you to bed."

Laurel laughed. "It would take that much, huh?"

"I'd do it for another kiss like the one you just laid on me. God, you look fantastic." Val reached up and touched the strings that hung from the peasant shirt.

"You look pretty handsome yourself. Need a little help there with those buttons?"

"Yeah, to undo them," Val said, dipping in for another kiss. Her lips met Laurel's with force.

Laurel met her with that same passion, and soon they were pressed close together. Laurel pushed her hand between their bodies and let her fingers slip into the open zipper of Val's pants. She pushed under the waistband of the boxer briefs Val wore. The second Laurel's fingers found wet heat, Val gasped. Pushing farther, she slid her fingers into Val's center. *I've never wanted anyone so bad in all my life. She feels so good.* Wrapping an arm around Val's waist, she held tight as her lover's legs went soft. Her palm found a hard clit, and she rocked her hand.

Val's head tipped back as she wrapped her good arm around Laurel's shoulder. "Baby, what are you doing?"

Laurel kissed her neck. "Relaxing you. Taking what I want and giving you what you need."

"Oh God, Laurel, don't stop."

Laurel stroked Val harder, feeling her tremble and collapse into her touch. "Let go, baby, I've got you." Val tensed and climaxed. Laurel kissed her, keeping her fingers inside to feel the powerful contractions. Val's breathing began to even out. She pulled back far enough to look into Val's eyes. What she saw there looked like peace. "You okay, Viking?"

As Val came back to herself, she looked deep into Laurel's eyes. "I'm better than you could ever imagine. You destroy me and save me in the same moment. I've never had anyone take me the way you do. I have no defenses against your touch."

Laurel withdrew her hand, licking each finger before zipping Val's jeans. She walked into the bathroom, washed her hands and returned to finish buttoning the form-fitting shirt. She kissed Val again. "I've never needed to have anyone the way I do you. It's a hunger I don't think I can ever completely satisfy. Now you're relaxed, and I'm satisfied." She kissed Val one more time, grabbed the leather jacket, and helped her into it. She stepped back, admiring the handsome woman before her. "You're so sexy. I'm going to have to fight every woman in there tonight."

"No need. I'm coming home with you."

"Just remember that, Viking, as you're turning heads tonight."

"My guess is the heads will be turning at the sight of you in those boots." She leaned in and kissed Laurel. "And the only head I want to turn is yours."

"Mission accomplished." *You've turned so much more than my head Viking, you've turned my heart.*

***

Val held Laurel's hand as they walked through the gallery. Jo's show was an obvious success, if the sold tags on many of the pieces were any indication. Liz stood by Jo's shoulder in a simple black dress and high heels, her left hand resting on the nape of her wife's neck. Two women stood close, valiantly trying to get Jo's attention. Val grinned. Their love, the knowing smiles and tender touches, were a beautiful thing to watch. Jo reached for Liz's hand and kissed the wedding ring she'd placed there.

Val enjoyed having Laurel on her arm. She noticed the appreciative looks Laurel received. As they stopped to look at another of Jo's pieces, Val placed her hand in the small of Laurel's back and rubbed small circles there. She could feel the heat of Laurel's body through her shirt. She wanted this woman so much. It was more than a want. It was a pure need. She could smell her perfume. It was light, with a gentle scent of the beach. It lingered with Val. She remembered smelling it in the hospital and had enjoyed waking up more than once to that scent with Laurel in her arms. Her mind started to scheme about feigning fatigue so they could leave. *That would be wrong. Laurel will worry.*

They'd walked around the entire gallery, admiring the intricate artwork. She was completely surprised at how well her new leg was doing. There were no issues like she'd experienced with her first one. She was completely content for the first time in a long time. They'd yet to talk with Liz and Jo, so they walked over to the couple.

Laurel leaned down to hug Jo. "You're an amazing artist. This is unbelievable."

"Thank you, Laurel. It took me a long time to get to this place. I never thought I'd have people showing up just to look at something I made."

Val rolled her eyes. "And here I thought all you were good for was giving me hell."

"Laurel, can you come with me?" Liz tilted her head in the direction of the bathrooms.

"Sure." Laurel leaned up, pulling Val's face to hers for a brief kiss. "I'll be back. You two stay out of trouble."

Val and Jo both mocked indignation then broke out into wide grins as Liz and Laurel walked away. As the two made their way to the bathroom, Val and Jo looked longingly after them.

"We're in so deep my friend," Jo said, taking Val by the hand and shaking it.

"Amen." *Deeper than I could have ever imagined.*

***

Laurel followed Liz into the rest room, where she watched Liz rest her back against the wall and close her eyes. They seemed to be alone as there was no conversation or noise around them.

Liz rubbed her temples. "I swear I'm not a jealous person, but if one more woman touches my wife, I swear I'm going to rip her arm off and beat her to death with it."

Laurel shook her head and laughed. "Jo only has eyes for you. We've been watching you as we walked around. No one should have any doubt how much she loves you."

Liz huffed. "One woman sat in Jo's lap!"

"And Jo quickly let her know she wasn't interested."

"The lack of respect for boundaries astounds me. For whatever reason, this show has been exceptionally difficult. She's done shows before, but tonight seems to have brought out all the hopefuls." Liz walked over to the mirror to inspect her makeup. Pulling her lipstick from her purse, she freshened it. "It appears that you and Val have a few admirers of your own."

"There've been a few that have given Val more than an appraising look."

"Oh, honey, it's not just Val who's been getting the attention. I saw more than one looking at you."

Laurel shook her head. "Yeah, probably wondering what someone like Val sees in me."

Liz stared at Laurel in the mirror. "Don't sell yourself short. You're a beautiful woman, and it's obvious Val's deeply taken with you. I wanted to check and see how you were doing."

Laurel blushed and ran her fingers through her hair. "I haven't let Val touch me yet. I haven't been able to bring myself to tell her about the surgeries."

"And you think her finding out is going to make her want you less?"

Laurel thought about Liz's question. "I don't know. Since I had the mastectomies, I've only been with a few women. None have had negative reactions. Gram spared no expense in finding me one of the best plastic surgeons in the business to do my breast reconstruction, but the horizontal scars are still red and I'm worried how Val will react. I'm falling hard for her, and it would kill me to know she was turned off by what she'll see. I made the choices I did so that I could be around to take care of Gram. I'd do it again in a second."

Liz raised an eyebrow at her. "I assume you've seen Val's scars?"

Laurel thought about Val's missing leg and the scars she'd seen marring the perfect body, including the recent ones. "I have. I can't even imagine what she's been through. She's incredibly strong and brave."

Liz looked at Laurel, resting her back against the counter, and snapping her bag closed. "And do you think she worried about you being turned off by them?"

Laurel rolled her shoulders, trying to relieve her tension. "She must've been concerned about me knowing she had a missing leg. If it hadn't been for this accident, I wouldn't have known. She never told any of us."

"And yet obviously, she let you see her scars and still make love to her."

A sudden recognition of Liz's point hit Laurel. *Oh. You're good.* "I know I can't wait much longer to find out, but I want to get her through this surgery tomorrow."

Liz touched Laurel on the shoulder. "Then you'll talk to her, tell her everything?"

Laurel once again ran her hand through her hair. "We'll see."

"Don't put it off much longer. From the hungry look in her eyes tonight, the sooner the better. Come on, let's get back out there before those two start wondering what we're up to."

They walked out arm in arm, Laurel still mulling over Liz's words.

**

Val looked at Jo and both let out an appreciative moan seeing their significant others walking toward them. *She's so beautiful. Somewhere the Norse Goddess Freyja is smiling on me.*

Jo absently turned her wedding ring. "Are we lucky fucks or what?"

"That we are, Jo. I'm going to suggest Laurel and I take off. I assume you'll be here for a few more hours?"

"If I had my way, no. Unfortunately, my agent has us going for drinks with a big gallery owner up in Baltimore. The house is all yours for at least four more hours. If I were you, I'd make good use of that time. Naked." Jo quirked her trademark grin as her wife reached her side.

Liz leaned down and placed a smoldering kiss on Jo.

Laurel tilted her head and looked at Jo. "I heard the word naked. What are you two up to?"

You'll have to ask Val." Jo pulled Liz into her lap and popped her signature wheelie while Liz wrapped her arms around her neck and squealed.

Laughing, Laurel slid her arms around Val's waist and stretched up to kiss her. "Are you ready to go?"

"More than ready." Looking over to Jo and Liz, Val tipped a small salute. "We'll see you two kids in the morning."

"What time is your surgery?" Jo asked.

Val returned Laurel's embrace. "According to Cat's secretary, 8:30 am."

Laying her cheek against Jo's, Liz looked at them. "Laurel, will you need any help getting her back to our place? I assume you'll spend the night and leave sometime the next day?"

"I think we'll be okay."

"Want some company? I'd like to come sit with you during her surgery."

"I know you have patients." Laurel shrugged. "If you want to drop by, you know where I'll be."

Liz winked at her.

Val squeezed Jo's shoulder. "With that, we bid you good night. The show was great. I'm proud of you."

"Don't do anything I wouldn't do, and that means make sure you name it after me. It's pretty easy, J-O. Even a Jarhead like you should be able to spell it," she teased giving Val the finger.

Laurel's face flamed. Val beamed and flipped her friends the feathers in response. "More like S-H-I-T-H-E-A-D, Dogface."

Val and Laurel made their way out, Val's arm wrapped around Laurel's shoulder, pulling her in close. Laurel's arm rested around Val's waist under the leather blazer, her hand in Val's waistband. They reached the Jeep and Val put her back against the door and pulled Laurel between her outstretched legs.

"Have I told you how incredibly sexy you look tonight?" Val reached in to kiss those soft lips and then down her neck. It was a rhetorical question. She'd made that compliment several times.

"A time or two. It certainly doesn't hurt a girl's ego to hear it."

Val's need to touch Laurel was growing stronger. "I can't help it. You are, and you've been driving me crazy all night. If you had put your hand in my back pocket one more time, I swear I was going to throw you down right there and make love to you on that gallery floor."

Laurel shook her head. "It wasn't my intention to make you crazy, just feels natural. Do you know what your touch does to me?"

Val ran her fingers into Laurel's hair and cupped the side of her jaw. "I've got a pretty good idea."

"You're pretty sexy yourself, Viking. And for the record, Jo wasn't the only one that was getting a little attention from the ladies tonight."

"Let's just say, the way you were growling at those so-called ladies, I think they got the message loud and clear." She kissed Laurel again, her tongue seeking entrance. Laurel's lips parted and she swirled her tongue around Laurel's, exploring the soft recesses. *She tastes so good.*

Laurel broke the kiss. "Let's take this somewhere a little less public, shall we?"

Val shivered and pressed her forehead into her lover's. Reaching behind her, she opened the driver's door for Laurel. "Your wish is my command."

Laurel let out a sigh. "Remember you said that, Viking."

"Why would I want to forget?"

Chapter Nineteen

LAUREL DROVE THEM BACK to Liz and Jo's while Val dozed. All the way home, Laurel's mind raced. *I'm out of time here. We're going to make love tonight and for the first time, she'll see all of me.* Her hands were sweaty on the steering wheel and her stomach felt like she was eight years old and on the Scrambler at the county fair. The streetlights cast shadows on the ground. They reached out and then retreated, just like her fears. *I want Val, and I want to be with her. I want her to know me, just like I told her I wanted to know all of her.* Val had never given her any indication that she cared about surface things. She wasn't about flash. She was genuine. Laurel rubbed her forehead. *She could be with anyone but she wants to be with you.* She remembered Gram's words. *'Never known ya to be a coward. I sure as thunder didn't raise ya to be one.'* It was time to find the courage she'd used to fight all those years ago. She'd need it again if she was going to have any future with Val.

They made it back to Liz and Jo's and up to their bedroom. Laurel kissed Val. "I need to get your meds and change. I'll be right back."

"For what I have in mind, you won't need pjs."

Laurel closed her eyes for a moment, reveling in the heady look of desire falling across Val's face. She sighed and rested her cheek on Val's chest. *The moment of truth.*

"What's wrong, love?"

Laurel took a shaky breath and leaned back in Val's arms. Give me a minute and I'll be right back. I need to share something with you. Something few people know about me." She ran her finger over Val's shirt collar and then left to retrieve the medicine and a bottle of water. Coming back into the room, she noticed that Val had a concerned look on her face, but her gaze encouraged Laurel to continue.

"Remember I told you my mother died of breast cancer?"

Val nodded swallowing the pills.

Laurel cleared her throat and she moved back into Val's arms. "I was in my sophomore year of college and I found a lump in my breast. I immediately made an appointment with my doctor. The scans showed a mass." She felt Val's body tense. "They were able to do a biopsy along with some blood tests, including a DNA test for the BRCA 1 and 2 genes. While the mass turned out to be just a cyst, unfortunately I came back positive for the BRCA 1 gene." Her voice grew soft. "That meant there was a good chance that eventually, I'd develop breast cancer. After a lot of discussion with Gram and my doctors, I decided to have double radical mastectomies to lower my probabilities. I couldn't take the chance I wouldn't be around to take care of Gram." She gave Val time to let the information sink in.

Val looked at Laurel in utter disbelief. "Honey, why are you telling me this now? Are you afraid I'll change my mind about how I feel about you?"

Laurel watched a look of fear cross Val's face. It was as if a dialog box popped up over her head. "Val, I'm healthy now. This happened a long time ago, I'm ok. I was worried you might..."

Tears welled up in Val's eyes. "I might what?"

Laurel's face grew hot, and her chest heaved. She tried to hold back the torrent that threatened. She looked at Val's face. The look broke the damn Laurel had been struggling to hold back. Tears poured from her eyes. *How can I make Val understand?* Her voice was barely above a whisper. "That you might not see me the same way."

Val stood silent for a few seconds saying nothing. Tears dripped off her quivering chin. "Laurel, you've seen all my scars and the pieces of me that are missing. You've made love to me more than once. Unless those are tears of joy for you surviving, you have nothing to cry about. Nothing." She lifted Laurel's chin, wiping the tears away with her thumbs. "Do you think this makes me want you less?"

"It's not that, it's just..."

Val pulled her even closer. After a second, Val forced her chin up and looked deep into her eyes. Her voice was soft, gentle. "Just what? Do you think that I won't still see you as the most beautiful woman I've ever known? That because you made a choice to save your life, I'd see you as less of a woman?"

Laurel heard Val's voice break and the words came with a touch of anger.

"You don't give me much credit, if that's what you think." Val released her hold and turned her back to Laurel, hugging her sides.

"Fuck, Laurel, I had my leg blown off in Iraq. I almost lost my arm. More recently I bounced off the blacktop." She turned back around. "Do you see me as less?"

"No," Laurel yelled, her hand covering her mouth. She couldn't hold back the emotion now. Her sobs filled the room and she dropped her head into her hands.

"Then why would you think this would change the way I feel about you? It makes me want you more." Val took her back into her arms and put her lips to her temple. "You're a warrior, honey. Your battle might not have been fought in the desert, but that doesn't mean you're any less courageous than anyone who has. Laurel, give me the chance to show you that no matter what is or isn't beneath your shirt, I love and care about you."

Laurel melted into her arms and sobbed, an immense weight lifted off her. Val kissed her. She felt warm breath against her cheek and a tongue trace the curve of her ear. She felt the words as much as heard them.

"I want to take you to bed and make love to you. I want you to feel the love I have for you in every cell of your body."

Laurel reached up and delved her fingers in Val's hair, holding her face to hers. She needed more and kissed Val, pulling her lower lip into her teeth, then drove her tongue into Val's mouth, expressing as much need as she could.

Val broke the kiss again and murmured against her lips. "I want to strip you down and make love with you until you scream, until you beg me to let you come and so much more. And after all that," she kissed her, "if you still doubt that I love you exactly as you are, then I'll start all over again until you do." Val pulled back and placed her hands on each side of her face. "I love you, Laurel. I have for a long time. I want you inside both my body and my soul. I want to drink you in until you're inside my every cell." Val took a deep breath and pressed her forehead to Laurel's.

Tears poured from both of their eyes as Laurel led Val to bed. She unbuttoned Val's shirt and ran her hands across the broad muscular chest that lay beneath. Her fingers brushed Val's nipples, and Val arched into her touch. A surge of power rippled through Laurel at the sight, erasing the tears. She undid Val's jeans and knelt to take off her leg and boot. She pushed Val up against the bed, letting the jeans fall to the floor. "Lie down."

Val did as she was directed, her eyes never leaving Laurel's. Laurel removed most of her clothes, leaving the peasant shirt hanging loosely on her torso. She climbed onto the bed and straddled her lover, taking in the sensation of Val's hands softly caressing her outer thighs. Laurel could see the scars on Val's legs and another that ran around her side. As Val reached her left arm up to touch her face, a third scar running up the back of her arm became visible. Val called her a warrior for the battle she fought. The real warrior lay beneath her, touched by the savagery of war. *She's so beautiful.* Closing her eyes tightly, she leaned into Val's touch. She turned to kiss the palm of her strong, yet gentle, hand, tears starting again and streaming down her cheeks. Opening her eyes, she could see the tenderness in Val's face. She trembled with anticipation and a hint of trepidation. Her body ached for Val's touch. Justified or not, her anxiety was still real.

Val sat up, wrapping her arms around Laurel. "We don't have to do this. I hate to see you this upset."

She ran a finger across Val's lips. "No, it's time. There's never been anyone I've wanted to share this with more. I'm just afraid and it's never mattered as much as it does now."

"Don't be afraid. Help me take off your shirt. I can't get my arm up that high."

Laurel hesitated and then crossed her arms to draw the shirt up and over her head, revealing her lacy red bra. She looked at Val knowing that, for the first time in her life, she was truly about to make love. She'd had sex before, but not with anyone she'd loved like this or who had shown her the depth of their devotion the way Val had. It was time to let the past and all her fears go.

Reaching behind her, Val undid the clasp, kissing Laurel's chest as she did so. "You're so beautiful." She reached up to draw the straps off Laurel's shoulders.

Laurel kept her eyes on Val's face, but her lover was no longer looking in her eyes. The lace fell away. The look of disappointment she anticipated never came. Val did look at her and desire was the only thing Laurel watched pass through her. Val's hands rose to cup her breasts and she saw a wince she tried to hide. "Watch your arm."

"I'm fine." Val leaned forward and kissed the scars. She looked up at Laurel and ran a gentle finger across them.

Laurel shivered at the touch of soft lips on her chest. She couldn't feel the touch on her reconstructed breasts, but she fantasized about the sensation. The visual impact filled her with desire. Val's soft voice reached her.

"These lines are more than scars. These lines are the ones you drew in the sand. They're the ones that bear witness to your battle, your desire to live." She kissed Laurel, long and deep. With her fingers, she traced each breast. "Can you feel me touch you?"

Laurel's breathing quickened. "The nerves were severed during the procedure. They don't respond like my natural breasts did. I can feel you touch me, but it's different than it used to be."

"I only care about now, love," Val said with a smile. "I want this to be pleasurable for you and if me touching you here makes you uncomfortable, then there are other places I want to run my fingers and tongue."

Laurel shivered. "You can touch me however you need to, Val. This is as much about your pleasure as it is mine. I need you to touch me." Laurel placed her hands on Val's shoulders as she rocked her hips into Val.

"You're the bravest person I know, love." Val softly kissed between Laurel's breasts and rubbed her cheek over the soft swells to each side of her lips. She licked the reconstructed nipple, sucking it into her mouth. The desire in her eyes clearly mirrored in Laurel's.

"Just watching you do that turns me on." Laurel cupped Val's face, holding it closer to her breast. Val lavished both breasts with attention, softly kissing both of them. Laurel watched as Val's eyes turn dark and her grin feral. With a shift of Val's hips, Laurel found herself under Val. Heat rose through her core. "Please be careful, love." Her hips bucked as Val's tongue stroked around the small gold belly button ring adorned with a pink ribbon dangling from it.

"I'm fine." Val tugged it with her teeth.

Laurel's hips bucked again at the first warm kiss placed in the hollow valley where her hipbone protruded. "Val."

Val held herself above Laurel. "In my wildest dreams, I could never have imagined how beautiful you truly are." She traced Laurel's breast with the back of her hand.

Laurel shuddered under Val's touch. Placing her hands on Val's shoulders, she pushed until Val settled her between her thighs. Allowing her knees to fall apart, she gave her lover access to her greatest need. Val's crystal blue eyes danced, locking onto her own. She watched with unbridled desire as Val stilled. She saw the predatory glint of a conquering Viking passing over her face. She felt her breath leave her chest in anticipation as she watched Val slowly lower her head. Warm breath brushed across her clit, seconds before a soft tongue found her.

I'm so gone.

*** *** ***

Using her hand, Val spread Laurel open and drank in the sweetness that flowed across her tongue. She licked and sucked until Laurel writhed beneath her. She tried desperately to maintain control, fighting her own growing need. She brought her good hand to Laurel's entrance and ignored the pain screaming from her injured shoulder as she moved it up to hold Laurel's hip. She wouldn't give into it and lose these moments. Sliding two fingers inside, the tense muscles closed around her. For the first time in Val's life, she felt connected body and soul to someone. Not just someone, this woman. She stroked through the tight muscles, feeling the contractions building. *I could never have imagined this.* She met Laurel's eyes and broke the contact her lips had with the swollen clit that called to her so strongly. The look in Laurel's eyes was full of need and want. "Laurel, I love you."

"Please, baby, please. God, please! I love you!"

A switch flipped in Val. She withdrew the two fingers and pushed three back in, stroking deeper.

"More!"

Val added a fourth finger and Laurel arched in pleasure, the tendons in her neck standing out starkly against the soft skin around them. Laurel's lips parted and her breaths came out in deep pants, her fingers digging into Val's shoulders. She threw her head back and closed her eyes.

Val gritted her teeth and ignored the fingers causing her pain, reveling only in the pleasure of Laurel's body and their mutual climb toward the epic release. She'd never experienced pleasure of this magnitude, nor the all-consuming need to claim and be claimed. She felt it starting, the clinch, the spasms, and the release. Watching Laurel, she knew she was right on the precipice with her. She took in a deep breath, surrounded by the scent of their passion.

"I am yours, body and soul. You're all I'll ever need."

She lowered her head, pulling Laurel's clit into her mouth and pushed the thumb of her injured arm against the tight ring of muscle to heighten the orgasm. She felt Laurel's body go rigid and rise off the bed.

With a massive shudder, Laurel went over and Val followed her, crashing into the pleasure that enveloped them. As the wave crested, ebbed and crested again, they collapsed back onto the bed panting in a desperate attempt to recover. Val lay with her head on Laurel's abdomen, her fingers still sheathed within Laurel's body, as the spasms tightened and released. She was overcome with emotion.

"I love you, Laurel."

Laurel whispered and with trembling hands reached for Val. "Hold me. Please."

She pulled her hand away from Laurel's heat and climbed up to cover Laurel's body, Val kissed every inch as she went, settling into the arms that invited her inside, wrapping her arms around Laurel's quivering body.

As Laurel's breathing settled, she kissed Val's temple. "I love you with every fiber of my being, deep in my soul."

"There's not much left of me, honey. I promise you, what there is, loves you more than I ever thought possible."

Taking Val's face in her hands, Laurel made direct eye contact. "What's left of you, Viking, is more than I ever dared dream of. All I want to do is love you as much as I can for as long as you'll let me."

The night settled in around them, their breathing falling into an easy rhythm. Sleep claimed them, arms and legs entangled, finding security in a love Val believed wasn't possible. She now knew it was, and that it existed between them.

Hours passed and soft light began to filter in the window around the shade. Val hadn't greeted the dawn, skin to skin, with anyone in years. She spooned tight up against Laurel's back. Her arm stretched across Laurel's body, her hand nestled between soft breasts. She felt her hand lift and warm lips kiss each finger. Keeping her eyes closed, she kissed Laurel's shoulder and rolled onto her back, pulling Laurel over with her. She groaned at the sensation of Laurel shifting on top of her and felt soft fingers run over her lips. She opened her eyes a fraction to watch as Laurel leaned down to softly kiss her.

Laurel snuggled even closer. "Hi."

"Hi, yourself." Val's eyes traveled down Laurel's body. *She's beautiful. Stunning.* Laurel's green eyes brightened and a slight flush rose up her chest at Val's appreciative gaze.

Laurel tilted her head. "What are you doing?"

Val pushed up to kiss her. "Enjoying the view."

Laurel ran her hands through Val's sleep tousled hair. "View's pretty spectacular from my vantage, too."

Val heard a sensual moan as she slid a leg between Laurel's.

Laurel shuddered and groaned. "God, I want you, but we don't have time. You have to be at the hospital in two hours."

"True, but I don't know that I can wait that long to touch you again." Val ran her hands up and down Laurel's body, stopping to hold her by the small of her back. "Trust me, I want this shoulder fixed so I can touch you without you worrying. I want a repeat of last night. Several, actually."

Laurel kissed her lightly and ran her thumb over Val's lower lip. "I can't say I'd mind that either. Unfortunately, you're going to have to wait. The next time we make love, I don't want you hiding how much pain you're in. I know you, Val. Let me take care of you."

Val sighed. "Nothing gets by you, does it?"

"I was raised by probably one of the most intuitive women in the world with eyes in the back of her head. She told me long ago I was in love with you." Laurel settled against her, breast to breast, crossing her arms and propping her chin on her folded hands.

"She did, did she?"

"Oh yeah, the last time you stopped. She'd been chewing on me to admit it and tell you."

"I knew I loved that woman for a reason. The day I walked into Cool Springs, I fell in love with you. I've traveled to hundreds of places and photographed more things than I can remember. Nothing holds a candle to you. Liz and Jo have known it since the first time I stopped. They've been hounding me for years to stop running away and tell you." Val reached up and ran her hand into Laurel's hair, sweeping it away from her face and behind her ear. "I've always been scared for someone to see my episodes. The things I've seen won't ever leave me. There are things that keep me unsettled, answers I need to find."

"Let me be by your side while you try and find your answers," Laurel spoke softly as she stroked the side of Val's face. "I want to be there with you."

Val said nothing for a moment. She'd spent her life handling and dealing with things on her own. It was part of the control she'd taken back in her life. "You are with me. I've never let anyone in this close."

"I get that. I want to know all of you. The things you don't show me, the things that scare you, the things that haunt you. I want you to know that no matter what happens, I'm going to be right by your side, anchoring you."

Val watched hopeful eyes and could feel her own heart begin beating out of her chest. The need was so great and somehow, her own self-doubt still clung to her like oil that couldn't be wiped off. Just when you thought it was gone, it rose to the surface again. The dread crept in, and she felt her pulse pick up as her vision narrowed. She heard a voice reach out to her like a lighthouse in the fog. *Laurel.*

"I'm right here with you. Touch me."

Val groaned as Laurel rose above her, placing her breast right above Val's lips. She accepted the gift before her. She ran her hands up Laurel's back as she sucked the soft flesh into her mouth.

Laurel's head fell back as Val's lips closed around her. Val cupped the back of Laurel's neck, bringing her down and crushing their mouths together, pushing past the barrier of those lips to taste and feel the warmth she found. Val rolled them both over and shifted so she could slide a hand between them. Laurel's legs fell open, guiding Val's hand to her center.

Val felt the warm, slick heat and felt her own center pulse. Somehow Laurel knew what would pull Val back from the darkness. *How does she know?* So many times, she'd fallen into the darkness, scrambling for something to hold on to. This time, she felt arms around her, pulling her safely away from the expanse, placing her own body in front of the abyss. The eyes that captured hers were bright green beacons holding her in place. Her terror faded away and desire replaced it.

She slid her hand down Laurel's body, smiling as she heard her lover's breath hitch and felt her body arch beneath her. She entered Laurel and began to stroke, all the while, sucking Laurel's soft earlobe. She tasted the hollow of Laurel's neck. *Salty and sweet.* Thrusting, she slid down Laurel's body stopping inches above her lover's need. Val withdrew her fingers and let all thought go, except for making love to Laurel.

Val's tongue slid through her folds and Laurel moaned with pleasure. She thrust back inside and was rewarded as Laurel writhed beneath her, hands clasped in Val's hair, crying out with each stroke. Val could feel the impending release as Laurel's stomach muscles became hard and the grip around her fingers grew tighter. Taking Laurel's clit in her mouth, she stroked the hard bundle of nerves until, with a great shuddering arch, Laurel came. Val held on and drank deeply. Laurel collapsed back into the bed, panting. Val met Laurel's eyes before lying her head on Laurel's rising and falling stomach.

"Come up here please," Laurel whispered.

Val made her way up and enveloped Laurel in her arms. *This is what she needs and so do I.* She kissed her temple over and over as they let the afterglow wash over them. Laurel drew lazy circles on Val's chest below her collarbone. For once, the world seemed to melt away. This moment, right here, right now, was all there was. Unfortunately, the clock ticked toward the time they would have to get up to leave for the hospital.

Propping herself up on an elbow, Laurel kissed her. "We need a shower."

Feeling playful, Val wanted to alleviate some of the tension of the upcoming surgery. "Are you offering to wash my back?"

"That and a few other places I can reach."

"With a proposition like that, we probably better get at it so you don't run out of time with all those hard to reach places."

Laurel laughed and smacked Val's chest. "You're so bad."

Val smirked. "And I'm sure there's never been any part of you that wanted to date a bad girl?"

"Only one, and I'm thinking she's not as bad as she wants everyone to think she is. I think she's beautiful, soft and tender. Leather or not, she's a bad girl with a huge heart." Laurel kissed Val again. Tender at first, but quickly descending into need. Laurel broke the kiss panting. "If we don't get out of this bed, we're going to be late."

Val rolled off Laurel. What she wanted to do was stay right here and make love to Laurel all day and deep into the night. She had to get this surgery over so she'd have two good arms to hold the woman who had come to mean more to her than anything. She needed two good arms to take care of Laurel and Ree. "Okay. Lead the way."

Laurel got up off the bed and pulled on her pants and shirt, sans bra and underwear. "I'm going to take a shower in my room so I can ensure we get out of here on time. Do you need any help?"

"Oh, I need lots of help. If we shower together, I can't be held responsible for my actions."

Laurel shook her head and left the room.

***

Closing the door behind her, Laurel looked up to see Liz was walking down the hall. Laurel nearly jumped out of her skin seeing her, and she put out a hand on Liz's shoulder to steady herself.

"Sorry, didn't mean to startle you. I wanted to tell you, I'll be able to come to the hospital around 9:00. I have an appointment early this morning, but I'm happy to say I was able to clear the rest of the day."

Laurel could feel her face flush and her ears went hot. She held her bra and underwear in her hand and obviously wore the same clothes she had last night. She laughed and shook her head. "I'm headed to get a shower. I told her if we attempted that together we would end up being late."

Liz looked at Laurel's hands and squinted. "I imagine so. You okay?"

Laurel could tell she was asking if having Val see her completely, was affecting her. "I'm better than I could have imagined. I told her everything last night."

"And how did she react?"

Laurel bit her upper lip. "She was upset at me for thinking she wouldn't want me the way I am. She reminded me that she had her own scars. She made love to me, showed me she wasn't turned off in any way. She even touched my breasts, like she knew I needed her to…just watching her touch them did something to me…ran chills straight through me." Laurel blush grew hotter. "I'm sorry this is probably TMI."

"Actually, it's not. Hopefully you consider me a friend." Liz slipped an arm around Laurel as they walked down the hall to her room.

"Of course, I consider you my friend."

"I'm happy for the both of you." Stopping at the door to Laurel's room, Liz squeezed her shoulder. "In true love, the scars become another piece of the landscape, and what we see is the love. Now get in the shower. You have plenty on your plate to deal with today. Jo's still sleeping, by the way. We're getting too damn old for these all-nighters." She laughed and blushed a little. "Correction, certain types of all-nighters. See you at the hospital."

Laurel chuckled softly. "Thank you, Liz, for everything."

Chapter Twenty

THE COUPLE SHOWERED, DRESSED, and drove to the hospital. Val held Laurel's hand in hers for the entire trip. Val enjoyed the fact that she wasn't behind the wheel. It allowed her to quietly observe the woman she loved. Laurel was focused, navigating morning traffic with a grin. *That smile might replace the sun.*

Laurel caught Val looking at her and arched an eyebrow. "What?"

"Have I told you how beautiful you are?"

Laurel blushed, redness creeping up her neck. "A time or two."

"You should hear it regularly, and I plan to make sure of that." Val raised the fingers clasped in hers and kissed them.

Laurel winked. "I could get used to that."

Twenty minutes later, Bethesda came into view. Judging from the tightness in her jaw, Laurel looked anxious about Val's upcoming surgery. Val leaned across the center console to kiss her cheek. *I'm so in love with her.*

After finding a parking spot, Laurel cupped Val's face in her hands. Val felt her moving her fingertips over every detail as if she was memorizing every line and feature.

"I love you." Laurel kissed Val on the mouth. "Now let's go get that arm fixed so we can go home."

"I'm all for that. You going to be okay with Cat?"

Laurel arched an eyebrow, a slight twist to her mouth. "As long as she remembers her place."

Val let a sly smile cross her own lips. "Her place, huh?"

"She's your surgeon, not your lover. That role is taken. I think we've firmly resolved who that title belongs to." Laurel ran a hand down the side of Val's face. "I think we're pretty clear on that point, don't you?" She tapped Val's chin.

Val laughed again and pulled Laurel into a passionate kiss. "Oh yes, my love, crystal clear. Did Liz say she was going to be able to come and sit with you?"

"Not initially. She'll be here around 9:00."

"Good, let's go do this. I have better things to do than hang out at a hospital."

Thirty minutes later, they'd registered and Val was prepped for her operation. Now they were in a small area waiting for the surgical team to come in and talk with her. Val watched the clock as her nurses worked to place an IV in her left arm. She watched them slide the catheter into her vein, remembering the medics jamming needles into her arm the day of the explosion. Sounds of the helicopter rotors filled her ears, sand stung her face and heat. *Searing heat.* A cool hand cupped her cheek, the thumb tracing her cheekbone. She leaned into the touch and kissed the hand that drove the memory into the background. *How does she know?* The nurses buzzed around them, leading them through the mound of initial paperwork. The anesthesiologist came in, asked a few more questions, explained what he'd be doing, and signed off on the chart.

He'd just left as Cat waltzed in. Laurel immediately went on alert. Val tightened her grip and fixed a wary glance on her. Flipping through the chart, Cat had yet to speak to either of them. She wore scrubs and rubber crocs in place of her uniform and high heels. She finally looked up at Val, ignoring Laurel. Untying the top of Val's gown, she pulled it down over her injured shoulder. With a marker, she wrote *Cat* on her skin.

"Marked you as mine." Cat smirked. "Any questions before we get started?"

Val stared at her, aware of her games and intent on making things perfectly clear to Cat. "Laurel and Liz will be in the waiting room. I want you to let them know how it's going. You'll tell them if there are any complications." She stared hard into Cat's amber eyes, making sure she had her attention. "Right?"

Laurel stepped to Val's side, taking her hand. Cat had yet to answer.

Val frowned. "Cat, I want you to keep them informed. This isn't up for discussion. Laurel and I are lovers. I'm asking you to respect that."

Laurel kissed Val on the head. "I think she's got the picture, love."

Cat crossed her arms. Tilting her head, she narrowed her eyes. "As you wish. I'll see you in the OR." She placed the chart back on the bottom of Val's bed and left the room.

Val reached out and pulled Laurel onto the bed with her. "Relax, she's trying to push your buttons. I'm yours."

"I know. It's taking every ounce of patience I have, though. I'd like to show her what happens to someone that sticks their toes in the pond that isn't theirs."

Val laughed and pulled Laurel down for a kiss. "I only love you. I'm only in love with you, and your toes are always welcome in my pond."

Laurel smacked her. "Terrible."

A few minutes later the anesthesiologist came back into the room. He had the nurse administer a vial of anesthetic. "You ready to get that shoulder fixed?"

Val was getting warm and sleepy but managed to nod.

Laurel kissed her forehead. "Close your eyes, honey. It'll all be over soon."

Val pulled her close and kissed her on the lips. "Don't worry."

Laurel's lips lingered then gently pulled away. "Sorry, it comes with loving you. Now go to sleep."

Val drifted, her heart firmly anchored in the woman she loved.

***

Laurel walked beside the bed holding Val's hand as the nurses wheeled her down the hall. After they reached the surgical area, Laurel was directed to the family waiting room. An elderly man sat holding a battered purse in his hands, a vacant look in his eyes. *Must be his wife.* She sat down, running a hand across her face. The TV droned in the background, some talk show she had no interest in.

She looked over at a woman holding a battered Army jacket and a faded stuffed tiger. It looked well loved. Its fur was matted and thinned, head lopped to one side. She was reminded of a passage from the *Velveteen Rabbit*, 'by the time you are Real, most of your hair has been loved off, and your eyes drop out and you get loose in the joints and very shabby.' Val was real and what they shared was too. She looked at her watch…8:30. Liz would be here shortly to wait with her. Laurel bit her lip, wanting Val out of pain and able to do the things she wanted to. *I can't wait to take Val home and away from that walking hormone Cat. I can take care of her and Gram together. It's time she knows what a real family is. I just hope she'll be ok.*

Pulling her phone from her bag, she dialed Beth and waited for the familiar voice.

"Hey, there. How are things?" Beth asked.

"They took her into surgery. This woman may be the best damn surgeon there is, but I don't like her a bit. She's tried to put the moves on Val at least twice. That was after Val told her that we were together and that she wasn't interested in Cat."

"Cat?"

Laurel huffed. "I think her real name is Catherine. All I know is if she keeps pushing my buttons, I'm going to release the banshee from within."

"And does she have a reason to think her actions are welcome?"

"Val said they spent a drunken weekend together and apparently Cat can't let go of the possibility of another one."

"And this is who is operating on Val's shoulder?" Beth asked, the incredulity in her voice evident.

Laurel rubbed her temple. A dull ache was taking hold. She was sure it was from gritting her teeth. "Val says she's the best. With all Val has been through, she needs to have some control in the process. Even if Cat refuses to see where Val's attention is, Val's made it clear we're together."

"How's that?"

"Damn hard to ignore once she flat out told her we're lovers. She even made Cat promise to come to the waiting room to tell Liz and me how the surgery went. If Val says she's the best, then I have to trust that she is. All I care about is her getting better. If that means putting up with a woman who has an orgasm looking at Val, then I will."

"Lovers, huh?" Beth's voice lifted a bit, and Laurel knew her friend had a wide grin on her face.

"That's a story for another time. Right now, all I can deal with is the fact that Val's on an operating table and that Lothario has a scalpel in her hand." Laurel pushed harder against her head as the headache ratcheted up.

"I seem to recall the last time you wanted to serve up a knuckle sandwich was when someone picked on Wunder. She's got you wrapped, doesn't she?" Beth laughed over the phone to break the tension.

"I'd forgot about that one. I was remembering defending your honor from that jackass you were dating. I'm pretty sure he got the message, because I don't remember him ever laying a hand on you again." She paused, trying to settle her nerves. "Gram close by? I know she'll want an update."

"Yup, she's right here. Love you, Laurel, be careful. I'll get the bail money ready."

Laurel laughed so loud the nurse at the desk turned her head. She silently apologized and waited. A few seconds later, the voice Laurel had loved to hear all her life came through the phone.

"How are ya, liebchen, and how's our Viking?" A little trepidation came through in Ree's quivering voice.

"No word yet. She's only been gone a few minutes, and I have no way to know how long the operation will be. I'm sure that'll depend on what damage they find after they get in there. As for me, I'm worried silly and homesick. I miss you, Gram, and so does Val. I'm hoping if Val's able, we can get a jump on coming home in the morning."

"That might be too soon for her to travel pain free, honey. Play it by ear. We're fine here at the store. Ya tell that tall drink of water I expect her butt back here and in therapy as soon as possible. Now how's my little girl doin'?"

"I'm fine, worried but fine."

Ree sighed. "Yeah, that's what your mouth said, now I wanna know about your heart. It's hard knowing the one ya love is in pain. Nobody knows ya like I do, honey. Your heart's in that operating room."

Laurel took a deep breath. "I told her everything."

"Everything?" Ree's voice raised.

"Yup, I told her about the DNA tests and the decisions made. To avoid embarrassing myself by talking about my sex life with my grandmother over the phone, let's just say it didn't matter to her at all."

"Praise the Lord and halleluiah. Have ya told her why ya didn't want anyone that close to ya?" Ree probed.

"No, I figured she had enough on her plate right now. She knows I love her, and I know how she feels about me. That's enough for now." Laurel didn't want this conversation to go any deeper. "I'll call you as soon as I have more news. Don't worry, Gram, I'm bringing her and my heart home with us."

"That's my girl. Just remember I raised ya to live child, not watch others do it. Call me later."

"I will, Gram. I love you and so does Val." Laurel disconnected and looked up as a shadow crossed by her.

Liz took a seat at her side. She was dressed in a pencil skirt and light green silk blouse. Laurel looked up to see the elderly man look Liz over. He smiled and then went back to watching TV. Liz was a beautiful woman. "Everything okay?"

"Yeah, they took her in about ten minutes ago."

Liz gave Laurel a hard look. "And how was Cat this morning?"

Laurel rhythmically flipped her phone over, touching each corner to her leg. "Infuriating. This morning she basically refused to acknowledge I was even in the room. When she marked Val's shoulder, her comment was, 'marked you as mine now.'"

Liz's jaw clenched. "I remember how I felt watching Cat come on to Jo. She's seduction 101. Val put her in her place, right?"

"Oh yeah, she told her we were together and that she was to come and let us know how the surgery went and any complications. If I'd any say in this, she'd be seeing another surgeon."

"She's the best I've ever seen. She'd be fascinating to analyze, although I don't think I could stand to be in the room with her that long."

"She may be the best, but if she makes another overture today, she's the one who's going to need a surgeon." Laurel winked, and they both stifled laughter.

Two nerve wracking hours later, Cat walked into the waiting room to give an update. Laurel and Liz both stared at her as she came in and pulled up a chair near them.

"Good to see you, Liz," Cat said.

Before Liz could answer, Laurel asked, "How is she?"

"She tore it up worse than we thought." With a voice devoid of any emotion, Cat described the surgery. "We had to do a lot of restructuring. She had a complete subscapularis tear. We had to put things back together so she'll have a functioning arm. There were two tendons that were retracted, forcing us to anchor them. I'm going to recommend a few specific courses of treatment for therapy. She should let this heal completely and do the physical therapy correctly or we'll be right back here in a few years putting in a new shoulder joint. We didn't run into any complications beyond the mess we found. She's headed to recovery, and they should start waking her up after that."

Laurel felt a wash of relief and ran her hand around the back of her neck, trying to rub out the tension. "Can I see her now?"

Cat shook her head and rose. "In a little while. They'll want to observe her to make sure she's stable. I'll have someone come to get you as soon as she's ready. I'll need to see her in two weeks if she doesn't have any complications before then."

"Thank you." Laurel moved unsteady hands to her face and brushed her hair behind her ears.

"There's no thanks needed. I've had to cut off her leg, replace her elbow, and now this. Although I enjoy seeing her, under my knife isn't exactly what I had in mind."

Cat turned and headed out of the room, Liz and Laurel staring after her.

Liz let out a slow breath. "Guess I was right, she hasn't changed a bit."

Laurel shook her head. "I guess to be a surgeon, there has to be a bit of cockiness and belief in yourself. Good Lord, that woman rubs me the wrong way."

"I know what you mean, but if Jo or I needed surgery, Cat would be the one we would want. Val was in good hands. Now we need to get her home with you, where she'll be in even better ones."

Laurel gave her a grateful smile and breathed more easily than she had in hours. She needed to see for herself that Val was ok. Only that would calm the ache she felt at being separated.

***

Over the next few hours, Val slowly woke up, performed all the necessary functions to be able to leave the hospital, and signed out. She groggily watched the landscape pass by while Laurel drove them back to Liz's. They both collapsed on the bed, exhausted. Neither bothered to undress, removing nothing more than Val's leg and their shoes. Laurel curled into Val's side with Val's arm tucking her in securely. Around two, the white-hot pain in her shoulder woke Val with a gasp. She was still groggy and her stomach rolled. *Anesthesia always makes me sick.* She took a few deep breaths in through her nose, exhaling through her mouth to try and settle the nausea.

Laurel sat up, wiping the sleep from her eyes. "What's wrong, baby?" She looked at the clock. "It's time for your pain medicine. I'll be right back."

Before she could make it to the door, Liz appeared with a sandwich for each of them, along with cold glasses of lemonade and a pill for Val.

"Thank you, Liz. I was just getting up to do that."

"I figured a good rest was what you both needed." Liz handed her the tray and ran a hand down Laurel's arm.

"I need her too, Liz." Laurel smiled at Liz and took the tray to the bedside table. Val opened her eyes.

"Hey there, sleepy head. I need you to eat something so I can give you a pill." Laurel ran her hand across Val's forehead and down her cheek.

Val shifted, grimacing from the pain, but she took the sandwich half from Laurel and devoured it. She would have eaten a kitchen table if put between slices of bread. Not being able to eat before surgery had made her ravenous. The small amount of juice and pudding they'd given her at the hospital after surgery had long since worn off.

"Slow down or you'll choke. I promise, you can have more." Laurel chuckled.

Val slowed her chewing. "Sorry, I'm starved."

Laurel waited until she'd chewed the bite of sandwich to hand her the lemonade. After it was handed back, she leaned in and kissed Val. "So am I, and it's not the sandwich I'm talking about."

Val groaned in appreciation and moved her hand into Laurel's hair. She pulled her closer and was surprised at the resistance she met.

"Not yet, love, we need to let this shoulder settle down. I promise once it's safe enough, I'm all yours." Laurel pulled back.

Val grinned. "If you think I'm waiting until this shoulder is healed to touch you again, we'll need to have a talk. I want you so bad, I'd starve to death if it meant being with you one more time."

"Is that so? Since I have no intention of letting you starve," she held the other half of the sandwich to Val's lips, "we'll just have to see what we can do to keep your hunger under control."

Val raised her eyebrows and took a bite from the offered sandwich. Every time she looked into those emerald eyes, she saw her future. She could only hope that Laurel did, too, but somehow, she could still feel there was a part of her she was holding back. Val made a silent vow to break down whatever barrier Laurel threw up. She wanted this woman completely. *How can I make this happen?*

Laurel settled on the edge of the bed. "I called your mom and let her know you were out of surgery. She thanked me and wanted me to tell you to get in touch as soon as you feel up to it. She also said something about peppermint shoe polish." Laurel shook her head. "I have no clue. I also called Gram. She said for you to get healed up quick as there's some crisp waiting and she can't wait for us to come home. Told me to tell you the gang from the store misses you too."

"I wish I felt like traveling three hours tonight. We'd go home."

She let that word roll around on her tongue. *Home.* She hadn't considered any place home in a long time, probably not since her grandmother's house while she lived with her as a teenager. She'd never had a permanent home as a marine, instead, she lived in the barracks if she wasn't traveling for a story. She didn't own much, Maggie May, a few electronics, and her cameras. As she chewed, she thought about her simple life on the road. She spent the winter on the west coast and the spring, summer, and fall on the east coast. She slept in hotels or in a tent in the more unpopulated areas.

Her memories kept her moving. Staying still gave her brain time to recall the horrors of war and that fateful day. The slideshow from her camera played over and over. Images out of focus and at odd angles. Never showing the face of the soldier with the child in their arms. The box of crayons held tightly in the hand of the lifeless form. She could smell the cordite and burnt flesh. The taste of blood in her mouth. The sounds of war consumed her. The muted shouts for medics and cries of pain. She could feel the desert heat on her skin and her lips cracking, like all the moisture had been sucked out of her skin. She could see the child, soot stained tears running down the face, blood coming from the nose. *Medic!* A voice called her but she couldn't tell from where. She looked frantically across the courtyard but she couldn't see and then there was Laurel, her hand outstretched and calling her name.

"Val, come back to me. I'm right here. There is no danger, there are no explosives, and no kids are hurt. Come back, love. You're safe. You're here with me at Liz and Jo's. You're ok, honey, I'm right here."

Laurel's voice was calm. Val felt arms wrap around her, but it didn't help. Val was still stuck in the throes of battle, in the heat and the terror and the pain. After a moment of silence, Val heard a second voice. *Liz.*

"Val, there's no danger. You're not back in Iraq. You're here in my home. You're safe. There are no suicide bombers, there are no children in danger, and you're not dying. You're all right. The woman who loves you is at your side. This memory is not happening now."

The woman I love? That snapped Val back, but she was still confused. Still worried. Her right hand embraced Laurel's. Her body softened from the rigid posture. She licked her lips and blinked. Tears rolled down her cheek.

Liz spoke again. "You're here in my home, Val. Laurel is at your side. You're in no danger."

Val heard the mantra breaking through the sand and heat. She could feel the soft mattress beneath her and the warm body up against hers. She blinked several more times and looked at Laurel. Her fear apparent, Val tried for a small smile. She was rewarded with the look of relief. Against the pain, she leaned forward to kiss Laurel.

"Welcome back, Val." Liz handed the lemonade to Laurel, who brought it to Val's lips.

Val drank greedily and sat back against the headboard. "I'm sorry." The lemonade quenched her thirst and cleared her head some.

Laurel shook her head. "You have nothing to be sorry for. There's no way you've completely purged the effects of the anesthesia."

Liz reached out and held Val's hand. "I was afraid Bethesda might throw you back into it. Seeing Cat as a surgeon likely triggered this. If you're feeling up to it, I'd really like to do a session tonight with both of you, together. I want to deal with some things before you two head back home, instead of waiting for it to rear its head later."

"Val?" Laurel squeezed Val's arm.

"Yeah, I think that's a good idea. Right now, I just want to finish that sandwich and go back to sleep. I feel like I went fifteen rounds." She was tired of these flashbacks and the energy it took from her. She wanted peace and stability. *I wish my mind would catch up with my body and realize I'm out of the marines.* She'd paid a heavy price for her service and wanted nothing more than to forget that day.

Laurel reached for the sandwich and again held it to Val's lips. "Good thing I'm here then. Your one wing is in a sling and the other is right where it's supposed to be." She indicated Val's hand that was resting against her hip.

"I'll leave you two alone for a while. Jo has burgers planned for supper later, around 5:00. If either of you need anything just call." Liz gave Val one last look and walked out of the room.

Val looked at the concern etched on her lover's face. She rubbed her thumb across the frown lines between Laurel's eyes. The worry she saw broke her heart. "I'm sorry, baby. I don't usually have these many episodes so close together."

"You could have them every day and it wouldn't change how much I love or care about you. I'm here to help bring you out of them and love you while I'm doing it. You don't have to hide this part of you from me. I love all of you, the dark and the scary parts too. Together we'll make our way through this."

"I'm not sure how I found you, but even a blind..."

"Dog finds a bone?" Laurel finished.

Val stared at her. "Wow, now you can finish my sentences?"

"I saw a picture in Liz's study where you were toasting them at their wedding. She happened to mention that line."

"I fit the category of a blind, one legged dog and somehow I still got lucky the day I stopped at Cool Springs."

Laurel held the sandwich so that Val could take the last bite. After doing so, she pulled Laurel's fingers into her mouth, tasting the salt and watching Laurels eye's flitter closed.

Laurel shivered. "Stop that. Your mouth is writing a check your body can't cash right now. How about we put this on simmer? Rain check?"

"Definitely." Val wanted nothing more than to empty the entire account.

***

Laurel led Val down the stairs to enjoy Jo's grilling skills. She opted for a beer, while Val settled for iced tea. The meal consumed, they concentrated on cleaning up and putting the dishes away. Jo headed to her studio for a bit while the other three headed to the study.

Val sat on the couch, her good arm around Laurel who sat with her bare feet curled under her, leaning against Val. Laurel needed the physical connection to calm her nerves. The heat they created together warmed her from the inside out. She took a deep breath and looked at Liz.

Liz opened the discussion. "How are you feeling now, Val?"

"Pretty wiped out. Between the surgery and the flashback, I'm exhausted."

"How about you, Laurel? This is as much about you as it is her."

Laurel started to say something and stopped. Liz was right. Loving Val meant being able to help her through the flashbacks and anchor her in reality. She needed to be totally honest. "Scared." She felt Val stiffen. She reached up and cupped Val's face. "I'm scared I won't know how to take care of you during one of these flashbacks. That I won't say or do the right thing, and you'll hurt yourself."

Val put her forehead against Laurel's. "You bring me out of them so much quicker and more completely than anyone in all the years I've had them. That's saying a lot."

"She's right, Laurel. I've seen her at her very worst with her flashbacks. I've never seen her calm down or fight to come back to the present the way she does with you near her. It really doesn't matter what you say while she's flashing, but we need to work on something that's uniquely yours. What she needs to know is that she isn't back in the desert, she isn't in danger, and there are no children hurt. These are the foundation. Val, let's start with you telling Laurel about that day in more detail."

Laurel looked at the woman she loved, wanting to take this pain from her.

Val took a deep breath and closed her eyes for a moment. "We were in Toraq. The unit was visiting a small education center to present supplies to the kids. My lieutenant was making the presentation. The kids were there, about fifteen or twenty, all smiling. Layfield was translating and helping pass out the supplies to the kids. They were so happy to be getting simple things like pencils, notepads, and stickers. I was taking pictures. Our protection unit was outside the interior courtyard. Corporal Taylor was acting like a big a kid passing out the bags. He was twenty. He and his wife were expecting their first child."

Laurel watched a blank stare develop on Val's face.

"This guy appeared from one of the interior doors. He has this look on his face. Pure disgust. He and the leader started arguing and our protection unit closed in. The guy raised his arms toward the sky and yelled something in Arabic. The world exploded. I think my finger must have still been on the trigger because we found distorted images on the SD card.

Laurel watched her body tense up. Worried, she looked to Liz for reassurance. Liz raised a hand to let her know it was all right.

"I remember the pain and the fear. Yelling for the medic."

Val paused for a moment and Laurel watched as her eyes shifted rapidly from side to side and her breaths became ragged and short. It was like someone watching a terrifying movie and she wanted badly to reach out and sooth Val. She looked to Liz who mouthed she was alright.

"I can see this kid, can't be more than nine or ten. There's blood coming out of his nose." Val blinked rapidly. "I can see that damn pack of crayons in his hand. I brushed the dirt out of his eyes. He's so small. I can't feel any heartbeat. I tried mouth to mouth but I couldn't get him to breathe. I screamed for help and tried to get up. I couldn't for some reason. So, I held him and cried. He was a child. All he wanted was some crayons and that bastard killed him!"

Laurel watched in horror as Val's chest rose and fell in desperate heaves.

Liz leaned forward in her chair. "Val, if you can hear me, I want you to lift your left index finger."

Val didn't respond, so Laurel tried.

"Val, it's Laurel. I'm right here. Your arm is around me. Lift your left index finger, honey."

Laurel held her breath and waited. Seconds later, Val lifted her finger as directed.

"Val, I want you to count out loud back from five and exhale after each number, slowly. Laurel will count with you."

Val and Laurel began to count following Liz's direction. "Five, four, three, two, one."

Liz said, "I want you to tell me your full name and how old you are, where you're from, and where you are now."

Laurel held her breath, wishing for all the world she could take this from Val, to bring these nightmares to an end. She heard Val's voice and looked into her eyes. They were cloudy, but not as dilated. She was pale, although Laurel couldn't tell if this was from her episode or from the surgery.

"My name is Valkyrie Vör Magnusson. I'm forty-four years old. I'm from Seattle, Washington, and I'm in your home in Annapolis, Maryland."

Liz nodded. "Who is at your side?"

"The love of my life, Laurel Anastasia Stemple."

Laurel buried her face in Val's neck and tried to control her own tense breathing.

"Val, close your eyes. I'm going to count down from five and when I reach one, you will open them and feel at peace and settled. Five, four, three, two, one."

Val opened her eyes, sobs escaping her body. "I was holding the kid. It was me!"

Laurel could feel that this was a major breakthrough. She kissed Val and put her arm around her neck, holding onto her. Val was shaking uncontrollably.

Finally, Val's sobs quieted and her breathing settled. Liz spoke to her. "I'd long suspected it was you holding the child, Val. Your subconscious wasn't ready to accept it. My guess is during the blast you dropped the camera and it fell against something that kept the shutter pushed. You were the only one still alive in the courtyard after your protection detail got to you. Gamble, Layfield, and Taylor all died in the blast. Apparently, you were far enough away that you didn't get the full brunt of the explosion and you probably dragged yourself over to the child to render aid. I believe the serious concussion you suffered kept this memory hidden. The one you suffered during the motorcycle accident brought it back to the forefront."

Val shook her head. "I'm not sure I'm ready to accept it as fact, but it does make sense. None of the pictures show the soldier from the waist down or the face. The hands were too blurry to be able to tell if they were mine or not. I need to figure out how to process this." Val let her head rest back on the couch, tears still running from the corners of her eyes.

Laurel curled closer into her side. "I love you, and I'm right here beside you." Laurel was trying to process it herself. What it all meant for her, or for that matter, them, was unknown. *All I know is, I'm going to be right by her side through this, come hell or high water.*

"I also suspect that the love you have in Laurel allowed your subconscious to release this memory, knowing you had a support system to hold you up." Liz nodded in Laurel's direction.

"I just don't know, Liz, I've been searching for this answer for a long time. I have a hard time believing it's true, but I know it must be." The tears rolled, and Laurel pulled her closer, stroking her neck and face.

Liz nodded. "All we can do is learn to manage your flashbacks to lessen their impact on your life. You have a family that loves you. They're what matters. Not a memory of a past you can't change."

Laurel kissed Val as she sat up. She reached out and dried the tears on Val's cheeks. Interlacing their fingers, she pulled Val's hand into her lap. She turned to Liz. "Tell me how to help her."

"First, I always confirm that she isn't in Iraq and what the present situation is. We ground her in time and place as well as acknowledge who she is. Assure her what's she's seeing is in the past. The where she's from, is to test her long-term memory."

Laurel bit her lip. "So, if I told her it was me, that she was at Cool Springs, and that she was safe, would that do it?" Laurel wanted to confirm that this simple phrasing wouldn't make the situation worse.

"It's possible. She responds to your voice and your touch. I've seen her flashbacks go as long as fifteen to twenty minutes. Every time you're with her, it's so much shorter. That's remarkable. Sometimes it may be just you reminding her that you love her. The key is you, Laurel."

"I'm all for that." Val leaned in and kissed Laurel's temple.

"After you get home, I want to do a few video sessions. I don't think these flashbacks are over. With this new revelation about the child, it's possible even Laurel will struggle to bring you back. I think with her help, we can bring you through this together."

***

Val appreciated the stress relief her friends could provide. She needed a break from trying to process everything. The rest of the evening passed quietly. Jo and Val bantered back and forth while the women who loved them just shook their heads. They told dozens of stories on each other.

"So, we go to this jeweler and Jo is as nervous as long tailed cat in a room full of rocking chairs. The guy at the counter was more feminine than both of us combined. Jo's looking at this gorgeous rock, and he looks up at me and says it will look fabulous on my finger. I damn near choked. Jo looks at him…" Val gazed over her shoulder at her friend.

Jo shook her head and grinned. "I say, 'Do I look like I go for the butch type, bub? The woman I'm proposing to looks like a model in little black dress with come-fuck-me heels that put yours to shame. I'll take it.'"

The room roared with laughter.

Val needed this. The images of that day had haunted her for years. The answers that had been revealed still didn't alleviate her anxiety about what she'd lived through. The banter and the humor were as important to her well-being, as the sessions she and Liz scheduled. She needed to laugh. Some of her memories were so graphic that they caused her not only emotional pain but physical at times. The moments she could spend reliving good memories chased the shadows away and let the sun stream in as the darkness threatened to drown her. *Best medicine ever invented, next to love.* She looked at Laurel and knew what she felt for her was stronger than any medication known to man. Jo's voice brought her out of her musings.

"And we haven't even gotten to the stories in the hospital."

"With that, I think it's time we all go to bed. I'm tired." Val pointed at Liz and Jo. "And you two need your house back."

Jo pulled her wife into her lap. "You're always welcome here. We expect to come and see you two soon."

Laurel reached out her hand and touched Jo on the arm. "Gram would love to meet you both. I think she'd give you a run for your money, Jo."

Jo hugged Laurel's neck. "I'm guessing that apple didn't fall far from the tree. What time are you leaving?"

"I'm hoping to get on the road by 9:00 and praying the morning commuters will already be at work. That puts us home around noon." Laurel stood beside Val, her hand tucked into Val's waistband.

Val melted at the familiar feeling, craving the contact.

"So, we'll see you guys for breakfast. I have a few pieces I need to finish up tomorrow, and Liz here has a full schedule, so we'll be up early. See you in the morning." Jo popped a wheelie with her wife in her lap and rolled them both to the elevator.

Laurel turned in Val's arms. "I'm going to go get your evening pills and we can go to bed."

"I like the sound of that. First, I'm going to call my mother."

"I was hoping you would do that. I'll give you some privacy. I need to call Beth, catch up on what's been going on with the store, and talk to Gram. I'll see you upstairs." Laurel stood on her tiptoes and kissed Val. "I love you."

"I love you too." Val watched her climb the stairs, a million things going through her head. She sat down on the landing with her phone pressed to her forehead. The revelation that she was the one in the pictures had shocked her to her core. Even now as she sat here, she could see him in her arms. Knowing the truth filled a good bit of the void she'd floated in for a long time. She still didn't have all the answers and might never have them. Those answers tempered the nagging feeling that something was missing.

She looked up at the ceiling and stared at the ornate plaster adorning it. The plaster was a façade for the wooden lath that lay under it. It had small spider cracks that snaked across it in fine lines. She'd been like that. A façade covering over imperfections and flaws. Window dressing to what skeletons lay beneath. It had been a long time since her boots were filled with sand but the cracks that developed in that harsh land were deep and started just below the surface. She stared out into the empty room and realized, *Laurel is filling those cracks*. Filling them with love and devotion until they were much less noticeable. She'd come to believe she could depend on Laurel to cope with her flashbacks. She shook her head and dialed her mother.

"Valkyrie, how are you?"

"Hello, Mother, just wanted to let you know I'm fine. We made it to Liz and Jo's. If all goes according to plan, Laurel and I will head back to West Virginia tomorrow."

"Did Dr. O'Neil think that was a good idea?"

"The only restriction I have is movement of the joint for the rest of the day." The ache in her arm reminded her she would still need meds before she could get any sleep. "She wants me in therapy as soon as possible. So, we have to go back to West Virginia where the therapist Laurel lined up is."

"Have you checked out this therapist or the facility?"

"I trust Laurel. She's confident Fallon is the best. That's good enough for me." Irritation nettled Val at her mother's constant questioning of her decisions. She was an adult and had been taking care of herself for a long time. Amanda had never been attentive and her mothering now felt more like meddling. The more she listened, the more it became white noise with no meaning.

"You'd have so many more options if you stayed there in Maryland or in Seattle."

"You're pushing."

There was a long silence between them.

"I'm sorry, Valkyrie. Forgive me for being your mother."

Val blew out a breath and stared at the ceiling. She closed her eyes and counted to ten before speaking. "Mother, it's okay to care. It's okay for you to want me to have the best. It isn't okay for you to second-guess my decisions. I'll call you in a few days."

"I'm sorry, Valkyrie. Just because your children grow up doesn't mean you stop wanting to protect them. I've tracked down your grandmother's salve. I'm ordering it. Where should I send it?"

For once she heard what her mother had said. Warm memories of her grandmother pulling it from her purse and putting it on her lips as a child, flooded her. "Thanks, Mother, I'll text you the address after I get it from Laurel."

"Sleep well, Valkyrie. Call me with an update if you can."

"I will, Mother. Good night." She stood, looking down the stairs, still trying to put the emotions her mother raised in check.

Laurel came up behind her and pressed close. "You okay?"

I am now. Val took a deep breath and blew it out slowly. Her mother tested every bit of patience she possessed. What she needed now was right behind her. "I'm fine. Talking to her raises my blood pressure. Can we go to bed? I really need to hold you."

"I can't imagine anything else I'd rather do."

Val took her hand and walked her to the bed.

Chapter Twenty-One

THE NEXT MORNING AFTER an extended goodbye over breakfast and coffee, Laurel and Val got on the road and headed home. Laurel weaved through beltway traffic and then settled in for the drive. She kept one hand on the wheel and the other hand in Val's. She noticed the woman beside her seemed relaxed, and not in any major discomfort. She'd taken the maximum dose of her pain medicine, and Laurel hoped it would be enough for the ride. The miles passed as the scenery changed from cityscape to trees and roadside streams. The flat gray land of the city gave way to the green rolling hills of the countryside.

Val smiled as she slept. *I hope it's me she's dreaming of.* Laurel was doing everything she could think of to keep Val safe and happy. In the back of her mind there would always be a chance her body would betray her and the cancer would show its ugly head. Looking over at the sleeping woman beside her, she pulled her thoughts away from the dark corners of her psyche. *Live for today.* It was more important to enjoy the things that were far more than chance. She was in love with Val and she'd keep loving her as long as she could. The day that Val rode into Cool Springs, her life had changed forever.

About thirty minutes from Aurora, Val stirred. "Where are we?"

Laurel squeezed her hand. "We're outside of Oakland, Maryland. Almost home. Anything you want before we get there?"

"I've got all I need." She kissed Laurel's fingers.

Laurel smiled at her. "Gram's going to be happy to have us both home. I want to do something special for Beth for watching over her while we've been gone."

"I've missed everyone down at the store. Can we stop there first?"

"You feel up to it?" Laurel smiled at Val's desire to reconnect with the people she cared about.

"I do."

Laurel nodded and continued to drive. Ten minutes later, she pulled into the store. They both stared at the sign above the door that welcomed them home. It might as well have said, *"Come on in, we've missed you."*

Just steps inside the front door, a collective cheer went up from around the potbelly stove. Ree came out of the kitchen, wiping her hands on her apron. Val and Laurel walked over to the stove area and patted Mule and Bobeye on the back. Ree walked up to Val and gave her a gentle hug.

Beth wrapped her arms around Laurel, holding her tightly. "How are you, hon?"

Laurel took a deep cleansing breath, familiar scents enveloping her, hotdog chili, apple pie, and today's special, fried chicken. "Really good. She's on the mend and that's all that matters."

Ree walked up to her and Laurel fell into her embrace. "Oh, Liebchen, I've missed ya. It's good to have ya home. And look, ya managed to drag the Viking with ya."

"She insisted on stopping in here before I took her to the house. I think she missed you all, too." Laurel laughed, and they looked at the others. Mule was staring at the display Val handed him. Laurel remembered Val asking Jo to create a special shadowbox. Inside was the rubbing Val made of his brother's name and a few pictures she had taken from the Vietnam Wall. He held it to his chest. The sight took her breath.

***

Everyone took the opportunity to tell Val how glad they were that she was doing well and back home. She was just as grateful to be in a place she looked forward to being. Ree took her into the kitchen. She smiled as the octogenarian dished out a large portion of her favorite dessert and topped it with ice cream. *I've missed this.*

Val spooned the first taste up to her mouth, closed her eyes and groaned. She looked at Ree who stared back at her with a twinkle in her eye. "What?"

"Good to have ya back, Viking. Ya in much pain with that shoulder?"

"At times. The ride home wasn't too bad. I had an excellent

chauffeur. It's good to be home." The words left Val's mouth before she even had a chance to analyze what it meant. *The truth will set you free.* She'd been thinking of what the word home meant, a great deal lately. Never had any place felt so right.

Ree placed her hand on Val's forearm. "Val, I love ya like one of my own. I can see how much ya love my granddaughter and I want ya to hear this straight from the horse's mouth. I approve. I want ya to feel like ya belong here. I want ya to know ya can stay, however long those rambling boots will let ya. Finish your crisp so Laurel can take ya up to the house. Ya look about as worn out as the belts on a farmer's hay baler."

Val hugged Ree with her good arm. "Ree, in all the places in the world I've been, there's no place like this in my heart. I do love Laurel. We're just figuring out what all that means. She's one incredible woman who was raised by another exceptional one."

Ree smacked her arm. "Flattery will get ya everything, honey."

Val let out a long breath, her heart warmed by the affection. She loved Ree. Shoveling the last few bites in, she rose and took her bowl to the big stainless-steel double-bowled sink. She started to wash the bowl one handed and laughed as Ree shooed her out of the kitchen.

Val exited to find Laurel at the counter with Beth, looking over the order forms for the following week. Mule and Bobeye sat around the stove, arguing about something in the newspaper. Wunder bused a table and made a small child laugh. All of the sights and sounds around her were comforting, like a long-lost friend. She felt an arm glide around her side and could tell who it was by the soft whisper of vanilla and coconut.

"You about ready to go home?" Laurel asked. "You look a little pale. I want you to take a pill before we go. Let it get into your system. After we get to the house, it's straight to bed."

"I like the sound of that." Val wagged her eyebrows.

Laurel blushed. "Your thoughts are writing those checks again. Behave. I'll be right back." Laurel went to pour Val a glass of chocolate milk. Wunder stood near the dispenser drinking his own glass. Val watched as Wunder spoke to Laurel and took the glass from her. He came over to where she was standing and handed it to her. They sat down in the chairs near the checker board and Val dutifully took out her pills, downing the milk slowly. She looked back up in time to see Laurel head through the swinging doors into the kitchen.

***

Laurel allowed the doors to swing closed behind her, relishing the familiarity of the kitchen. The heat from the deep fryers turned the whole place into an oven and the smell of fried chicken filled the air. *Home.*

Ree walked up beside her. "I sure have missed ya. Val looks like she's doin' good. She's hidin' how much she's hurtin', though."

"I had her take a pain pill. By the time I get her to the house, she'll pass out for a few hours and will look better this evening."

"How about you? Ya look like ya haven't got much sleep of late."

Laurel hugged her grandmother tightly, allowing herself to become lost in the arms she'd sought solace in so many times. "She's got things eating her up inside. She has flashbacks and crawls across the floor looking for cover. She'll break out into a sweat, and her mind's right back there in the desert. We stayed with her therapist and best friend. Having to go back to the hospital where so many things happened was hard. The surgeon who fixed her shoulder is the same one who amputated her leg in Iraq. I've seen her terrified, and I'm helpless to do anything to stop that." Tears welled up and sat heavily on her lashes.

"What did her therapist say?"

Laurel stood, wiping tears from her cheeks. "Liz said I actually help bring her out of it faster. She taught me a few things to say."

"Let's walk out back for a minute. I need some air. This kitchen is blazin' with the twins workin' on the fried chicken."

Each took a rocker as they reached the wide back porch. Laurel had snapped and shelled more beans than she could count here since her childhood. It looked over the park area of the attraction. Steam engines, iron tractors, and other equipment dotted the tree-covered area. Children climbed on the seats and let their imaginations take them to a different time as they ran around on the sun-dappled grass.

After a moment, Ree spoke. "Now ya also know I'm one ta speak my mind."

Laurel laughed. "You speak your mind? I'm shocked."

"Don't you be sassin' me, Liebchen, I can still send ya to cut a sprig of forsythia."

They both raised their pinkies, laughter rolling off the porch. Laurel grinned with deep affection for the woman beside her. "I'm not sure how many switches I cut as a kid, but damn if I can ever remember you using one on me."

"A lot of that was bluffing. You and Viking slept together yet?"

Laurel's faced burned. It wasn't as if she and Gram never talked about sex. Gram was the one who'd explained the birds and the bees to her, talking to her as she'd grown old enough to need answers. This seemed different in some way. "Yes."

"And she knows everythin'?"

"Not everything. I haven't told her my fear of the future."

"How'd she react?"

Laurel laughed. "Pissed. Put me in my place, right proper. Reminded me I'd seen all her scars and didn't see her as less than a whole person." She dropped her head back and closed her eyes, remembering the first time Val had touched her. "She made love to me in a way I never thought was possible. I didn't think about the reconstruction or the cancer possibilities. All I could think about was how she made me feel."

"Then it's love." Ree put her weathered hand on Laurel's cheek. "I best get back to it. You go take our girl home."

Laurel rose and clung to her grandmother, letting the words sink in under the caress of her weathered hands. "See you at home."

After they reached the house, Laurel took Val straight to bed and settled her under a light sheet. The room smelled of the mountain laurel planted outside the open window. "I'll be right back. I want to put something in the oven for dinner, then I'll come and lie down with you." Laurel leaned over and kissed Val. Her eyes were already growing heavy, but she held on to Laurel. "I promise, I'll be right back."

Val released her and Laurel made her way to the kitchen. She was just as comfortable cooking a meal here as she was helping in the kitchen at the diner. She pulled out the Crock-Pot and went about filling it with ingredients for a pot roast with the vegetables she and her Gram grew in their own garden. *Gram always said that fixing someone a meal was an intimate thing because they would feed their body and spirit from what you'd prepared.* Thinking about all the meals her Gram fixed made her smile knowing she was now doing this for her family. Laurel placed everything in the slow cooker and poured some beef stock in with it. She changed into a pair of shorts and crawled into bed with Val.

Sliding under the sheet and into Val's open arm felt so natural. "You okay?"

Val hummed.

"I'll take that as a yes. Get some sleep, love." Laurel kissed her cheek and let her own exhaustion take over.

Both slept until they heard car doors three hours later. Laurel urged Val to stay in bed while she went to catch up with Beth. Val nodded and drifted back to sleep. Laurel went to the kitchen and helped unload groceries. Everything was put away and Gram went to catch the evening news before dinner. Beth and Laurel made their way to the swing on the front porch.

They had been best friends since infancy. There were no secrets between them and there was no embarrassment as they talked of love and sex. Laurel thought she'd been in love with Beth at one time. As they grew older, it was obvious the love wasn't sexual in nature. It was a kindred spirit love that allowed them to be more than friends, more than sisters.

Beth rolled her head to the side. "Ok, fess up, how was the sex?"

"Mind blowing. I've never felt that way. It's not like I slept around. The last one I let touch me never made me feel that way."

"Abby?"

"Yeah. It wasn't that she wasn't attentive or acted turned off, it's just the difference between the way Val touches me and the way Abby did. There's no comparison. Val engaged all my senses. For once, none of the other mattered except her touch."

Beth flapped her shirt away from her body. "Whew, I need a cold shower now."

"You jerk."

Beth gave her a little nudge. "I'm happy for you. So, when does she start therapy?"

Laurel sneered. "Cat didn't want her to wait too long. We have an appointment with Fallon tomorrow morning. They may not start yet, but she needs the consult so they can set up a course of treatment and appointment schedule."

Beth furrowed her brow. "Every time you say the name Cat, you might as well be taking a spoonful of cod liver oil. You really don't like that woman."

Laurel's jaw tightened and jumped. "That's an understatement. That woman makes the hair on my neck stand up. She's used to getting her way, but this time, she's met her match."

"That's my girl. Now let's go back in and see if Ree needs anything. I'm no substitute for you, that's for sure. I think we've done pretty well. I'm positive I got on her nerves. I wasn't about to let anything happen to her while you were dealing with Val's surgery." She lifted Laurel's hand and clapped hers against it. "Tag, you're it."

They both laughed and went back inside. They found Val up and in conversation with Ree in the kitchen. Laurel walked around to Val's back and her hand squeezed Val's neck as she kissed her on the head.

"Need anything?"

Val raised her eyebrows up and down provocatively at Laurel. A smile quirked across her face.

With the roast almost done, they set about making rolls. Laurel cut some greens for a salad while laughing at the stories being told. Val had many adventures that never made it into the magazine, making them all new to the three women involved in the food preparation. She helped set the table after Laurel carried the plates over. The kitchen smelled heavenly as the roast was sliced and everyone made their way to their seats. Ree announced that she wanted to say grace. Around the table the four held hands, with Beth placing a hand on Val's injured arm.

"Lord, we have much to be grateful for. My girls are home, and Beth didn't kill me for treating her the way I do Laurel. We're thankful to be able to be together, and we ask you to watch over us. As my momma used to say, thank God for dirty dishes, they have a tale to tell. While others may go hungry, we're eating very well. Amen."

Laurel chuckled a little and touched Val on the arm. "Need me to cut your roast?"

Val shook her head. "I saw the way it came out of that pot, practically falling apart. I'll try and see if I can cut it with my fork ."

Laurel leaned over and kissed her on the cheek. It was a simple thing, a meal with your family, and Laurel felt like the luckiest woman alive to have the people she loved most around her.

Ree looked at Val and Laurel. "You two can come to the store after your appointment. Come have lunch and let me know how it went."

Dinner was finished in comfortable companionship. The dishes were washed and put away and the four sat talking over coffee. Beth yawned and excused herself to go home. Laurel took Val by the hand and directed them both to her room.

"Ree's not going to be upset if I sleep with you, is she?"

"Did you hear Gram make the statement that she wants great grandchildren? I think she'd be pissed if I don't sleep with you."

Val shook her head in laughter. "I heard. Even if I sleep in the same room with you, I'm not sure we're going to be able to accomplish that." She walked to the bathroom to brush her teeth. She was getting better at doing this left handed. The movement was still jerky and foreign to her, resulting in as much toothpaste on the outside of her mouth as was in. She looked to her side to see Laurel stifling laughter with a hand over her mouth. "Think this is funny, huh? You try brushing with your left hand."

Laurel watched Val and knew she'd never grow tired of lying down with Val every night for the rest of her life.

Chapter Twenty-Two

MORNING CAME ALL TOO quickly and another day dawned. Val rubbed a hand across her face to clear the sleep away as she walked to the kitchen.

Laurel gave her a light kiss. "Morning. How are you?"

"I can tell it's time for a pain pill. Think we can we cut them in half? I get too groggy with a whole one."

Laurel frowned. "We're going to see Fallon. She might want to manipulate that joint, and you don't want to do that un-medicated."

Val rocked her head back and forth. "I'm pretty good at judging what my pain tolerance is. I think I'll be okay. Worst comes to worst, we can take the other half right before we go see her, agreed?"

"You know your body better than anyone." Laurel smirked. "At least parts of it, anyway."

Val gathered her closer. "I'm hoping you get to know it a whole lot better."

Laurel pulled away with a groan. "Breakfast time. Sit down. I'll get you some coffee."

Ree walked by her and touched her good shoulder. "How'd ya sleep?"

"Good. I slept like a baby."

"The mountains can do that to ya. They have a special way of making ya feel protected and a part of something deeper than yourself. They ground me." Ree sat a plate of bacon and eggs in front of Val.

Val looked at the two women around the table. "In all the traveling I've done, I don't know that any place ever called to me the way this one has. I have no doubt it's more about the people I've found here than the place itself." She bit into the biscuit, dripping with homemade strawberry jam. An explosion of sweet flavor hit her tongue.

The back door opened, and Beth strode in. She kissed Ree on the cheek and took her place at the table. Beth and Laurel started talking about something from the store. Val envied the two women. It was obvious they were as close as any sisters could be. She was grateful Laurel had Beth and having more people as close family made her happy. Her closest friends were Jo and Liz. *Not sure where I'd be without those two.* She wanted to call them after therapy and fill them in on the course of treatment. She also needed to call her boss. There was no way she'd be back on a motorcycle any time soon, but she couldn't disappear from her readers. She needed to write a short story of what happened, explaining she'd be four wheel bound for a while. She had another idea rolling around in her head though, a series of quirky articles about the store and its characters. A fellow journalist friend had been trying for years to get her to expand her work to include some feature pieces for the magazine. Maybe she should explore that. Her mind was lost in a million possibilities. The sound of her name brought her back to the present.

"What do you think, Val?" Beth asked.

"I'm sorry. I was lost in my thoughts. What did you say?"

Laurel's brow furrowed. "You okay, honey?"

"I'm fine. Just thinking of a series of articles. Now what did you ask, Beth?"

"A man came by a few days ago wanting to upgrade our postcards. Said he had a new series of images."

Laurel broke in. "We've been using the same company for years. They sell okay, nothing to write home about, excuse the pun."

Val rolled her eyes. "I've got a better idea. There are companies out there that will turn photos into postcards for you. Personalized with a message from the store. I could take the photos and we could offer larger prints for sale too. There are dozens of places around this area to take wildlife and nature photos."

"Oh, Val, we couldn't ask you to do that," Laurel said.

"Are you going to let me pay you for room, board, and travel while I'm here?"

Ree sat back in her seat, lips pursed. "That jam go to your head in a sugar rush, child? There'll be no paying for ya being here."

Val turned her palm up. "Then how can you not let me do this for you? I'll need to replace my camera lenses anyway. Digital photography makes it cost effective, and I already have the editing software. If I truly am part of this family, then let me pull my weight. Right now, I'd only be a terrible bus boy, an inept waitress, and you don't want me anywhere near a cook stove. This is what I do. And I'm good at it."

Laurel chuckled. "Well played, Viking."

Val grinned. "Now for a while, I'm pretty sure I'll have to have someone drive me. It won't be too long before I'll have both my arms back in working order. Then I can do a lot of this on my own while you guys work at the store. I need to take some time to work on Maggie May with Bobeye, and even Wunder's offered to help."

Ree crossed her arms and squinted at her. Val could see the gears turning. She could also see the woman coming to a decision.

"I'll agree to this with one condition. Ya put the picture postcards thing together. Ya get the sale on them prints you're a talkin' about. Now ya mind me, no sweet talk's gonna work." Ree pointed her finger between the two other women at the table. "Ask both them younguns' there." She looked at Laurel and Beth. "Once I make up my mind, there's no changin' it."

Val looked at the two women between her and Ree.

Laurel held her hands up. "Don't look at me. I learned a long time ago, you can't move a mountain. You can go around it or over it. Either way it's easier to accept that the mountain is there and work with it." Laurel grinned and squeezed Val's hand. "I suspect you're starting to see that I come by my stubbornness honestly."

Val shook her head and took another bite of biscuit. "Agreed."

"Now that we've settled that, we need to finish up and get a move on, Beth."

Beth smirked and finished her breakfast.

"I'll get the dishes. You two head out to the store. If Val feels up to it, we'll drop by there after her appointment." Laurel rose and hugged her grandmother.

The four women finished breakfast in comfortable silences. Val had never, ever experienced such warmth and concern. She caught Laurel looking at her and reached out to hold her hand. The look that passed between them was pure love. Beth and Ree left as Laurel began to clear the table.

Val picked up a plate. "I can at least help with the clearing. I'm not sure how good a one-handed dish washer I'd be either."

Laurel smacked her forehead. "We should talk to Daren. He's probably analyzed the data from the last twenty-four hours." You need to go get ready. I'll clean up the kitchen. Your appointment is in two hours. Cat said there was a specific course of treatment she wanted you to follow. Something about teaching your deltoid muscle to assist the damaged tendons and muscles. I didn't understand all of it, but Fallon will."

Val kissed her and kept kissing her until Laurel's lips parted to allow her tongue to enter. With her good hand, she reached under Laurel's shirt to find the bare skin of her lower back. She let her fingers play in the hollow dip at the base of her spine and watched as Laurel's face took on one of desire. She kissed her again.

Laurel stepped back and took Val's hand out from under her shirt. "You play dirty, Viking. Go get ready."

Val leaned forward to kiss her again. "Yes, love."

Laurel finished everything and joined Val by the laptop at her bed. They found the cord Daren had given Val and logged onto The Bodyshop's website, entering the secure portal. They uploaded the data from the microprocessors in her prosthesis and were surprised as a video feature popped up with Daren's face. "Hey, Daren."

"Hey yourself, Val. Hi Laurel, everything good?

"Good to see you. I'm trying to make her behave. I've got a tough job."

Daren laughed, shaking his head. "No doubt about that. How'd the surgery go on the shoulder?"

Val looked thoughtfully at her friend. "Good. There was a lot more damage than expected. She thinks with therapy, I'll get full function back. How's the data look?"

"Looks like you have a pressure point down near the bottom. I'm going to make a slight adjustment. Try it today and we'll reevaluate. Other than that, it looks spot on. How's it feel?"

Val was pleased with how comfortable the new leg was and wanted to tell the world about it. "Really good. Maybe we should do some follow up articles on, you guys. I know the *Marine News* would carry it, as would *Stars and Stripes*. Maybe we could talk to some of the vets."

Daren nodded. "Get healed up first. You've got plenty on your plate, and we're about maxed out on how much work we can handle. We're considering opening up a branch office to help cover the need."

Laurel ran a hand through Val's thick hair. "That's fantastic, Daren. Give our love to Anya and Charley. I've got to get this one to therapy."

"Be a good girl, Val. Looks like your care is well in hand. Hugs to you both. I've got a dozen more of these to go. I just wanted to pop in and see how you were doing. Watch for red spots on your skin. They're pretty good indicators we need to adjust."

"Will do. Over and out." Val laughed and Daren signed off. "I need to get a new laptop, have my camera examined, and purchase some new lenses. The insurance company for the car that hit me basically said they would pay for replacements. I haven't talked to them about Maggie May. They may total it, but they aren't getting her. I'll take a settlement on it and fix her. She will ride again and so will I," Val said, her confidence soaring.

"You'll have plenty of time. Now let's get on the road." Laurel kissed her and pulled her up into her arms.

Tucked into Laurel's embrace, Val sighed. *No place I'd rather be.*

Twenty minutes later, they sat in the waiting room of Backbone Mountain Physical Therapy. Val needed Laurel to fill out most of her paperwork as she was right handed, but she didn't mind and looked around the waiting area instead. A young man sat with them, his young son on the floor between his feet coloring. Val watched the small dark-haired boy, his small hand clasping the bright red crayon. Her pulse began to race. She licked her lips and reached for her lip balm, putting on layer after layer. She began to become uncomfortably warm and pulled at her shirt. She could smell the explosives. Her chest began to heave. She felt a hand in hers and heard a far-off voice in the back of her mind.

"Val, you're in no danger. You're here with me, not in Iraq. Lift your right index finger up if you can hear me."

Val struggled to orient herself, the voice pulling her away from the darkness. Her lips felt so dry, and sweat rolled down her face.

"Val, you're at the physical therapist's office. You're in no danger, and I'm right here with you. Lift your right index finger."

The room came back into focus and the little boy held up the picture for his dad to see. Val felt Laurel's hand in hers, and she lifted her right index finger.

"Tell me who you are, where you were born, and why we're here."

"Valkyrie Magnusson. I was born in Seattle, Washington. We're at the physical therapist's office in West Virginia, and you're the love of my life, Laurel Anastasia Stemple." Val turned her head to Laurel, grateful for her lover's intuitiveness to her distress. Laurel was like the sunrise that broke the darkness of the night, flooding everything around it with warmth and light. Right now, Val could see the worry that shadowed her eyes and rubbed her thumb in those increasing frown lines between her eyes. She tilted her head. "I'm okay, promise." She watched Laurel visibly calm and slow her breathing.

"I'm going to get you something to drink. Sit still." Laurel got up and went out to the vending machine, returning with a bottle of orange juice.

Val accepted it and drank it down. She hadn't even realized how parched she was. The sharp tang tasted good. "Thanks. I don't know what happened."

"I think it was seeing the little boy and the crayon. You came out of it quickly," Laurel told her. "I'm still worried. Your color still isn't right."

Val closed her eyes. "I'm sorry." She didn't want Laurel to worry about her so much. The juice that had tasted good going down now turned to acid in her stomach.

Laurel's eyes grew soft and her face relaxed. "Love, there isn't anything to be sorry for. We'll deal with this together. You have a family who loves you, and there's nothing we won't do for you."

Val let all those words sink in. Family. It had never been a word to bring her comfort. Thinking of her father never brought a single kind word to her mind. Her mother, on the other hand, seemed to be trying. Not since her grandmother had she really thought about family and home. Laurel and Ree offered her a warm, loving home with people who weren't afraid to show their deep affection for each other.

A few minutes later, a tall athletic woman with a million dollar smile stepped through the waiting room door. "Hi, Laurel, this must be Val. I'm Fallon."

Val waved. "Val Magnusson. Nice to meet you."

"Come on back. Laurel's welcome to come with you if you want," Fallon said.

Val took Laurel's hand. "Can't imagine doing this without her."

They followed Fallon back to a treatment room. Val was still a little shaky from her flashback, but the feeling of Laurel's hand in hers helped her believe everything was possible.

Fallon read over Cat's surgical report and ran Val through a few range-of-motion tests. "This will need time to really heal before we can do much in the way of serious physical therapy. I'm sure they told you not to move your arm away from your body. Keep it protected in the sling. No driving for at least a week. We'll start you out with some cold therapy to decrease the swelling and then small exercises. If you work with me, I believe it will be fully functional after we're done."

Laurel spoke up. "Anything we can do at home?"

Val watched her lover with pride. *She's taking the bull by the horns that's for sure.* It had never been her way to let anyone else do things for her, but watching Laurel take care of her made her heart swell with deep affection. The therapy didn't worry her. She'd come through worse. Nothing could be as difficult as learning to walk without her natural leg. This would be a piece of cake.

Fallon made some notes. "A few small exercises and some cryotherapy. I'll show you what to do with a detailed list for you to follow. If we can, we'll meet twice a week."

"Laurel, will you be able to bring me?" Val asked, knowing she had the store to tend to.

Laurel squeezed Val's knee. "Won't be a problem. We'll make it happen."

Fallon rubbed her hands together. "Ok, let's do some measurements and an ultrasound treatment."

Val mentally prepared herself for the road ahead of her that would lead to being able to hold and touch Laurel with both arms, pain free. She looked at Laurel and reached for her hand. "Bring it on."

***

After the therapy session, they drove back to Cool Springs. Val settled in one of the rockers with her arm propped up on a pillow.

Laurel adjusted it. "You okay here?"

Val smiled at the adjustment, thinking about the care with which Laurel did everything. "Yeah," Val replied. "Do you have a laptop I could work off of to order a few things?"

Laurel ran her hand up and down Val's forearm. "Sure. I'll be right back."

Laurel weaved her way through customers who greeted her like a long-lost friend. She welcomed them all and checked on their needs. Val watched her lover, fully in awe of the woman she'd fallen head over heels for.

Wunder stopped by, handing her a glass of chocolate milk. "How's your arm?"

"It's on the mend, Wunder. Had a chance to go see the bike yet?" Val was confident of Wunder's ability to fix Maggie May. She couldn't wait until she had two arms to be able to help. She knew how to tear both the Indian's engine and fuel system down and put both back together.

"I stopped over on my way home the other day. It'll take some time, but don't worry. I ain't met a motor or a machine yet I can't get running." He shuffled his feet a bit, and then that peculiar look came over his face. "I was wondering, why is it that superheroes wear their underwear on the outside of their clothes?"

Val laughed and shook her head. "Beats me, Wunder, beats me."

Laurel came back with a small collapsible table and a laptop computer. She set it up in front of Val. "If you get tired, I can always run you to the house. I've got some accounting I need to do, and then the lunch crowd will invade."

Laurel headed back to the office area, while Val pulled up various sites to purchase a new laptop and some other equipment. She placed her order, pulled her phone from the breast pocket of her shirt, and dialed the office in Camarillo, California. She shifted in her seat. *I hope Jenny's in.*

"Rider Magazine, how may I direct your call?"

She smiled hearing the distinct California accent. "Hi, Angie, it's Val."

"Val! How are you? We've all been so worried about you." Angie covered the main desk at the home office.

"Had the shoulder repaired a few days ago, so I'm pretty sore, but I'm on the mend. Unfortunately, it's going to be a good while before I'm back up on two wheels."

"God, Val, we're all so sorry. You'd think all those public service announcements we do about watching for bikes, these accidents would go down. Anyway, I'm glad to hear you're up and around. Who'd you want to talk to? Mark and Greg are out. How about Jenny?"

"Jenny was exactly who I was looking for. Thanks, Angie."

A few seconds of southern rock wait music and Jenny's voice came on the line. "Val, how are you?" Jenny Smith was the current managing editor of *Rider Magazine* and a good friend of Val's.

"Hey, Jenny, slowly on the mend. Stopped in today to set up physical therapy sessions."

"Sounds like you're going to be sidelined for a while."

"Yes and no. I won't be able to ride until this shoulder is healed. I've got an idea, and I need a favor. Val tapped her fingers against her thigh as she waited for Jenny's response.

"Hit me."

"I'm staying with Laurel at Cool Springs. You remember that quirky little tourist trap I've written about?"

"Sure, it always gets great feedback from our readers."

Val knew Jenny was a great sounding board. More than once

they'd worked through an idea so that both parties came away with a good understanding of the final product expectation. "I'd like to do a series of articles about the store, the area attractions, and the off the beaten path rides. A little more in depth than normal since I won't be leaving this area for a good while." Val heard Jenny crack the gum she was chewing. It was a habit she had come to expect any time Jenny was contemplating something.

"I think we could make that work. You sure you're feeling up to that?"

"I think so. This area has all kinds of attractions like Blackwater Falls, Seneca Rocks, and Smoke Hole Caverns. I think it would shine a light on the area and expose our readers to a few things they might not see on a ride through on the main roads."

"I think it has great potential. The visuals should be fantastic."

Val went on to ask for her spare camera to be shipped and could hear the scratch of Jenny's pencil on paper.

Jenny sighed. "I was afraid you were going to tell me you were taking a complete break. You're our most popular contributor. We need to do an update on your accident so the readers know what's going on."

A warm feeling of appreciation washed over Val. "I thought of that, too. I'll work on it. Tell the boys I'm sorry I missed them."

Jenny snorted. "They're out testing the new sport bikes. I drew the short straw."

"Well then I'm happy to brighten your day with my call."

"Oh yeah, this was so much better than taking the new Ducati a few laps around Ventura." Jenny's sarcasm was legendary.

"Wow, you really did draw the short straw. Thanks again, Jenny."

"Take care, Val. Give us a call every once in a while. I'd rather hear your voice instead of just reading an email or text."

"You got it."

Now that her backup camera equipment would be shipped to her, Val could concentrate on getting her primary in for repair. She sent an email to the camera company, requesting a packaging set she could put her damaged items into and mail back. She was grateful most of her data was stored in the cloud, and she made arrangements to extract the rest of the information from her trashed external hard drive. Her new computer would be mailed to Ree and Laurel's, arriving in a few days. She'd need to have Laurel take her vehicle shopping at a later date.

The next item on her to do list, was to call her attorney who was dealing with the insurance issues from the accident. Smiling, she decided to do something nice for Laurel and Ree instead. There was a beautiful deck off the back of the house with a worn set of deck furniture that could use an update. She looked through several sets and found one that seemed to match the style of the house. She'd more than likely take an ass chewing for this one but still she clicked the purchase button. *Worth it.*

Laurel walked toward Val carrying a bowl of Frito pie. The dish involved corn chips, chili, melted nacho cheese, and a dollop of sour cream. She also carried a large glass of chocolate milk. Sitting it all down on a small table next to Val, she took the laptop and sat it off to the side. "You need to eat something and take a pill. I tried to come up with something you could eat one handed."

"Thanks. I haven't had this in a long time. You actually introduced me to this delicacy." Val grinned as she dug her fork into the lunch, recalling the first time she'd tried this meal years ago. She loved the way the corn chips crunched and blended with the sour cream. Laurel left her to her meal, pulled away by customers.

A few minutes later, Ree came out and pulled up a rocker, wiping her hands on her ever-present white canvas apron. "How ya feeling, Viking?"

"A little tired and glad to be back here. After I get the use of both of my arms back, I want to help out however I can. I love her. That goes for you too."

Ree had a big smile on her face. "Ya can help out by keeping my granddaughter happy. Don't have to tell me what I already know. I like seeing her smile. I don't want ya doing more than you're ready for. Ya gotta take time to heal up right or it's going to keep poking its ugly head up."

Shoveling another bite of Frito pie in her mouth, Val nodded. After taking a few minutes to chew, she looked at Ree. "I promise, Ree, I'm going to do everything in my power to keep that smile on her face."

Ree grew solemn. "She's got fears she hasn't told ya about yet, I'm sure of it. The fear about what might come in the future holds her back." Her tone grew stern. "You're the first person she's let in this far. I need ya to understand what that means."

This wasn't something that was easy for Ree to talk about, and the fact she was taking the time to enlighten Val didn't go unnoted. Ree was a woman who'd lived a long time and suffered more heartache than most. The loss of her husband at an early age, both of her daughters passing before her, and the concern for her granddaughter, shaped

Ree's life. She didn't take anything for granted and made sure those around her didn't either. She was allowing Val into her own personal demons, and Val felt unbelievably privileged. "Ree, I won't let her push me away. I've spent a lifetime running until I pulled Maggie May into your parking lot almost years ago. I love her in a way I didn't know was possible. I haven't figured out how to make everything work yet. Rest assured, I plan to be by her side if she'll have me. If she tries to push me away to protect me, I'll fight for her."

"I'll hold ya to that, Viking." Ree sat back in her rocker and closed her eyes.

Val finished her lunch while Ree swayed in the well-used wood rocker, her feet gently lifting and falling in a rhythmic pace as her hands rested on the smooth arms. Val noticed the laugh lines that creased the edges of her eyes and the corners of her mouth. She loved Ree and would hold the trust Ree put in her as one of her most treasured possessions. She got up to carry her dish to the kitchen and found Laurel stirring a large pot of hot dog chili. "Anything I can do to help?"

Laurel gave her a slow smoldering look. "Not a thing, but thanks for the eye candy."

Val raised an eyebrow and pulled her shoulders back, increasing the stretch of the t-shirt across her broad chest. "Glad to be of assistance. I'm going to grab a bottle of water. I suddenly feel a bit warm."

"Get out of here before I mess up an entire batch of chili." Laurel walked over and gave Val a kiss, pointing her out of the kitchen.

"I can see you're impervious to my charms today."

Now it was Laurel's turn to laugh. "Shows how much you know, Viking. All I'll say is, if you don't get out of here, I'm likely to take you into that back office and do unspeakable things to you."

"Hmm, then I'm not sure I want to leave."

"Go, you sweet talker."

Val winked and walked back through the swinging doors.

Chapter Twenty-Three

OVER THE NEXT FEW weeks, Val had slowly been working into therapy. She and Laurel had gone vehicle shopping, where she'd purchased a new Jeep Scrambler pickup just recently released to the market. She was still learning how to get in and out of it without the use of her right arm. Most days, Laurel drove. They'd all settled into an easy routine of family dinners using the new deck furniture she'd ordered, and nearly had to cut her own switch for. Ree had conceded, eventually admitting that it was now one of her favorite ways to spend an evening. She spent time at the store, and touring around the area. Her new magazine articles were becoming part of her routine.

Val placed a call to her editor and waited for the secretary to put her through. Hearing the familiar greeting, Val spoke up. "Hey, Jenny, it's Val. You should see my latest showing up in your inbox."

Jenny opened Val's latest submission. "Got it. The readers are loving this, Val. We've had great feedback. They seem particularly taken with Wunder and those hysterical questions. Several have commented on the recipes from Ree. I think we have a real winner here."

Val smiled at the praise. "I'm glad it's working. I've been basing all the routes from Cool Springs, trying to include a tidbit about the store, a recipe, a photo, or one of Wunder's questions." She'd seen the tremendous amount of light-hearted feedback. Wunder would beam as Val shared it with him. She'd even created a small icon of him with a glass of chocolate milk scratching his head to accompany the inquiry.

"How's the bike coming?"

"Wunder and I've been working on Maggie May every evening before he goes to watch his niece and nephews." Val marveled at his intuitive mechanic skills. "Bobeye's turned out to be an unexpectedly good body man. He's currently painting Maggie May's tins. It's slow progress, but we're getting there. I'll send some pictures with the next article." Val listened to the characteristic creak of Jenny's office chair. She could picture her leaning back and propping her feet on the desk, the same way she'd witnessed it many times in person.

"I'm glad things seem to be on the mend. You take care of yourself, Val."

Val was grateful for her friend's concern. "Thanks, Jenny, talk with you later."

Val likened the bike's restoration to her own healing process. Her body and head had been battered. She'd lost pieces of herself and needed replacement parts. Some parts still weren't working like they should. Yes, she and Maggie May had a lot in common, but she truly believed that her two-wheeled love was on the mend and so was she. Her friends and her lover were restoring her, piece-by-piece. The rough edges were being sanded and smoothed and the mechanics refined and tuned. Her flashbacks were far less frequent, and it took very little for Laurel to bring her out of them. Sometimes just the touch of her hand and a reminder she wasn't alone would do it. Laurel would have her focus on her face and that quickly made her realize she wasn't in Iraq. Every day that passed, they grew closer. Today, Val had plans for Laurel. She planned an entire day of touring activities throughout the area to take photographs and write up a few segments for the magazine. She also had a special event for this evening that kept her grinning.

A week ago, she and Laurel had traveled back to Bethesda for a follow up with Cat. She shook her head as thoughts of the appointment and how it had ended came back. Val could now laugh at the memory. At the time, it was anything but funny. The possessive kiss Laurel planted on her still lingered in her memory, seared into her skin. Eyeing her outfit, she got dressed for their adventure. Laurel convinced her to buy a pair of hiking boots and even tried to get her to wear shorts, at least around the house. Val had never gotten to the point she'd wear them outside, though. She was a quiet person by nature and wasn't ready for the questions or stares. Laurel tried to convince her that she was a hero, but Val didn't feel heroic and preferred not to talk about her military service too much outside her close circle of friends. Today she decided on a pair of light hiking pants and a white tank top. Part of the adventure was actually walking to the top of Seneca Rocks.

Laurel was in the kitchen preparing their backpacks with some snacks and travel essentials. A few pieces of Val's camera equipment would also be in there. Val was including a monopole she'd used occasionally in her work to avoid supporting the new camera body with her limited movement. The repair shop reported that the damage to her old one was too extensive to repair. She'd kept her damaged one as a reminder of all they'd seen together. It now proudly hung around the neck of the deer head wearing the Viking helmet with blonde braids at the store.

Laurel stood in the doorway, clad in hiking boots, a pair of pants that converted to shorts by zipping off the material at the knee, and a sleeveless shirt. "You about ready, baby?"

"Yup, I still can't button my pants." Val lifted one eyebrow. "Somehow, I think you enjoy doing that yourself. Interesting that the last jeans you bought me were button fly. Are you are taking advantage of my weakened condition?"

Laurel sauntered over and reached for the button at Val's waist, sliding her hand lower to cup her first. Val took in a sharp breath. Laurel bit her lip. "Would I do that?"

"You most certainly would. You'll hear no complaints from me. Although if you keep your hand where it's at, we won't be going sightseeing anytime soon." Val kissed her and slid the tip of her tongue across Laurels lips.

Laurel moaned. "You taste like peppermint. I think I'm starting to be like Pavlov's dog. Every time I smell peppermint now, I want to kiss you." She squeezed Val's backside and pulled the can out, opening it and using her finger to rub some of the peppermint balm across Val's soft lips.

Val's mother had found her grandmother's brand of the rosebud/peppermint balm and was sending her some every few weeks. She carried a can of it with her in her back pocket no matter where she went. Her jeans sported large worn spots resembling a smokeless tobacco ring. Liz had determined that the can acted much like a security blanket that her psyche used to soothe her mind anytime the flashbacks became too strong. Val's mother also sent along a card keeping her up to date on her own life. They got along much better now and communicated regularly with calls and email. She was even talking about coming to West Virginia for Christmas, if her schedule allowed.

Val kissed Laurel then pulled back. "Come on, I really want to climb today and if we don't get going, we won't be able to get to all the other things I want to see before we head to the meadow." Tonight was supposed to be perfect viewing conditions for the Perseid meteor shower, and Val didn't want to miss it.

Laurel's jaw fell open in mock disbelief. "Spoilsport. I never thought

I'd see the day you'd turn down getting naked with me for climbing a mountain."

"There's nothing more I'd rather do than make love to you. Don't ever doubt that." Val threaded her hand into Laurel's hair and tilted her face up. She and Laurel spent a few hours last night exploring every inch of each other's bodies before falling asleep with arms and legs entwined. They hadn't slept a night apart since they had stayed at Liz and Jo's the first time. On their last trip to Annapolis, Liz insisted on taking Laurel shopping, leaving Jo and Val to their own devices. Val used the time by taking Jo with her to do a little shopping of her own. "For now, this kiss is just a prelude to later." She kissed Laurel again, pulling her into her embrace.

They gathered their things and headed to the truck. Val opened Laurel's door, helped her in, and walked around to the driver's side. They drove to Seneca first, where they climbed to the top. Val was more than grateful for the latest micro adjustments Daren made to her leg. Sometimes she completely forgot about the prosthesis. The new sleeve and socket were beyond comfortable and allowed her to enjoy whatever activity she was involved in, without being consciously aware of it.

After a good hike, they reached the tower of rock known as Gendarme. They took a break from the heat. The sun was out and large white clouds floated across a vibrant blue sky. Val took out her camera and captured photos of peregrine falcons as they flew below her. She'd also turned the camera on Laurel several times without her knowing. Just as she turned the camera away from Laurel, her lover turned and sent her a blazing smile. *How many photos have I taken of her? And how in heavens name did I get this lucky?* She'd fallen in love with this amazing woman and everyone at Cool Springs with each click of her shutter. A slide show of images flooded her mind. She realized for the first time in her life, frame by frame, she was truly at peace.

Laurel blushed. "What are you looking at?"

Val leaned on the monopole and grinned back at the woman who'd captured her heart and freed her own damaged spirit. "The most beautiful thing I've ever seen. The woman I love."

"You looked like you were lost in a memory."

"No, love, just the opposite, I was found in one." She watched as Laurel furrowed her brow, but she kept the rest to herself, grabbing Laurel's hand instead and guiding her along.

They spent the rest of the day traveling to a few more sites before driving back toward home. They stopped at Hellbenders for supper on the way, enjoying the company of fellow diners while they watched the Pittsburgh Pirates and the Cincinnati Reds play baseball.

They finally arrived at the meadow Ree had named for her granddaughter. Laurel's Meadow was a beautiful rolling pasture with lush green grass and mountain laurel growing at the edges among the oaks and maples. At one time, the meadow was home to the cattle Ree and her husband owned. After his death, Ree sold some of the cattle and butchered a few, canning and freezing a good portion for use at the store so that nothing went to waste. Now the meadow was brush hogged off a couple of times a year by Mule and used to make high-grade hay for horses. They chose a section of the meadow that gave them a panoramic view of the mountains around them.

"Here, you blow up the mattress," Val said as she placed her camera on a tripod and adjusted the different settings to capture the meteor shower. She hoped to create something really special for Wunder and the kids. She'd grown fond of the three small children and found herself becoming the chief storyteller anytime the kids came by. She and Laurel had even taken them and Wunder on a few small adventures to places they'd never seen. They'd gone so far as to replace the Jeep Laurel owned, with one that could accommodate six passengers. She shook her head as she thought of Allie, Aaron, and Andru. She'd never thought about wanting children and there were days those three could try the sainthood of Mother Theresa.

Laurel set about making things more comfortable for viewing as they lay in the truck bed. "What are you smiling about?"

"I actually was thinking of the three musketeers." Val had given them the nickname and even tried to teach them the motto, *all for one and one for all*. Most of the time, the phrase didn't come out clearly or in the correct order as they tried to repeat it.

"What about them?"

"Just how much fun it is to watch their world open as we read to them."

Laurel wrapped her arms around Val's neck looked up at her. "Wunder, too. He hangs on your every word. Soaks it up like a sponge."

"He's a lot brighter than anyone gives him credit for. Not from education, I know. He's got an uncanny intuition. I'm not sure I've ever met anyone like him." She kissed Laurel, deepening the kiss by pulling her close.

As their lips separated, Laurel looked at her. "Wow. Where did that come from?"

Val pointed to her heart. "Here." She pulled out her phone and brought up a playlist of songs her grandmother had loved. Ones she'd heard many times when she was a child. She hit play and Nat King Cole's "Unforgettable" came pouring out. "Dance with me?"

Laurel nodded.

Val slipped her healing arm around Laurel's waist. She protested, only to be silenced by Val's lips against hers. "It's okay. There's no pain." Val pulled her closer and Laurel slipped both arms around her neck, her head on Val's chest. They swayed as Nat crooned. Next came a series of songs by Patsy Cline.

Laurel smiled. "Who knew you were such a romantic, Viking."

"Card carrying, for you and you alone." Val kissed her softly, allowing her tongue to seek out the depth of Laurel's mouth.

Laurel drew her tongue in and matched it with her own. As their bodies parted, she said, "I love the feeling of your body against mine. Just a few years ago, I could never have imagined loving anyone the way I do you. I wouldn't have allowed myself to imagine a future with anyone. Now I can't imagine not having you in my life."

"Me either, love." Val grinned at the way they'd settled into a relationship that filled all the voids in her heart and soul.

The music changed to a song by the band Halestorm, and Laurel leaned back to look at Val. "That's a pretty big style swing."

"True. Listen to the words closely," Val whispered, feeling the pressure of the small box in her pocket as she pulled Laurel tighter to her body. They swayed, listening to Lzzy Hale sing *I Am Beautiful With You.*

Val felt the words begin to wash over her about feeling beautiful because the one looking at her saw her exactly the way she was. As the song got to the part about her lover seeing all of her scars and still making her feel beautiful, Val kissed Laurel and then pulled back enough so she could tilt Laurel's head up to meet her eyes. She watched as tears rolled down Laurel's cheek.

"I want you to know that when I hear this song, I'm the one who feels beautiful, despite all my scars and imperfections. I'm the one who feels blessed because you see me exactly as I am, broken and yet mending. You bring me back from a world of death with a simple touch of your hand. Pull me from my nightmares with only the sound of your voice. I'm so deeply in love with you that I can't imagine a day without you in my life." She pulled out of Laurel's arms, reached into her pocket, and dropped to her good knee, feeling more confident about this than anything she'd ever done. "Laurel Anastasia Stemple, I've traveled all over the United States and places beyond our borders. I've never called anyplace home until I met you. I've never truly loved anyone until I met you, and I can't imagine spending a day without you by my side. Will you marry me?"

Laurel brought her hands to her mouth.

Val stayed on the bended knee and looked at her. After several late-night chats with Ree, she'd come to a full understanding of Laurel's fears. She and Laurel had talked about it, and she wanted her to have no doubts of how she felt. "I know your fears. I know you're afraid you'll develop cancer and leave me. Laurel, tomorrow I could do the same. I could drop over with a heart attack or something else. Whatever time I have left on this earth, I want it with you by my side as my wife. If that's one more hour, one more day, or one more year, then that's what I'll have. Say you'll fill those minutes, hours, and days with me." She pulled the diamond ring out of the box and held it up. "Say you'll marry me?"

Tears poured down Laurel's face as she stared at the engagement ring. She raised her eyes to Val's. "Yes, I'll marry you."

Val stood, her heart bursting with joy. The smile she felt was so wide it almost hurt. Against Laurel's protests about her shoulder, she picked her up and swung her around as meteors shot across the blackened sky above them.

She kissed Laurel then yelled to the heavens, "She said yes!"

"Put me down, you fool, before you hurt that shoulder." Laurel pulled her head down for another kiss.

She stopped spinning, allowing Laurel's body to slide down hers. With sure and steady hands, she grasped Laurel's left hand and slipped the diamond solitaire ring onto her finger.

Laurel stared at it and the tears began to fall again as Val's arms enveloped her. She placed her hand over her mouth and cried into Val's chest. "I love you, Val. I love you with so much more than I knew was possible."

Tears fell down Val's face too, a warm feeling spread from her chest as her resolve grew even stronger. "I feel the same, love. I spent years wandering around trying to find something I'd already found. I just couldn't bring myself to acknowledge it. I've loved you from the first day I saw you serving hot dogs and chocolate milk."

Laurel laughed and so did Val. "Oh, Viking, I wish I could have captured a picture of your face the second I offered you that combination." She kissed her and wiped at the tears rolling down Val's cheeks.

"It was a shock, I'll tell you that, but it was just the first leap of faith I wanted to take with you."

The two stared at the obsidian sky dotted with tiny pinpoints of light. For this one perfect moment, no more words were needed.

***

Laurel stood encircled in Val's arms, her head resting against Val's broad chest. The heartbeat below her ear was relaxed and steady. She looked at the diamond ring on her finger, closing her eyes against the rush of emotions she felt. Val asked her to marry her, to spend the rest of her life with her. It wasn't something she'd ever envisioned. To be honest it'd rarely seemed more than a distant possibility. Now she was committed, heart and soul, to the woman who held her.

She whispered into the hollow of her lover's neck. "I love you, Val." She kissed the tanned skin as her own breath quickened at the salty taste on her lips, and she began to open the buttons on Val's shirt, walking them backward toward the truck.

They crawled onto the air mattress and quickly divested themselves of the clothes separating them. Laurel settled herself on top of Val, straddling her and running a finger down her cheek, over her neck, and between the breasts that lay exposed before her. She kissed Val, sealing her lips to her lover's. She moved her hands to Val's breasts and rolled the nipples between her fingertips. Val's hips arched. Laurel sat back, reaching for her own breasts, touching them for Val's pleasure. She'd discovered this made Val's eyes go dark with desire and in turn, increased her own arousal. She touched herself as Val's hands roamed up and down her sides.

Val began to undulate her hips, grinding their centers together and wetness escaped from Laurel. Val slipped a hand between them and entered Laurel, who in turn rode Val's hand, clenching down on her lover's fingers. Laurel reached between her own legs with her left hand and brought the soaked fingers to Val's lips. Laurel felt her greedily suck them into her mouth and tongue each of her fingers along with the diamond ring.

"Like that?" Laurel whispered, smiling.

Val groaned and protested when Laurel removed her fingers, wet them again, and brought them back to her lover's lips once more. Val tensed, urging her to move up her body.

"Val, your shoulder."

"It's fine. Please? I want you in my mouth."

Laurel could no more deny Val this than deny that she loved her with all she was. She was still worried about causing Val pain. As soon as Val's tongue hit her center, all thought shattered. She spread her hands on the truck bed and allowed Val to devour her. She felt the soft tongue stroke her and enter her, driving her to release with broad strokes and light flicks over her clit. Her breath quickened. She looked down at Val whose eyes met hers. Her orgasm built. Val again drew her clit in between her lips. Laurel's body shook and stiffened as the orgasm washed over her.

She threw her head back and cried out into the star-filled sky. Crying one name. The name that meant more to her than life itself. "Val!"

Val changed her stroke to soft passes allowing the climax to be drawn out. Finally, the tremors subsided and Val urged her down and into her arms. Laurel's rapid breath calmed and the pulse pounding in her chest slowed. After a few minutes, she kissed Val's chest. "That was incredible."

"Yes, you were." Val grinned, raising Laurel's left hand so that they both could look at it.

Laurel buried her face deeper in Val's neck. "Not something I expected, Viking."

"I know. I'm beyond happy you said yes. Every time I came back, I was trying to show you how much you'd come to mean to me. Ree's crisp is amazing, but it wasn't what brought me back time after time."

Laurel rose up on her elbow, staring at her, realizing her love for Val had grown deeper over the years and the need for her had grown larger every time she rode away. "I was so scared when I thought I'd lost you."

"The accident made me realize I couldn't keep riding away from you."

Laurel settled back down into Val's arms. "What do we do now, Viking?"

"For right now, we lay here and watch this incredible nature show above us. I take a few more pictures and then we make love until we fall asleep."

Laurel snuggled into Val's side. "I like that idea. I was thinking a little farther than just tonight. Are you really ready to settle down for good? I have Gram and the store. I can't take off and follow you."

Val entwined their fingers. "I've never been more ready in my life. I've never called any place home before because no place has ever felt like home until I came here. Home is where you and Ree are. I asked her permission to marry you, you know."

"What?" Laurel tried to sit up, but Val held her tighter. *She asked my grandmother? Oh Viking, you never cease to amaze me.*

Val chuckled and kissed the top of Laurel's head. "I said, I asked Ree for her permission to marry you."

Laurel smiled at the sweet gesture and kissed her. "Thank you, baby, for including her." She started to think about all the other parts of Val's life. "What about your work?"

"Ree is a big part of who we are as a family. Now in reference to work, I've talked with the magazine. I'll do a few feature pieces a couple of times a year. I'll expand the blog and believe it or not, I've had requests for more of the post cards we've been selling at the store. I can expand the nature shots and maybe sell them to a few of the magazines I've submitted photos to over the years. The point is, I have my marine disability, my photography, and blog enterprise. That's not even mentioning the substantial trust fund that Grandmother Magnusson left me. Our family claim to fame is holding several patents on specific gel inks. The family we create won't have to worry about money."

Laurel squinted at Val. *Trust fund? She's never mentioned that. Was she afraid I was a gold digger?* "Val, I don't want your money. I want you."

Val reached to her side and drew the sleeping bag over them both. She shook her head. "I know that. I didn't mention it because it's never been important to me. Most of the time, I don't even think about it at all. The majority of it I haven't even touched since I've spent most of my life in either the military or on the back of a bike. Now that money can help do a lot for any renovations we would want to the store or the house. I asked you to marry me and you said yes without knowing I had a single dollar to my name." Val traced her lips. "Once we're married, that money will be used for building the life I never knew I could have. My grandmother would have wanted that." She stroked Laurels cheeks with her thumbs and smiled. "Or it will make a nice college and trust fund for our kids."

Laurel propped herself up on her arms, her mouth fell open. "Our kids?"

Val smirked and tapped the end of Laurel's nose. "Don't tell me you don't want them. I know better. I've seen you with the three musketeers. I want them, too. If you don't want to carry them, then we'll adopt. There are thousands of kids that need good homes, and we could provide that. You don't have to decide tonight. I know you and I know me. I also know there's a five foot nothing spitfire who wants great grandchildren." She held up Laurel's left hand. "I'm pretty sure once Ree sees that ring, she's going to start knitting baby booties and quilting a baby blanket."

Laurel laughed and rolled to Val's side, looking her in the eye and kissing her softly. "Valkyrie Vör Magnusson, have I told you how much I love you?"

"Yes, but I could stand hearing it a few million times more."

Laurel pulled on Val's hand and encouraged her to roll on top of her. She began a slow smoldering kiss that she knew would lead them back to the edge of ecstasy and beyond.

***

The next morning, Val woke up spooning Laurel's back. It was warm inside the sleeping bag.

"We've got to get up." Laurel pulled Val's hand tighter between her breasts.

"I know. Just not ready to go back to the real world. I want to spend a few more minutes with my bride-to-be."

Laurel raised her hand and gazed at the diamond ring. "How soon were you thinking we should have the wedding?"

Val kissed Laurel's bare shoulder. "The sooner the better. I've spent enough time without you. We need to decide soon so we can give everyone enough notice. Liz and Jo, and my editor, Jenny."

Laurel turned her head slightly toward Val. "And your mom. I'm not going round and round with Cruella because you didn't invite her."

Val snickered at Laurel's nickname for her mother. "I know. Anyone else on your list?"

"You've met the people who are important to me."

Val stretched and shifted. "I want Jo to stand with me, figuratively speaking. Although she does have that fancy chair she built to help her stand."

Laurel rolled on top of Val, resting her head on her crossed hands. "Bobeye and his family. Mule, too. Allie can be the flower girl! She'll love that. I think at six she'll know what to do, right? The boys can walk with her as our ring bearers. I'll ask Beth to be my maid of honor, and Liz can be a bridesmaid. Oh, and the crew from the store has to come."

Val laughed at Laurel's rapid fire thought process. "Liz and Jo will have a few things to say about me popping the question. They even had a hand in this proposal. Jo went with me to pick out your ring while Liz kept you busy shopping on our last trip."

"You're kidding. Those sneaks! I love them both. Thank you for bringing them into my life." She wrapped her arms under Val's shoulders, allowing her head to settle just under Val's chin. "And I love you, more and more every day."

Val kissed Laurel. "I love you too. I'm not sure how Jo and I kept a straight face that night."

They lay together as the sun came up over the horizon, eventually deciding it was time to head to the house to shower and get ready to go to work at the store. They knew both Ree and Beth would be beyond excited, and they wanted to announce their engagement to everyone. That would lead to figuring out a time and place to hold the ceremony. It was a little past seven as they made it back home. Ree and Beth were gone.

Val watched as Laurel stared at the ring on her hand. She drew Laurel's hand in her own and kissed each knuckle. "Believe it, and this. I'll marry you today, tomorrow, or whenever you want. I'll spend the rest of my life waking with you every morning. We'll laugh and cry together, because a love this strong has no choice but to grow."

"I love you so much, Val. Unfortunately, if we don't finish what we came in here for, we're going to be behind all day."

They needed to get to the store. Gram would be busy baking pies, and Beth would be running things until they got there. Val wanted to write up yesterday's adventure for *Rider Magazine* and work on Maggie May after Wunder finished his shift.

Val smiled as Laurel rested her hand on her thigh while they drove. She kept stealing glances at the sparkling diamond, her heart filled with warmth. She remembered sitting out on the deck with Ree a few weeks ago.

Val raised a glass of lemonade gathering her courage. "Ree, I need to ask you something."

Ree sat flipping cards on a table in a game of solitaire. "Ask away. Ha! Ace. What can I do for ya?"

Val sat up straight and put her hand on Ree's arm. "Ree, you know I love Laurel, don't you?

"Never had any doubt. Ya gonna tell me something I don't know?"

Val shook her head and laughed. "Ok, how about I want you to know I'm hanging up my rambling boots." She turned the formidable woman to her. "Ree, I'm asking for Laurel's hand. I want to spend the rest of my life right here with her and all the rest of you I've come to call family. May I have your permission to ask Laurel to marry me?"

Ree narrowed her eyes and smiled at Val. "Well, it's about damn time."

Val was stunned. In all the time she'd known Ree, she'd never heard the woman cuss. She broke out into a shaking laugh. After she'd been able to bring herself under control, she hugged Ree. "I have to agree. Now, I've got some planning to do."

"Penny for your thoughts." Laurel took her hand from Val's leg and pulled off the leather ball cap. Placing it on her own head, she ran her fingers through Val's hair.

Val stuck her tongue out. If someone told her seven years ago, she'd be engaged and settling down in the mountains of West Virginia, she'd have told them they'd lost their mind. Here she was, putting down roots in a place where her wife-to-be's family had been born and raised.

"I was thinking about your roots. They run over a hundred years deep in these mountains. Now here I am, being grafted into this amazing family I never knew I could have. I'm thinking about how damn lucky I am."

"It's not just you. I've spent most of my life believing I was living on borrowed time, constantly waiting for the other shoe to drop." At that statement Val furrowed her brows and Laurel paused. "Oh, I didn't curl up in a corner. I just wouldn't let myself believe I could share my life with anyone. I thought it wasn't fair, because I might not be able to give them long. And then this tall Viking rode up on a gleaming black Indian. She was decked out in black leather, wearing a million-dollar smile, and that all went out the window."

"Thank God." Val laughed and pulled into the store.

They came in the back door so Ree would be the first one they would see. She was leaning over the counter, her hands covered in flour.

"Morning, Gram."

"Morning, you two. How was the star gazing?" Ree rolled out dough for fried apple pies.

Val walked over and popped a piece of scrap dough into her mouth, trying to hide her grin.

"Pretty spectacular if I do say so myself. Funny thing, one of those stars fell out of the sky as a diamond and ended up right here." Laurel reached out and put her left hand down on her grandmother's arm.

Ree's eyes lit up, and she yelled for joy. "Hallelujah. I got to thinking I was going to have to pop the question for both of ya. Gracious. Oh, honey, I'm so happy for ya." Ree wrapped her arms around her granddaughter and held her tight. She extended an arm and pulled Val in with them. "I've thought of ya like family for a long time, Val. Now ya officially will be."

Beth walked in and saw the embrace. "Hey, am I missing out on a group hug or what?"

Laurel tilted her head out of the circle, grinned at Beth, and held out her hand.

Beth's eyes grew wide, and her hand shot to her mouth. "Oh my God, Laurel!" She ran across the kitchen stopping to kiss Val on the cheek before wrapping her best friend up in a hug. They jumped up and down. "Jumping off Seven Island bridge doesn't hold a candle to this!"

Val couldn't help but smile. She looked at Ree who had her arms crossed.

"Those two sometimes don't use the sense the good Lord gave them." She rubbed Val's back and went back to rolling out her dough.

Val had to hold the stitch in her side that developed while laughing at Ree's assessment.

Beth peppered them with orders and questions. "We've got so much work to do. We have to plan the wedding and the reception. We have to go shopping. Where are you going to have it? When?"

Val laughed, crossing her arms. "You tell me where to be and the time to be there. If you need help, ask. I have no doubt the two of you will have it in hand."

Laurel and Beth both turned to Val, hands on hips. "Oh no you don't. This wedding is yours too." Laurel squinted at Val. "Your list is coming, trust me."

Val raised her hands in surrender. "Name it, and I'm on it."

They spent the rest of the morning and afternoon working at the store. Val had set up a small work area over in the sit-a-spell. Her cellphone rang. She looked at the display and laughed. "Hey, Jo."

Jo's voice boomed. "Don't hey me. Give! What did she say?"

Val fessed up. "What do you think she said? She said yes!"

She could hear Liz yelling in the background over Jo's congratulations. "Fantastic. When's the hitchin'?"

"We haven't set a date yet, but we're working on it. I imagine it's going to be an evening ceremony so everyone here can attend if they want. Where, I have no idea. I do have a question for you. You'll stand with me, won't you? I've already told Laurel I want you to, but I wanted to make the formal request."

Jo chuckled. "It would be my honor to stand beside you. Someone has to keep you from making an idiot of yourself."

"Then the job's yours. She was quite happy with the ring we picked out."

"Told ya. You let us know the date of this shindig, and we'll be on our way. Any clue about the dress code yet?"

"Uh, no. That's Beth and Laurel's department. I have a list of things that I'm responsible for, although I have yet to see it."

"We're so happy for you. I can tell you from experience, there's nothing like it."

"Amen to that, Jo. I best go check with the boss of me to see what my marching orders are. I'll let you know details as soon as I get them. My love to Liz there in the peanut gallery."

She could hear a faint, "Love you too," as they said their goodbyes.

Val worked through the day on her story and her postcard venture. Laurel called her into the back for a late lunch, and they ate together around the island. Ree was baking cookies with the biggest smile on her face Val had ever seen.

After lunch, Val went to find Wunder so they could go work on the bike at Bobeye's garage. Val's current job was sanding the fenders Bobeye had painstakingly pounded and rolled out and back into their original form. She laid the fender across her lap and wet sanded the primer. It brought her great satisfaction to be making progress on the bike. Wunder had the engine block out and was working on the cylinders, rings, and pistons. The smell of the grease and oil put her at ease. She was fascinated watching Wunder work. He'd already taken apart the fuel system and replaced anything that couldn't be fixed. Val had found a site on the internet that specialized in vintage motorcycle parts.

She cleaned her hands and dialed. They knew her by the sound of her voice. "Hey, Terry, I've got a few things for you to look for."

Terry Austin owned Vintage Iron in Boise, Idaho. He was a magician at finding rare motorcycle parts and accessories. Val tried to imagine what the gruff voiced man looked like. He answered in his deep Midwestern accent.

"Hey, Val," Terry growled. "What impossible to find part are you looking for today? You sure don't make it easy on a guy."

She placed an order for a few things and then asked about something special she wouldn't reveal to anyone until she was sure it could be done.

Val held the phone with her shoulder as she went back to sanding. "You think you can find one in the next few months?"

"I wouldn't get your hopes up too high. It'll be a challenge, and it won't be cheap."

"You just find it, Terry, and I'll worry about the cost." Val always tried to picture the man she'd been doing business with almost once a week for the last month. She could only imagine a hulk of a man typing hunt and peck style on a dirt stained keyboard.

"I'll see what I can do, Val. How's the Indian coming?"

"Every day, she's a little closer. We're taking our time to do it right."

"Nothing else would do it justice if you didn't. I'll get to work finding what you need. I'll call you in a few days to let you know if I have any leads."

Excitement coursed through her. "Thanks, Terry, talk to you in a few." She disconnected the call, looked over at Wunder, and waited.

"I wonder, since everybody says that's the best thing since sliced bread, what do you reckon was the best thing before sliced bread?" He went back to the engine block.

Val glanced at Bobeye who was doing his best to stifle a chuckle. Shaking her head, she went back to sanding.

Chapter Twenty-Four

THREE WEEKS LATER, VAL waited at the back of the chairs lined up among the trees in the play area of the Cool Springs Store. They'd set the wedding near the big steam engine adjacent to the water wheel. Laurel, Beth, and Ree were inside the store. Marion and John had ridden in for the occasion. Ree closed the place for the entire day so they could do food preparation for the reception and no one had to work the evening shift at the diner. They'd put up road signs all around the area about the store being closed for a private event, alerting those passing through. They'd even advertised it in the paper and posted notices on the community bulletin boards.

The store had only been closed three times since Ree had owned it. The first time was after her husband had been killed and the other two times were for the funerals of her daughters. Ree was happy, for once, to be closing for a joyful occasion. Most everyone from the area was aware that Laurel Stemple was marrying the woman from Seattle who'd stopped there almost five years ago and stolen her heart.

Val's mother straightened the black bow tie at her neck and ran her hands down Val's silk lapels. "You look handsome, my dear, even if you are wearing blue jeans." Amanda smiled. "Grandmother Magnusson would have been thrilled to be here."

"I feel her here." Val pulled out the tin of peppermint balm and smoothed some over her lips. "And this," Val held up the tin, "makes me feel like she is." She reached out and hugged her mother. It was unusual for them to display any kind of affection, but Val wanted her to know how happy she was for her to be there. For the briefest second, she felt her mother stiffen, and then finally relax into the embrace.

"I can still see the tomboy running into the house with her camera, excited to have me send the film off to be printed."

Val laughed at the memory. "Thank you for being here, Mother."

"Oh, Valkyrie, I know I haven't been the mother you needed or deserved. Somehow, we've found our way back. I'm grateful that you still let me be a part of your life. Almost losing you twice made me realize how precious you are to me. I'm sorry for all those years we spent at odds." Amanda's eyes misted.

Val looked into her mother's eyes, her own eyes watering a bit. "I am too, Mother. The past is just that. I'm glad you're here."

Jo wheeled up beside her. "It's time."

The music started and Val's heart raced. Soon, she would stand in front of her friends and family waiting on the woman who had made this miracle possible.

***

Laurel grinned as Beth fussed with the hem of her wedding dress. The dress was a simple ivory eyelet design that fell softly on Laurel's shoulders, tapering in at her waist and then flowing down to just above her knees. Her long hair was pinned up, chestnut ringlets falling around her face and neck.

Laurel looked up at her grandmother who stood close to tears. Her heart melted, and she felt her chest grow tight.

"Not sure where that little girl went who'd sit at my side for hours listening ta my stories. Seems like yesterday she was runnin' through the yard at dark catchin' lighting bugs in a mason jar." She reached into the pocket of her dress, pulled out a delicate handkerchief and wiped at a tear threatening to escape. "I declare, I might be a bit partial, but you're the most beautiful young lady I've ever seen. I love ya honey, and I couldn't be happier to be here to walk ya down the aisle."

"Gram, I don't know that I've ever been this nervous in my life."

"Do ya love her?"

"Oh God, with all my heart."

"Do ya want to be with her for the rest of your days?"

Laurel's face beamed with happiness. "Without a doubt."

"Do you believe she loves ya?"

"Unconditionally."

Ree scoffed and reached out to hold Laurel's hands in hers. "Then that's as clear as mud. I could see why ya'd be nervous. Honey, she loves ya and thinks ya hung the moon and stars. Perfectly good reasons to be nervous." Ree looked at her granddaughter and shook her head.

"I get it, Gram, I've never been so sure of anything. My lingering doubts about my health, Val's devotion and what it all means, are gone. Today I'll say 'I do' to the woman I love more than I knew was possible."

Ree released her hands and held out her arm to Laurel, as they headed to the door. "Times a wastin' so let's get this shindig started. I've got dancing to do afterward."

Laurel looked at her grandmother who'd raised her to be the woman she was and said a silent prayer of thanks that she was still here today to walk her down the aisle. She kissed her temple as she threaded her arm through the one that had held her as a child. "Lead on, Gram."

***

Val took her mother's arm as the quartet from Aurora Celtic played "Aurora Morning." Allie, Aaron, and Andru walked down the aisle with Wunder with Liz behind them, spreading mountain laurel all the way to the altar. Val thought the boys looked adorable in their blue jeans and bow ties. Jo wheeled down the aisle with Beth at her side and they took their places. Val escorted her mother to her seat in the front row and took her place beside Jo, who'd used her chair modifications to stand at Val's side. She could feel the butterflies fluttering through her stomach and pulled at her collar. She couldn't wait to see Laurel, who'd forbidden her to even peak at her dress before the wedding.

"Don't lock your knees. You'll faint," Jo chided.

Val shook her head. "How would you know, goofball?"

"Just trust me. I almost fainted watching Liz walk down the aisle to me and was mighty grateful for this chair to hold me up. You go down and I'm taking pictures, Jarhead."

The music changed to John Legend's "All of Me" as those in attendance got to their feet. Val got her first look at her bride to be and felt her knees go weak. Laurel stared back at her with a wide smile and a twinkle in her eyes so bright, it could outshine the stars. Her dress was perfectly tailored for her gorgeous figure. Val watched as she came closer, holding on to Ree who was sporting an equally wide smile. The glisten in her eyes almost broke Val. She staggered ever so slightly and felt Jo beside her.

"Told ya," Jo said, putting a hand on Val's back to steady her.

As the music played, Laurel walked arm in arm with her grandmother until they reached the altar. Ree put Laurel's hand in Val's and pulled both women down for a kiss. She turned and took her seat.

Fallon's wife, Lindsey, was performing the ceremony and looked at both women. "We're gathered here together to join Laurel Anastasia Stemple and Valkyrie Vör Magnusson in holy matrimony. To seal their bonds of commitment and devotion by the giving and receiving of rings. The words they will speak and the observance of those who will bear witness to this day, will stand forever in time as a turning point for them both. No longer will they travel life's road alone. Hand in hand, they'll greet each moment knowing they have someone to lean on."

Val looked at Laurel and was barely able to draw a full breath. Even though she could hear Lindsey, her voice sounded a million miles away. All she could see was the beautiful woman before her, about to become her wife. A gentle squeeze of Laurel's hand brought Val back to the present just in time.

Lindsey looked to those in attendance. "Laurel and Val have chosen their own vows." She stepped back.

Laurel drew in a deep breath. Her voice trembled. "Val, they say that to appreciate what you have, you must let go of what you have lost. For a long time, I thought it unfair to take someone's heart if there was a chance I'd break it by dying. You made me realize that if you don't live, you're already dying each day. You made me see a future, a life of love and passion. I'll love you in this life and whatever life comes next with all my heart. To you, I give my solemn vow to love, honor, and cherish you, in sickness and in health." She turned to Beth and took the ring from her. She slipped the wide gold band, embossed with mountains and the sun, on the ring finger of Val's left hand. "With this ring, I bind my heart and soul to you."

Val turned to Jo who winked at her and handed her Laurel's wedding band. She took a deep breath trying to calm her nerves and remember all the things she wanted to say. "Laurel, family is an interesting word. There's family that you are born into," she paused and looked at her mother and smiled, "and family you choose." She looked over to Ree, and then turned back to Laurel. "I'm grateful to have both. I've seen sunrises on the east coast and sunsets on the west, so magnificent in color, they would rival any artists painting. I've seen triumph and tragedy in a land far away. I've had hopes and dreams realized and dashed. I've seen love in the faces of families all over. I never realized how badly I needed my own family until I met you and Ree. You also helped build the bridge between my mother and me. I fall asleep each night secure in the thought that I'm loved beyond what I ever deserved. I rise each morning with a fire inside of me that no cold can drive out, because it's fed by your love and the family we've made."

She slipped the matching gold band onto Laurel's ring finger. "To you I give my solemn vow to love, honor, and cherish you, in sickness and in health. With this ring, I bind my heart and soul to you."

Lindsey stepped back to them and wrapped their crossed hands with a wide navy-blue ribbon, trimmed in gold. "This tie isn't the one that binds you to one another. It's merely a symbol of the vows you've made. Love binds you together. As your hands are bound, now your hearts are also. Your hands are crossed as symbol of infinity. The life energy flows out of one and into the other and back again, continuously. What has been bound together by love cannot be torn apart. By the powers vested in me by the State of West Virginia and by the constitution of the United States, I now pronounce Val and Laurel wed. You may seal your vows with a kiss."

"Thank God," Val said, stepping forward and drawing Laurel into her arms. Their lips met in a passionate kiss interrupted by wolf whistle calls from the crowd. Shouts of congratulatory joy rose from those gathered, along with loud clapping of hands and Jo's ear-piercing whistle.

Val tucked Laurel's left hand into the crook of her arm and led her back down the aisle between their friends and family. Reaching the last row, Val kissed Laurel and turned to the crowd. "Come on everyone, the party's just getting started. You're all welcome to join us in the tent set up out back."

Laurel and Val positioned themselves at the entrance to the tent so they could greet those in attendance and accept their congratulations. As each person filed past, the words of wisdom and happiness filled them both. The meet and greet finished, Val cleared her throat. "Laurel and I thank you all for being here. Please feel free to dig into the buffet while we take some photos."

There had been another photographer hired to take pictures of the ceremony and the reception, but Val had asked Jenny to take a few personal photos, too. Jenny was just as proficient with a camera as Val. They posed for family pictures with Ree and Val's mother, including the wedding party. The others went back inside and the couple took a few simple shots gazing at each other, the rings on their hands, and a simple kiss. Val picked Laurel up and swung her around filled with pure love and tremendous joy.

Laurel squealed. "Val, put me down!"

Ignoring Laurel's protests, Val continued to hold her, one arm around her back and the other under her knees, cradling her like a precious gift. "Not a chance, my love. You belong in my arms."

Jenny's shutter clicked rapidly, capturing every unscripted moment. They stood on the front porch of the store to snap a shot of the quirky Cool Springs sign.

Laurel cupped Val's chin. "You tear that shoulder up again, and I'll kill you."

"I'll die a happily married woman." Val squeezed Laurel tighter.

They finished the photo session, and grabbed plates of their own. Val had only been able to manage a few pieces of toast for breakfast because her nervous stomach had threatened a revolt at anything beyond that and coffee. Starving and looking forward to sitting down, the couple found a seat with Ree in the middle of the crowd. The local fire department roasted a pig for the large BBQ style buffet, and Ree and the twins had prepared an array of side dishes from baked to green beans, wilted lettuce salad with hot bacon dressing, potato salad, biscuits, and an assortment of desserts. They'd catered the cake out and had a special cake topper ordered with one figure wearing a motorcycle jacket and the other an apron. Aurora Celtic was playing for entertainment after the meal, so Val encouraged them to eat with the guests. After Val finished eating, she made her way around the crowd, making sure to thank everyone for coming. She looked up and saw Laurel waving for her to come to the front.

"Hi, baby," Laurel said, kissing her.

"Hello, my gorgeous wife. What can I do for you?"

"It's time for the toasts and to cut the cake."

Val beamed. "Okay."

Jo rolled up beside Val and used her chair to stand up. She raised her glass and began to speak. "I met Val several years ago, as we both were recovering at Bethesda. To be honest, she was probably ready to kill me, because I forced her to get up and chase me around the wards. I knew she had so much more life to live. I remember the day I was positive Val was in love. She stopped at our place after one of her cross-country rides and all she could talk about was this little store that served the best chilidogs she'd ever eaten. She also told me there was a woman there who was like warm sunshine."

"After meeting Laurel for the first time, I knew exactly what she meant. Laurel and Val, I wish you both a lifetime of love, happiness, and the laughter to see you through any storm." Jo looked to Liz who handed her a basket with three items. "The Italian in me, and at a threat from Noni Romano, blesses your marriage with the following. The bread is so that you will never know hunger. The salt is so your marriage will always have flavor, and lastly the wine is so that you will celebrate your whole life through. Laurel, good luck with this one. You've got your work cut out for you. Val, even a blind dog finds a bone every once in a while, and Jarhead, somehow, you and I managed to do just that." Jo raised her champagne glass. "Salute!"

Val turned and hugged Jo, with Laurel following suit. "Thanks, Dogface," Val whispered to her friend. She was grateful for Jo to see her at this stage in her life knowing she'd witnessed a big part of the worst of it. Now she got to see the best of it.

Beth stood and wiped tears from her eyes. She reached for Laurel's hand. "How do I even begin? Laurel and I have been like sisters for over twenty years. We've laughed more times than we can count. We've shared our ups and downs, our heartaches, and our most incredible moments. There's no one I trust or love more. You made me a part of your family and now you've expanded it by taking the biggest leap of faith in your life. I know you have a lifetime of adventures yet to come with Val at your side. You will always have each other. Val, I trust you with my sister and best friend. I know you'll keep her safe and protected. I know you'll love her, and be in love with her for the rest of time. I've watched this love grow for five years, waiting for one of you to wake up and realize what was right in front of you. I'm grateful we don't have to wait any longer." Beth turned to the crowd laughing. "Raise your glasses in a toast to Laurel and Val."

Cheers went up throughout the crowd as they toasted the couple. After the toast, they cut the cake and both sweetly fed the other a small piece without smearing it on each other's face, although Val did put a little bit of icing on Laurel's lips so she could kiss it off. The band began to play, and the couple took to the floor. For their wedding dance, Val and Laurel had asked the band to play Stevie Nicks and Don Henley's *Leather and Lace*. As the voices crooned about being lovers forever, Val pulled Laurel close to her and held her left hand to her chest as they danced, occasionally kissing her bride. Even with her prosthetic, Val was a good dancer. The two women melted into each other.

Val whispered, "Hi there, Mrs. Magnusson-Stemple, how do you feel?"

"Magnusson-Stemple, huh?"

"I've thought a lot about it. It's you that has the deep roots here where we will make our home. If someday we decide it's time for kids, I want them to have the Stemple name."

Laurel buried her face in Val's neck, tears trickling from her eyes. "Good thing I don't wear mascara, because it would be running down my face. Have I told you how much I love you?"

Val kissed her. "Yes, but I'll never get tired of hearing it."

Their wedding dance ended, and Val took Laurel over to her grandmother so that they could share a dance. Val reached out her hand for her mother's. Amanda blushed and then stepped into her arms.

"It was a beautiful ceremony, Valkyrie. You're lucky to have found your soul mate," Amanda said as they danced.

"That I am, Mother. I'm glad you enjoyed the wedding."

Amanda leaned back to take in Val's wide smile. "I enjoy seeing you so happy, that's all a parent could ask for their child."

"I'm happy, Mother."

Val looked over at her wife dancing hand in hand with Ree. Their smiles were wide, and she could tell Ree was having a great time. The band had struck up Patsy Cline's "Walking after Midnight." It was quite a sight to see Ree kicking up her heels and spinning out on her granddaughter's arm.

They invited the crowd to join them and soon everyone was doing the 'Electric Slide' and a few other group dances. They delighted in the sight of the three musketeers holding hands and dancing in a circle, shirttails untucked. Val helped Allie dance on the top of her shoes while Wunder and the boys danced with Laurel. Jo had Liz in her lap, spinning around the floor.

Laurel and Val had asked everyone who wanted to give them a gift to fill a large pickle jar with donations instead. The money would be divided between Gary Sinise's charity and Betty's Bus, which offered free or low-cost mammograms to women whenever the mobile clinic came to their community. Surprisingly, everyone complied with the newlyweds' wishes and soon a second jar had to be found.

It was closing in on midnight when Val and Laurel announced they would be leaving. Val had one more surprise for her new wife and she was buzzing with anticipation. There was a crew on standby to clean everything up after the last reveler left and a group of designated drivers to take partygoers home or to rented cabins. Val kissed her mother, thanked her for coming, and then kissed Ree. "Thank you for believing in me and making me a part of this family."

Ree patted her hand. "No thanks needed, honey. Take care of my Laurel there. That's all I can ask for."

"That's a promise."

Ree opened her arms and Laurel stepped into them. "Liebchen, I couldn't be happier for ya. Live every day, child. This is the ice cream on the crisp."

Crying, Laurel choked out her reply. "I will. I love you, Gram."

Within minutes, Val and Laurel were headed up the mountain. They turned off the highway and onto the road leading to Laurel's Meadow. Laurel glanced over at Val. "I'm going to be patient because this is your surprise, my love."

Val grinned. They broke into the clearing and Val headed toward a glowing tent, glancing every so often at the look of awe on Laurel's face.

"What in the world?"

Val chuckled, hefting a bag she'd hidden in the back of the truck and motioning her forward. "It's called a yurt. I wanted something different that we could stay in whenever we needed to get away."

Laurel put her hands on her face, staring. "Oh, Val."

They walked up to the tent-like structure. "I stayed in one out in Montana once." Val thought the cloth and wooden structure fit perfectly in with the surrounding landscape. "It gives us more room than a camper, and it won't feel like a box."

Val swept Laurel up into her arms. She cradled Laurel, kissed her, and carried her across the threshold.

Chapter Twenty-Five

LAUREL HELD TIGHTLY TO Val's neck as she was carried into the yurt. She loved the soft glow it gave off. She ran her fingers through her lover's hair as Val laid her down on the bed, lying down and hovering above her. "I love you."

"I love you too, my beautiful wife." Val's eyes smoldered with desire. She rolled over onto her side and propped herself up on her left elbow.

"My wife. That sounds so good coming out of your mouth." Laurel traced a fingertip across Val's lips. She kissed her. The minute their lips parted, she rose and undid Val's bowtie, leaving it hanging loosely around her neck. "You looked so handsome today. I know your mom hated the jeans, but I couldn't imagine you any other way. The tux jacket was damn sexy." Laurel ran her fingers down the buttons of Val's dress shirt.

"You pretty much took my breath away. If Jo hadn't been there to hold me up, I swear I'd have passed out." Val ran a hand lightly down Laurel's arm until she held the hand that now wore her ring. She kissed it and held it tightly to her cheek. "I never dreamed I'd have someone to wear my ring."

"I never dreamed I'd find someone I was willing to take the chance with." Laurel removed the pearl studs of Val's shirt, dropping each of them on the teakwood floor one at a time. After removing the last one she stood. "Unzip me, please?"

She watched Val sit up. As Val unzipped the soft eyelet dress down to the small of her back, Laurel felt Val kiss her bare skin. She leaned into the touch and shivered with pleasure at the light bite and lick that followed. Laurel turned and pushed Val onto her back. Laurel watched Val's eyes as she drew the dress over her right shoulder then her left, letting the fabric pool at her feet. Laurel stood before Val in a sheer white teddy and her high heel shoes. Val's eyes widened. Her hair was still up and Laurel pulled the pins, letting it fall to her shoulders, and heard Val's breath hitch.

Laurel stalked around the bed running a single fingertip up the inside seam of Val's jeans. She watched as her lover and wife shuddered at her touch. Reaching for Val's belt, she single handedly undid the buckle and slid it free. She slowly popped every rivet on the button fly jeans, all the while watching Val's chest rise and fall in an uneven rhythm. She put a knee on the bed between Val's legs and leaned over to lightly kiss her abdomen, running her tongue teasingly around the belly button. Her hand brushed over her lover's chest as Val ran her fingers into her hair. Val pulled her hand up and kissed her palm. The touch of Val's lips to any part of her skin made her shiver with anticipation.

"No touching, lie still." Laurel pushed back Val's shirt and the tux jacket, until her breasts were exposed.

The desire Laurel saw was pure hunger. Val obeyed her order to remain still, as Laurel stalked up her body, stopping at her breasts and placing soft lips over a taut nipple. She teased it by licking, sucking, and biting it, all while locked onto Val's eyes.

A look of intensity passed over Val's face, and it nearly took Laurel's breath away. She watched those eyes flutter shut and her back arch as she ran her fingers over the waistband of Val's silk boxers under her jeans. Val gasped as Laurel slid a finger under the elastic, her hips rising to meet the touch.

Laurel seductively licked her lips. "What, love?"

"Laurel, please, touch me."

"I will. Eventually." The power she felt at controlling this strong, handsome woman was intoxicating. Laurel kissed her way back down her body and heard a moan from Val.

Val trembled at the touch and grasped the sheets. Laurel removed Val's gleaming leather boots, letting them thud to the platform floor. She ran her hands up the outside of Val's legs and grabbed the jeans tugging them down and off, leaving Val in her shirt, tux jacket, and black silk boxers.

Laurel removed Val's prosthesis and sat it on the floor. She ran a hand up through the boxer legs, brushing Val's center, feeling the wetness that gathered there. Val gasped and bucked with pleasure. Laurel withdrew her fingers and licked each one, as the other hand pulled on the boxers until she lay naked from the waist down.

Laurel rose over her and smiled. "You okay?"

"Fuck no, I want you," Val hissed.

Laurel held up her left hand and rolled her wedding ring around her finger. "You have me."

Val squirmed. "You know what I mean."

"Oh, I do. Right now, I want you." Laurel settled herself again between her legs running the tip of her index finger over Val's center. A smile crossed her face as Val arched into the touch. Laurel withdrew, prolonging her seduction. Laurel's hand brushed Val's soft sandy triangle and curled her fingers in it. She let her thumb brush lightly across the swollen clit. Pleasure spiked through her and she licked her lips. When Val let out a whimper, Laurel knew she was close to breaking. Laurel moved down and held her face inches above Val's clit, her tongue extended. So close that with the smallest of movements, she would be able to taste her. She blew warm air across the heated flesh, making Val shiver and give another pleading moan.

Laurel released Val's curls and used both hands to expose her. With the tip of her tongue, she separated the silky folds and licked. Val let out a guttural moan as Laurel's tongue drove deep inside her. The feeling of stroking Val, combined with reaction of Val's body, drove Laurel to the edge.

Laurel stroked Val with her tongue as she slowly began to enter her. Val grasped for Laurel with her right hand. She saw tears flow down Val's cheeks as she entwined their fingers together, binding them in yet one more way. Laurel locked eyes with her. What she wanted Val to see was love and security. She channeled every ounce of love she could into her gaze. *Surrender.* With the unspoken request, Laurel watched as Val's body tensed. She felt muscles clamp hard around her fingers and Val slipped over the edge. Laurel followed her with blinding intensity, giving in to her desire. They lay there panting together. Laurel crawled up Val's body and kissed her. "I love you Val." Hearing her wife murmur the same, they fell asleep, secure in the love that surrounded them both.

It was still early when they woke. Sometime in the night, they had shed the remainder of their clothes. Laurel lay on top of Val, rubbing small infinity symbols on her chest with the tips of her fingers. "You hungry?"

Val kissed her head and moaned something unintelligible.

Laurel snickered. "Was that a yes?" Her laughter shook the bed. She raised her head and propped her chin on Val's chest. She traced Val's lips with her fingers and stretched to kiss her.

Val wagged her eyebrows. "Depends on what type of hunger you're talking about."

Laurel dug her finger into Val's side. "You're insatiable."

Val's eyes roamed her body. "With all this at my fingertips, can you blame me for enjoying the bounty?"

She met Val's eyes and watched them darken with desire. "I love you."

"I love you, too, more than I ever knew I was capable of."

Laurel slid up Val's body, straddled her hips and cupped her face. "Just so you know, that feeling is mutual." She kissed Val again and looked at the ring on her finger. "I know it's real. Somehow, I still can't believe it. We're married, you're my wife."

Val's hands traveled up Laurel's sides. "So do I, and she's without a doubt the sexiest woman alive."

Laurel fell forward burying her face into the crook of Val's neck. "I'm of the opinion that I have the sexiest woman alive as my wife. God, I love the sound of that."

Val intertwined their hands. "Say it as often as you like." Her stomach growled.

Laurel tried to suppress a laugh, failing miserably. "Sounds like that," she said pointing to Val's stomach, "is indicating you have another type of hunger. Is this place stocked?"

"I had them put the essentials in. You should find eggs, cheese, milk, assorted vegetables, and bread, I think. There's probably more there than that. I didn't get to do a pre-honeymoon inspection."

Laurel looked around at the cozy set up that was beginning to lighten with the rising sun. It was a wide-open space with a small kitchen off to one side and a table that folded up, saving space. Colorful tapestry rugs were scattered around the room and a small walled off area was to the right of the bed.

"I can't believe you had this built. It's incredible." It smelled like fresh linen and sunshine.

Val stretched, pushing the covers off them both. "I wanted to give you a memorable wedding gift. It has all the conveniences of home." She laughed. "Aside from a short gray-haired firecracker."

Laurel thought about what she had for Val and wondered when would be the best time to give it to her. She'd agonized over what to do and had spoken to Liz about it several times. "Stay right here, I have something for you too." She kissed her, got up and reached into her overnight bag. She pulled out a thick letter size envelope. When she crawled back onto the bed, she handed it to Val.

Val eyed the letter. "What's this?"

"My wedding gift to you." She propped up the pillows and helped Val sit up. She curled up beside her love so she could be close in case what was in the letter threw Val into a flashback. *I hope this brings her the closure she needs to heal.*

***

Val tilted her head and squinted at Laurel as she tore open the envelope. She pulled out the few sheets of paper and unfolded them. Something fell out of the folds. She stared at the picture of a young man. He appeared to be a teenager, with dark brown skin, straight shiny black hair, and deep brown eyes. He was dressed in dishdasha, a long-sleeved robe, and some loose-fitting pants. He held something in his hands. Val turned to look at Laurel with an unspoken question.

Laurel cupped her cheek and tapped the papers with her other hand. "Read the letter, my love."

Val let her eyes drift to the papers.

Corporal Valkyrie Magnusson,

My name is Amal Al-Jamil. I'm happy to finally make contact with you. I was the child you helped save in the schoolyard in Toraq. I have only recently learned your name. I have no real memories of that day, other than being given school supplies. After a long recovery in the infirmary, I was finally able to return to school. I have recently graduated. I wanted to thank you for caring for me that day. They tell me you stopped the bleeding in my damaged leg. The doctors told my parents that without your intervention, I might not have survived. Unfortunately, I lost my leg, but I'm grateful to be alive. I want to attend a university next year, and I hope to become a doctor so I may help my people. I hope to meet you some day. Until then, I can only express my extreme gratitude for your kindness.

Amal

Val's hands shook as she held the letter. A tightness built in her chest and darkness closed in. Her vision was closing down. Her breathing was rapid and shallow, her chest burned, and the room disappeared. She felt the warmth of Laurel's hand on hers, penetrating her conscious.

"Honey, It's Laurel. I'm right here, Val. You're not in Iraq, and there's no danger. Look at me, Val, I'm right by your side. We're in our bed, and you are so loved."

Val turned her head and focused on Laurel, seeking the warmth of her eyes. She heard Laurel tell her to stay in the present. The soft voice drew her back.

"You're safe."

Finally, the fog in Val's eyes cleared. She shook her head. "Laurel?" Her face finally came clearly into view. She rubbed her temple with her fingers, letting the letter fall in her lap.

Laurel reached up and clasped Val's shaking hands. "I know baby, I know. It's a lot to take in. I hope it brings you peace. Amal is alive and well, thanks to you."

Laurel's eyes drew her in, locking them together. "I don't know what to say." Val pulled one of her hands from Laurel's grasp and scrubbed her face. "It wasn't that long ago that I realized it was me holding him."

Laurel shifted closer and shrugged. "I had to do some digging to find all this out. I remembered you told me this all happened at one of the events you were covering for Gary Sinise's charity. I enlisted Liz and Jo to make contact with Tess."

"Tess?"

Laurel winced and let go of Val's left hand, smoothing out a wrinkle on the bedsheet. "Don't be mad. Liz and Jo helped me."

"Oh, honey, I'm not mad." She leaned forward, kissed her forehead, and rested her own there. "I'm just surprised you remembered her name and where she worked."

Laurel placed her palm on Val's face, tracing her cheekbone with her thumb. "Love, there isn't anything you've told me about your past that I've forgotten. All of those things make up who you are."

Val felt the terror melt away. She shook her head in confusion. "I still don't know how you found all this out."

"I asked Jo and Liz if they knew Tess. When they said yes, I asked them to have her call me."

Val rolled her eyes back and shut them. "That had to be awkward."

"Not as bad as I expected. She actually said she was really happy for you. Shocked, but happy. She told me you had a bit of a commitment aversion."

She felt Laurel trace her eyebrow and opened her eyes to see earnest green eyes staring back at her.

Laurel smiled sheepishly. "She said that if I'd managed to capture your heart that I'd never have to worry about you not being around. Tess honestly said that what happened between you two, as far as parting ways, was amicable. She also wanted you to know that she and Kelly were getting married."

Val opened her eyes wide. "That's fantastic news. Kelly is great. Tess deserves what I couldn't give her. Now that I look at it, I couldn't give what I didn't have. I didn't realize what I was missing until the day I met you. After that, it all came together. I knew where I wanted to be. I knew who I was and where my future was." She watched Laurel shake her head and grin. She grabbed Laurel's hand and stroked the knuckles with her thumbs. "I know, it took me a while to get there. What I can see so clearly now, was that it was all worth it to be right here, right now." She picked up Laurel's hand and held it to her face, kissing the palm.

"There's something else in that envelope."

Val shook it and another picture of Amal fell out.

"That's Amal getting his new prosthesis," Laurel explained and pointed to the picture. "Look at that smile. You should recognize a few people in that picture."

Charley, Daren, and Anya stood around him, grinning from ear to ear. Val looked up at Laurel, confused. "He's here in the States?"

Laurel shook her head. "He is, and will be for the foreseeable future. He and his family are trying to immigrate to the United States. He's anxious to meet you."

Val pointed to her chest. "Me?"

Laurel placed her palm against Val's chest. "You saved his life."

Val sat for a minute, saying nothing. "I..." She stopped.

"Just think about it, baby. You don't have to, and Amal isn't expecting it. We didn't say anything to him. He was sponsored by one of the international charities to come here and be fitted for his new leg. Anya worked with Tess to get all his documentation together. His family is working to bring his two sisters and his father over. Right now, he's here with his mother."

Val shook her head and leaned it back in an attempt to stop the tears threatening to fall. "Gotta love my Bodyshop family."

"When the crew heard that this was the kid you saved over there, they got to work on helping him out. Charley swore me to secrecy. I hope you aren't upset at us."

Val pulled Laurel into her arms and held on as the tears broke over the dam of emotion. Her sobs shook the bed. All the years of confusion and doubt flooded her system. An end to her nightmares and some form of closure seemed within reach and was overwhelming.

Laurel stroked her back. "It's okay, baby, let it out. I'm right here."

Val cried until she had no more tears and fell asleep in Laurel's arms as exhaustion took over, food forgotten for the moment. Val needed time to process everything. As she drifted off, she knew Laurel would give her that time and whatever else she needed.

***

A few hours later, Laurel stood near the stove in nothing more than Val's tuxedo shirt when Val woke and stretched. She watched as Val sniffed the air and propped herself up on one elbow.

"That smells so good. By the way, you look sexy as hell in my clothes."

Laurel watched her, spatula in hand, and sucked her bottom lip. "You look good in our bed. I thought you might like breakfast there." She finished frying the bacon and brought it over to Val, retreating to bring two steaming cups of coffee to go with the bacon.

Val held up a hand. "Stop right there."

Laurel tilted her head, letting a sly grin form as she watched the hunger in Val's eyes. "Like what you see?"

Val's shirt was too big, but it felt comfortable on her. More than that, it smelled like her wife and she felt wrapped in her love wearing it. She had the collar turned up and the sleeves folded back. She'd managed to find a few of the studs on the floor to hold it together at her breasts. She watched as Val's eyes glinted.

Val leaned back and put her hands behind her head. "You're the picture of beauty and femininity. You make my mouth water."

Laurel swayed her hips provocatively as she made her way to the bed. She handed Val her coffee and leaned in to kiss her. "That's probably the bacon making your mouth water. Be careful, it's hot," she said, allowing the innuendo to hang in the air.

Val sipped her coffee. "The coffee isn't the only thing that's smoking hot."

She blew on her own coffee to cool it and let her eyes roam over Val's body as she carefully sipped the rich hazelnut flavor. "I agree with you."

They both laughed and dug into the crisp strips of bacon, feeding each other until the plate was empty and each of them had devoured two cups of coffee.

"So, what do you want to do today, my love?" Laurel asked.

"My only plan is to keep you in this bed with me."

"Oh, that's an enticing proposition." She took Val's empty coffee cup and placed them both on the bedside table. She came up on her knees and straddled Val's lap taking her face into her hands, bending her head to capture the soft lips that still tasted of bacon and coffee. She slipped off her lap and sat up beside her. "Did you equip this splendid love shack with any entertainment?"

Val's eyebrow went up. "Like what?"

Laurel smacked her shoulder. "I mean, is there a TV here that we can watch cheesy chick flick movies?"

"Your wish is my command." Val sat up and looked around. "I know where my pants are, got any idea where my leg is?"

Laurel moved and settled back under the covers. "It's standing up at the head of the bed to your right."

Val leaned back and kissed her. "What would I do without you?"

"God willing, honey, you'll never have to find out."

Val slid into her sleeve and socket. "If I live to be a hundred, it won't be enough."

Laurel watched the muscles in Val's back and legs as she walked in the direction of the shelves lining part of the yurt and slid back a panel, revealing a forty-inch TV. *That's all mine.*

Val turned to face her. "So, what do you want to watch? *First Wives Club, The Proposal, Mamma Mia*—"

Laurel cut her off, appreciating the front of Val's naked body with an obvious stare. "Right now, I like the show I'm already watching."

Val wagged her eyebrows and posed for her. She gestured to the movies.

"*Mamma Mia*, please."

Val chuckled. "Admit it, you're a closet ABBA fan. I've caught you more than once singing 'Dancing Queen.'"

Laurel's face heated, and she covered her face with the sheet. "I refuse to answer that on the grounds I may incriminate myself."

Val howled with laughter. "*Mamma Mia* it is."

.

Chapter Twenty-Six

VAL AND LAUREL SPENT the next two days lounging around, watching movies and making love. They'd christened several places in the yurt, but the hot tub proved to be one of their favorite places. Laurel treated Val to several strip teases. They'd taken walks around the property and Val used the opportunity to do some photography work and sneak photos of an unguarded Laurel as often as she could.

They were walking hand in hand down one of the logging roads close to the yurt, soaking up the sun and the crisp mountain air when Laurel posed a question to Val about Amal. "Honey, we haven't talked much about Amal's letter. Are you okay?"

Val felt her pulse race a bit, and she stopped to look up at the bright blue, cloudless sky. The racing was calmed by the support she felt holding Laurel's hand. "I think so. I probably need to talk to Liz about it. I was thinking maybe we'd take a day this week and go over if she has time. I know the store needs you, but..."

Laurel stroked down Val's cheek with her free hand. "You're not going anywhere without me, especially if it involves things like this."

Val smirked. "I thought it would take more time for you to be able to read my mind."

"Nope, marrying you gave me super powers." She stood on her tiptoes and wrapped her arms around Val's neck to kiss her.

"Super powers, huh?" Val licked her lips, absorbing the heat Laurel left behind.

"Oh yes, I can read your mind, I can hold you in place with a single finger, and I can render you breathless with a kiss."

"Guess I'm lucky you use your super powers for good." Val's smile widened so much she knew it brought out the rarely seen dimple in her cheek. "I thought maybe after I check in with Liz, we can try to make contact with Amal and his mother. I'm not sure how this is going to affect me. Somehow it feels like it could lead to closure. After that, maybe a new beginning." She started walking again kicking at the rocks and leaf litter on the ground. Ferns grew out of the bank and waved gently in the slight breeze that cooled her neck.

Laurel pulled close to her and rubbed down her arm with her free hand. "I think you're right on all accounts. I don't think your mind or heart will be at peace with this, until you see him. When do you want to go?"

Val leaned over and kissed her temple. "I'll call Liz today and see when she has time. After that, we can visit the crew over at The Bodyshop and figure out how to make contact with Amal." She stopped and picked a single white daisy for Laurel. Val put it in Laurel's hair behind her ear. She smiled as Laurel reached up, and clasped her hands behind her neck and graced her with a soft kiss.

Laurel leaned back. "No need. I've got the contact for Amal. Tess gave it to me. Now all we have to do is get you ready to meet him, mentally and physically."

Val thought about how many times she'd read the letter, still trying to process it. She still couldn't fit all the pieces together. Frequently, she saw the actions as single frames, moments in time, captured by the click of a shutter. She shivered and held Laurel a little tighter.

They walked back and closed everything up. Val turned on the solar electric fence that surrounded the dwelling to keep bears and other unwanted four-legged visitors out. They drove back to the house, made a call to Liz, and discovered she could see them tomorrow afternoon.

Val had one more surprise up her sleeve. "Mind if we go down to Bobeye's and see how Maggie May's coming?"

"Sure. I need to go check in on the store anyway. We'll go to the garage and then go on over."

As they drove to Bobeye's, Val couldn't help but chuckle to herself. She was looking forward to seeing Laurel's reaction to the bike. Val shut off the engine and came around to open Laurel's door, helping her from the truck. She'd texted Bobeye that she was bringing Laurel to see Maggie May. She knew he'd have the bike waiting front and center, gleaming in the sunshine.

Laurel put her hand over her mouth as she saw the vintage bike, completely restored and now sporting a shiny black sidecar. Val drew her over so that she could see the two photographs affixed to the tank.

The first was the black and white photo of Lorraine and Maggie. Just below that was one of Val and Laurel on their wedding day.

Laurel reached for Val's hand. "It's beautiful. Now I know why you had Jenny take those pictures."

"I thought you might like it. Maggie and Loraine should be riding with people who will remember them." Val paused, silently hoping Laurel would grant her this request despite her previous trepidation. "I know you've always turned me down when I've asked, but would you do me the honor of accompanying me on her first ride? We won't go far, just down to the store."

Laurel's eyes grew bright. "I guess you finally found the day where 'someday' falls between."

Val shook her head, remembering how many times Laurel had said that in the past. She'd repeatedly asked where 'someday' fell in the week. She reached into the sidecar and pulled out a gleaming black helmet with mountain laurel airbrushed on the sides. "I had this made for you."

"It's beautiful." Laurel slipped it on, and Val helped fasten the chinstrap.

"Does it feel okay? It needs to be snug, but not so tight it gives you a headache. There's a built-in intercom system so we can talk. Its voice activated, so all you have to do is talk and I'll hear it in my helmet."

"Oh, wow, it fits fine."

Val pulled her new helmet on, the back of it airbrushed with wedding rings and their wedding date. Laurel squealed when she saw it and hugged Val.

Val climbed on, kickstarting the big Indian. When it roared to life, Val couldn't help but let the smile take over. She'd missed the feeling of the bike's raw power and the freedom that traveling on two wheels offered her. Now she could share this with the one person that gave her peace like she'd never known. She reached for Laurel's hand and helped her settle in on the seat behind her. "Ready?"

Laurel looked perplexed. "Why not in the sidecar, isn't that why you had it put on?

"And miss the chance to have you snuggled up against me for your first ride? Not a chance. Plus, there's something in the sidecar. Now, hang on." She felt Laurel wrap her arms around her waist and squeeze as she pulled out slowly onto Route 50. Val didn't even go the speed limit, trying to let Laurel get the feel of traveling on the bike. The only adjustment Val had to getting back in the saddle, was in how the bike handled as she steered. It wasn't as aerodynamic as it had been without the side car. The resistance drag she felt, made her tighten her grip on the handlebars. "Lean into me and you'll naturally roll through the curves."

After a few minutes, Val would've sworn Laurel had always been on the bike with her. The feeling of Laurel pushed up tight against her with a warm hand resting under her t-shirt, was causing her to use a lot of focus to avoid crashing them into a tree. She tightened her grip. The dance they were performing was maddeningly arousing. Val powered through the turns. After a short ride, they pulled into the store. Val got off and helped Laurel dismount. They walked in the back door to the smell of frying meat and spicy chili. Ree came around the wood topped island, kissing them both. Val had one final surprise she hoped would be memorable for all of them. "Ree, how would you feel about taking a ride with Laurel and me?"

Ree put her hands on her hips. "On that motorcycle? I may be small, but I'm guessing our butts won't all fit on that seat."

"Oh, I took care of that." Val could tell by the shocked look and broadening smile on Laurel's face, she now understood the sidecar.

Laurel shook her head and laughed. "Gram, you'll have to come and see. Just trust her. I did."

Ree squinted at them. "What are you two up to? Ya both look like the cat that swallowed the canary."

Val protested her innocence with a scout's honor sign. "Not a thing, Ree, not a thing. Follow me. I think you're going to like it. Come on. Come outside with us."

Ree walked to the small hand sink by the door, washed and dried her hands, and removed her apron. "Lead away! I'm not getting any younger."

Val crooked her elbow for the elderly woman's hand. The three of them walked outside, and Val pulled a custom helmet for Ree from the sidecar. On it, the words "Cool Springs Queen" had been painted, with a spatula and a mounted deer head. She handed the helmet to Ree, whose smile was as wide as the Cheat River.

Ree put her hands on her hips. "Now how am I supposed to get in that contraption? I'm an old woman."

Val opened a small door to show Ree she could step in and sit down. Val helped her put on her helmet and a pair of goggles that looked similar to a long-ago aviator. After she was outfitted, she led Ree over to the sidecar and helped her get in. She latched the side door shut. Ree giggled like a schoolgirl, her hands covering her mouth, as Laurel and Val mounted the bike.

Several people gathered around, having come out of the store to see what was going on. Beth, Tilly, and Wunder stood on the porch while Mule leaned against one of the supports. Beth had the camera and snapped pictures while Wunder made a video with the small camera Val had given him. They posed for Beth so she could get a picture of this adventure. Val had plans to add one of these photos to the tank as well and a story about Ree's first ride for the magazine.

With the occasion thoroughly documented, Val started Maggie May and looked at Ree. Deep affection for the elderly woman warmed her entire body more than the sun shining down on them. "Ready?"

Ree waved her arms. "And waiting. Come on. Let's get this show on the road. Not every day do ya get to see an old bird like me fly."

Val maneuvered them out onto Route 50 and onto the long black ribbon that wound into the sunshine. In all her rides across the mountains and plains, she'd never enjoyed one more than this one with her family surrounding her.

***

The next morning, Laurel rode the majority of the morning's trip to Annapolis with her left leg folded under her and Val's hand tucked into the crook of her knee. She ran her hand in Val's hair over and over throughout the trip. Val once mentioned how much that simple touch soothed her, and Laurel vowed to herself to do it as often as possible.

Liz met them at the door and hugged both. "How was your trip?"

Laurel tilted her head back and forth. "Pretty good. The new corridor makes quick work of it."

Liz turned from Laurel to eye Val. "I'm glad. How's the shoulder?"

"Still a little stiff. We're down to one therapy session a week. Still working to get the strength back. At least I can lift it over my head now." Val demonstrated by raising her arm to touch the door header.

"Fallon says she's been a model patient." Laurel stepped into the house. "Correction, as model as a Viking chomping at the bit to get back on Maggie May can be. We took her out for a test drive with Gram in the sidecar. Unfortunately, we passed Fallon. Val got an ass chewing from her. Says Val needs another month before she feels comfortable with her on it. So, for now, Maggie is parked in the garage."

Val looked sheepishly at her boots, a smile curving up at the corner of her lips. "Where's Jo?"

Liz pointed up. "She's in the studio. If you wait a few minutes you can follow the noise. Now you see why I have an office out back. When she starts hammering and grinding, I can't hear myself think."

"I'm going to run up and say hi." Val leaned over, kissed Laurel and headed for the stairs.

Liz and Laurel walked arm and arm into the kitchen. "Care for a glass of iced tea or coffee?"

Laurel relaxed into Liz's embrace. "Iced tea would be great. Thanks for letting us crash here again."

"Laurel, you're always welcome here." She poured a glass for Laurel and led them to the table. "How's she taking the news about Amal?"

Laurel looked around the comfortable kitchen. The granite counters sparkled, and she eyed the two matching blue coffee cups sitting there. "It's hard to say. When she read the letter, she started to flash. I was able to divert it, but I think it was quite a shock. She's still trying to process that the person she was searching for all along was her. She's still sketching. We brought her pad with us."

"I'll take a look when we sit down to talk. How are you handling it?"

"It was interesting talking to Tess. She wished us well and told me she and Kelly had a date set for their wedding. She was very helpful in trying to track down all the pieces. Hearing from Amal shook Val pretty good. I think knowing he survived has to be a powerful thing to process. In his letter to her, he mentioned that if she hadn't stopped the bleeding, he likely would've died. Now he's getting ready to go to college." Laurel put down her glass and pushed her hair behind her ears.

Liz looked at Laurel. "I imagine it's a lot for her to take in. However, you're avoiding answering my question about how this is affecting you." Liz pointed to her.

Laurel looked at Liz, then away. Her finger traced a pattern in the condensation on the glass. "Caught that, did you?"

Liz quirked a smile. "I'm trained to, remember?"

"Nothing gets by you. There are nights I lay awake watching her fight in her sleep. Most of the time, I can rest my hand on her chest and tell her she's safe, but it kills me to watch her suffer. I'm so grateful I can help bring her out of it. I'm hoping once she meets Amal, many of the demons she runs from will find their way back to hell." Laurel wiped a tear from the corner of her eye. "I think she still questions if it was her in those pictures. Sometimes she stares at them for hours at a time. I've caught her reading the letter again several times. She gets this look. It's not long after that she takes to her sketchbook."

"I'll talk to her. We'll work our way through this together." She reached out and held Laurel's hand.

Laurel gripped the fingers tightly. "Thank you, Liz. If not for her, then for me. I'm grateful you'll be there." She sipped the iced tea Liz refilled for her and looked into the back yard where the mid-day sun was just reaching its highest point.

***

After supper, Val, Laurel, and Liz made their way to the study and sat down in their usual arrangement. Val handed Liz her sketchbook, and she flipped through the pages. Several were sketches of Laurel in unguarded moments. Other scenes were from her time in Iraq. Val watched as Liz stopped on one that showed a familiar scene of the child in the soldier's arms, then turn back to an earlier version and compare the two. The earlier one showed the child and a soldier from the waist down. The more recent one showed farther up the chest, though no face had been drawn. The name Magnussen was on the clothing.

"Val, talk to me about these two sketches."

Val furrowed her brow. "They're the same."

"Not exactly. More of the soldier is revealed in this one. Your name is on the identifiers." She paused. "You still haven't drawn in a face. We've confirmed it was you in those pictures and yet you still doubt."

Val put her head back and began to search her pocket for the familiar tin of lip balm. She put layer after layer on until Laurel reached up and stopped the movement.

Laurel reached for the tin and closed it, holding Val's hand in hers. "I'm right here. You're safe. You're my wife, and I love you."

Val took several steadying breaths as a whiff of copper teased her senses. She looked at Liz, fighting to keep the black at bay. The feeling of Laurel's warm hand connecting them centered her as the room came back into focus. She saw Liz looking at her and stretched her neck by pulling her head side to side, clearing her throat. "My heart wants to believe the person who helped Amal was me. My head still refuses to comprehend it. I don't remember crawling over to him. I know I must have, but I can't wrap my head around it."

"There were only four American soldiers in that courtyard, and three died in the initial blast. You were the only survivor. It wasn't your fault that your fellow soldiers died, Val. Amal lived as a direct result of your actions. He's grown into a fine young man with dreams. Like you, he lost his leg that day. Like you, he's never let it stop him. You made that possible."

Trying to force the acceptance, Val blinked hard. She clenched her other hand into a fist and then released it. The walls of resistance her subconscious had built were slowly being dismantled, brick by brick. She pictured the fall of the Berlin wall and thought about the symbolism of combining two completely different ideologies into one belief. Squeezing her temples with her free hand, she felt the tears coming and sliding out beneath her palm.

Laurel leaned up to kiss her. "I love you, baby. It's going to be all right."

Val turned into Laurel's arms, sobbing.

When she began to quiet, Liz spoke to her again. "Val, it's time to forgive yourself for something you couldn't have prevented. It's time to realize you weren't responsible for the loss of your fellow soldiers and it's okay that you survived when they didn't. It's time for you to remember and celebrate that you saved a life. A young man who has so much promise and may go on to do incredible things. Those things are possible because of you."

Val looked at Liz with puffy, red-rimmed eyes. "I don't know that I can. I keep trying and failing. I don't want it to affect Laurel or those around me, so I keep pushing it down in my gut."

"Pushing it down is the equivalent of poisoning yourself. If you had a cut that was gangrene, you wouldn't sew the wound shut. This is no different, Val. It will slowly poison you from the inside out, day by day, destroying all the good things until there isn't anything left but guilt over something where no guilt is warranted."

Val sat forward leaning her elbows on her knees, her hands covering her tear streaked face. *Worse it will affect my relationship with my wife.* She felt her Laurel's hand rubbing small circles on her back. The warmth radiating from that small hand spread throughout her body. Her knee began to bounce with nervous energy. "How, Liz? How do I do that? I'm desperate. I don't want it to poison me or my marriage." She turned and looked at Laurel, managing a small smile. "It took me too damn long to find her as it was."

"The first step is to meet Amal, talk with him, and let him tell you how thankful he is that you were there that day. After that, we need to concentrate on replacing your guilt with feelings of being at peace. I think it would be a good idea if I accompany you and Laurel, just in case the meeting triggers a severe flashback."

"I'd like that. I trust your judgment, Liz. I really do." The relief that passed over her was like a cool breeze on a warm night. She scrubbed her face and ran her hand through her hair dispelling the feelings of dread. *One step at a time, I will get past this.*

Liz nodded. "Good, then let's see what we can do about setting up a visit with Amal. They're staying with a host family for now. The whole family is trying to immigrate. It's a long process."

Val's mind raced with thoughts of how she could help support their efforts when she heard Laurel speak.

"Do they need a second sponsor family?" Laurel sat up a little straighter and leaned forward.

Val leaned over and kissed her temple. She marveled how the woman she loved could read her mind so well. This was one of the things she adored so much about Laurel, her giving spirit. *Love in the purest form.*

Liz handed Val back her sketchbook. "It would make it easier. Even with one, it's still not a guarantee."

"I want to help, however I can. I'm not sure how that all works, but I want to try." Val reached for Laurel's hand, and they exchanged a grin.

"Tomorrow, we'll see what we can find out. For tonight, I think we've dug up enough."

The three of them made it to the kitchen where Jo sat poring over the newspaper with a beer. Liz walked over and kissed her on the top of her head. "Any news in there that's worth reading?"

"No. My Jets still suck," she pointed to Val, "and as far as I'm concerned, your Seahawks do, too."

Val laughed. "I can't remember the last time I watched a game."

"You're not missing anything. Ready to go to bed, love?" Jo asked Liz.

"Yup." Liz sat down in Jo's lap and kissed her. Jo wheeled them back toward the elevator while Laurel and Val followed.

Val just shook her head at her friends. "You two kill me. Even a blind dog..."

Jo finished the thought. "Finds a bone, or a boner."

Laurel slapped Jo's shoulder. "Behave, Romeo, or I'll bet the only bones you'll soon find, are the ones in your chicken wings."

Liz covered her mouth but couldn't manage to stifle her laugh.

Val laughed, and then sighed. *I need to laugh more.* She relished the relationship she had with Liz and Jo. The humorous banter back and forth they frequently engaged in, had long kept her from losing her mind. The fact that Laurel could be so easily drawn into it with them, constantly reminded her of one more reason she loved her.

Chapter Twenty-Seven

THE NEXT DAY VAL, Laurel, and Liz arranged to meet with Amal and his mother at the host house. Val bought small welcome gifts. They pulled in front of the house, and Val looked out the window. It was a small brownstone with connecting units on both sides. Her body tensed. She reached for the peppermint salve in her pocket. She felt Laurel reach over and put her hand over her own shaking one, squeezing gently.

Liz spoke up and broke the silence. "Val, I want you to close your eyes and try to quiet your mind. Go back home and hear the sound of the birds greeting the morning, the sound of Ree fixing breakfast, and Laurel getting ready for her day. Remind yourself you're home and safe, not back in Iraq."

Val did as requested, concentrating on the visuals Liz described. She could feel the tension leave her body. *It's time to do this.* She squeezed Laurel's hand before climbing out of the Jeep. They stood on the front porch as Val pressed the doorbell. A few moments passed and the door opened.

A petite woman in a long pale green tunic greeted them. Her dark eyes sparkled. "I assume you're Corporal Magnussen?"

Val shook her head and smiled. "Not for a while, ma'am. I'm no longer in the marines. You can call me Val. This is Laurel and Liz."

"I'm pleased to meet you all. I'm Kalani. Amal and his mother Rahal are in the living room. I'll act as your translator. They speak little English."

"Thank you. I brought this as a gift to your family for hosting Amal and his mother. I'm grateful."

"No thanks needed, Val. I truly appreciate the thought." Kalani accepted the small wooden box with intricate carving on all sides.

"It's not much, but I hope your family will enjoy it."

Kalani ran her fingers over the carvings. "It is very beautiful. Thank

261

you."

Val nodded and followed her through the small hallway to a spacious living room where Amal and Rahal were seated. They were both in traditional garb in shades of tan and light gray. Rahal wore a traditional head covering. When they entered the room, Rahal stood. Amal looked at Val, a wide smile breaking over his face. He struggled to stand, and his mother offered her hand to help him. He shook his head and grabbed the arms of the chair to pull himself up instead. Amal stumbled a bit and his mother reached for him. He held up his hand to stop her. With a beaming smile, he found his footing and looked at Val. He pulled up his pants leg and showed off his new prosthesis. It was ornately decorated with a soccer ball theme.

A broad grin crossed her own face as she pulled up her own pant leg to reveal her own prosthesis. She looked at the young man before her and saw the small child she'd held so many years ago. Images of that day slowly filtered through, filling in the missing frames in her memory. His dark hair, skin, and hands filled her mind with new photos to replace the ones that haunted her. *He's alive and thriving.* They stood staring at each other for a few long minutes. Amal took four tenuous steps toward her, reaching out his hand. Val joined him and took his hand in hers. The handshake turned into an embrace.

Rahal covered her mouth. Amal looked at his mother and spoke in Arabic. Kalani translated, "I consider her family. She, like you, gave me life." He turned to Val and spoke while Kalani translated. "It isn't customary for a young man to embrace a woman who isn't family. You, my new friend, will always be family to me."

Val couldn't stop smiling at Amal. They used pantomime to convey things beyond words. They'd both survived. They hadn't let their loss take their will to live or their will to persevere. They had a lifetime to experience everything that lay ahead of them. She had so much she wanted to tell him. Now, she'd have the time to do that. Val turned to look at Laurel and saw her most treasured reason to live. A reason that a few years ago, she wouldn't have dared to imagine. Now she couldn't imagine a life without Laurel.

For the next hour, Amal and Val conversed with the use of the translator. Liz and Laurel sat next to Val, making her feel connected, but she kept her focus on Amal. She learned through Kalani's translation that he'd graduated with honors and was applying for a student visa. He'd taken entrance exams to nearby universities. Amal's dreams were to help others who'd been hurt by war and he wanted to work with

Doctors Without Borders. Val made a promise to herself that she would help make that happen.

Val reached out and squeezed Liz's arm. She looked at Laurel sitting beside her with her hair tucked behind her ear, smiling at Amal and his mother. She turned to Val. The love Val saw in her eyes warmed her entire body. She'd captured thousands of photos in her lifetime but couldn't remember a single image she wanted to remember more. The miracle was that Laurel was much more than a photograph. She was flesh and blood in living color. She was her present and her future. *And in love with me*. Her time in Iraq would fade into the background and her future lay in front of her waiting to be lived to the fullest. She had survived and now...she could thrive.

Epilogue

IT WAS EARLY IN the morning and Val lay on their bed with Laurel. Her head was propped up on one arm. She was looking at her beautiful wife, her right hand caressing Laurel's protruding belly. She couldn't help but smile. They would be expanding their family soon by two. Anastasia Marie and Johann Valkyrie Magnussen-Stemple would be coming into world.

Laurel had been ordered to bed rest. Her pregnancy had been unremarkable until a month ago, when she developed some bleeding that concerned her doctor. She'd promptly been sent to bed and watched like a hawk by Val, Ree, and Beth.

Laurel scowled. "I want to get up."

Val sighed trying to placate her. "I know."

Laurel raised an eyebrow. "I'm not kidding."

Val tried to hide her smirk. "I know."

Laurel shifted and scowled. "You're not going to let me, are you?"

"Nope." Val leaned over and kissed her pregnant wife. "Whatever you need, I'll get for you." Laurel had been uncomfortable for months, struggling to do many things that Val adored doing for her. In the last few weeks, everything she did got on Laurel's nerves, but she didn't care.

Laurel huffed and smacked the bed. "What I need is to get out of bed."

Val tilted her head, trying to be supportive. "It's just for a little while."

"I'm tired of lying around."

Val reached up and brushed the hair back from Laurel's face. "I know, love. Our wee ones in there aren't quite ready to come out and play. Right now, they're hanging out in a heated swimming pool." She leaned down and kissed Laurel's belly. "Isn't that right, guys?" At that exact moment one of them chose to kick their mother in the ribs, directly under Val's hand that rested there.

"I think I'm carrying at least one soccer player, unless they were making the turn for the next lap. Laurel's smile broke over her aggravated face. "It felt like they were doing the backstroke all night."

Laurel stroked Val's shoulders as she lay with her head by Laurel's

265

belly. "You're going to make a great momma."

Val looked up at Laurel. "You're the one who's going to make a great mom. You've had a great teacher. I, on the other hand, did not."

Laurel pulled Val up to her. "We'll learn together."

Val watched her run her own hand over her swollen abdomen. She put her hand on Laurel's cheek, letting her lean into the touch and sigh. *She's more beautiful than ever before.*

Laurel shifted again. "These little ones are going to be the two most loved babies ever born."

Val placed her head very close to the babies. "If we have anything to do with it, that'll be the truth." She dropped her voice and spoke directly to her children. "Gram, Beth, and Wunder are bursting to meet you."

"And their other grandmother, Amanda," Laurel added, poking Val's shoulder.

Val shook her head, smiling. It was such a strange thing to watch her mother now. Soon after they'd become pregnant, she'd left her home and job in Seattle, settling in Morgantown, West Virginia. She visited frequently and was as excited as Val and Laurel were. She'd taken a teaching job at West Virginia University, while still doing some freelance writing. She'd finally divorced Val's father and enjoyed life for the first time in many years. "Yes, and my mother."

Laurel fidgeted again, holding her side. "My back is killing me."

Val sat up. "Want me to rub it?"

Laurel grimaced. "Not sure how you're going to get to it."

Val kissed her. "Just roll on your side as best you can, and I'll do the rest."

Laurel started rolling over, stopping short and going wide-eyed with alarm. "Val."

"What, love? Are you okay?"

"My water broke."

Val returned the wide-eyed look, nervous energy prickling through her. "Your what? Your water broke? But it's not time yet."

Laurel hugged her belly. "Honey, whether it's time or not makes no difference. My water broke and that means these babies are coming."

Val jumped off the bed and fell on the floor, forgetting she didn't have two legs. Laurel covered her smile as Val looked up at her sitting on the floor, pulling on her leg and then her jeans.

"Where's the bag we packed? Are you in pain? How far apart are the contractions?"

Laurel burst out laughing. "You're adorable. The bag is in the closet, I'm not in pain, and I have yet to time them."

Val fumbled to button her shirt, missing several of the buttons and misaligning those she did manage to bring together. "Shit. Ok, I'll go get the bag. You time the contractions." She held up both hand palms out to Laurel. "Don't move. I'll be right back."

Laurel laughed again. "Val?"

"Yes?" Val turned to her, a hand driven deeply into her own hair, fingers curled tightly in anxiety.

"Take a deep breath and calm down."

Val stared at her, the heart in her chest threatening to burst out. "Calm down! How can I calm down? My babies are coming!"

"Yes, and I don't need you having a stroke beforehand. Call for Gram. She can help me while you go get what we need."

Val put her hands to the side of her head. It was swimming, and she felt slightly sick. "Gram, good God, I forgot. I'll be right back. You stay still."

***

Laurel watched Val rush out of the room in a panic, happy she'd finally given in to her grandmother's prodding's to call her Gram. Gram had even shed a tear the first time she'd done it. Laurel chuckled, and one of the babies gave her a swift kick to the ribs. "All right, you two, settle down. We need to make it to the hospital before you two decide to make your appearance and your momma passes out." She sat up on the edge of the bed and rubbed her side.

Gram came in the room, smiling from ear-to-ear and shaking her head. "You'd think that Viking was carrying these babies. I've never seen her so flustered. Did ya see her shirt?" Ree was pointing to her own buttons. "She went to get the Jeep. I've called Beth. She's going to meet us there, and she's calling Amanda. How are the contractions?"

Laurel felt her grandmother's soothing hand rub her lower back. "Not too bad now that I know what they are. They're pretty far apart."

"Val said your water broke?"

Laurel grimaced as a contraction hit. "Yes, I was rolling over."

Ree shook her head and helped Laurel stand. "Let's get you changed, Liebchen."

Laurel hugged her and let out a sigh. "Changed and then a lot less pregnant if you don't mind. Thanks, Gram, I couldn't do this without

267

you."

***

Val flew out of the Jeep, nearly forgetting to put it in park before she tried to get out. She fumbled trying to get the door open, accidentally locking herself in. She ran a shaky hand through her hair and took a deep breath. "Staring down the Taliban wasn't this terrifying." She bounded back up the ramp and into the house. Gram and Laurel were coming down the hall. She quickly made her way to her wife's side. "Just breathe, in and out. Slow."

Laurel shook her head. "Val?"

"Yes?"

"Momma, take your own advice or you'll be the one passing out before your children arrive." Laurel laughed and put her hand to her cheek. "Calm down, we have time."

Val took a deep breath and shook her head. She couldn't help being nervous and excited. She was about to become 'Momma' to someone. Two someones. At the same time, she was scared to death for her wife. The babies were early. The doctors told them they mostly likely would be. She calmed herself, knowing Laurel needed her to be strong, not a stark raving lunatic. She kissed Laurel and again took a deep settling breath.

Laurel nodded. "That's better. Now let's go before I have these babies at home."

Val's stomach dropped. She leaned down and whispered to Laurel's belly. "Don't you dare."

They piled into the Jeep and made their way to Garrett Memorial where Laurel was admitted to the Labor and Delivery unit. Amanda was there, as was Beth. They sat in the comfortable room decorated in pastels and furnished with small home-style touches, like a sofa and some recliners. Laurel rested in bed and Val sat next to her, holding her hand.

Doctor Brannigan came in, looking at the monitors and Laurel's chart. She turned to the couple and grinned. "I thought we were planning on keeping those two baking a little while longer."

Laurel rubbed her belly. "I think they have other plans."

"So it seems." She made a note on the chart. "We'll watch you for a while, monitor their heartbeats, and as long as they don't drop, we'll try to let them come on their own terms. If it drops, we'll have to take them by cesarean. I need to see how far you're dilated."

Doctor Brannigan examined Laurel and gave them the results, saying she was two centimeters. It would be a while. They sat through the next several hours. Val's nerves stretched thin, and Laurel sent her on several errands just to get her out of the room. The contractions came closer and closer together. Finally, Doctor Brannigan came back and examined Laurel again.

"Okay, I think it's time we bring these two into the world." Dr. Brannigan smiled. "We're going to take you to the OR in case we have to change direction in the middle of the stream."

Val's head buzzed, and she felt sick.

Laurel squeezed her hand. "Honey, it's going to be okay."

Val tried to put on a brave face. Her fear that something would happen to Laurel or the babies was overwhelming. She took a deep breath and gave Laurel a tremulous smile. "I know."

Doctor Brannigan released the brake on the hospital bed. "Okay, you two, let's go have some babies."

As they readied Laurel to be moved, Amanda stood and walked to Val's side. She rested her hand in the small of Val's back. "It's going to be okay."

Val melted into her mother's reassurance. She felt part of the tension leave her body, and her resolve strengthened. She stepped up to the bedside. Looking down at Laurel, she kissed her lips. "I love you. Let's go meet our kids."

A few hours later, a grinning Val came into the waiting room, dressed in pale blue scrubs adorned with zoo animals. She pulled off the surgical cap and looked at her family that sat before her. "They're fine, both of them. Anastasia Marie weighs four pounds, three ounces, and Johann weighs four pounds, four ounces."

"Did they have to do the C-section?" Ree asked, her hands clasped in front of her chest.

Val breathed a sigh of relief and leaned on the doorframe to rest. "No, they behaved themselves and came into this world the way we'd hoped."

Ree wrung her hands. "And Laurel?"

Val stretched out her hand and took the older woman's weathered ones in hers. "Exhausted, but right as rain. In an hour or so, she can have visitors one at a time. Ree, we got permission for you to see her now."

They made their way to Laurel's room and found her dozing with a double bassinet beside her. The babies were bundled up, foreheads touching, sleeping peacefully. Val gazed down at her children and then over to her wife, who'd opened her eyes. She reached for Laurel's hand, and her heart filled with an overwhelming joy. Ree bent down to kiss both of her great grandchildren, tears trickling down the wrinkled cheeks. She picked up her namesake, Anastasia Marie.

Val couldn't believe how fortunate she was. If not for the love of Laurel and Ree, she might never have known what being a family truly was. She blessed the day she'd rode into the parking lot of the Cool Springs Store. She thought she ought to alter the sign out front. *Good food, groceries, ice cream, hardware, feed store, taxidermy, gifts, gas and 'family.'* Somewhere that sign needed to reflect that love could be found, not on the shelves, but in the people who graced its visitors. Looking at her family, Val was grateful for the day she climbed off Maggie May and found that, frame by frame, she had finally come home.

The End

About CJ Murphy

I grew up a voracious reader, feeding my imagination with books. I spent hours exploring the woods around my farm, pretending I was "Hawk-eye", surviving in the wilderness. I climbed into the hayloft of our barn, looking for "Charlotte" among the spider webs. Later, I looked in every wardrobe I could trying to find "Narnia and Aslan". As an adult, I can still remember reading my first novel with a lesbian character and how it made me feel to finally identify in an entirely new way.

My adventure into writing came at the suggestion of my wife. Several years ago, she asked me to write her a story. I began crafting her personalized gifts for holidays and special occasions, by writing stories for her. I'd weave in pieces and parts of our life. My brain started asking *"what if"* after she mentioned forgetting I'd written the story until something sounded familiar.

My wife and I are part owners of an active produce farm and a U Pick strawberry operation on my wife's family land all while I continue into my twenty fifth year as a full-time firefighter. On top of all that, we built our dream home in 2016, on property we've been clearing and preparing for fourteen years. Now we reside on 221 acres of woodland in the mountains of West Virginia, with three cats as I pine away for another promised Border Collie. We love to go watch our Mountaineers, Pittsburgh Pirates, and Steelers. We love leading our great niece and nephews on adventures to fuel their imagination and creativity as we watch them grow.

Connect with CJ:

Email: cptcjldypyro@gmail.com

Facebook: CJ Murphy

Note to Readers:

Thank you for reading a book from Desert Palm Press. We have made every effort to edit this book. However, typos do slip in. If you find an error in the text, please email lee@desertpalmpress.com so the issue can be corrected.

We appreciate you as a reader and want to ensure you enjoy the reading process. We would like you to consider posting a review on your preferred media sites such as Amazon, Smashwords, Bella Books, Goodreads, Tumblr, Twitter, Facebook, and/or your blog or website.

For more information on upcoming releases, author interviews, contest, giveaways and more, please sign up for our newsletter and visit us as at Desert Palm Press: www.desertpalmpress.com and "Like" us on Facebook: Desert Palm Press.

Bright Blessings